MW01128389

BOOK 1

Chronicles of
ALLUVIA

———————❧———————

BIRTHINGS

JCM

PAGE PUBLISHING
Conneaut Lake, PA

First originally published by Page Publishing 2022

ISBN 978-1-6624-7602-0 (pbk)
ISBN 978-1-6624-7605-1 (hc)
ISBN 978-1-6624-7604-4 (digital)

Printed in the United States of America

The telling of this story would not be possible without the feedback, encouragement, and the voluntary and willing help of the following individuals:

Deryl Conrad (aka Barbacoa), one of my best friends online who read the first raw addition and encouraged me to continue writing and to publish. I could not have completed this without your encouragement, my friend. My memories of online gaming with you are among the most fabulous.

Drew Timmerman, for being my first willing victim to read and critique the original draft, a good friend of my son's, and a fine friend of mine. A special thanks for immortalizing the word "Freegin" during our roleplaying weekends.

Cori Edwards, the first person to provide me editing and encouragement to continue writing. I will always appreciate your critique and encouragement, my friend.

Elijah Murphy (my son), for taking the time to read and provide feedback, for always enjoying my role-playing adventures, and for being an encouragement in my life. I'm very proud of you. I love you, buddy!

Janelle Murphy (my wife), for listening and critiquing as I read every chapter to her. She is a remarkable woman and a persistent encourager who loves me in such a remarkable and spiritual way.

Joshua Murphy (my son), who continued to badger me about completing the first book and demanding I not kill off "G. G.," his favorite character. Josh's encouragement kept me thinking about the story and was part of what motivated me to publish this book. I love you, Josh, and true to your request, I did not kill off G. G. in the first book.

My ex-wife, I appreciated and still appreciate the excitement she showed when I told her I was writing this. Life changes, and so do people. I wish her well.

There were others along the way who encouraged the work this became. I appreciate all of you.

CONTENTS

Prologue...vii

Alluvia..ix

Chapter 1: Ashes..1

Chapter 2: Commencement...5

Chapter 3: Representatives...20

Chapter 4: Adversary and Counterpart 36

Chapter 5: Birthings Two...53

Chapter 6: Entrapment...103

Chapter 7: Woman-Child 137

Chapter 8: The Tempering..171

Chapter 9: Messene and Nanling 223

Chapter 10: Progression 253

Chapter 11: Camen 264

Chapter 12: The Artist..281

Chapter 13: Gerald the Good 292

Chapter 14: A Paladin's Contemplation 304

PROLOGUE

A wizard's warning:

Be warned, fair traveler, the world captured within these confines has marked my spirit and will steal you away without regret or compunction. Think well before stepping into the realm of Alluvia for there are treacheries afoot, lives entangled in a web, not of their own making. It may be impossible to alter what has occurred yet, such is my endeavor. My words, quiet in the din of humankind, rarely matter... They carry on the wind to nowhere unless embraced by another soul who finds value in their meaning and purpose in this pursuit. If you choose to enter, I cannot be held responsible or accountable for the consequences to or for your well-being. Alluvia will seep into your soul and never fully set you free.

M...

ALLUVIA

———————— ❈ ————————

Alluvia, mysterious and chaotic, consists of multiple dimensions, bound and chained through parallel layers of magnetic and magical energy. The resonance of which creates lesser echoes of the inner most dimension, its core. Spirit energy combines with the flux flowing around, and through Alluvia's dimensions balancing all but the outer shell, an unstable miasma of swirling chaos. Tendrils spiral upward from Alluvia's surface connecting to dimensions of similar worlds, a phenomenon that remains a mystery even to the brightest of the inner core. Each tendril, a time-limited corridor able to be traversed by the skilled and the brave…or fearless. It is this chaos, the unpredictable and often-unstable nature of Alluvia, that resists balance and creates vulnerability all the while strengthening her inhabitants.

Through the generations, many have attempted to conquer and claim aspects of Alluvia. Conquests, involving a single dimension as well as multiple dimensions, have been attempted, but Alluvia has not ever been conquered in total. Alluvia's layers serve as protective barriers to reaching Alluvia's center. In addition to the natural protection provided by Alluvia, a strategy, intended to balance good and evil was designed by the most powerful beings of Alluvia's core, the Grand Council and the Council of the Acquired. The strategy was named the Certamen of Stratera (Latin words for game of balance), the "game" as it is commonly referred to.

Alluvian lore suggests the existence of three hundred dimensional layers, like the skins of an onion, echo outward its core. The dimensions, each contiguous to a greater and lesser variation of the core, have not been fully mapped nor is communication between each of the dimensions normally possible. All the dimensions are inhabited, rich in diverse flora and fauna, humanoid life, cultural variations, magic energy, social and emotional expression, and civilizations diverse in their folkways, mores, and lore. A small number of extremely rare individuals can pass through the dimensional walls, arcs, and rifts or create momentary portals to other dimensions. It is this capacity that makes the conquest of Alluvia, theoretically, possible.

The Certamen of Stratera, the game, was designed, as part of maintaining a balance between good and evil, to regulate the conflicts for dominance and restrict those conflicts to one dimension at a time, all under the purview of the Grand Council. Abkhas and Messmor were chosen to represent the opposite ends of the continuum to presumably bring balance to conflicts that would arise in each of the dimensions. Unfortunately, the Grand Council did not anticipate the methods by which Abkhas would undermine their intent and orchestrate repeated defeats of Messmor… The result of which has been the conquest of 250 dimensions as well as subjugation of the civilizations within… Messmor had not ever been given resources equal to Abkhas to defend his position. The rules of the game require he seek representatives not native to Alluvia, draw "birthings" from the representative's bloodlines to defeat Abhkas and its minion leaving Messmor significantly overmatched.

Each dimensional rotation begins with the Grand Council ending the previous and announcing "Commencement" of the next rotation. All the while, a large tendril seeks the magnetic and magical energies of another world from which the representatives will be brought through.

It is here our journey begins…

CHAPTER 1

————— ✴ —————

Ashes

He stood in silence, nostrils filled with the stench of conquest and funeral pyres not of his making but in some way his responsibility. "How many echoes of Alluvia... How many civilizations...will suffer this fate without intervention?" he pondered as he unconsciously twisted and braided bits of chin whisker with his right hand. His long white beard, styled in the fashion of his unsocialized ancestors, dual braids, an unruly mixture of unattended growth, and freshly woven hair. Each braid picked, pulled, and spun into small outer quill-like points of white and gray marking him as a warrior in many realms. Flames flickered in the darkness. "Abkhas' signature, funeral pyres, death, and subjugation." Messmor pressed the rough edge of his left palm's heel against the twin braids as he tucked them beneath his long cloak. Messmor pulled the gray-brown hood over his head, all the while keeping his staff upright. "So much carnage...so much sacrifice to what end?" he whispered as magical energies arced along the curve of his fingertips.

Piercing eyes, midnight blue mixed in hazel and grey, understated the intensity of the moment, the purpose of his presence. The gnarled wooden staff tipped in onyx and ivory, gripped tightly in his left hand marked him as a wizard and a member of the Court of the

1

Acquired. The depth of his despair, nearly lost in the flickering of firelight, dimmed his vision. The dampening failed to diminish the pain or obscure the memory of what had occurred. He understood he'd failed himself—he'd failed those whom he'd intended to protect. He failed the court.

"How did I get here?" he muttered to the embers burning near his feet.

His eyebrows furrowed, remembering his departure from the confines of parental expectation to blend into a world he barely understood. The lessons were harsh. He could feel the scars, physical as well as mental. Yet he maintained the resolve to keep moving forward as well as to keep his capacities hidden. There were exceptions where he had no alternative but to utilize those skills despite his desire to remain anonymous. Unfortunately, as inconspicuous as he intended to be, he was recognized by many associated with the Grand Council as well as the Court of Acquired. Obscuring his staff with glamour and adorning the appearance of hooded beggar or monk of some remote clan would not fool those few. He reached inside the cloak, unconsciously fiddling with his beard, a habit he could not seem to break particularly in times more serious than the court could comprehend or that he could resolve.

He knelt beside the small stream and gathered a cupped hand full of water, braid tips swung free from beneath the hood, soaking in a drink of their own. Noting the quills above the braids in his reflection, he chuckled out loud, remembering a comment made by a long-dead compatriot: "Ahh, thot beard o' yours looks like a porcupine's arse with two tails." *Humor*, his thoughts shifted back to the present, *an odd place for it*. He stood. *Never lifts the burden of death, just avoids the truth of it*.

Thermals swirled through the carnage in the valley below. He failed to notice the ashes falling gently around him or the sound of the water trickling behind. He could not blink away the harshness of smoke, the sharpness of defeat, or the stench of death that filled his nostrils. Though the valley had been silent several hours, Messmor could not escape what he'd witnessed or push the sounds of death and enslavement from his mind. He bowed his head slightly, inhaled deeply, and pressed his eyelids with the back of his thumbs to resolve the tears. He'd been here many times before…echo after echo, each civilization subjugated without recourse once Abkhas' conquest was achieved. The Certamen of Stratera…the struggle for balance between good and evil devised by the Grand Council had evolved to accommodate this horror of tyranny… Venatus Tyrannide…a game of tyranny, a gambit with the lives of the unsuspecting. A game of conquest rather than a system of balance. Conquest, the goal to which his nemesis dedicates its existence.

His left hand squeezed his staff. "How many more times must I witness this before momentum swings center? How many more times will I have to sacrifice others to end the Venatus Tyrannide?" He gritted his teeth, knowing he must leave the desolation, regain his composure, and meet with the Grand Council.

"Another game another gambit," he muttered to himself. He would, once more, be faced with devising a plan where the players might actually survive. He rubbed his chin. "And achieve the balance," he whispered, "precisely what the Certamen of Stratera, 'the game,' had originally intended."

Messmor grimaced. He would likely find himself standing on a precipice overlooking the carnage when those selected fail. Messmor looked toward the horizon. "Am I the only being who weeps for the dead?" he whispered. "Well…AM I?" he bellowed, arm wide. Silence, greeted only by the fading returns of his voice. "No answers," he muttered. "There are no ears to hear, only the clicking of buzzards and the carcasses of those who thought their sacrifice could make a difference." He paused. "At least to someone or something more than I."

A carpet of ash at his feet, remnants of volcanic eruption, and fires of war still falling. *How ironic,* he thought as he glanced to the ash that had fallen on the top of his left hand. *So soft and fragile… No hint of the life that preceded it, only the being that caused it.*

He felt the familiar sharpness of talons press upon his shoulder. Jeb, Messmor's familiar, a small leathery pseudodragon, shifted his weight. "I know," Messmor responded to Jeb's shifting. "I should not dally, Commencement awaits." Messmor closed his eyes, gathering in the memory of the valley before he bowed respectfully to the dead.

"May ye rise again in an afterlife free from the burden that brought us to this end." He opened his eyes and pulled back his hood.

"We go to the Grand Council," he announced to Jeb.

Messmor's staff touched the ground, and the two shimmered away.

4

CHAPTER 2

───────── ❧ ─────────

Commencement

Perplexed, still reeling from his last failure, Messmor entered the courtyard of the Grand Council. The guards said nothing as the large door creaked open to the Council Chamber. The members of the Grand Council were just now moving toward their places beyond the table of subordinates where he would find himself in a few steps. He noted the shimmer of "It" as Abkhas appeared behind him. *Always the dramatic*, Messmor thought to himself as he pulled the high-backed chair from the table and sat. He did not like being here again, facing the rules of the game again, listening to the antics of Abkhas, but it was his place and obligation. He hadn't lost all faith but had to admit to himself he was wearier than ever before.

Messmor pulled the large bound books and manuscripts close and began organizing his thoughts as the Council Chair called the meeting to order reciting the usual reviews of meetings past. Messmor intentionally appeared to be absorbed in the review of the Rules of Engagement. He found it difficult to give the chair's recitation the attention required while still shaking free from the sight of oppression and the smell of carnage fresh in his memory. The desperation to win an end to the suffering was equally distracting at a time when Messmor needed to have his wits about him. He bent his head slightly to hear the proceedings but not so much as to provide a clue to anyone that he was truly listening.

"One more rotation approved!" Abkhas, arrogance without limits, slammed a rendered hand atop the Council table as It stood fully erect, eyeballing the Council with disdain.

"I accept the Grand Council believes Messmor to be worthy." It leaned forward. "But consider history. Messmor is suuuch a pitiful player." It laughed. "I shall offer twoooo civilizations against the two pending in a double or nothing rotation."

Abkhas ended its outburst standing directly behind Messmor, rocking on its heels, and picking at its fingernails. Abkhas scoffed at Messmor.

Bending forward, It murmured, "My silent, hunched over, caricature of an opponent."

Messmor, though fearful of this round's conclusion and hating the carnage that had occurred previously, was secretly pleased to have been granted another opportunity to continue the Certamen of Stratera. "I may finally be able to solve this dilemma," Messmor mumbled purposefully. "Hmmm, yes, possibly with another rotation," continuing to mumble to himself yet just loud enough to be heard by those close by as he turned slowly to the Council. Appearing a bit forlorn, dejected, yet not despondent, Messmor responded flatly, "I agree to the terms." Appearing to be much older than one would expect, he turned the page of the large volume very slowly and carefully, as if fully occupied, with not tearing a page of the Rules of Engagement.

Maintaining the charade, seeming to be oblivious to his surroundings, but perplexed by the discussion, he adjusted his posture and squinted at the text feigning a deeper interest than what existed. Noting Abkhas had hesitated to look more closely, Messmor began reading the text in mumbled whispers, right elbow resting on the table, right hand pointed upward and fingers moving, hand waving slightly in an exaggeration of the eccentricity most assumed wizards would have while he listened intently. Abkhas, particularly satisfied with Messmor's apparent sullenness, snorted, shifted his attention away from Messmor, and began to expound upon It's remarkable ability to mastermind what it confidently referred to as Messmor's final humiliation.

Abkhas strutted back and forth, swirling its arms, accenting each bit of verbosity with an echoing nonverbal crescendo. Council members attempted to resist Abkhas's melodramatic oration with greater difficulty than any would have initially imagined. Messmor noted that more than half of the members seemed unaffected, yet several struggled to repel Abkhas's influence, losing track of the conversation, preoccupied with not being swept away by the weave of It's words. Messmor noted with some despair that Abkhas was gaining influence where he should not have had the opportunity to do so. Some members were repeatedly unsuccessful in sustaining their thoughts, catching themselves bending to Abkhas's charisma and enchantments—It's persistent subliminal enticement to yield freely to Abkhas's desires. Other members were equally distracted, preoccupied with the failings of those who were bending to Abkhas. The total effect was to cause the Council to focus more on Abkhas's influence of the Council than Abkhas itself. Abkhas, understanding the benefit, purposefully continued bending the Council toward It's design. Messmor truly hated Abkhas but had not ever underestimated nor failed to respect It's cunning or It's ability to obscure It's true intent even in the face of higher authority or, in certain circumstances, potentially greater power. Today was no exception. Abkhas's weave masked It's intention and, despite determined opposition, was successfully moving the agenda forward in a direction it favored. *It would eventually dominate even the Council*, Messmor thought to himself.

Abkhas, an odd orator, an accomplished politician, continued to effectively obscure its ambition to dominate and, eventually, destroy the Council to ultimately subjugate all that exists. *The Council would see what the Council chooses to see*, Abkhas thought. *They will continue to believe that my only motive is to humiliate Messmor...which will, of course, occur.* Abkhas, without the slightest indication of its hidden agenda, smiled, decayed lips stretching agonizingly over yellow broken teeth, as it continued its performance deftly misdirecting the Council toward the obvious. "Pooooor, pooor, Messmor, dost thou lose thy passion for the game?" Abkhas placed his face close to Messmor's left cheek. "Protector…O Protector…dost thou lose faith in thy name?"

Abkhas stood erect, bending slightly backward, arms wide, yawning an exaggerated yawn. "I grow weary of this distraction. In Messmor's defeat lies my satisfaction. While my spirit soars, Messmor's mourns. I grow weary of this affair and move we adjourn." Abkhas walked to the door that exited the hall, hesitated, then turned its head slowly, dramatically, to face the Council. "Well," It added, "is there a second?"

The chamber resonated with arcane energy as the Council Chair rose from the first station in the Council Chamber. The floors of the chamber vibrated, wisps of light and power seeped from the Council Chair's silhouette.

"ABKHAS," the Council Chair's voice sizzled. "Do not assume you are more than what you are, or I assure you, I will render any semblance of your existence a memory to all who behold the pitiful remnants of what you once were." Abkhas seethed with anger, "How DARE YOU humiliate me in the presence of my foe." It pointed at the Council Chair. "You favored Messmor from the beginning, but now you know that it is Abkhas who is winning, Abkhas who ascends. Now…NOW you employ theatrics? Believing your elected authority is sufficient to muzzle ME?"

Abkhas stepped toward the Council's table, opening its hand's palms out, arms wide. "The smell of arcane and the twitch of your fingers. This is the demonstration of your power, and you expect to bend MEEEE? You…"

The Council Chair clenched his fist. Abkhas's retort was cut short. The Council Chair lowered his hand. Abkhas was pressed to its knees. "Do not tempt me, Abkhas. You are a dog in his master's house and Messmor no more than another mongrel bred for our entertainment. Take your place as you were told. The Certamen of Stratera proceeds as the Council allows. You exist because the Council allows."

The compulsion to kneel subsided. Abkhas stood slowly, arcane aura arcing on all sides until It managed to regain control. Abkhas proceeded to its designated place at the table.

Its consistent ascension to power had been obvious, but the Council, much to Abkhas's disdain, still possessed the ability to contain—a condition that It intended to be permanently remedied if it could keep everyone's focus on the game and away from its ascension. It realized today had been a miscalculation. It should have used better judgment, but be as it may, It would not admit it as an error, only as a premature demonstration of arrogance and authority that would eventually be scripted as normal by all concerned.

Messmor sat up straight, taken by surprise by the Council Chairs' movement. *What's this?* he wondered. Messmor watched the exchange between Abkhas and the Council Chair. Messmor had not seen this sort of display at any point in the Certamen of Stratera. *My god*, he thought, *they are actually taking notice of It... Keeping the upstarts in line...I wonder how much the Council fears It will have to contend with a rogue of their creation?* Messmor pondered what had taken place and the millions of possibilities that would ripple from such an unusual incident. *Hmmm*, he thought, *and what do they think of me?*

"CONTINUE THE PROCEEDINGS," the Council Chair's voice boomed.

Messmor felt the psychic nudge as the Council Chair looked in his direction. The Certamen of Stratera, in Messmor's opinion, though continually more frustrating remained virtually unchanged. Abkhas would challenge. Messmor would respond. The Council would continue to enforce rules that favored Abkhas because of their belief that good always overcomes evil. *An illogical imbalance...to provide an advantage to evil simply because of some past life's romantic belief that good shall always prevail. This is the true idiocy*, Messmor thought as he shuffled through one of several volumes related to the current worlds on the table and prepared to select his representatives.

"There," he stated as he withdrew the rules sheet for this particular rotation of the game.

"The rules allow me to select Abkhas's Adversary, and in this case two, Adversary and Counterpart," he mumbled as he read. Though restricted from interfering directly with Abkhas, Messmor's (aka Messmorizer) task, by rote, had been to pick an adversary from the ranks of a civilization not native to Alluvia. Their objective would be to defend the current dimension and civilization from Abkhas's domination. Messmor's deliberation was abruptly interrupted by the Council Chair's directive. "SUMMARIZE ALOUD, MESSMOR."

Messmor, startled by the resonance, quickly followed the Council Chair's instructions. Clearing his throat, Messmor began, "**The Council allows**," his voice boomed. "Messmor to select Abkhas's Adversary, and in this case two, Adversary and Counterpart." His voice vacillated between mumbling and talking very loudly as if to forget then realize he'd been commanded to speak loudly by the Council. Messmor smiled inwardly, knowingly, he continued to project the persona of an eccentric wizard whose intellect was immense, but the command of that intellect left something to be desired. Once again allowing his voice to boom initially, Messmor's voice gradually faded to mumbling as he continued to read the text. The Council Chair began to rise. Messmor's voice immediately amplified. The Council Chair returned to his seat.

"In this case, I will visit Earth, a parallel universe, to choose two adversaries that will defend the world within which the Certamen of Stratera is initiated. Alluvia, the host of the two hundred and fifty-first and fifty-second dimension acquired, is the host of the civilizations selected. The adversaries will defend Alluvia first and then, if necessary, earth itself."

Messmor hesitated. "Earth itself? You are allowing Abkhas to travel the corridor and attempt to subjugate the dimensions of earth?"

Messmor's facade was completely shaken. He stood shaking his fist. "When have the worlds attached ever been part of the Certamen of Stratera? NEVER before!"

Messmor's face reddened as he realized he was speaking out of character and was being muzzled by the Chair at the same moment. Messmor sat abruptly.

"Please excuse the outburst. I am a being of order and unnerved by change!"

The Chair nodded. "Proceed."

Messmor flinched. "I am allowed to nurture powers, skills, and characteristics already possessed by the individual or evidenced somewhere in their lineage. I cannot push any individual beyond its, his, or her natural ability but can elevate each to their fullest potential."

Messmor hesitated while Abkhas laughed aloud, then continued, "My final rule," a rule that caused Messmor considerable consternation, "forbids me to tell any of the birthings about Abkhas."

Messmor believed a loophole existed in this rule but was under compulsion to desist in divulging even a hint. Messmor's cheek twitched with anger that this rule continued to be employed. He felt the compulsion press against even thoughts of divulging anything about Abkhas.

"I still believe a weakness exists, but this damnable compulsion to desist divulging even a hint continues to oblige me to follow the rule or suffer the pain of retribution any time it's stretched," he muttered loud enough to cause two of the Council members to frown. Messmor smiled toward the council members. He could manage the pressure of the compulsion for short periods, but eventually, he would have to desist or be broken completely.

"Stop that." Messmor swiped his hand backward toward his shoulder as he barked to his familiar. Jeb, a miniature pseudodragon, appeared from nowhere to perch upon Messmor's shoulder and, in his usual fashion, greeted Messmor by finding some grooming irregularity that needed to be attended to. Jeb clucked as he slurped down a coarse white hair approximately three inches long that had formerly been embedded in Messmor's right ear, all the while transmitting mind pictures of the two Council members who had heard Messmor's last comments. The remainder of the Council members turned quickly to the source of the interruption. Abkhas, momentarily startled, eyed the pseudodragon perched on Messmor's shoulder with contempt. Abkhas had always had difficulty knowing where and when Jeb would show up. Abkhas silently recommitted himself to eliminating that winged nuisance before returning his attention to Messmor. Messmor, realizing that Jeb had possibly rescued him from disaster, continued to mumble the rules aloud as if nothing had happened.

"Where was I? Oh yes, yes, here." Messmor's voice increased in volume.

"Abkhas, on the other hand, is restricted by nothing but two rules and its unnatural abilities." He hesitated a moment thinking to himself. *A host of abilities it has... No one is sure what Abkhas is. Demon, mage, sorcerer, or the combination... It is an abomination.* Abkhas took the hesitation as an opportunity to remove himself from the table and resume pacing all the while sustaining an air of omnipotence. It turned its back to the Grand Council, an obvious show of disrespect then strolled to the archway, hesitated, finally turning to lean its atrophied hand on the wall and face the Council once more. The Council Chair did not appear to take note of Abkhas's bravado, but Jeb repositioned his talons several times, nervously watching the anomaly grin at the Council.

Clearing his throat, Messmor continued, "Rule number 1, there must be a means of escaping every situation. Rule number 2, Abkhas cannot take the souls of the Adversary, Counterpart, or their birthings."

This final stipulation caused Abkhas considerable duress. Past grumbling to the Grand Council had not resulted in a ruling in its favor. The birthings were, after all, manifestations of the parents. Abkhas abruptly stopped rattling its deformed fingers on the wall adjoining the archway to the door, reasserting the aged argument.

It billowed, "The birthings souls should be mine! The birthings"—Abkhas pacing back to the Grand Council's table, bent toward the Council Chair's face—"are, after all, manifestations of the parents. When the parents looooose this game, theeeeiiiirrrr birthings are irrelevant." It stood, arms to its side, yet palms up and forearms slightly forward. "They...they are but emanations of the parent. They do not even have a soul of their own for all you know. They may simply have an echo of their lineage, a feeble and frail human spirit... Is that a soul?" It addressed the entire Council, "I don't think so! What harm would this final reward be?" Abkhas finished by grinning and spreading its hands wide in its usual way. Messmor could not determine who disgusted him the most, the members of the Grand Council with their analytical detachment from any entity or Abkhas in its total obsession with dominating all that lives.

Silent nods all agreed. The Grand Council's gavel fell. "The rules stand as written. Abkhas is denied. Is there a motion for adjournment?"

"I so move," a Council Member offered.

Abkhas growled, slamming its atrophied hands on the Council table. The Council Chair stood and faced Abkhas, energy began to coalesce.

"I second," another member offered.

The Council Chair remained stationary. The entire chamber was stricken with the intensity of what they sensed to be building. The Grand Council gavel fell. Cloaked in a haze of nebulousness, none to be recognized, the vote concluded, silent nods in anonymity agreed. Commence the Certamen of Stratera! Abkhas shimmered away. Messmor and Jeb sat watching the Grand Council as all the members but the Council Chair vanished.

The Council Chair stood motionless, power continuing to radiate though very slowly diminishing in intensity. The Council Chair regained composure as the last bit of radiated energy crackled its way to being re-absorbed within the hooded cloak. The Council Chair turned toward Messmor and held out his arm. Jeb immediately flew to and landed on the outstretched perch, carefully avoiding gripping the forearm with too much pressure. The Chair of the Grand Council stroked the pseudodragon's back gently, smiled, then placed a silver ring over one talon. The moment the ring snugged on Jeb's talon, without explanation, the Council Chair shimmered away. Jeb flapped his wings startled at the abruptness of the Council Chair's departure, landing firmly on the floor. Jeb eyeballed the ring, lifted the talon to beak, and tried to peck if free. Jeb jerked his head backward startled by the initial shock, only to be shocked sternly a second time by a small bolt of lightning from what seemed to be a tiny living band of silver. Jeb, still standing on one foot staring at the ring-bearing talon, squawked in agitation but did not strike the ring a third time. He simply returned to Messmor who was equally intrigued by the gift. Messmor examined the ring without touching it. *How unusual... This day is odd in every way*, he thought. He reached to touch the ring. A small viper's head emerged. The miniature snake's tail twitched as Messmor's nose closed the distance between the two. Messmor, fascinated by the change of appearance, reached out his finger only to retreat quickly, narrowly escaping the fangs of the little beast.

"Hmm...and to whom do you belong? What is your purpose my little vagabond?"

Messmor stood upright. "Well, Jeb, the Game's afoot no sense wasting time trying to make sense of the senseless."

The trio shimmered out of the Grand Council chamber.

* * *

Zeeba could not understand why the master would part with her. They'd been together since her beginning. The parting left her confused and uncomfortable but in no way despairing. Zeeba did not understand despair or many emotions beyond those that one could describe as accrued by simply existing. She was born to serve and had been given the freedom to accomplish whatever task she'd been given in any way that the task could successfully be accomplished. She experienced satisfaction when the task was accomplished to the master's liking and dissatisfaction when the task was accomplished to the master's dismay. She did not know failure because she'd not ever failed to accomplish the goals or objectives assigned and the methods were of her own making.

She held tight to the winged being's toe and resisted any effort the being made to dislodge her. She held tight even when the winged being summoned the white-furred beast, its master. No being but the master would remove her. If she departed, it would be her choice, her time, her method, and all would be as required to accomplish the task she'd been directed to accomplish. Zeeba kept all the master's directives quiet, sealed in the sacred place the master had created for such things. No being, not even the other Council members, could invade that place as long as Zeeba kept the door shut. Keeping the door shut is what pleased the master the most. She struck out purposefully, missing the white-furred beast warning it to keep its distance. She was not entirely repelled by "White Fur" or the "winged one." Neither smelled wrong. White Fur smelled like the master, but that would not cause her to abandon her task or her loyalties. It would only keep her from killing White Fur outright. Killing White Fur was not part of her directive. She could remember other directives where killing was also not part of the task but was necessary to accomplish the master's desire. She would accomplish the master's desire at any cost. The master was all that mattered.

* * *

Messmor shimmered into his abode, a short distance from the large bookcase and carved wooden table near the fireplace. Still contemplating the actions of the Council, he scanned the library quickly and completely taking in the position of his belongings. The practice had become automatic and unconscious since his dealings with the Hag's servants before he'd managed a truce of sorts. Very tricky creatures they were, thieves and glamour weavers. They'd taken several of his books to the Hag's library weaving glamour to camouflage each book's absence. Regaining the books and establishing a truce with the Hag was an adventure he did not want to have to repeat. With a wave of his hand, the wood ignited in the hearth. Satisfied nothing was missing from his study, Messmor pulled a small bit of kindling from the flames and lit the large candle setting on the upper left side of the table next to a set of quills and varied colored inks. Spinning chin whiskers, Messmor sat in his favorite chair, bent forward, and removed one of the quills. After testing the tip for sharpness, dipped the quill in dark ink and proceeded to write the Council of the Acquired, the small group of wizards who desperately wanted to return life to that which existed before the Certamen of Stratera's creation and, without reserve, remove Abkhas and his minion from existence. Messmor touched the quill's tip to parchment.

Council of the Acquired

Please forgive the scrawl of this quill. My hand trembles as I embrace the undeniable evidence that the Certamen of Stratera is most certainly nearing an end, and I sadly cannot scry or anticipate the conclusion. Tyranny is no longer out of bounds after conquest occurs... The Certamen of Stratera has changed. Abkhas now refers to it as the Venatus Tyrannide... Game of Tyranny, to which It takes considerable delight. I digress...

The Certamen of Stratera, as old as our father's father, claims new victims and creates new heroes yet, incredibly, was intended to bring balance to our existence, an equilibrium between the factions of good and evil. Is it chance, or is it destiny? Could it be a divine edict or simply the outcome of our collective ignorance? I find no satisfactory answer to this conundrum. Is it impatience or arrogance that causes the Certamen of Stratera to be continually extended and the stakes gradually increased rather than achieving and being satisfied with the recurring balance as originally contrived? Yes, increased, not balanced, increased even beyond my vision. Abkhas's influence has permeated the game in a way I cannot seem to counter.

It, the thing known as Abkhas, and to you, as my nemesis, believes each populous is ignorant and ill-equipped to manage their or any world. Abkhas, through diligence and my error, has subjugated civilization after civilization, mercilessly enslaving each to do its bidding subsequently reinforcing its belief that the ignorant are incapable and that ignorance abounds no matter the rift or dimension. The chattel should be relegated to do It's bidding and satisfying that bidding their only measure of worth.

Abkhas has not experienced loss in the past 250 cycles, gods, 250 civilizations subjugated...

It now believes a loss is beneath its stature and ultimately impossible given It's abilities. That loss can only and purely be experienced by those opposing It's will. It believes that the Grand Council still has the power to command but no longer the ability to defeat. It intends to avoid the endearing qualities derived from the humiliation defeat would bring... Humility is beyond It's capacity.

Please excuse my demeanor. I grow weary of living through reoccurring waves of despair... I hear the voices of the oppressed, cannot escape the images of so many dead or the smell of funeral Pires... The years of challenge, forced patience, subdued frustration, and aloneness that accompanies this deed with or without the cooperation of the Grand Council.

I, as you know, am of the belief each world, each race, can succeed if given the freedom and the opportunity to utilize their inherent strengths. I have attempted to free the captured by developing and utilizing those attributes however, as you are also aware, I have been unsuccessful on the larger scale. Abkhas controls, and I have not prevailed in the face of Its' domination.

I, though freshly defeated, am no fool, understand that the Certamen of Stratera is out of balance. I have no choice but to play, however unfavorable the odds, if not for me Abkhas would continue unopposed. It already has attained power sufficient to proceed without regard. No one could resist It for long. Abkhas has enslaved an unknown number of beings, many more than the 250 worlds we have cataloged. His lieutenants have journeyed across the riffs of ten spheres. Even now, It contemplates crossing dimensions and may have pooled enough resources to accomplish such a feat. It has amassed a dominion that no single civilization could oppose. Only its addiction, the Venatus Tyrannide, as It describes the game, prevents complete eradication of freedom in any world it would choose to append. Its need to torture the subjugated and respond fervently to any irritant provides an opportunity for diversion and possibly more time to devise a plan that could be successful. I realized early that my only hope of success hinged on my ability to challenge Abkhas, to be an irritant to such an extent It would maintain It's interest in the game.

So describes the dilemma. I must gain time to accomplish the impossible. I must discover players able to challenge the most formidable player the Certamen of Stratera has ever engaged. Players, lacking experience in or awareness of the Certamen of Stratera, limited to relying on their inherent traits and the unique abilities or characteristics of their ancestors. A special set of strengths that in combination could neutralize or defeat Abkhas and his minion. Exceptional players with extraordinary attributes that together create a synergy greater than I can contemplate and sufficient to defeat It...

Gods! Is it a wonder that selection for this round has escaped me? I have discovered and rediscovered several individuals with qualities that I, and many others, would have believed to be sufficient only to witness their utter destruction despite incredible courage. I would prefer to face my adversary singularly, but that shall not occur within the construct of the Certamen of Stratera though the very nature of the game seems to be reshaping.

I am again faced with the task of finding a new set of qualities and another set of individuals to sacrifice. I cannot help but wonder if I will be successful. It is more and more difficult to believe that heroes exist who possess or can recall the attributes of their ancestors in such a way as to influence the outcome positively...to press forward and believe balance could truly be restored.

The arrangement causes me great pain. As you are aware, once selected, the chosen must marshal their strengths, those innate characteristics, find one another and defeat an adversary that I have not defeated in 250 cycles. I weep for their sacrifice. In the end, I may have only forestalled the inevitable...to further complicate this wretched interplay...if by some ridiculous twist of destiny they achieve the impossible... Well, you know what would have to be done...gods forgive me.

Are our hands innocent? Are we as guilty as those we oppose? Each defeat has "player" casualties on both sides, but we remain safe... We sit comfortably, insulated, watching, and commanding without pain or risk. At our worst, we experience little more than a bit of frustration or a sense of loss while their lives expend without even a moment of remorse...no tears for the marionettes.

Again, please forgive me, I digress.

My last failure nearly caused Abkhas to desert the Certamen of Stratera. There would be no greater disaster. I am thankful It revels in my defeat. Abkhas, though, arrogant beyond description, is intelligent yet confused by the ease with which It has been successful. It believes I am feigning.

If the chosen fail, It will realize I have not been feigning. It will forgo the game to acquire all that is left. It will construct an even greater empire, sovereignty that includes domination of all within its vision...all of yours and all of mine.

I am not optimistic, yet I remain encouraged by the faith of those who have challenged before me and the knowledge that somewhere in the cosmos is a greater force for good that will, as we all believe, prevail despite the shadow of Abkhas and its minion. Let us keep our faith and pray desperately for the success of these birthings. If they fail, we have failed. If we have failed, I know not what the outcome will bring, but I can assure you life, love, and any spark that separates humanity from barbarism will be extinguished the instant that failure is realized.

I have nearly exhausted my resources. I fear the Grand Council is either utterly influenced or incapable of stopping Abhkas from dominating existence. Your consistent support provides the only sustenance from which I draw strength to continue. For the first time since the original commencement, your assistance may be required.

Keep thee safe.

Yours in spirit,

Messmor

CHAPTER 3

---※---

Representatives

On his way out, Greyson Mirphey pulled a stack of envelopes from his small business mailbox, walked to his automobile, and sat them on the seat of his Honda Civic. "I can't wait to check my inbox at home." He laughed aloud. *More bills I suppose*, he thought as he rolled up the window. "Burr, that northwest wind's a hummer!" he muttered as he flipped the heater on high, shifted the Civic into first gear, and pulled away from the mailbox. *I can't believe I got up so early on a Saturday! I should have grabbed the mail yesterday when I was here*, he thought. *I wonder whether the Vikings will win tomorrow?* Greyson pulled out of the parking ramp, glanced in both directions, and headed toward his home on the very outskirts of town. Greyson casually aimed his pointer finger and jabbed the radio On button.

"ARE YOU TIRED OF THE SAME OLD THING? DAY IN AND DAY OUT, BLAH, BLAH, BLAH, NO EXCITEMENT, NO STIMULATION, JUST THE SAME OLE ROUTINE? HAVE YOU FOUND YOURSELF GAINING WEIGHT AND GAINING YEARS? IF SO, DO WE HAVE AN OPPORTUNITY FOR YOU!"

Click! The radio silenced abruptly.

"Same old BS." Greyson snorted looking out the window at gray skies and grayer dirt-stained snowdrifts. After a brief silence, Greyson's thoughts wandered back to the radio announcer's enticement. Rattling fingers in contemplation, Greyson finally succumbed to his boredom or the announcer's sociopathy, he could not figure which and snapped the radio's On button. *It would be nice to do something out of the ordinary, something exciting*, he thought. "OUR INVITATIONS," the announcer offered with a bit too much elasticity, "IF YOU RECEIVE ONE, JUST REMEMBER YOU'LL NOT RECEIVE A SECOND, AND THERE ARE ONLY TWO OPENINGS! THE FIRST TWO INDIVIDUALS MEETING OUR REQUIREMENTS WILL END THIS AMAZING OPPORTUNITY. Dum, dum, da, dee, dumm, dumm. Jumpin' Jack Flash is a gas, gas, gas." Greyson grimaced and silenced the radio. "Another gimmick!"

Curiosity, unfortunately, had always planted seeds that blossomed at an amazing rate with the Mirpheys. He tapped his fingertips on the steering wheel one more time as he drove the Honda into and up the driveway, parking in the back of his modest yet cozy country home, Greyson lifted the seat lever and tilted the seat back momentarily, closing his eyes and taking a deep breath.

What a day, he thought. "Well, wonder what's in the inbox?"

He contemplated aloud, "Paper first, electronics second."

Sitting forward in the seat, Greyson unlatched the car door and proceeded to the garage, deciding for some unknown reason to use the garage side door rather than parking the car inside. Greyson, always a bit hypervigilant, smiled at his "security tape." *No one home I see.* He removed the piece of masking tape from the top right-hand corner of the door, stepped through, closing the door behind, and glanced down to check the paper mail. Sure enough, a stack of envelopes begged his attention. Thoughts of the radio announcers AMAZING OPPORTUNITY pressed him to hesitate only briefly before following the impulse and shuffled the envelopes half smiling at the silliness. There, as if intentionally separating itself and appearing from the middle of the stack, was an emerald green letter sealed with a red stamp.

"What's this? A Merry Christmas card." He laughed. "I don't know anyone that would send green envelopes even if I am Irish!" Greyson lifted the envelope. "For Pete's sake, it's," he muttered, shaking his head, "it's one of those letters! They can't really believe I'd be interested."

Greyson pressed a finger beneath the flap and ripped, permanently destroying, the expensive envelope as he pulled the letter free with a bit more vigor than he'd anticipated. *Curiosity again*, he thought as he began to read:

Mr. Mirphey,

> *You and a few others bearing unusual characteristics have been determined likely candidates for our new position. We assure you this is a legitimate opening for which only the rarest is qualified. We've researched your history extensively and believe that you could be the person we're looking for! We will be interviewing Saturday, November 18 from 10:00 a.m. until 2:00 p.m. There will be no other interview times scheduled despite inconveniences or emergencies. This is a face-to-face interview process. We will not be accepting any other forms of making your acquaintance.*
>
> *We hope you will find time to attend. If not I'm sure we will find a suitable candidate.*

> *Yours in affinity,*
> *Mr. Messmor*

"Incredible... I don't bel...," he stuttered with agitation. "RESEARCHED MY HISTORY! Can you believe these guys!" He crumpled the letter and pitched it to the corner of his workbench where it caromed off a trophy from years past, rattled its way to the box of full contact gear, concluding its trip resting comfortably between a book about the philosophies of man and another book about basic survival. He shook his head.

"You reading my mind?" he offered to the crumpled ball of paper formerly known as an invitation.

"Well, they can shove the opportunity, but they'll get a piece of my mind. I'm not the man I used to be." He laughed aloud. "But then again, I have my limits."

Glancing at his watch, Greyson calculated, "It's 10:15 a.m. Let's see twenty minutes to Parker Avenue, five minutes on Parker, three minutes on Clark, and two minutes to park the car. A hell of a place for an interview!"

Greyson fumbled through his pocket for his keys, pulled the garage side door closed, reconnected his security tape, and jumped into his Honda. Greyson took a deep breath after getting seated and situated then shifted Honda firmly in reverse, backed out of the driveway, and sped away, tires squealing their resistance to his heavy foot and dry bits of pavement.

* * *

Miriam McDermott had also heard the radio advertisement and received a letter though the content was considerably different:

Dear Miry,

We've researched several individuals with admirable skills and intellect but were very much impressed by you! We are required by the selection committee to interview for all positions in our company, but I must say, you'd be a sure fit! No matter what your current situation, I'm sure you'll find this position more exciting and possibly more rewarding than any endeavor previously experienced. Unfortunately, we are only able to schedule interviews between 10:00 a.m. and 2:00 p.m. Saturday, November 18. We certainly hope you'll at least meet us. We will be serving those selected Therian Shelless Escargot and other delicacies.
We're looking forward to meeting you.

In hopes of a partnership,
Mr. Messmor

Though not familiar with Mr. Messmor, Miry noted the invitation was sent from the office of Brigham Johnson Institute, one of the most respected investigative journalistic agencies in the world. The institute's endeavors covered a wide range of topics from current events to scientific discovery to paranormal and metaphysics. Miry had recently submitted an application for an investigative assistant's position working on a project with Elam Brant related to metaphysics. Her initial suspiciousness fostered by the shallowness of the advertisement was abated by the exciting possibility of going to work at the Brigham Johnson Institute. Miry wasted no time getting to the ballroom. She'd always dreamed of doing something unique rather than the mundane that seemed to be offered to most women in *Independence*.

Through more than the usual self-examination, Miry knew she was socially assured yet not aggressive, and underneath her very well-kept exterior existed a carefully guarded and tender heart—one surrounded by love or sturdily protected by glacial barriers depending on the situation. She smiled to herself, how much she cared about certain things or people tended to surprise her, but her ability to instantly erect those icy barriers did not. She knew she was intelligent, sharp-witted, yet she was not as confident as she should be about becoming successful. *Time for preparation, positive thoughts, breathe, deep breath.* Miry inhaled deeply and exhaled slowly. *I'm going to take this position, and I will excel.* She smiled, dabbing a bit of lipstick from the corner of her mouth. Miry's smile broadened as she flipped her brush on the dash. Miry was very nice-looking but not strikingly beautiful, yet there was something about her personality that seemed to make the rest of her even more attractive to men, and she knew it. Being in her early forties had not affected her self-assurance when it came to dealing with men. She had not found her "true love," was not even certain he existed, but she was never short of dates. She was not prone to flirt yet was not opposed to having fun. Her blue eyes twinkling, Miry mused aloud, "You'll knock 'em dead!"

The ballroom was full. *Will you look at all these people! I've not ever seen such a hodgepodge.* Miry stared silently into the crowd.

"Excuse me, miss, MISS!" the doorman nudged Miry who was startled when he poked his finger to her ribs.

"What!" she asserted a bit more aggressively than she'd intended.

"Your number," he retorted, scowling.

"My number," she returned. "What number?"

The doorman rolled his eyes. "Are you all alike, or is this just my day for airheads?"

Frowning his disdain, the doorman, moving much more quickly than Miry was prepared, pointed at the sign, and advised Miry the number was for her interview. Spinning abruptly on his heel, the doorman quickly separated himself from Miry. He greeted the next applicant before Miry could comment. Miry's number was 71. *Great,* she thought. "Now what?" she muttered, scoping the room for some clue of the procedures. Miry noted several lines of chairs numbered, separated by gender, and situated contiguous to adjoining meeting rooms. The lines of chairs only met in two places and chair number 71 anchored the south side of one of the intersections. Miry followed the numbers chronologically ending at 250. She could not help but notice that people of all shapes, sizes, and intellect seemed to have been sent invitations or were showing up unannounced, looking for work. She leaned next to the wall just inside the entry to the large waiting room and searched through her purse for breath mints.

You can't be too careful, she thought. *Suppose I meet the man of my dreams in addition to getting the job of my life?* Miry chided herself humorously. *You should have known this would not be what you expected.* Miry gave the gallery a once-over then proceeded to her designated chair and began preparing for what would likely be a long wait as well as a less-than-desirous interlude with an idiot rather than the man of her dreams.

Miry located her folding chair, swept her coat next to the back of her legs, simultaneously spinning, and sat down. In a moment, she was looking into her compact, hands nestled atop her purse. *I wonder what the qualifications are,* she thought, glancing into the compact's mirror. *I wonder what the expectations are.* Her eyes widened slightly, then she smiled. *It won't be anything I can't handle,* she thought. Miry pressed her back firmly in the chair, crossed her legs, and exhaled, finally feeling comfortable in the chair, glanced one more time into the mirror. "Besides, you're just fine, and you look marvelous, simply maaaaaarvelous," she whispered with a chuckle and a wink into the compact, not paying attention to her surroundings.

"Better than that," announced a short balding man carrying card number 72 as he, too, sat down in the appropriate chair. Both faces turned bright red.

"I'm sorry," Greyson offered, stumbling over his words, his red face, and the awkwardness of silence. He suddenly found it difficult to maintain eye contact. "I…I didn't mean to sound quite…that way. I normally wait for a woman to make conversation, uh…I try not to make a fool out of myself from the start."

Miry smiled, the redness receding. "I admit you caught me off guard, and I'm not sure I'm comfortable with what you said, but… my name's Miriam, Miry for short…and I'm usually not this vain." She quickly closed her compact and dropping it self consciously into her purse.

"Well, I can certainly understand why you are." Greyson's face lit completely red. "I'm, I'm…dang, I did it again!"

Miry laughed aloud, feeling some relief that this guy was not only embarrassed but self-conscious and, to this point, seemed harmless. "I think if you stop trying to be Casanova. We'll get along fine, and you won't be permanently red-faced." She smiled, carefully reaching her fingertips to lightly touch his wrist, attempting to put Greyson at ease yet not introduce more to the relationship than what had already been established.

Greyson silently pledged, *I'll not say another word*, as he sat back cross-armed in the chair. *You certainly are the fool, Mirphey*! he chastised himself.

Though Messmor's invitation was allegedly sent to a select few, the ballroom overflowed with people milling and bumping yet cordially making their way in and out of the interview stations. Greyson sat quietly, trying to catch bits and pieces of several conversations occurring simultaneously. Miry, a bit impatient, fidgeted in her chair. She looked toward the balding slightly gray-haired man next to her, guessing he was in his middle forties.

"I didn't get your name," Miry offered.

"Greyson…Greyson Mirphey," he quietly replied, avoiding eye contact, watching the crowd.

"Irish, huh?" Miry asserted.

"Well, Irish as any American can be." Greyson smiled, still having difficulty maintaining eye contact.

"My last name is McDermott," Miry added.

"You're Irish too?" Greyson responded with genuine interest.

"No." Miry frowned. "I'm Scottish, but we're close to the same heritage, though don't let my relatives know that!"

Miry's smile returning. "I guess I'm more American than Scottish, but I kind of like being a Scot."

Greyson chanced eye contact. "I know what you mean. I'm proud of being Irish, but I'm not sure what it means here in America. I've always wondered what it would have been like actually living in Ireland, but I won't get the chance… Can't afford it."

Miry nodded, and Greyson continued, "Not that I'm poor, I'm just saving to build a larger house. Anyway, I don't like the fact that England has oppressed Ireland for such a long time, and I think I would have liked being part of pressing for freedom."

Miry flinched. "You're not one of those guys that will blow up my car if I disagree with you, are you?"

Greyson laughed aloud. "No, I wouldn't blow up your car, but I might ask you to join me for dinner and debate the issue in a more relaxed atmosphere than this place." Greyson's face pinked. "I hope you don't think I am being too forward. I was just saying I like good conversation, something I find less of more and more these days."

Miry tilted her head slightly to the left. "You're not being too forward, but I doubt that I'm your type."

Just as Greyson opened his mouth, he was interrupted by the intercom. "71 and 72 please," a voice boomed over the PA.

"Well, it's our turn, and thanks for the conversation."

Miry stood up, opened the compact, reviewing for final touch-ups.

"You look great. Any more preps and you'll overdo it. Being real is…um…never mind." Greyson took a deep breath, stood up, and offered his thoughts without any innuendo beyond genuineness. "I hope you get the job…and…that you'll consider another conversation over dinner to celebrate or just to talk. I enjoy intelligent people."

Miry turned, a bit closer to Greyson than she'd anticipated, and squarely met Greyson eye to eye. Miry's intention to accept the compliment but end the exchange dissolved in the recognition of Greyson's genuineness and integrity.

That rare sort of integrity, the kind found in old movies and first loves, in any case, rare these days, Miry thought to herself.

"You don't sound like you're much interested…in the job I mean," Miry responded, wondering whether it was simply his genuineness that attracted her.

"I'm not"—his eyes smiled—"in the job." Greyson blushed a bit but managed to maintain eye contact. "But I would like to know how they found out so much about me…and from whom."

Greyson dropped eye contact. Glancing slightly down, he asked, "So what about dinner?"

Miry placed her brush neatly in her purse. Hesitating slightly, she contemplated Greyson's offer. *Deep blue eyes…windows to a romantic soul…the kind you fall into and never out of…*, she thought then smiled, reconsidering.

"Let's talk after the interview. Who knows maybe we won't be celebrating." She offered to shake Greyson's hand.

Greyson took Miry's hand and, much to Miry's surprise, kissed the hand just above her knuckles gently.

"I look forward to that discussion, M'Lady Miry of Scottish descent."

Miry, caught totally off guard by such a chivalrous gesture, blushed and laughed in delight before she realized she had. She had not ever experienced or developed a defense to this sort of romantic gesture. She stood speechless, heart racing, and blushing even more deeply at her physical response to her very keen awareness of the warmth of Greyson's lips. She slowly pulled her hand from Greyson's touch. Still speechless, knowing that Greyson had certainly seen her reaction, Miry smiled what she'd originally planned to be the final smile, eyes twinkling, and turned toward the interview station. Greyson's expression remained open and accepting. He straightened, then bowed slightly, motioning his arm as if clear the way and beckon Miry forward. Miry smiled spontaneously.

"I think I might actually enjoy dinner with you, my Irish knight."

This time, Greyson blushed, knowing he could not keep his attraction from his eyes and understanding equally well that Miry was very aware of its presence.

"I know you don't want the job, but good luck anyway," Miry offered as she turned and walked toward the interview area.

Greyson watched Miry walk away and, for an instant, lost track of why he was here in the first place.

Smiling about the interlude, he whispered aloud, "Lovely woman…truly lovely." It took Greyson a few moments to shake off Miry's effect. He stood motionlessly as he watched her make the final turn to the interview area. He smiled to himself delighted that he might be spending time with this woman. He was not interested in employment, but he definitely was interested in discovering the heart of the woman who caused him to feel such genuine attraction and, more puzzling, the unexpected comfort he felt in her presence.

Greyson attempted to shake himself loose from the Miry effect and returned to contemplating the task at hand. "Back to the cattle shoots," he muttered. He began rehearsing what he intended to say to the interviewer when he caught the fragrance of perfume that was the same as Miry's. He shook his head. "Come on, Mirphey, you're not sixteen again," but he could not completely shake the thought of Miry. He wondered why she'd made such an impression particularly when she was a total stranger met in passing. "Scottish, huh? I wonder if the countryside is as beautiful as the woman… Ah, Glaayson me, lad, put yoor mynd on the tosk at hond." He smiled at the sound of the brogue. Strolling toward the voice calling his number, still inhaling the memory of Miry's fragrance, he moved forward fairly quickly, managing to only stumble into a few chairs along the way.

Miry found the interview waiting room and a chair next to the corner of the wall directly across the door to where the interviews were taking place. A young woman, very beautiful, huffed out of the interview, picked up her jacket slinging sleeves toward Miry's face. *I thought she was going to be a model,* Miry thought, staring briefly at Linzey Sharf, Miry's next-door neighbor.

"NOT ACCEPTABLE!" the young woman exclaimed. "What the hell do they want! I'm the best-looking woman in this place. I could have practically any job!" She powdered her nose as she paced back and forth without noticing the other interviewees attempting to avoid a collision. "What do they want? Who could they want?" Linzey opened then snapped her compact case shut over and over, fuming about her rejection. She paced, debating whether she should barge back in and demand an explanation. Linzey stepped forward, nearly tripping over Miry who was also eyeing her compact trying to catch any imperfection in her lip gloss. Linzey obviously expected that all would move aside without question, even those who were sitting. Miry, paying little attention, was unaware of her neighbor's outrage or painful rejection.

Linzey waited impatiently staring icily at Miry. Miry, feeling the coolness, looked up to see her neighbor staring at her with disdain.

"Is there something I can help you with?" Miry asked as she dropped the compact into her purse.

"Not unless you can get me this job."

Miry smiled thinly. "I may be interested in the position myself, Linzey," she offered more cordially than the situation called for. "But if it's not for me, I don't mind putting in a good word for you. What would you like me to tell them?"

The woman laughed. "YOU MIGHT BE INTERESTED, BUT YOU WOULDN'T MIND PUTTING IN A GOOD WORD FOR ME? Aren't we self-absorbed. What makes you think you would even have a chance if they wouldn't accept me?"

Miry shook her head. "Linzy…you've had everything handed to you, and the only reason you want this job is that they said they didn't want you."

Linzy leaned down very close to Miry's face. "Well, daddy's little girl, Mirrryyyy bbbaaabbbyyy's just jealous because she's never had anything given to her. Pooooor, lonely, deprived thing." Linzy straightened up. "It's obvious they weren't looking for class when they sent you the invitation."

Though Miry had successfully fended off several of Linzy's attacks over the years, she found herself having a particularly difficult time dealing with this one. "Why **did** you apply for this one then?" Miry responded, attempting to keep her agitation hidden.

"For the same reason you did! If you had a brain, you'd have realized that from the beginning!"

Miry laughed. "It's obvious that they weren't looking for beauty alone. You'd have won."

The young woman backed up a bit, believing she'd somehow been complimented but couldn't believe that her low-classed neighbor would say anything positive.

"Number 71?" an elderly gentleman offered, looking for an appropriate response from the applicants.

Miry nodded, locking eyes with the younger would-be debutante, and continued, "And if it were intellect, it's just as obvious why they didn't!"

Without waiting for a response, Miry smiled generously to the elderly gentleman. "I'm number 71."

Miry managed to look back in time to see Linzy's lips part, but her retort was interrupted by a very drunk unkempt middle-aged man who appeared to have slept two or three days in the suit he was wearing.

"I could finnnddd jo...jooo...hic...a, umm, a yea, that's it...a jooobbbb, bbbaaabbbbyyyy. Juss gab yur purse an folla me to da bar cross da street." He smiled, wiping a bit of spittle from his chin. "Come onnnn, honey, there'sss nothin keepin' you here."

Linzey pushed the man aside, spilling the drink in his left hand, as she exited the interview area.

"Ohhh, I sse seee playin' hard ta get, huh?" The more-than-slightly-intoxicated gentleman gyrated in Linzy's direction as only individual swimming in drunkenness could manage without falling over.

Miry smiled. *Maybe there is some justice in the world after all,* she thought to herself.

Greyson walked into the room marked number two. *And behind door number two, you'll find an opportunity of a lifetime selected especially for you,* Greyson thought, smiling and tensing simultaneously. *This is absolutely ridiculous!* He found a chair he liked, turned, and thumped himself into it.

"Don't get comfortable. I doubt you'll be staying long," said the tall, slim austere man dressed in a double-breasted tweed suit.

"Well, Clayton Irvine, you applied for this hoax too!"

"I suppose you did not," Clayton asserted in his usual haughty manner.

"As a matter of fact, no, I did not. I'm not interested," Greyson said smoothly then grabbed the *Independence Gazette*.

"I wouldn't be so sure." Clayton's eyes twinkled. "If they didn't accept me, you're just the kind of person they're looking for, devoid of intellect, finance, and breeding!" Clayton laughed as only Clayton could.

Greyson dropped the paper into his lap, looking quietly offended. "Clayton, do you ever get sick of the 'I'm better than you are' gig? I'm happy that you have money because it somehow makes you believe you're somebody, but I'm not interested in your opinion about me or your views of your fellow human beings."

Clayton pulled a monogrammed handkerchief from his sleeve, very slightly dabbing his nose, and cleared his throat. "Come now, Greyson, you have to admit that you are not exactly a refined individual, and you would much prefer having the means to do the things I can do rather than trying to live on the pittance you generate. Look at you. One would expect to see a face like that on an IRA poster or a 1950s dock worker article, not applying for a position that is obviously appropriate for the more elite."

Greyson sat up in the chair, tilting his head slightly cocked to the left, glancing slightly at the floor. "Clayton," he offered, slowly lifting his head to make eye contact, "there are some days I can deal with your bullshit, and there are some days I think you should have your ass kicked. Today I think you should have your ass kicked."

Clayton smirked, continuing to dab his nose with the monogrammed handkerchief. "Very Neanderthal of you, Greyson."

Greyson laughed as he moved with surprising quickness from the chair to within a foot of Clayton.

"Mr. Mirphey?" the usher called.

Greyson snatched the bottom tip of the handkerchief just as Clayton was blowing his nose. "And someone probably would kick your ass if you would quit covering it with your handkerchief."

Clayton stared hostilely as he pulled a tissue from a box next to his right hand and attempted to wipe the snot from his face. Without a word he watched as Greyson turned toward the usher.

"That's me," Greyson replied.

"Follow me, please." The usher led the way.

"We're off to see the Wizard… Wonder if he'd like a mono-grammed handkerchief?" Greyson hummed as the door closed.

"Wizard INDEED!" The man grinned, whose back remained exposed to Greyson. "How perceptive of you. Please be seated, Mr. Mirphey, and no, I have a handkerchief of my own, but thank you for the consideration." The man motioned Greyson toward a chair without looking in Greyson's direction.

"Messmor?" Greyson inquired as he seated himself. "I'm not interested in the position. I appreciate the offer, but I'm sure there are people more qualified than me."

Turning toward Greyson and nodding, "That's probably true," Messmor responded flatly. "But I'm curious, so let's just find out, shall we?"

Greyson began to protest as the man turned to face him. "That's okay, I really don—YYEEOOOWWW!"

Messmor's gaze transfixed Greyson. "RELAX, Greyson," he commanded with authority.

Greyson, still shaken, asked, "Did everyone else see you?"

The man laughed. "First, let me answer your first question, yes, I am Messmor, and your second question, of course, they saw me."

Greyson blinked. "But your eyes." Greyson pointed.

"Oh, they'll not remember my eyes. In fact, they'll only remember the coffee was excellent, I was handsome, and the job had been filled by someone in the next room. Now shall we proceed?"

Messmor's eyes, ocean blue and deep as an Alaskan night, enveloped Greyson. Greyson blinked, attempting to avoid eye contact and to resist whatever Messmor was trying to do.

"We're finished," Messmor stated.

"Already?" Greyson retorted, glancing at his watch to discover forty-five minutes had elapsed.

"I'm glad I didn't get the job. You'd be a difficult man to work for, Mr. Messmor." Greyson began rising from his chair. "No offense."

"No offense taken, Greyson. Unfortunately, or fortunately, however you choose to perceive the conclusion, you are the only one qualified to work for me. You are, in fact, the Adversary." Messmor's eyes remained focused, yet his mind was elsewhere.

Greyson, now standing, stepped backward. "Adversary? What do you mean Adversary?"

Mr. Messmor smiled. "I'm sorry, Mr. Mirphey, it's not for me to explain. That will be done by the Antagonist."

Greyson's jaw tightened. "Adversary! Antagonist! What kind of a game is this? I'm not into games, and I think this whole thing is nuts!"

Messmor remained seated, looking calm, self-satisfied. "Well, you're right to an extent. The game is…uh…nuts, but on the other hand, I'm very sane, and you will battle the Antagonist."

Greyson blanched. "Battle? What is this…some sort of joke? You probably know I have some experience in martial arts, but I haven't fought in more than fifteen years!"

Messmor smiled a relentless smile. "I'm not selecting you because of your martial arts experience…," Messmor hesitated. "Yet it is a desirable characteristic"—he scratched his chin—"one worth exploring." With a slight wave of the left hand, Messmor motioned Greyson away, adding, "Let's hope you remember well."

The room spun. Greyson felt his body ripple, and the floor give way. He dematerialized.

* * *

Miry walked into the interviewer's room. Without turning, the man in a very elegant high-backed Elizabethan chair advised Miry of destiny. "I'm glad you're here. As the letter stated, you'll fit the position nicely. I sensed your presence when you arrived. You are indeed a special counterpart."

"Counterpart?" Miry's left eyebrow elevated slightly.

"You are the other half of a team destined to enhance or resolve a conflict. The rest will be explained by the Antagonist." The man's chair began to turn in Miry's direction.

"Antagonist? What are you talking about?" Miry inquired, not yet panicked but preparing herself for the unexpected.

"I'm sorry Miry, you've been hired, and you must leave immediately."

Miry, caught by Messmor's piercing blue magnetizing eyes, could not respond. Messmor smiled an emotionless smile. "I wish you victory."

The room dimmed. Miry opened her mouth to speak, but before any sound emerged, her body shimmered and dematerialized.

CHAPTER 4

※

Adversary and Counterpart

He flexed his back muscles and pushed himself up from the floor. His ribs ached. Stomach muscles trembled from overexertion and a growing weakness resulting from the lack of nutrients. He hadn't eaten in sixty-one hours. The room, as he perceived it in the darkness, was six feet by six feet. The cold blackened walls perspired from his body heat.

How long have I been here? he thought. "How long? What do they…," he muttered, thinking back to the interview with Messmor. "What does he want from me? I'm no one special."

He rubbed his eyes, clearing away the sweat, and attempted to stare through the darkness. "At best, I'm ordinary…just ordinary," he muttered, shaking his head while grasping the back of his neck with the right hand. *I must be asleep*, he thought. *This is too bizarre to be real.* Suddenly feeling weak and ill, his stomach lurched and trembled, legs gave way. He spun and fell for what seemed an eternity. The wind from falling rippled across his face, producing a false euphoria, the illusion of freedom. He smiled just before his body struck the floor firmly, muscles cascaded from the impact, startled and confused, tears trickled over his beard. He could taste the salt, but he was too exhausted to attach an emotion to what was occurring. Reality, a recurring part of this new cycle of life, pressed more and more diligently, eventually forcing Greyson to embrace it.

"What is it that Messmor truly wanted? Why am I the one chosen?"

He laughed. "I am just an ordinary man."

He pressed himself up from the floor to his knees. "One of the guys, no one special, no one unique. I can't be qualified for this. I can't be here." He stood back against the wall. "But I must be because here I am…"

Cradling his head, eyes down, forehead resting on forearm, he tried not to allow the tears to fall but could not stop the flow despite being confused about the intensity of the emotion. He could understand the despair that resulted from his predicament but not the intensity of the emotion that was bringing the tears forward. He stood, numb to his existence, and attempted to reconcile this senselessness with logic but sane logic, no matter how he applied it, failed to bring explanation or relief.

"WELCOME TO MY DOMAIN, ORDINARY MAN." The projection shimmered and materialized. Face then eyes like embers of emeralds dipped in a carnal fire, a nearly featureless black shroud grinned, lips appeared, bits of flesh stretched agonizingly over broken yellow teeth, a long arm with exposed tendons, atrophied hand, and decayed fingers seized him by the throat quenching his lungs of oxygen. Greyson did not attempt to move. His mind remained strangely detached as if watching something occur outside himself until he realized he was smothering. *What do you want from me?* his mind screamed. *"And let go of myyy THROAT!"* he commanded.

The anomaly laughed a deep resounding guttural explosion, "I AM YOUR KEEPER. YOU ARE MY SLAVE. I AM THE REAPER. YOU ARE THE KNAVE. YOUR WORLD'S A SLEEPER, BUT IF YOU ARE BRAVE, YOU'LL SATISFY MY CRAVINGS, AND I'LL DIG YOU A GRAVE."

The answer, so absurd, so demeaning, and so absolutely challenging that even as an ordinary man, he was not prepared to take it without some sort of retaliation. Greyson had prided himself about the changes he'd made since his violent and chaotic childhood, but nothing prepared him for what he was experiencing. Oddly, his mind wandered to a much younger time when being beaten by thugs several years older when he refused to allow them to insult his father. This was much different from those days on the street, but the oppression was just as real. Greyson's anger surpassed his sensibilities. He erupted losing emotional control, kicking and swinging only to witness the anomaly shatter and reform without completely losing its grip. Abkhas slapped Greyson, sending him back into the wall.

Exhausted, Greyson slid down the wall, ending the physical assault, but his anger increased. "Kill me and be done with it, or stay the hell out of my mind!" Greyson screamed, tears continued to trickle over his beard while blood oozed from a bruised and swollen lower lip. These tears were from anger as rage began to build.

The anomaly's hand loosed slightly. Hot stale air invaded Greyson's lungs. Abkhas, emerald eyes danced a sadistic jig, leaned forward. "I AM YOUR KEEPER. YOU ARE MY SLAVE. I AM THE REAPER. YOU ARE THE KNAVE. A MAN, YES, BUT NOT SO ORDINARY, FOR IN YOU LIES MY ADVERSARY...MYYYY ADVERSARY." Abkhas laughed, a deep resounding guttural resonance, then, suddenly, pulled Greyson's face next to the broken yellow teeth. "MY ADVERSARY! CAN YOU IMAGINE THAT? YOU...NO MORE THAN FLY SEED, A MAGGOT! IN YOUR FRAILTIES AND STUPIDITY. WITH YOUR POORLY DEVELOPED INTELLECT, THERE IS NO RESPECT. YOU ARE NOT A CHALLENGE. YOU ARE A HIDEOUS JOKE, AN INCONSEQUENTIAL POKE, A COUNTERCHECK CONJURED BY MESSMOR TO PROTECT HIS FEEBLENESS...TO TEMPT MY WRATH, BUT NOW YOU ARE ON THE PATH TO FEED MY DESIRES NO MATTER HOW MUCH YOU RAVE. NO ONE LEFT TO SAVE...WHEN I DIG YOUR GRAVE." Fetid breath fogged, coiled, and swirled about Greyson's face.

"I don't know what or who you're talking about. I am no one special. I'm flesh and blood." Greyson's bruises were more and more evident.

Abkhas smiled insanely wide. "YOU'LL KNOW SOON ENOUGH, KNAVE." Abkhas dropped Greyson back to the floor. "I AM OBLIGATED BY THE CERTAMEN OF STRATERA TO OFFER YOU CLUES, TO POSSIBLY LENGTHEN YOUR EXISTENCE, BUT MARK THIS TRUTH, DESPITE MESSMOR'S INSISTENCE, HIS CARD IS NOT TRUMP. YOU ARE MINE IN THIS INSTANCE." Abkhas gazed, eyes unseeing. "MINE, I TELL YOU.

For now, you know me as *Abkhas*, a fictitious name of course." Abkhas moved its atrophied hand with a deftness lost in the darkness. It began nonchalantly picking remnants of its last meal from between broken teeth as it spoke. "From where I come is the source of your pain, of your agony, and you, though very ordinary"— smiled—"are named '*Omurcada*' for the seed you carry. You are chained to the wall in the Province of Mull. Your being will be encased in darkness for the knave that you are until you give birth to the three. Zen the Mage Born, Gerald the Good, and Camen the Chameleon. In the millennia of their birth, you will be charged with the task of orchestrating my destruction. They are your questors. I am the Antagonist. Your destiny will reveal itself. My death or the death of your world will signal the completion of your quest. Your death is no longer possible, but you shall wish you were dead should you not accomplish your goal. For my reward is your destruction or eternal…slavery."

Standing fully erect, still aggravated by not being able to have the souls of the Messmor's representatives, Abkhas put his hands behind his back, unconsciously picking at the nail of his middle finger. "I have fulfilled my honor, such that it is, you have been advised." Abkhas ceased, picking at his nails. "The game begins. I am destined to win, and you…human feces are destined to lose. Remember, human, you are mine. I *am* the keeper. You *are* my slave. I *am* the reaper. You *are* the knave. Your world's a sleeper, but if you are brave, you'll satisfy my cravings, and I'll dig you a grave."

Abkhas shimmered very gradually, leaving all but a vague silhouette of self adrift in the darkness.

"Wait!" Omurcada slammed his fist to palm in an unsuccessful attempt to control his panic. "Wait! You can't do this to me. I'm not part of your ridiculous game!" Omurcada's anger pressed as his fear dwindled, and with it, his panic gradually subsided, replaced by an uncharacteristic calmness. "I'm not Adversary. I have no hope of contending with you," Omurcada offered quietly. The deep guttural laugh, though not as forcefully as before, echoed slowly, fading into infinity.

It was difficult to determine whether hours or days had passed in the darkness. The iron couplings gouged his wrists, blood trickled over slick, malnourished skin. Omurcada wept. "It's truly happening to me. I'm here." He gestured in the darkness. "How can it be?" He muttered his new name, "Omurcada," before, again, sagging to his knees. "It can't be real, but it is. Give birth? How can I give birth? I'm a man." Omurcada sat back, drifting aimlessly into hopelessness. "I can't give birth. I'm a man…a man. I'm doomed."

* * *

She opened her eyes. Remnants of an unfit sleep blurred her vision. Her nails ached. She felt as if they'd been levered backward against their natural position, nearly torn from her fingers. She felt numbness at her fingertips. Analyzing the rest of her body, she discovered either her left leg was deeply cramped or the femur was broken. She had not been violated sexually, but her body pulsed with pain. The peripheral nerves seemed to be on fire. Her stomach wrenched, but she could not vomit. Dizzily, she fell to the floor with a thud. She smiled and thought, *Maybe I'm dead*, then laughed hysterically. She could not determine the size of the room but guessed it would be about the size of a prison cell. The black cool wall to her back bled from her perspiration.

"Why in god's name am I here?" she muttered.

"FUNNY YOU SHOULD ASK. WELCOME TO MY DOMAIN," a voice from an unknown source boomed through her consciousness as a specter shimmered into existence. She pushed her body to the wall opposite the shimmering force. The edifice shifted as the creature took form—a large black anomaly stood translucent. Those eyes, like embers of emeralds, dipped in a carnal fire—lips grinning stretched agonizingly over broken yellow teeth, long misshapen arms showing tendons attached to atrophied hands and decayed fingers, wrapped tightly around her ribs and squeezed the oxygen from her lungs. Her mind screamed out in indignation. *Get your hands off me, you bastard!* Its grip tightened.

"Damn you!" she screamed.

She attempted to grab and gouge what appeared to be a face finding no resistance where flesh should have been. The anomaly laughed a deep guttural resonance.

"I AM YOUR KEEPER. YOU ARE MY SLAVE. I AM THE REAPER. YOU ARE THE KNAVE. YOUR WORLD'S A SLEEPER, BUT IF YOU ARE BRAVE, YOU'LL SATISFY MY CRAVINGS, AND I'LL DIG YOU A GRAVE."

One side of her mind fought to regain her wits and her freedom the other detached, searching for a means of safety. She struck the anomaly with the palms of her hands, grabbing, twisting, turning to no avail.

"You bastard! LET GO OF ME!" Miry sent knees and elbows to places that would render a lesser being helpless—nothing changed.

Its grip undulated ever so slightly, just enough release of pressure to allow her to gulp air sufficient to launch another verbal assault. "Satisfy your cravings? I don't know what you have in mind, but I'll not give you anything willingly, or is it you are depraved enough to find joy inflicting pain?" It backed Miry against the wall. She aimed her knee, nearly losing her balance meeting very little resistance as it traveled upward, missing Abkhas altogether. *I'd kick you in the groin if you had one*, she thought, continuing the struggle to gain freedom. *Have to breathe*, she thought, her brain felt as if it would burst for the need of precious oxygen. The anomaly loosened its grip. She gasped for air. Emerald eyes danced a sadistic jig.

"I *AM* YOUR KEEPER. YOU *ARE* MY SLAVE. I *AM* THE REAPER. YOU *ARE* THE KNAVE." Abkhas laughed aloud, pulling Miry to its chest then launching her back into the wall. Miry's body shuddered at the impact. Upon rebound, it caught her elbows and pressed its face close to hers. She gritted her teeth and shifted her angle, keeping the hip pointed at her assailant.

"DO NOT TEMPT MY RAGE, YOU INSIGNIFICANT TWIT. THE CERTAMEN OF STRATERA HAS RULES TO WHICH I MUST ADHERE, BUT SUFFERING IS ALLOWED, AND SUFFER YOU WILL, MY DEAR," Abkhas bellowed, the walls reverberated as it picked her up by her chin and eye sockets. It grinned, momentarily holding her aloft, then dropped her to the floor. "Such a pity I cannot have my pleasure. You ignorant bearer of pestilence. When the game is done, I will dip you in your incontinence." It grinned, again pressing its face closer to hers. "Then remove your skin bit by bit, strip by strand while you live, screaming through the time that spans my pleasure...without peace or sanctuary." It grinned at its mental picture. "You are indeed pitiful. To think the Messmor believes you are the seed, the medium, the Counterpart of my Adversary." It spread its arms wide and turned slowly circularly as if addressing the masses in a large auditorium. "You who lack imagination, cunning...skill. You who fancy yourself unique among your kind."

Abkhas grunted with disgust, dropped its arms to its side, then turned to face Miry who remained seated below him, tilted back, trying to find a way to move away. It bent slightly toward Miry. "By the precepts of the Certamen of Stratera, I am obligated to offer you clue to lengthen your existence, but I will triumph. My wrath will be satisfied despite your resistance." Abkhas straightened, smiled, totally preoccupied. "For now, you know me as Abkhas." It stepped back a step. Miry returned to her feet and pressed backward until she felt the wall's support. "A fictitious name of course. From where I come is the source of your pain, of your agony, the origin of the game, and you, though so very self-emancipating will be called peace. You are chained to the crease in the wall in the Province of Llum. You will be encased in darkness for the absurdity that you are until three birthed women come, Wigan the Sorceress, Nanling the Artist, and Messene the True. The hope of a civilization...echos of you. In the millennia of their birth, without instruction, you shall be charged with producing the seed of my destruction. They are your questors. I am the Antagonist. Your destiny will reveal itself. My death or the death of your world will signal the completion of your quest. Your death is no longer possible." It hesitated, grinned, stepped forward, then trailed its broken atrophied fingernail down her nose to her throat.

Peace tried to remain calm outwardly. If it hadn't been for the wall, she was certain she would not have been able to control the trembling or the fear that made her want to scream aloud. It stepped backward.

"BUT YOU SHALL WISH YOU WERE DEAD SHOULD YOU NOT ACCOM-PLISH YOUR GOAL. FOR MY REWARD IS YOUR ETERNAL SLAVERY. I HAVE FULFILLED MY HONOR, SUCH AS IT IS, YOU HAVE BEEN ADVISED. THE CERTAMEN OF STRATERA BEGINS. I AM DESTINED TO WIN, AND YOU… HUMAN DECREPIT…ARE DESTINED TO LOSE. REMEMBER, HUMAN, YOU ARE MINE. I *AM* THE KEEPER. YOU *ARE* THE SLAVE. I *AM* THE REAPER. YOU *ARE* THE KNAVE. YOUR WORLD'S A SLEEPER, BUT IF YOU ARE BRAVE, YOU'LL SATISFY MY CRAVINGS, AND I'LL DIG YOU A GRAVE."

The anomaly shimmered slowly out of visible existence.

"Wait!" Peace stepped forward. "What am I to do? Why am I here? Riddles? Riddles are all I get?" Peace, frightened beyond imagination, mustered the strength to feign regret, hoping to find out more about her captivity as well as the role of the Antagonist. Peace, consciously holding hatred and fear in check, decided to try a different tact. She slumped down against the wall. "I'm, I'm…afraid," she offered.

"SO SWEET IS THE SOUND OF COURAGE LOST." The deep guttural laugh echoed, slowly into infinity. Her jaw clenched.

It was impossible to determine how many hours or days had passed in the darkness. The iron couplings bit her wrists, blood trickled down her bruised yet savory arms. "Peace, what kind of a name is Peace?" She sat, still shaken from the appearance of Abkhas. *Harmony*—she smiled as she tried to make sense of what was happening—*isn't exactly how I would describe my life. Maybe Abkhas is referring to my body.* Peace shuddered as she redirected her thinking and pulled on the chain that bound her. *I'm still chained to this wall for goodness' sake.* She laughed. *For goodness' sake…I doubt goodness has much to do with these chains.* The room was devoid of light. She could see nothing. The only scent was that of her perspiration. "I stink." She wrinkled her nose. "I don't suppose a Jacuzzi comes with the room." She laughed aloud on the verge of hysteria. She knew the wall was made of stone, the floor earthen, and the air noticeably fresh despite the absence of light. *None of this makes sense... Even the riddles make no sense*, she thought. "Give birth to three women? How am I supposed to give birth to three women? If it were possible, and it is not, why would I pick those names? Who's the father going to be...?" Her face reddened. "Oh god, not Abkhas. It probably can't breed anyway." Her fear dissipated ever so slightly.

The room darkened mysteriously, black on black. The anomaly smiled that hideous smile then whispered, "No, my sweets, I shall not sire your offsprings. They will spring from a womb of your own making. If, however, this is the most cataclysmal you can imagine, I have truly won. Peace for one, peace for all, except the peace on the wallllllll."

The room hummed like a tuning fork as Abkhas shimmered and was gone. Several hours passed before Peace was able to relax the muscles that pressed firmly against the resistance of the wall.

Her eyes hurt from the strain of attempting to see. Her mind hurt from trying to logically embrace her surroundings with all her senses. Her imagination, not her worst but a very capable enemy, kept her busy discounting every sound, even her breathing. She was continually forced to prepare for a visit from a thing, a horrible visage, all the while pressing her vivid imagination into submission instead of allowing it to simply make things all the worse. Exhausted, she lay prone resting her forehead upon her arm. Her wakefulness gave way to the exhaustion of stress as the memory of Abkhas's last visit carried her into unconsciousness. Its final statement reverberated drifting into her subconscious. "Peace for one, peace for all, except for the peace on the wall. My peace, haaa, haa haaaaaaaaaaaaaaaaaaaaaaaaaaa...," ending thickly in a silence nearly drowned by the residue of insanity.

* * *

"A void or a vacuum, I must be in a void... I can breathe, and I'm still chained to this wall." His mind continued to wander. "Omurcada...why does that seem familiar? Maybe something from my Irish ancestry… Who knows? What could Abkhas want from a coward of an Irishman?" The thought of coward and Irishman in the same sentence caused Omurcada laughter juxtaposed with instant regret. "The Irish are anything but cowards… It's me." He chuckled once more, staring out at the darkness. "Wanna fight?" The chuckle left nearly as quickly as it had arrived. "I had courage once…but no more and not twice." He cackled deliriously. "Maybe it's because I'm short. That's it! That overgrown son of a bee wants a toy, better yet, A PET to play with." He sifted through memories of distant and not-so-distant past. *I used to have anger—no, not anger, it was a rage. It wasn't even an emotion, really… It was a place I'd go when I needed to disconnect myself from the moral responsibilities of hurting someone else. I had a reputation…part fiction and part reality…and that rage…a rage that would cause most to think twice before challenging me.* He smiled. "A little street survived," he mumbled, admitting to himself he was still a little proud in the reflection. *I was a kid…just a kid.* That seemed so long ago. "I really didn't like fighting," he explained to the darkness. "I just didn't know how else to deal with life," he muttered. *Too much life way too early*, he thought. Omurcada grimaced, lifting the chain slightly to touch the gouge on his right wrist. "What a past… What a present! I must be in hell," he offered to his captivity.

Omurcada fingered the wrist cuff, peeling what he believed to be chaffed skin. Though futile, he inhaled deeply then stared with intensity, attempting to penetrate impenetrable darkness by sheer willpower.

"Hell…," he exhaled. "Of course! That's it! I'm in hell! That's why I won't die. That's why I don't need food. That's why…" His stomach seized, the sharp pangs of hunger caused him to tremble. He felt as if his ribs were bound tightly together only separated by his backbone. "Hunger? I'm hungry!" he exclaimed, pushing himself off his knees. "I must be still alive… I'm hungry!" He attempted to dance what seemed, in his delusion, to be an Irish jig, but the chains, reasserted their authority, restricting his range of movement and dampening a small but vital bit of hope that resulted from realizing he was still alive. "Damn chains!" he exclaimed while returning to a kneeling position and rubbing the chaffed skin below the ankle shackle. *If I am hungry, I am also able to starve myself.* He sat thoughtfully. *I'll show that sturgeon-faced pile of blubbering dung I'll starve myself.* He stood, self-satisfied, though frowning a bit at sounding so much like Abkhas. "I must be nuts. I'm sounding like him, and I smell like him! I smell like dead carp…like…like…old vegetable beef soup, and so does he!"

Omurcada laughed until ribs hurt from more than a lack of sustenance. The room filled with a familiar fetid scent. *That can't be,* he thought. *It would be too easy.* Omurcada sensed a presence.

"Abkhas?" he ventured, but no answer came.

Still sensing the presence, Omurcada braced for an assault. When no assault occurred, fists clenched and opened repetitiously. On the verge of becoming completely irrational, Omurcada outstretched his arms and bellowed, "AABBKHAASSS, LET ME SEE YOU!"

Abkhas radiated darkness. "AH, HOW THE RAGE SEETHES WITHIN YOU, LITTLE ONE. YOUR RESPONSE HAS NOW BEGUN. FROM WITHIN YOU, THE EMANATIONS COME. YOU'LL FIGHT ME, MY LITTLE CELT, AND YOU'LL WISH THIS WAS THE LEAST PAIN FELT. AS FOR STARVING"— Abkhas grinned audaciously—"YOU'LL EAT WHAT I CONJURE, BE IT ROOT OR SLUG!"

Omurcada clenched his teeth to no avail. His jaws slowly opened against his will. His tongue lurched forward and seized the slug as a frog would flick a fly. The tongue retracted, Adam's apple shifted, and Omurcada swallowed. He gagged but was unsuccessful in regurgitating. Abkhas proceeded to force-feed Omurcada much like a mother robin would force regurgitation down the throat of a chick, emotionless—the act was simply a menial requirement of the Certamen of Stratera. Without any hint of agitation, yet a directness that could not be mistaken for anything less than a frank expression of reality, Abkhas spoke, "I PLAY THIS TIME. I PLAY NO MORE. THE BIRTHING IS ROOTED IN YOUR CORE. YOU CANNOT STOP IT. YOU CANNOT DIE, BUT YOUR PAIN WILL PLEASURE THIS EMBER-RED EYE. IF YOU CONTINUE TO TEMPT THE ROOT OF MY RAGE, I WILL FORGO THE GAME, AND YOU'LL BE MY SLAVE…TO FEED AS I WILL TO A FIRE IMMENSE OR NOT QUITE DROWN YOU IN YOUR INCONTINENCE. I LEAVE YOU NOW,

MY ADVERSARY. TAKE YOUR STRENGTH. REINFORCE YOUR SOUL FOR ITS ENCHANTMENT IS MY GOAL." Abkhas flickered and was gone.

The air in the room cleared, but Omurcada's memory of every aspect of the event remained sharp—sharp as a knife's edge. In place of the fear was rage, a cold, logical but very dangerous response. *No one…no being should have the power to inflict injustice to such an extent on one so inferior.* He clenched his jaw and his fists. A largely forgotten rage sparked to life, ever-so-small yet distinctly vital, this remnant of the past reemerged, fed, fumed, and underpinned an intense rage in the present. *Survive, yes, survive I will, and as you say, the game has begun. I don't know how I can give birth, but I will. With all that is in me, I will, and…I will defeat you, Abkhas.*

Omurcada hung from the chains. His mood altered between determination and bewilderment. Rage seethed and ebbed, never quite relinquishing its influence upon his thinking. Omurcada experienced a good deal of difficulty, sustaining focus on anything other than what he'd just experienced. His mental state, not quite sane yet, not entirely insane, swirled between an intellectual reconstruction of his captivity to a broken thought process—at one moment, babbling in incomplete sentences; the next moment, reciting the "Gettysburg Address." Omurcada's emotional control slipped as he grinned a bit of lunacy. *Fourscore and seven years ago, our forefathers brought forth upon this continent…continent…incontinence… Hmm… Can courage…courage forgotten be regained? Is it possible I am here destined to fight a being I can't hope to defeat? A new nation conceived in liberty… I'm in captivity… Maybe I'm a modern-day Peter? Wait…"* He paced, wringing his hands. "Am I someone's champion? Whose champion am I? Tune in next week, same Bat Station, Same Bat Channel." He laughed aloud as he sat back against the chilled wall of his imprisonment. *Time to get serious,* he offered to himself. *Break's over back on your heads!* he addressed an imaginary audience. *I am someone's champion.*

The thought died as Omurcada for the first time since his imprisonment contemplated his dilemma, his part in the game, and the game itself as a reality. "The birthing is rooted in your core… in your core," Omurcada repeated Abkhas's phrase over and over.

"What could he mean, my conscience or my body, hmmm, my conscience or my body, who knows?"

Several days passed, Omurcada contemplated his existence. "I can't believe it, but I'm feeling stronger," he murmured as he pulled himself up on the chains for the fiftieth time. He could feel the tendons in his stomach tense then ripple. *When I started in here, I thought I was going crazy, you know. For Pete's sake, don't babble to yourself! Oh, what the hell—seventy-eight, seventy-nine. The blackness is the most treacherous. I wish I could see. Encased, It (Abkhas) stated, encased in darkness until I give birth to…to…Ben. No, that's not right. Gen—no, ah, Zen, yes, Zen, the firstborn. Wrong again.* He closed his eyes and concentrated. *Zen the Mage Born. Mage Born, right. I'm supposed to give birth to three men, and this one is supposed to be a magician!*

Though Omurcada seemed to undulate between being rational and irrational, his rage, that quiet rage of a man caged, burned ever brightly beneath the surface. He'd managed to stop the ravings, fending off the insanity of his anger. He embraced it, held it, formed, and forged it into a disciplined, yet quiet, symbiosis of self and lethal energy. Self-renewing energy that, in turn, focused his cause, honed his conviction, and fueled self-righteousness. His anger, his rage, had become a creation practically of its own consciousness—a consciousness he talked to, took energy from, and found sustenance within. Omurcada had become a man with a goal above the mores of right or wrong, the whims of other men. A goal, a determination to right the personal injustice, and destroy the Antagonist. He smiled.

"Yes, that's it, 'Mage' for magic or wizardry. I wonder which, or is it witch?" He laughed. "This is truly insane, to think I can give birth to such a being without a counterpart… Anyone wants to volunteer?" he addressed the empty room as if expecting to hear a woman's voice. "No takers? What, you don't like my living quarters, or is it my personality?" He shook the cold sweat from his head. "Give birth… This really must be a very bad dream," he muttered, knowing that he was not dreaming and would not likely escape the entrapment anytime soon.

Omurcada scooped and released handfuls of silt. Granules trickled out of his clenched fist. No matter how much he attempted to keep the floor uniformly smooth, he was defeated by his daily ritual of standing, sitting, sagging, and shuffling. The silt persistently shifted shapes…loosely gathered then pressed into the shape of his hands or feet, forming small malleable peaks he marveled at in the darkness. He allowed particles of silt to flow through his fingers, relishing the newly found ability to feel each individual particle pass through the byways and crevasses of his now coarse palms. His imagination had developed considerably since his captivity. He could bring forth memories in vivid detail. He reviewed the events leading to his captivity over and over, finding no explanation for the entrapment or Messmor's decision to choose him above the other candidates. His imagination, though sharpened, was difficult to manage.

At times, he felt utterly defeated and imagined killing himself—simply ending the game by default. He could not, however, ignore Abkhas's declaration, the fact that he could not die if he wanted to. The thought periodically caused thoughts and feelings of omnipotence to overtake him. He imagined he could perform superhuman acts. After all, he would become the proud father—and mother—of three men without the assistance of another human being! Omurcada's mind wandered, undulating with feelings of omnipotence and inferiority. He contemplated, with questionable lucidity, *I could build a mud mannequin cemented by spit and will it into life. Maybe that's the way to give birth.* He shook his head as if to clear the delusion and pitched the remaining silt in the air, treasuring the gentle rain against his face as well as the infinitesimal percussion of a thousand little drums ricocheting to the limits of his captivity. *But that probably wouldn't work.*

"Three hundred and fifty-one, three hundred and fifty-two, these damn chains and this eternal darkness are going to be the death of…my world… My world, my world such as it sucks snail shit!" The darkness, a nothingness that enveloped his awareness. The blackness, almost physical, impenetrable, continued to press in. Stretching sinew against the chains, he bellowed in frustration. He could imagine each and every link straining, yet he could not pull free. The chains were too strong. The darkness continued to etch away at his awareness, dim reality, and mask his world—so complete in its touch it smothered all sight. It seemed to dampen and muffle the sound.

The effect was profound, but it could not stifle Omurcada's growing desire to win the game. Beneath that desire, the rage seethed. *I wonder if I still have eyes, five hundred and one, maybe when I can do five thousand of these, I'll be able to pull myself free. Then Abkhas.* He hung for a moment in the chains. *I'll figure out a way to see through this darkness.* "Yes, Abby, baby, then it's your ass!"

He slumped in the shackles and resigned himself to eat slugs from the tray that suddenly appeared. "If they feed me three times a day, then I've been here for 231 days. Damn, I feel like it's been an eternity." The room wreaked with his body odor but somehow did not smell of human waste. Regardless of where or how often he relieved himself, the feces and urine disappeared immediately. "A miracle of modern toiletry," he offered in a deep Louisiana Southern drawl to his imaginary audience. The entire affair was as confusing now as it was in the beginning, though he was adapting to his environment. At times, it was almost too much, yet he found comfort knowing he could contemplate the Antagonist and the Adversary without distraction. His body was numbed by the exercise. The massive musculature that had developed since his captivity drooped in exhaustion. Though beaten down for the day, he still took pride in the consistent increases in endurance. "My day will come. My day will come…," he whispered as he drifted again to that sweet respite, his only freedom, blessed and pure—sleep.

* * *

Oooooh…my head, she murmured as she raised her hands to her temples and opened her eyes. Nothingness surrounded her, the chains that held her wrists and legs helped her distinguish between dream states and reality. *I'm still here.* Tears filled her eyes then flooded her cheeks. *My god, why me?* she thought. Taking a few moments to gather her thoughts, Peace opened her eyes. *Be strong even if you don't believe it, but you're not strong, or you wouldn't be here.* Disheartened, she trembled, unable to stop her teeth from chattering. She felt her panic rising. While outwardly she managed to appear in control, she struggled against being overwhelmed internally. Peace pressed her lips even more tightly together to prevent the panic from causing sound. Squinting her eyelids tightly and repeatedly telling herself, *I am in control, I am in control,* that she could be strong, she managed to contain the voice from within. Hopelessness picked and pushed but was unable to cause her misery to deepen, yet her despair filled the room over full. Silence, unkind and cold, mocked her in the quiet echoing of her entrapment. When she did speak, the room amplified her mutterings redundantly, unemotionally, apathetically, tolerating the sound without giving value to her existence. Anguishing silently, she stood rocking back and forth, attempting to console herself and generate warmth rubbing her arms with her hands. The anguish combined with physical weakness was nearly her undoing.

She sensed herself falling. Physical pain, a welcomed distraction from emotional incapacitation, registered as her leg and ankle twisted. Cold sweat covered her body. She could not speak. Her tongue swelled. As her body convulsed, she collapsed only to relive the entire incident over and over. Amidst the confusion, she realized a presence had entered her chamber, infusing her mind with hallucinations and pain. None of this was real.

"I am strong," she muttered then regained control, lifting her head upright. "Release me!" she exclaimed.

The anomaly's hand covered her mouth. The taste of decayed flesh invaded her sensorium. She tried to vomit, only managing to taste bile.

"Peace scots, lady," Abkhas roared, and Peace's body collapsed, yet she remained conscious.

Her body warmed and healed itself. Abkhas, a juxtaposition, seemed to enjoy having her healed as much as causing her pain. The thought was a distraction. She had been returned to, actually had not ever departed, captivity. Chains still restrained, but the pain and anguish were gone. "Don't thank me for your repair, my lady of despair," Abkhas offered whimsically.

"Get away from me, or get this over with," she stated flatly, attempting to stare through the image whose eyes glowed but appeared as a silhouette in the darkness. "If I'm going to die here, then do it now."

"Die!" It laughed. "I am your keeper. You are my slave. You cannot die, but there is pain. Five days more would have driven you insane. I enjoyed your agony, but you've delayed too long. It is time to move forward to interrupt your pitiful song."

She dangled in the chains as Abkhas squeezed open her jaws and force-fed her. She began to grope for the food despite of herself. Her body yearned for nutrients. Angered by her cooperation, Abkhas slammed her into the wall.

"Piglet," It mumbled.

She healed instantly. Realizing Abkhas's vulnerability, she smiled. Angered again by her impertinence, Abkhas expanded and engulfed her.

"Stop! Stop!" she screamed.

The chains began to heat red then orange and finally yellow. She felt the heat creep slowly toward her wrists. Just as the pain became unbearable, it ceased. Abkhas's mouth opened and closed without uttering a sound. Only the hiss of air being forced over serrated yellow teeth interrupted the silence. Abkhas stopped, regained composure, and smiled very thin-lipped.

"I'll have time enough when the game is done to continue this delight and have my fun."

Peace lifted her chin slightly. "I'll not participate in your game. I will not be your pawn... I can't be," she said, momentarily losing composure.

"Your decision is of no consequence. There is no longer recompense. If there were, it comes too late. The birthing is started it won't abate. Enjoy your world, though dark and drab. Is all the peace in this world you have."

She said nothing. Abkhas was gone. Despair remained.

CHAPTER 5

—————— ✳ ——————

Birthings Two

Omurcada woke, counting softly. "Three thousand six hundred and forty-eight, three thousand six hundred and forty-nine, three thousand six hundred and fif—what the heck are you doing?"

He suddenly realized he was still doing pull-ups as well as conversing with himself. Omurcada gulped air, feeling as if he were slipping under, drowning in the sudden realization he was moving closer, much closer to losing his sanity.

"I can't lose it," he mumbled. "A prison of my own insanity would be a fate worse than Abkhas," he offered aloud, stretching the ache out of his forearms. "You are not crazy, and you won't go crazy." Omurcada tensed. *I just answered myself again*, he thought, biting off an impulse to give in to the insanity altogether. *Yes, you did answer yourself,* the voice came. Omurcada felt his mouth move, but those thoughts were not his thoughts. *Dribbling Druids, I'm hallucinating!* he thought.

In three dimensions, the voice echoed.

Omurcada stood, left hand raised, and pointer finger perpendicular to the side of his nose as if he were about to scratch. Every muscle remained tensed, body flexed as if frozen amidst the act of movement. He slowly turned his head to the right, sensing duality, concentrating, pupils as large as saucers, attempting to perceive what was not perceivable in pitch blackness. More to the right—nothing. Turning to the left, glimpsing something that glistened.

"What's this…?" Omurcada stared. He felt the blood move from his face to the back of his skull. "It can't…can't…be…?" Omurcada stared, eyes wide, directly into his own eyes, screamed, and lost consciousness. An ominous shimmer vaguely interrupted the void. Not a sound, not a figure, yet a presence shifted the blackness. The silence trembled ever so slightly in response to the soundless laughter of one who had played a joke that only It could appreciate.

When he awoke, he was still counting. "Four thousand nine hundred and eighty-one, four thousand eight hundred—no, nine hundred and eighty-two, four thousand nine hundred and eighty thre—aaaa, DAMN! I'm doing it again!" He shook his head. *This is nuts… I am nuts! I'm crazy… I've finally lost control of everything. I'm talking in my sleep. My arms continue to pull me up even against my will, and I'm hallucinating! What do you think, Sigmund?*

"Definitely fixation in the anal stage," the darkness murmured.

Omurcada pressed his back and head against the wall. Petrified, he warbled, "AAAAABKKKKAAAASSSS, is that you?"

Silence emanated. The room remained devoid of all sound, except the rhythmic thump of Omurcada's heart. Omurcada finally, very cautiously, released his breath, trying to suppress the sound of his heart pounding in his ears.

"I suppose you think this is funny?" His voice reverberated, yet no answer came. Sucking in wind, jutting chin and chest forward, he bellowed, "YOU! YOOOUUUU!" So filled with anger, his eyes bulged, his brain blackened the room to a deeper pitch. He could perceive nothing, yet something was with him. What that something was, he was unsure. It didn't matter. He would smite it with his rage alone. Pushed to a frenzy by his captivity and the audacity of his captor, Omurcada concentrated with mind and muscle. He screamed and pulled against the bindings. The chains creaked and turned but would not release him. The greater their resistance, the more urgent his frenzy. Omurcada inhaled, audibly, until his lungs were about to burst as he prepared to break free from the chains or lose his limbs in the effort.

Omurcada's mind, body, and spirit rippled against the chains. He felt his bones begin to bend and flex. His tendons vibrated in agony against the pressure. Suddenly, the resistance subsided. His chains reeled forward an arm's length before stopping abruptly. The release caused Omurcada to dive forward, his body quickly reaching the end of the slack created by the release only to be snatched backward by the wrists. Omurcada's feet slide past his torso, escaping fully forward. He realized he'd hit the end of the chain fully at the moment he realized he was fully extended horizontally four and one-half feet above the floor. His heart and mind rejoiced despite the knowledge he was about to establish a concrete relationship with the floor. He'd gained freedom. As small as it was, an arm's length signified a victory. It was the first step in winning the game and ending the fear of insanity. His body absorbed the impact at the conclusion of his fall, but Omurcada barely noticed. The pain in his wrists and forearms abated as he straightened. His body repaired itself.

Omurcada sat on his haunches, grinning. Oblivious to all but what had just been accomplished, he smiled completely over full and pleased with his newly found freedom. *It is possible. Yes, it is possible.* He smiled. "All is well in Gotham City." A new hope took root in the dunes of his desperation—a hope nourished by the knowledge he could win if only one small victory at a time.

* * *

She woke to a smothered distant almost imperceivable cry of another being.

"Who's there?" Peace ventured, muscles tensed in apprehension and anticipation of struggle. No sound. No answer. *I must have been hearing things. It only stands to reason. I've been here for months... or years...who knows? Even the food's tasting better. God, what I'd do for a toothbrush. It's a wonder I can eat for the moss on my teeth."* She thought quietly about her captivity. *It's strange. I never thought I'd enjoy being alone. I guess I have not ever had this much time to get used to it.* She smiled as her eyes filled. *Part of me enjoys this mending body and growing strength. Part of me wishes for a friend to touch and to hold. Part of me hates the smell I seem to be spreading throughout this room.* A solitary tear slipped over her cheek, gliding near her nose, and finally bouncing over lips to the edge of her mouth. She wished she was not quite so familiar with that salty taste. *Oh well, no sense contemplating the impossible. I wish I could find an answer to this riddle. Maybe I can sweet talk high pockets into another clue!*

"Abkhas," she called in a voice as sweet as honeydew. Silence. "Abkhas, please," this time, a bit more restrained. As she prepared to call, the distant cry resounded. Peace flinched, positive she'd heard the same cry earlier. Though nearly out of ear's range, she strained to locate the voice's origin.

"Abkhaaaa—" Peace was suddenly lifted directly up from the floor, spread-eagle, then stretched full length and dangling by the chains coupling her wrists. Her shackles abraded, digging deeply into her wrists and ankles. Her shoulders pinched. The shackles throbbed with each beat of her heart. Peace, wracked with fear and practically unconscious from the onslaught, continued, "Abkhas, nooooo! I only wanted to talk!" Her voice pushed forward horse from exertion. The pressure grew. She felt as if her vertebra were being slowly but progressively separated. Blood flowed more quickly, jelling the shackles.

Peace pulled with all her might without success. Slowly, inch by inch, she was being lifted from the floor. Clawing, pressing her hips against the wall, digging in her heels, the pull was relentless against her will. Peace continued the struggle, expecting Abkhas to appear at any moment, grinning with those broken yellow teeth. She could no longer resist physically. Peace attempted to pull herself up by the chains, hoping to relieve the pain from metal biting into her wrists. The pain did not subside. She screamed silently, desperately wishing someone or something would intervene, end this torture. Her desperation grew to a frenzy. Resisting the push to lose consciousness, she focused her remaining will upon attaining freedom. Peace closed her eyes, recalling the events leading to and beyond her captivity— to the words uttered by Abkhas as well as Messmor. *There must be an answer*, she thought. *Something they said…some sort of clue.* The answer must be somewhere within her lineage. *But that makes no sense at all*, she thought, yet she knew an answer, a solution existed.

The pain intensified. "Noooooooooo!" she forced through clenched teeth. From deep within her persona, a coldly calculated sense of purpose and logic grew. *I will not allow this!* Her mind wheeled. Her wrists began to warm, the chains and couplings began to vibrate and blur. The links began to hum, gradually glowing brighter from the friction. She screamed, shaking her head, slinging droplets of perspiration in all directions, frantic for freedom. The chains glowed ominously, each link slowly being enveloped by energy resembling St. Elmo's Fire inching its way up the chain. She felt psychic energy ebb and flow, wax and wane, gather and release like a blast furnace and bellows. Parts of her mind worked in synchrony as she concentrated to contain and manipulate the power all the while struggling to determine whether the psychic energy was real or hallucination. She extended the energy partially from fear of being overcome if she did not release it and partially to extend her awareness through the links of the chain. She could sense an entity equally chained, equally trapped, and equally desiring freedom at any cost. She hungered to end its existence. Peace teetered on the verge of unleashing the building blast furnace. Should she unleash, willing the other entity's destruction or allow life? She reconsidered, "Freedom first," she offered aloud. Instead of ending the life of an entity, her power was diverted to the links that bound her. The chains lengthened!

Stunned, she realized she had actually lengthened the chain, and someone else was held captive. *Another being*, she thought. *And it wasn't Abkhas!* Her mind quickly refocused upon freedom, the psychic energy, the odd sense of duality. A second scream drifted through her imprisonment from the entity she'd sensed earlier. Peace's mind took in the scream, a distraction, but did not shift from contemplating the discovery of the power, and even more so, her ability to use, or better describe, manipulate the psychic energy. Chains cooled. "How in the world did I do that!" Peace pushed the chains aside and sat in wonderment, feeling her wrists healing, a subtle and once-irritating itch.

After a very short bit of contemplation, she frowned and resolved. "I couldn't have done that…"

She puzzled onward, hoping for some sort of revelation. "Then who could have? One of the birthings? Abkhas? Someone or something else I cannot see?" Peace's brow furled once more. "Or…maybe someone else was also chosen… Someone able to cause the chains to move or lengthen…" Peace stood and paced the length of the chain and back. "A birthing…unreal…yet…maybe real if I accept the rest of this as being true. It must have been…well, maybe, maybe not."

Something from deep within rumbled. Peace hesitated. She unconsciously placed her hand over her stomach.

"Is it you, little one?" She ached for company, camaraderie, and began to believe with certainty not only were the birthings possible but that the first one. Wigan…was with her.

"Well, Wigan…baby girl…if it was you…I need you now more than ever."

The thought of Wigan, as far-fetched as it seemed, filled her heart with that for which she was named, Peace.

* * *

Omurcada closed his eyes and contemplated what had happened. "Extra chain? Nothing's free around here. What do I need extra chain for?" He stretched the muscles in his back. "If only the girls could see me now." He stared blindly at his massive forearms and torso. *I can't see them, but I know they're twice the size they were…and that I'm smiling about it!* The room seemed to change. *Something's different*, he thought quizzically. *That smell? It smells like a foundry.* The chains began to quiver. "Now what? Fun and games again, Abby?" The room smelled more and more like an ironwork. The crude acrid scent of metal being heated and alloys being undone wafted through the cavern, irritating his eyes and burning his nose. Omurcada cringed, wrinkling his nose in an effort to avoid both the aroma and the burning sensation. He avoided breathing through his mouth, yet breathing through his nose brought little relief. He coughed out to whom he believed to be the source of irritation.

"What is this, Abby?" Omurcada cupped his hands around his nose and mouth, attempting to force his voice to carry. "You planning to poison me?" He reached up for another section of chain, only to find the temperature of his metal bond was climbing. With a moment more of inspection, he concluded the room temperature had risen...and was steadily rising!

Omurcada's fingers itched as the heat traversed link to link, ebbing ever closer. The links closest to his shackles were the first to cause pain. Omurcada stared, straining to see the length he'd been carrying, which extended several inches above his wrist. Hissing and popping, the moisture that had formed a barrier of sweat dissipated. His skin undulated, stretching closer to forming blisters. Sweat beaded, trickled, then streamed down his rib cage and back. He released the length of the chain to wipe sweat from his eyes and forehead.

"First, blind me, then poison me, then turn the place into a sauna." He shook his head. "What next?"

Omurcada wiped the salt from his eyelid, careful not to drop any from his fingertip, then touched the droplet to his tongue, smiling. "A little seasoning before lunch."

He reached again to shorten the length of the chain.

"Yeeooww!" he exclaimed, quickly releasing the chain and blowing on his freshly singed palms. He gingerly grasped the chain just above the coupling. "Warm and getting warmer." Fully expecting to see nothing through the impenetrable darkness, he squinted, unconsciously searching to see what was happening to the chain. Omurcada exhaled slowly.

"I'll be...," echoed near soundlessly. His eyes, attempting to adjust to the vague light, focused upon a nearly invisible yet definite hair-thin outline of chain link appearing out of the darkness. The red-rimmed silhouette of the chain emerged ever so slowly, deepening in color and brightening until the chain was completely visible and more. The links, fully luminous, lighting the room, sent shadows dancing in every direction. He rubbed his eyes, believing the sight to be another hallucination.

"Lo-Lo-Lor-Llloorrrddd, I can see!" he exclaimed. Just as suddenly, he thought, *But what is it I am seeing?* The chains trembled as one link's red hue morphed to orange as the next link morphed to red. The pattern continued repetitively, with each red link moving ever closer to Omurcada's wrist. Stunned to silence by what was happening, he eyed the pattern as it undulated in color and form—dull red link to luminous red to an orange hue to an orange glow. The final link continued to be enveloped by finely spun green tentacles, snapping, gripping, lacing spinning, and etching intricate delicate yet deadly designs. The kaleidoscopic dance of tentacles was underscored by the constant and deliberate progression of heating metal. The design complexed, web upon web, glowing incandescently and emitting a radiant pulsing vitality that, in turn, caused the chains to glow and to undulate in intensity as well as color.

Omurcada's wrists began to itch. *To near the heat*, he thought. Caught between the horror of being burned by near-molten metal and the exhilaration of recapturing sight, Omurcada cringed backward then, hesitantly, reached to touch the green webbing. Before he sensed danger or pain, he smelled the hair at his wrist singe. Quickly jerking his hand back, he discovered the coupling was beginning to heat. His curiosity almost was overridden by the fear of being consumed by what now appeared to be an iridescent mist devouring the chain link by link. "Damn," he muttered. *What could be causing this?* he thought. "Abkhas...ABKHAS! You dung heap! Stop toying with me!"

Omurcada's body pressed and pulled against the chains and heat while his mind continued to distract and revel in the sight of the room. He had not had sight for what seemed to be months. His entire orientation was to the dark dimensions of the room and the restrictions of the chain. Omurcada, despite the pain of hot metal to the flesh, was more fearful of the return to blindness. Though his eyes ached from the brightness, he hastily attempted to commit the room to memory. It was much larger than the six-by-six cell he'd originally imagined. Distracted both by panic and pain, he attempted to gauge distances from the wall to the contiguous wall. He pressed his mind away from the distraction to determine the physical makeup of the walls and floor and to determine the distance to the ceiling.

Omurcada closed his eyes for a moment, attempting to commit to memory each of the room's irregularities. He could feel the heat from the chains and was very aware the room temperature had increased by ten to fifteen degrees. His calculations were abruptly interrupted by a surge in the mist, a sudden and intense increase in the flow of heat as the tentacles leaped down the chain. Omurcada's arms, and body for that matter, were immersed in sweat. The heat, practically unbearable, was dramatically increased by the mist's presence. He pulled viciously against the restraints, right arm then left arm, then both arms together. The chain refused to relinquish. The green mist continued to undulate, actuating more and more rapidly toward Omurcada.

He could hear himself screaming, feel his body resist the chain, and sear from the heat. He could not accept what was happening until the mist leaped from coupling to his elbows then onto his face. He tried to scream—nothing. He tried to breathe—nothing. He pressed against the chains to the point of dislocation—nothing! Mentally, he howled, *THE GAME, ABKHAS! THE GAME! WHY KILL ME NOW?* His legs burned from the exertion. His face burned from the heat. *You'll not die*, a distant yet distinct voice audibled from somewhere within his mind—their mind. Omurcada dropped to his knees, grabbing and prying at the mask of mist, attempting to survive the webbing that had enveloped his face. His panic was nearly incapacitating, and his sight narrowed from lack of oxygen. Omurcada could feel an excess of synaptic activity. The other voice seemed to detach from and observe the event with an analytical coolness and an even more determined callousness. *You'll not die, Sensi.* His rage, and logic, driven by survival, coalesced into a consciousness of its own.

Omurcada's body now lay on the floor of his prison. His face expressionless, his form motionless, he no longer felt in control. His detached mind surmised that his life was ebbing, being sucked away by the webbing that had enveloped his mouth and nose. Inside, though outside consciousness, an alien yet familiar entity assumed control of Omurcada's body. Without pain or inhibition, the entity raised Omurcada's hands. Massive fingers wrapped around the glowing mask tearing it from his face. Mechanically, the hands moved to the chains and quenched the fire. *I...am...here...* The other self-addressed the phosphorescent anomaly. *Sense my presence... Release myself and Sensi.* A cold logic permeated Omurcada's conscience. The statement, though simply a statement without malice, betrayed a determination that would be brought to fruition now and into the future. The mist resisted only momentarily. Seeming to sense and understand the entity's purpose, it began to recede, evaporating slowly then rapidly. The room cooled and returned to near-total darkness. All that remained was a phosphorescent sphere glowing and undulating rapidly two meters in the air. The orb was the size of an acorn, golden radiance surrounded by what appeared to be St. Elmo's Fire. *What the hell is that... It*, Omurcada thought, clearing his mind and reveling in the presence of oxygen.

He tentatively reached his right hand, forefinger extended, to touch his guest. The entity zipped instantaneously to the tip of Omurcada's nose. Startled by the sudden movement as well as the speed in which the orb repositioned, Omurcada tensed. The sphere glowed golden, radiating kinsmanship, cold, factual assessment with an absence of warmth on a physical level, a loyalty mixed with detachment on an emotional level. A strange symbiosis seemed to exist between the orb and Omurcada. Omurcada could sense part of himself fused within the psyche of the orb, yet the entity had a mind of its own, apart from the fusion. Like a son to a father. A strange inner connectedness coupled with a stranger who needed to be separate all the while interdependent upon one another. Omurcada pressed himself to his feet bringing the orb to eye level.

The orb and the ordinary man observed, touched, probed, and examined one another. An empathy of sorts was being established. Omurcada found the experience unsettling, flinching with the sudden changes in mood and emotion being expressed by the orb. Rage then logic, emotional attachment then detachment, unity then fear, continued to radiate from the orb. The orb seemed to be searching Omurcada's thoughts for an anchor, a direction, a certain kind of connection to make it complete. Omurcada tried to open his mind but could not bring himself to trust anything even something of himself that completely. He thought of Abkhas for just a moment.

The orb radiated extreme hostility and an absolute conviction that this was his enemy. Omurcada stepped back from the intensity of the interaction. Before he could express himself, his thoughts touched the orb, advising it that all beings are not like Abkhas, but it is not easy to determine the difference. The orb seemed settled…complete with the interaction. The entity touched Omurcada's cheek ever so softly then vanished.

Omurcada flinched, covered his eyes, then doubled over from the pain. "My eyes… God, MY EYES!" He could only see pain, sterile, flash of white, pain as bright as lightning's core. It seemed to burn through his brain to the back of his head. Tears burst forth, but the pain would not be quenched. With great restraint, Omurcada managed to resist digging out the pain. "Calm, stay calm," he repeated the mantra as his fingers unconsciously flexed into and out of a fist. Just when he believed that he could no longer hold out, his eyes began to adjust. Blinking and rubbing provided some relief, but he could not bear to open them completely. Again, the detached side of himself offered aloud, "Zen?" just before losing consciousness and collapsing to the floor. The orb returned for a millisecond, flashed brightly, then disappeared.

* * *

The birthing bubble enlarged and dissipated, releasing the birthing fully grown at the beginning of his journey. Zen Murcada sat cross-legged, the third branch up a downed fir tree, contemplating his existence. "There's no sense wondering how you arrived or why you're here," he said to himself while fidgeting from the onslaught of pine needles. "Funny, I remember darkness. I know my name, first, darkness then this overgrown hunk of pointed shrubbery," he said, staring at the tree, fingering the needles of the Douglas pine. Zen sat scratching his head, wondering how he knew this was a Douglas pine and that it was out of place. It should have been located in colder more northern climates than he was experiencing. He shifted his weight, attempting to disallow the bark from biting into his rear posterior. He examined his short squat thick-skinned yet muscled body. "I'd better find some clothes. This birthday suit"—he glanced down—"and loincloth will never do."

After scanning the countryside, Zen, five foot seven, all two hundred pounds, dropped from his perch, avoiding pine needles with much more control than one would anticipate to the ground not far below. Zen, with no knowledge of purpose or probable destination, could only sense destiny was to the north. Without a second thought, he cat-rolled silently to his feet, pausing just long enough to determine which direction was north then strove forward. Rhythmically heel met path, dust puffed then settled. Zen's image diminished into the foliage. *Slightly west,* Zen thought to himself. His eyes flickered rapidly side to side, accounting and discounting all that he encountered. The sensory hypervigilance was as natural as his birthday suit, which caused Zen to be more and more aware of the need to find clothing quickly or be a bit better at evading stands of raspberry bushes and those pesky little bugs equipped with a drill and pump. He had only so much blood and was not inclined to share. He hesitated just long enough to remove the vagabonds that had attached themselves to his legs. "Thorns," he muttered. The glen teemed with life that Zen categorized quickly to be nothing more than non-threatening inconsequential distractions. He moved rapidly, yet methodically, careful to avoid twigs that crackle and branches that would announce his presence to the world. He innately understood silence as his friend. Destiny was calling, and dawn was breaking. Both warranted caution.

Zen spotted a small dwelling neatly camouflaged in the woods. The house was situated adjacent to an intensely entangled thicket. The dwelling was further obscured by ivy and small bushes. Six horses were corralled about one hundred feet to the east near what could best be described as a series of lean-tos. The lean-tos apparently had been built to provide some shelter for the horses but had fallen in from lack of attention. Zen could hear the wind gently puff its way through their disrepair. The lumber sagged, serving as a meal place for a host of crustaceans, slugs, and beetles. *The bugs and birds have enjoyed their stay,* Zen thought while scrutinizing the area. Zen's nose wrinkled, instinctively repelling the smell of wood rot and fermenting horse droppings. *Well, it's at least a roof over their head*, he thought, glancing back toward the house, he shifted his weight, turning in its direction, then squatted on his haunches rubbing his chin. Zen's hypervigilance, coupled with a keen sense of sight, brought clarity, a sharpness to his vision as he surveyed his surroundings. He remained motionless even as his cheek twitched to remove a mosquito that had landed for a moment. He was uncomfortable remaining in any one position for more than a few seconds. He understood that there were other beasts and beings with eyesight sharper than his own. Movement of any kind would likely draw attention. After a short while, Zen stood cautiously, then proceeded forward, scanning for anything unusual or what he believed might represent danger.

Though the house was generally dilapidated, the door, sturdily framed and barring entry, was constructed of heavy oak that had been recently cut. The house, better described as a small shanty with a door that did not match the dwelling, looked unoccupied. Zen scanned the area intensely, expecting to see some sign of life as he moved silently along the wood surrounding the glen. He continued to carefully avoid fallen twigs and downfalls all the while keeping his focus primarily on the shanty. Zen noticed the windows of the house were shuttered with pine and deer hide. The roof was thatch. *All that frailty and an oak door large enough to keep out a bear*, he thought, wondering about the motives of the occupants. Zen paused a moment as he reconsidered the shanty's construction, thinking, *Just what were they trying to keep out…or in?*

Zen sat back on his haunches a second time. Though at a moderate distance, he was still close enough to thoroughly observe the dwelling. No one was about, except a young boy carrying water and oats to the stock. Zen counted three horses in a smaller corral, ten pigs, twenty chickens, and one… *Big canine*, he thought. The family was small, based on the clothes strung across branches hanging to dry, grandmother, mother, two sons, and one daughter. The "old man" was either dead, gone for the day, or gone forever as it appeared. "Well, time's a-wasting," Zen offered. Quietly patting a giant oak with feigned affection, he made his way to the back of the dwelling, cautious to avoid detection by the boy.

Negotiating the thicket had been a bit more difficult than Zen had initially imagined, but he had successfully arrived at the rear of the dwelling with only a few scratches and less than a half dozen stubborn companions. Zen winced quietly as he picked the last of the thorns out of his backside, noting to himself that certain areas stung a bit more than others. Examining the inside of his thigh, he found himself wishing that he at least had had a little more loincloth. Noting other locations of scratches, one, in particular, he considered himself lucky to still be male. After thoroughly checking for nicks, bruises, and freeloading thorns or ticks, Zen returned to the task of silent observation, hoping to see or find something useful.

The bugbites were frequent and intense to the point of distraction. *Clothes*, he thought to himself, silently wishing the bugs would find another meal or that he would grow fur. Zen, hidden between the thicket, the back of the house, and a stand of corn to his left, eyeballed the stack of clothes. The sun was still high enough to make it difficult to make it to the house without detection. He knew he could not wait much longer. The bugs continued to present a nuisance, but the nagging compulsion to travel north was gaining intensity. Though he knew not his role or the nature of his mysterious existence, it was more and more apparent to Zen that his goal, whatever it might be, was time-sensitive, and the press to move onward was more and more persistent.

"Who are…" was all the young woman managed to voice as a startled Zen struck her squarely in the temple with a left-handed back fist.

"Damn," he mumbled, catching the young woman as she slumped toward the ground. He cradled her quickly and gently set her down, checking vital signs. Zen felt her throat for a pulse. *The heart pumps normal and strong*, he thought. Regretting the action, Zen tried to make the unconscious young woman as comfortable as possible by laying her on her side, resting her head upon her arm. She was already beginning to moan and focus her eyes when Zen, certain she was not seriously injured, made his move toward the house. He slipped past the garden to the side window where a stack of clothes was visible. He stood for a moment next to the wall, still shaking his head, disappointed that the girl was able to sneak that close to him. He had been too absorbed in obtaining clothes and entertaining the compulsion to go north. He was not prone to guilt but did regret striking the girl. He understood when she woke and reported his presence, there could be an additional complication.

Careful not to disturb the landscape or make unnecessary sounds, Zen ducked the window and made his way to the front entrance. He stepped gingerly on the first of four steps to a wooden platform that served as a walkway and a makeshift porch to the dwelling. Zen negotiated the first two steps when the third marked his weight and his arrival. *CREEEECK.* He stood motionless. Believing he was alone and no one had noticed the step's plea for relief, Zen made his way through the door. In moments, Zen reached his destination and quickly sorted through the stack of clothes, hoping to find something useful. Zen tensed, staring at the pant leg. The clothes he'd discovered, judging the size, belonged to a very large male. Even worse, nothing seemed to fit. The boy's clothes were too small, and the old man's? Well, *he must have been a giant*, Zen thought, trying to locate something that would allow a modicum of protection from the elements. Zen's lips twitched into a barely noticeable but authentic smile as he pulled a large blanket from the middle of the stack.

"You'll need more than a blanket to cover that arse." The grizzled old lady wheezed with a sound that may or may not have been a laugh. Zen sprang 180 degrees, somehow managing to tuck an end of the blanket under each arm covering his privates and landing in a full fighting stance. "I must be slipping," he said aloud.

Zen's face reddened as much from embarrassment for being nearly naked as from being discovered by the old woman particularly when he had been without a clue of the old women's presence. Regaining his composure, "I have no goods, no clothes, and relatively little recollection of my past. I'm honest enough," he offered while continuing to cover himself with the blanket, bowing slightly with respect, eyes aimed primarily at the floor. "And am willing to work long enough to fulfill my obligation for the blanket and clothes…if you have any that would fit me. I mean, you know harm, madam," Zen offered after he snatched up a piece of twine, forming it into a belt, folded over the blanket, and tied the blanket securely enough to allow movement without it falling.

"MADAM!" the old lady exclaimed. "A whorehouse, is it? You think this be a WHOREHOUSE!"

Zen's brows rose in surprise, followed quickly by anger. His eyebrows narrowed. "I said madam out of respect, not to infer a...a whorehouse." Zen regained composure and returned to the original subject. "My request remains the same."

"We get bounties for strangers around here"—the old lady squinted maliciously—"especially thieves such as the likes of you."

Zen's temper flared a second time as he became more perplexed with the old woman's attitude and more impatient with her continuous play on words. "Your opinion of my intent is in error, madam. In either case, you'll allow me the opportunity to pay by service or force me to take the stores I need... The choice is yours," Zen responded in a determined yet unabrasive manner.

The old lady scowled then grinned mischievously. "Well, laddie, you've never met my Frank now, have you? Me tinks it's time for introductions." The old lady struck her cane against the oak door, calling, "Frankey, ma darlin', there's a stranger out here who exposed himself to me! He wants to have his way! He's tryin' ta steal our stores!" she cackled.

Zen's jaw dropped almost as quickly as his face reddened. He was about to protest the ridiculous accusation when he was interrupted as Frank ducked his head through the doorway.

"'Tis a fine way to greet a neighbor...neighbor." Frank finished squeezing his enormous body through the doorway, not losing any time removing his shirt and proceeding to stretch his torso and crack his knuckles. He hesitated, staring at Zen, then rubbed both arms, smiling. "You'll be learnin' a lesson in manners, laddie. You'll be leaving these parts with no need of clothes." Frank stepped forward, adding, "If you survive your beatin', you'll be so blue no one'll tink you naked!" He laughed.

Frank popped the last of his knuckles, assuming a nonchalance but superior posture. Zen's eyes steeled as he very subtly switched to a rooted stance.

"Fra—" was all that Zen was allowed to say when Frankey stepped forward.

"I'm not in tha mood ta talk, laddie!" Frank barked as he began to rotate his fists in front of his chest.

Zen smiled a one-sided smile. His eyes twinkled as if enjoying what was about to happen. His demeanor radiated confidence and a lethality. "There will be no offer other than the one I gave the lady."

"Lady, is it," the old lady interrupted. "Well, now that's a change of heart. Me tinks he's learned respect, Frankey. I wonder if it is me or you that has changed his mind?" She laughed to the point of wheezing and coughing.

Frank simply resumed the conversation, "I tink you're finally usin your brain. I like your dress, but it will be of no matter, your breakin' will be done."

Zen stared through Frank, his voice cut the air crisply. "Horses break, not I. I'll warn you once and only once, I am no one's prisoner, and I have no enemies." Zen paused then added, "Living."

Frank's face lost its cheer and a bit of its confidence. Frank's facial muscles tensed as he stepped forward, intending to end the argument quickly. Zen leaped. In a single fluid motion, Zen slid his right heel into the base of Frankey's right knee, down the shin, finally crushing Frank's instep through the sides of his moccasin. The blow, without breaking stride, had dislocated the knee, removed all the flesh from the front of Frankey's shin, and broken his foot at the instep. Zen's right foot had no more than slid from the arch when his jump spin-side kick with left foot penetrated Frankey's solar plex, lifting and sending him into the wall next to the oak door.

Frankey's back hit the wall with such force the shack quaked and dust fell from the ceiling. As Frankey rebounded, Zen slid close, landing a spinning left back fist firmly between Frankey's eyes snapping the bridge of his nose, then followed through with a right palm heel to the heart. The blow could have killed, except for Zen's restraint. The palm heel was sufficient, however, to render Frank motionless while standing. Zen stepped away from Frank, smiled, then front kicked him firmly in the groin. Zen withdrew his right foot to the back position, remaining in a modified front stance.

Frank's eyes rolled up, ribs quivered. He bent over, falling directly onto the top of his head. Still conscious but completely incapacitated, Frank moaned and stared forward. Zen feigned a kick toward the old lady. She backed into the corner and cowered. Zen continued to watch her movement as he bent down next to Frank.

"I have a strange code of justice, FRIEND. You were only defending the lady's stupidity. The next time, you'll not be so ignorant. You live because I still call you friend. She"—Zen closed the distance between the old lady and himself much more quickly than the old lady could anticipate as she reached for the hammer that had been beside her rocking chair. Zen slammed her into the wall with palm heels under each of the woman's armpits. He grimaced hearing bones crack as she slid to unconsciousness—"should not have lied." Zen's rage pressed and nearly gained control before Zen mastered himself. Zen stared down at the old lady's body. He'd heard the clavicle break but could see nothing mishappen and for a moment thought her shape glimmered slightly.

Frankey gasped in horror. His urge to strike Zen left his eyes as quickly as it had arrived. Frankey sensed lethality in this stranger, and though Frankey had had his way most of his life brutalizing the weaker, this man was not weaker. Frankey's usual brashness was replaced by awe and fear. Zen turned toward Frankey, watching Frankey's eyes closely.

"You're learning," Zen muttered.

Zen stood silently and searched the area for additional danger. Glancing at the old woman, Zen bent down, feeling for the heartbeat. Strong and regular, Zen smiled, still wondering how the clavicle, which had been clearly broken, was completely healed. "Tough old buzzard." Lifting an eyelid and looking into her eyes, he noted no apparent concussion. Though she continued to appear unconscious, she seemed to mock him in her sleep. Zen again sensed a deeper strangeness to the old lady, something even more malevolent here than the old woman's manner. He shook his head, wondering at his paranoia.

After clearing his head with a few deep breaths, satisfied that the old woman was strange but no longer a threat, Zen turned to

Frankey. Frankey had not moved during Zen's interaction with the old woman. He remained very still but was conscious and aware. Zen glanced at Frankey and surmised that Frankey was in no mood to cause him further trouble. Though Zen believed he was safe from intrusion for the moment, his paranoia would not allow him to leave Frankey completely unattended or open to retaliate. Zen secured Frankey's hands to his feet with the remaining twine and maneuvered Frankey's bulk just out and to the side of the door. He glanced one more time at the surroundings. Satisfied he could reenter without further disruption, Zen reentered the dwelling.

It was fairly well-kept and appeared to be used by a larger family than the two who were present, three counting the girl. He tilted his head, four counting the clothes that would fit a boy. There were plenty of stores and extra utensils should he decide he needed them. He discovered two small hide pouches that would serve very useful in the journey ahead. Zen helped himself to the stores he required filling the pouches to over full with dried fish, jerky, a couple of apples, day-old bread, and a cornmeal biscuit. He bit into one of the apples as he glanced about the room.

"A quarterstaff." Zen smiled. He set the two pouches on the floor. He tipped the staff from its resting place, flipping the staff into the air with his left foot and catching it in his right hand. Zen twirled the staff in figure eights.

"I can't believe my fortune," he offered aloud, checking the staff for flaws and testing its balance. "There will be time for the two of us to get to know one another well I suspect." Zen's attention returned to the task at hand. Flour, bread, apples, onions, and a variety of dried meats were strewn along the countertop and adjoining table. Zen finished one apple and picked up another. He pressed the apple with his fingers, testing it for suppleness then bit a large chunk out. Juice flew forward as the apple snapped and broke into his mouth. Zen smiled at its richness. He continued his search, lifting keg tops and opening drawers, alternating apple from mouth to hand.

The shanty was very simple. Most of the families belonging were contained in hide bags and vine or grass weaved baskets. He glanced at the pouches then at the bags. He emptied two sizable bags.

Placing one inside the other, he added apples, bread, dried meats, and, for the time being, the pouches. Fumbling to figure out a way to attach the bag to the twine without losing his blanket, Zen turned back toward the door. Feeling the pull to go northward, he stepped to the doorway and nearly missed the bundle that had been very neatly folded next to a used but well-maintained sharpening stone and a small container of animal oil. He plopped the last bit of apple in his mouth, core and all, as he unwrapped the bundle. Zen grinned at the quarterstaff.

"Two of your friends!" Zen, again, could not believe his fortune in locating two engraved and rune-marked throwing knives, a matched set encased in open leather sheaths. "It seems a long time since I've embraced your sort," he muttered, examining the detailed design and assessing the quality. He did not recognize the craftsmanship, but the quality was unmistakable. Removing the knives very carefully, Zen examined the workmanship closely. He was amazed at their lightness countered by an incredible sturdiness. Each knife was balanced to perfection. Platinum-silver sheen emanated from the pair, making each line seem crisper than it should be and the multiple edges more vivid. The edges were honed expertly. No apparent abnormality from abuse or honing mistakes and razor-sharp. Zen flipped the knives in 360-degree spins, catching the knives by the tip without flaw. But…no signature from the smith.

Odd, Zen thought, realizing he was reveling too much in weaponry and not attending to the tasks at hand, regretfully, returned the knives to their appointed resting places. Each knife's sheath bore a resemblance of its companion etched in the rich leather surface. Otherwise identical the sheaths, as well as the knives, were the same in their intricacies except for a peculiar rune sign—one for male—a blue stone with an "O" etched on the surface above the outline of a man's face. "Hmm." He frowned.

"I-I know that face," he thought aloud, and one for a female with a "P" etched on the surface above the outline of a woman's face. Zen wondered why he knew that the runes were intended to represent a bonded pair and were likely bound in some magical or spiritual way. He decided he'd better leave the solving of what was becoming a reoccurring riddle, knowing but not knowing. He sheathed the knives and continued his search.

"I need boots, and those should fit." Zen picked up a pair of very worn deer hide boots that were propped in the corner next to a very new pair. *No sense taking his best*, he thought, slipping one foot on at a time. "It's a good thing my feet are big! I'm going to have to control that rage. It always gets the best of me," he continued speaking with himself. Zen paused. He could not stop his mind from wandering to the puzzle, knowing but not knowing, wondering how he knew so much about his rage and almost nothing about anything else, except weaponry.

"So my leathery friend," he addressed the boot. "What's your opinion? Will this take time to piece together or no?" he asked as he pulled the left boot onto his foot. "I see you have a tongue but no comment, then I believe you agree it will take time despite how aggravating that might be."

Zen cut slits into the leather bags and wove twine through each slit, carefully creating a drawstring and a loop strap to carry the bag cross shoulder, thereby freeing his hands. Zen tested the bag for sturdiness. Satisfied, Zen adjusted his blanket a final time placing one knife near the small of his back and the second in a pocket near the back of his boot. A final glance netted a flint and striker and a scarf.

"Time to move," Zen muttered and headed to the door once again. On his way out, he stopped and sadly saluted Frank. "Just one word of advice, Frank. Pick your friends wisely and always pick on someone your own size." One more step, Zen hesitated. "Well, it's probably too big, but I can always tuck it in. Thanks, Frank," Zen offered as he removed Frank's shirt. A few more steps, Zen stopped, returned to check the old lady. She was gone. *Hmmmm*, he thought as he tensed and scanned the area. No sign of the old woman. "I didn't hear her leave. Well, Frankey"—Zen bent down, looking Frankey squarely in the eyes—"I'm loosening the ties a bit, and you should be free in no time. Don't follow me. I doubt I'll spare your life a second time."

He noticed, in peripheral vision, the young woman peeking through the window, rubbing her temple but saying nothing.

Without looking up, he said, "I see you there, young one, and you are safe. I am sorry I hurt you. It won't happen again unless you decide to attack me." Her face vanished from the window. He could hear her back slide down the outer wall.

"I'm young, but I'm not stupid," she offered.

Zen chuckled, a sound he found unusual and a bit out of place. "No, you're not stupid... Tell your brother to leave me be and he will not be harmed."

She giggled. "I'll tell him, but he is stupid. Are you taking all our food?"

Zen grimaced. "No, just enough to keep me alive for a long trip." He did not understand where the feeling of guilt was coming from and squelched it nearly as quickly as it had surfaced. "Where did you put your grandmother?" he asked.

"Now you're being stupid," she replied. "I don't have a grandmother."

Zen turned toward the window. "Then who—never mind, go tell the boy to stay away... Tie him up if you have to. I'll be gone in a few moments."

He heard the young woman's footsteps trail off in the distance followed by an, "Ow! What did you do that for?" from a boy very dismayed with his sister's behavior. Grabbing one more apple, Zen stepped toward the door.

The growl no more than began when a startled Zen turned to face the family's snarling, drool-ridden Doberman. "More friends?" Zen's fear abated, but his annoyance was apparent as he slowly edged the staff into a position of advantage. The dog surged. Zen's rage emerged. The Doberman slumped, its skull reverberated from the single motion of the staff. "One not-so-big canine." His jaw clenched as the canine dropped to the porch floor. "I don't appreciate interruptions."

Stepping out of the front stance, his rage receded, grudgingly resisting imprisonment. Zen was certain the Doberman was dead. Again, he regretted losing control of the rage...but not the death of the canine. The boy appeared by the corner of the dwelling, then disappeared.

Zen continued to forcibly harness then squelch his rage. He'd managed not to blackout and remained aware but had not been able to control the intensity. He continued to reduce the rage as well as the anger counting backward from one hundred to fifty, concluding with a deep breath, *"woo that was intense"* he thought.

Zen managed to relax the tenseness, as he snatched up a second blanket, cut holes for his head and arms.

"I need to get hold of this rage," he said to himself as he slipped the shirt on tucking in the tails then pulled the newly made sleeveless over-garment over his head. He was not entirely uncomfortable with the singular clear-mindedness that came with the rage, but he was uncomfortable with not having the discipline to control it.

Rage…why rage? Something I need to conquer…before it conquers me, he thought as he stepped from the porch.

Zen crossed the meadow and entered the wood, thinking aloud, "I know I'm Irish." He danced a jig. "But I'll be damned if I know why or how I am Irish or how I got this crazy name! Zen, for Pete's sake… Why not Se'an or Erin or Matt… What is 'Irish' anyway?" He frowned. "And…who's Pete?" Glancing at the blanket that bounced over his knees, he grinned. "And this is a hell of a kilt. Hahaha!" His annoyance with the Doberman ebbed to mild disdain as the wood thickened, blocking his view of the dwelling and hiding his presence from the residents.

Zen's distant silhouette blended with then disappeared in the north woods when the old lady's body shimmered. In its place stood a black shroud. Abkhas glanced apathetically at the Doberman then to Frankey. "Idiots!" It thought, then vanished.

* * *

Peace felt warmth throughout her being. She had finally acquiesced to the reality that she was part of a "game." To what end, she could not imagine, but to be freed, she would have to bring the conclusion of the game to fruition. The combination of believing she was no longer alone coupled with the change in the routine of her captivity caused the captivity to be bearable and provided a satisfaction of sorts. The game had begun, and she was certain one of her birthings, Wigan to be more precise, was with her—part of her. She did not know exactly why she felt that the birthing existed and the birthing was Wigan. Call it women's intuition, call it a hunch, call it what you will, Peace believed that Wigan was present, and for the time being, that was enough to keep her sane.

She spent the better part of two weeks contemplating, examining, and eliminating arguments to Wigan's existence. Despite Peace's better judgment, she was much more confident that this sort of coalesced energy was real—not simply a delusion, and she suppressed any contradictory thoughts by pushing them from her mind forcefully. The ritual was as much a part of her daily meditation for sanity as it was a hope for future freedom. She obsessed about the birthings even through the feedings. She knew they must exist. She just needed to find a way to free them—to sustain her concentration while eliminating anything that disrupted or disturbed her focus, particularly thoughts that suggested she could be defeated. Those silent but unnerving doubts nipped at her consciousness and her defenses, but she held fast, forcefully pushing them aside and focusing on the game. *I know you are real... I know you are with me... I believe you sense me... I have to bring you forth...somehow free you*, she thought to herself as she spoke to what she believed to be Wigan, simultaneously, day in and day out.

Today was no different. The obvious necessity followed by the obvious obstruction. "How can I set you free?" she wondered aloud. "You're so close, but I don't know how to release you." Peace picked up another slug as much for the water within it as the food it represented, all the while not losing focus on the task at hand. "Thank God you're really from me and not part of Abkhas." Peace shuddered not altogether, certain that the birthings were not of Abkhas—or at least its influence. After sensing the energy, if that is an adequate description, she struggled more with the possibility that the energy was of Abkhas and Wigan a delusion, not real, who existed because she needed her to exist out of desperation—a manifestation of her subconscious desire to have company. "If this...this being is real...

how do I know it's Wigan? Could it be just another of Abkhas's games?" she asked herself over and over in the beginning.

Peace resolved the issue by deciding that if it were of Abkhas, she would not feel safe as she did in the odd duality. It was not that she felt incredibly pure, but she was certain she was not evil, and anything that had even a particle of Abkhas associated with its creation could not escape the overwhelming taint Abkhas brought into existence whenever it was present. Dismissing Abkhas, however, did not dismiss the possibility that this energy, this feeling, was not some sort of conversion hysteria where she was unconsciously willing Wigan into existence. Mumbling to herself, Peace continued to search for the energy's center. She could sense she was close to the heart of the being existing within her, a near yet incomplete duality. She imagined this would be the relationship she would have had with her unborn child if she'd ever been pregnant.

"I wish you would say something… Do something that would tell me for certain you exist and feel the same bond with me as I do with you." Peace closed her eyes and repeated the mantra she'd grown accustomed to. "Wigan…can you hear me…? Do you know me…? Are you here…? My name was Miry, but I am now known as Peace… I am your mother." She sighed. "I wish I could see. Maybe I could think better." Peace continued the mantra as she swallowed another slug. For the first time, something seemed to respond. Peace stopped mid-chew, opening her senses to detect any sort of communication that could be happening. A warmth, that Peace had isolated and identified as Wigan, seemed to mass itself in the small of Peace's back. Peace inhaled sharply. Fingertips touching her lips in anxious excitement, she swallowed, then cleared her mind.

"You can hear me?" she asked. The warmth intensified then abruptly cooled. "YOU CAN HEAR ME!" Peace exclaimed with excitement, standing up and turning as if to face the warmth. She stopped turning and laughed aloud, realizing as long as it was located in the small of her back, she could pirouette but would not ever quite face the warmth. "My daughter," she corrected herself aloud. She was certain this was no figment of Abkhas. "At least, if you are able, move to the front," she whispered. No movement occurred, but Peace was much more at ease knowing that the riddle had been partially solved and the game was afoot. No more loneliness. Time to think, time to plan, and time to be very wary of Abkhas. Her hackles stood at the thought of it being anywhere close by. A mother's instinct to protect pulsed through Peace. "Remember, little one, remember its name… ABKHAS…and be afraid, always be afraid it might be near because it could be the death of you," she mumbled without thinking while every sense strained to determine whether Abkhas was near.

Days passed, yet the warmth remained, evolving ever so slowly into a solid acorn size sphere of energy. The sphere traveled alternately either as a concentrated source of energy or a fluid wave of confined energy spreading then coalescing wherever it was destined within Peace's body. The warmth routinely moved to the front of Peace's body, settling just above the abdomen and radiating warmth when Peace's hand was near. Their communication had begun with the first realization that the warmth could hear and understand Peace's statements as well as some of her basic emotional desires. Peace and the warmth's ability to communicate improved substantially—to the point that Peace had attempted to communicate telepathically. On the first attempt, the warmth pulsed intermittently spreading itself throughout Peace's body as if searching for the voice. The warmth settled at the top of Peace's head, as near as Peace could tell, and spoke, "*Where you? What am it?*"

Startled by the response, Peace attempted to puzzle out how to respond while catching her breath.

"You can speak?" Peace blurted.

"*Where you? What am it?*" The warmth repeated with more urgency.

"I am here," Peace returned, "and you are part of me."

The warmth ceased pulsating. "*Where here…? What am it/me/you?*"

"It's a long story…daughter."

Peace began the telling actively addressed the sphere of energy as Wigan. She opened her mind to the first counterpart, telling her the history of their captivity to Abkhas and the game. Wigan struggled initially in her attempt to absorb Peace's statements. Peace's vocabulary and adjoining thoughts, which seemed to be a medley of word pictures, were difficult to match or make sense out of. Slowly, with certainty, Wigan puzzled out the meanings—first disjointed partial sensibility then, with great persistence, she began to understand all of Peace's offerings as well as the emotional impact of each statement as if she were part of Peace's psyche. Once the symbiosis became fully functional, Wigan learned quickly. Wigan enjoyed an openness with Peace yet struggled to understand Peace's response to certain ideas or conditions. Peace's undulation in mood was the most difficult to come to terms with causing Wigan to be somewhat cautious in what she asked and what memory she invoked. She, though not much more than a duality, did not divulge her awareness to Peace beyond the pulses of energy, a code that they'd developed unique to their relationship that, at times, was a much more complete communication than words could provide. As Peace relived the events, Wigan pulsed accordingly—immense heat during rage, coolness during despair, all-encompassing warmth in compassion, and a guarded radiance and tempering whenever Abkhas was mentioned.

Their relationship grew, truly as mother and daughter, Peace rejoiced in the symbiosis as well as the companionship. *I certainly love you, daughter*, Peace thought. Wigan radiated warmth. *I don't want you to go.* Wigan cooled then iced. Peace panicked. *I know you must. It's just I don't think I can bear the loneliness, the darkness most of all.* Wigan warmed slightly then began to pulsate rapidly. The little orb pulled itself into a solid ball of energy and proceeded to scurry rapidly, as if searching, throughout Peace's body and consciousness. Peace giggled, then laughed.

"Stop it! You're tickling me!"

Wigan pulsed through Peace's nervous system, jumping synapse, vaulting thresholds, then zipped to the top center of Peace's skull, just under the scalp.

"What are you doing?"

Wigan pulsed then flashed to Peace's eyes. Astonished, Peace blinked. Tears blurred her vision. "I can see! I can SEE! THE DARKNESS, it's, it's gone!" she exclaimed. The vision was short-lived. Wigan pulsed warmth and love throughout Peace's body then cooled. Peace's sight diminished as the warmth dissipated into coolness.

"*What is it you want?*" The orb quieted. "*You just want me to guess?*" The orb pulsed rapidly then stilled. "*You do want me to guess.*" The orb pulsed rapidly then silenced. "*All right.*"

Peace contemplated what it was that Wigan could be pursuing so diligently. Peace asked questions, brought forth memories for Wigan to review, and guessed at what Wigan would possibly desire, but all met with silence. Wigan's silence continued for several hours until Peace, throwing her hands up in frustration, barked, "What the hell do you want, girl! Abkhas, you bastard. You said the game had begun. How am I supposed to play it sitting in this dungeon? I want out of this place." At that instant, the orb pulsed furiously abounding to and fro between Peace's shoulder blades, again settling at the base of Peace's knowledge knot.

"You want out of this place?"

The orb pulsed warmth, filling Peace's eyes with vision then cooled, taking the vision with her. Peace shook her head. "All right. It's a deal, daughter. Your freedom for my sight. I'm not your keeper, though. If you really want to go, which you must, you don't need to be thinking about my needs. You need to take care of your own."

In that instant, the orb dashed from Peace's eyes.

Wigan was born. An emerald orb encased in a gold matrix of soft light. She pulsed and glowed then touched Peace's cheek. Peace's eyes teared from the joy of Wigan as well as the despair at the inevitable loss of companionship. Peace could no longer see anything in the darkness but the orb. Wigan slowly withdrew as if to say, "*Departure is truly a sorrow, but I must go. I love you, Mother and dear friend,*" then vanished. Peace wept in the darkness. "Alone again. You didn't have to take me at my word. I don't know if I can stay alive in this infernal darkness even if I must."

The chains seemed cold and lifeless, the room stifling. Peace wondered whether she would ever see again yet was grateful for the moments shared with Wigan. Peace smiled to herself, lifting her head she stood straight, proud, and determined. "One candle burning, one small light in the darkness"—she smiled—"and that small light defies the dark even if ever so slightly," she offered aloud to her captivity.

* * *

The matrix complexed and evolved, enlarging and shaping with every pulse until Wigan opened her eyes. Wigan, fully grown physically, remained enveloped by the sphere her psyche had been captured within. The sphere, considerably larger, served as a sort of umbilical bubble, now resting comfortably on the shore of a small brook. The sphere was permeable, allowing air in but keeping out whatever might be harmful to its occupant, including not being visible to onlookers, magically endowed or not. Wigan, without leaving the bubble, could see her reflection in the brook. She stared into the brook and marveled at her appearance. "I'm...beautiful... Such a gift my mother gave." Wigan flipped back her lush auburn hair. Below the shoulder in length, Wigan's hair lifted and swirled in concert with a gentle but persistent warm breeze that seemed to move through the bubble. Wigan curled strands of hair that had drifted over her high cheekbones to near the corner of her mouth and contemplated her body's reflection. "Green eyes. How appropriate." She smiled. "You shall see, Mother." Wigan closed her eyes, envisioning Peace's chains and darkness. "*Mother*," her mind called.

Peace, startled by the call, said, "Wigan? Is that you? You can STILL SPEAK TO ME."

"*Yes, Mother. I can speak, and you can see. There has always been light, but Ab—It prevented you from seeing. I'm lifting the veil.*" Peace was dumbfounded as the darkness lifted. The walls shimmered in phosphorescent light. The room was much larger than the six by six feet she originally assumed to dimensions to be. The walls were mortar, covered with moss and ivy, except for the harsh stone wall to which she was chained. The room was tidy with three chairs, one on either side and one directly in front.

Peace, significantly distracted by her new awareness, quietly responded, "Thank you, Wigan. If I never see you again, I'll cherish this gift throughout my existence."

"We'll see each other again, but when I cannot be sure." Wigan's voice faded. *"It takes too much of my strength to maintain contact,"* she shuttered with weakness. *"I don't know when or if I can again... Remember... I... love... you... and... thank... you... for... my... l-i-f-e..."* Wigan, gasping for breath, sent one final message. *"I... look... for... Zen... and... wait... my... sisters."* Wigan slumped, palms on temples, and head pounding from exertion.

Peace responded, "Zen? Who's Zen?"

"The one." Her voice grew faint. *"The spirit you sensed in the beginning."* The voice faded into silence.

"The spirit I sensed? Wigan? Wigan!" No answer. Silence engulfed the room. Peace began retracing the time before Wigan's birth. "What being? Who in god's name is Zen?" She paced the length of the chains, concentrating, attempting to contact Wigan without success. "Zen... the 'one' I sensed?" Peace spent the next several hours attempting to recall any clue to Wigan's reference.

Peace had not realized she'd fallen asleep until her head slipped from the palm it had rested in. A table shimmered then materialized in front of her. Peace found herself being supported by a deeply cushioned feather pillow and chair. Roast duck appeared where the slugs had once been. For just a moment, the chalice of wine shimmered. Green eyes silhouetted by auburn hair appeared.

"I cannot break your chains, but you'll never be alone. A gift of love from your firstborn!" Wigan smiled. *"The gifts would not have been possible without your help. They were in your mind. I guess you're tired of the Therian Shelless Escargot!"* Peace laughed aloud, marveling at her good fortune and the love of a daughter she had not expected to have. *"I do not believe I'll be able to create any more for you, Mother. I don't know how I managed this, but I feel it could not be done again, and it would not have been possible without you... The images in your mind... I love you, Mother..."*

Wigan's smile faded as her reflection vanished from the chalice. "Thank you, Lord, for this respite in my misery, for a daughter I've never deserved... and for this duck... Can you believe the size of that thing!" Feeling like a teenager, she laughed aloud, stripped a piece of the duck's breast, giggled, and recited, "Look out, teeth. Look out, gums. Look out, stomach, here it comes!" Peace ate the duck's meat in its entirety, one strip at a time savoring every tidbit. "If this is a dream, I hope it is reoccurring!" She sat, almost miserable after stuffing herself with roast duck, spinning circles in the duck grease that had begun to jell. "I am too lucky for my own good?" She smiled at her surrounding as well as at herself. While licking the final bit of residue from her fingers, Peace noticed one more gift. A package containing items she recognized immediately. Picking up and holding the gift next to her face, tears overflowed—a toothbrush, a tin full of something that resembled toothpaste, and a cup. "Oh, Wigan, you're an angel! Thank you... Thank you..." Peace wiped tears with her wrist but could not stem the flow.

Wigan opened her eyes then smiled. Exhausted yet fulfilled by the love shared and the experience with her mother, Wigan stood up, straightening the emerald-green dress, turned, tossing a well-fluffed feather pillow to the portion of the bubble directly before her. "It's a good thing Mother has imagination and you," addressing the orb, "the ability to transmute!" The orb pulsed warmth toward Wigan. Wigan believed she could replicate what her mother had been thinking because they were relatively close but could do very little more. She was considerably exhausted. She knew, without understanding, that she possessed a knack with energies—"magic" if her mother's memories were correct, and the sphere worked like an oscillator shifting radiant energies and magnifying magical emanations. She could not determine, however, the extent or permanence of her abilities. She believed herself safe within the bubble but noticed the protective energy that had emanated from the exterior of the bubble was significantly depleted. She felt compelled to relinquish its protection soon but knew that she needed rest. The bubble was very comfortable, the atmosphere perfect, and the membrane soft. Sleep was not a problem. She did not and could not perceive the bubble was also invisible to all that would attempt to see it or anything it contained.

Wigan woke after several hours, feeling that pull to leave the bubble but did not understand where the pull was coming from. She surmised that it was her internal clock and compass telling her it was time to leave this protection and journey forward. As Wigan probed the bubble for weakness, two very blue eyes shimmered into view. Wigan stepped back, attempting to gather energy without consciously realizing what she was doing, to defend herself from whatever it was.

"Careful, little one," the voice soothed as Messmor shimmered into view. "You are much more than even I could anticipate, but you are much less than you believe yourself to be," the voice concluded.

"Who are you? I have not permitted you to enter my...my... home!" Wigan pushed her chin forward, hands on hips, attempting to look absolutely in control.

The voice laughed. "I am a friend of sorts, but that is not important. You need to rest and leave the bubble tomorrow, or It will find you." Messmor peeled the tip of a nail that was a bit too long from his middle finger and, as if out of habit, placed the remnant in his side pouch.

"What do you mean...It will find me?" she responded.

Messmor glanced around the bubble. "Interesting abode." He pressed the side of the bubble, watching the skin accommodate his hand then immediately return to its original shape. "You already know the answer to that question, little one. You just have not teased it out of that more than full of yourself head of yours." Mesmer smiled disarmingly then chuckled to himself. "I must be going, but I'm glad you appreciated the gifts I arranged for your mother. Did you really believe you were able to do that?" He could not contain himself. His laughter boomed. "My, do we have an excessive self-concept!"

Taken back and confused by the comment, Wigan screeched, "You don't know what you're talking about! I saw those images in her mind, and I created what I saw!"

The voice soothed once more, "There, there, little one. You did see the images in your...mother's mind...but I saw the images in yours, and I was close enough to her to transform organic materials near her place of captivity."

"I don't believe you!" Wigan screamed, stomping one foot and biting her lip.

"Suit yourself, but ask Peace whether she's noticed the small strip of cloth missing from the hem of her dress and/or that the chain on her left wrist is free of one of its links."

The voice faded as Messmor's image became translucent. Wigan noted the mage's lips moving ever so slightly as he recited the very subtle incantation. "If I...if"—she pulled off her shoe and threw it through the apparition—"I had something that would hit you, I would."

The last bit of Messmor's image faded, but his smirk was undeniable. Wigan sucked in air, preparing for a scalding retort but released the would-be assault slowly as she sat speechlessly, knowing it would not be heard. Her anger pressed her to talk to her mother. Her common sense, the little bit that managed to intrude from time to time, wrestled the anger for all it was worth and for once won the battle. Wigan decided that she did not have the energy to attempt to contact her mother. Though she was admittedly extremely flustered, she was too exhausted once again to avoid sleep. Whomever her "visitor" had been was neither friend nor foe...and he may have been telling the truth but *Why was I so tired after making those things? Why did the bubble pulse? Why did the energy swirl around me so if HE was the one doing it?* Wigan planned to stand and demand the visitor return, but the magically induced compulsion to sleep was simply too much to resist. If her mother had been close enough to hear the last words muttered as she realized the compulsion was causing her exhaustion, well, Peace's face would have reddened at the thought her daughter actually learned such language from her mother.

* * *

Trees of every variety thrived in the woods—conifers, redwoods, maples, elms, mulberries, ash, birch, and poplar. The woodland was magnificent in the diversity yet unusual in that all trees flourished fairly close together. The terrain included a variety of soil types also uncommonly found together in such an expanse, at least from Zen's perspective the root of which he had no idea. Zen stared skyward in admiration. *This redwood must be seven hundred years old*, he thought quietly. *I've never seen a place such as this.* He chuckled. "Of course, you haven't seen a place such as this... You don't know who you are or why you're here." He shook his head, stepping over a fallen branch, trying to understand his existence. Loneliness tugged gently at his heart. "Loneliness? For what and for whom...? I have no time for this," he told himself, simply denying the need of anyone or anything but himself. "What use would someone else be to me?" The emotion seemed foreign, out of place. "I have a destiny. I don't know what it is, but it certainly does not require fellowship, or," he shuttered, "a mate! What and who would I be lonely for anyway. I don't know where I'm from or if I even know anyone...AND if I do know someone, how the hell am I going to know that?" Disgusted with the state of his memories and further frustrated by unwanted emotions, Zen yelled at the sky, closed his eyes to regain balance, and focused on the journey to somewhere unknown. He pushed the complexities of his existence aside. Hands spread, "Onward," he offered to the forest, dodging branch and thorn bush with an uncanny deftness.

Zen traversed down the high creek bank, surprised that such a thin trickle of water could ultimately move the amount of landscape required to create an embankment ten feet high. He hesitated a moment then knelt to sample the water. *Cool, clear, and clean.* It quenched his thirst. Zen scanned the distance in both directions. Calculating distances, balancing the need for sustenance and supply, he decided to make sure the creek was always within a day's travel. Fresh water would be important as would be nourishment from plants and animals the meandering trickle of life attracted. The forest was thick but not so thick he could not catch a glimpse of blue sky through the treetops that shaded the creek. He resumed his journey toward the opposing bank and made his way silently over rocks in the creek bed, avoiding wetness, all the while searching for memories of self and his past. *How do I know what to do? What drives me forward, northward?* He contemplated his fighting ability. *Obviously more than an ability. It was training... Training in some kind of martial art*—an art he had no awareness of until challenged by Frankey. He bent down and wiped fresh mud from his hands onto a tuft of grass secured to the top of the creek bank. In a single motion, Zen grasped the unsoiled portion of the tuft and launched himself atop the bank. Landing smoothly, he proceeded in a northerly direction.

Zen flicked a droplet of sweat from his brow, continuing to contemplate what had occurred earlier in the day, yet sustaining a persistent awareness of his surroundings. Zen thought his hypervigilance to be unusual yet effective, an ability common among the rarest of professionally trained combatants. He couldn't imagine himself a member of that group. *Innate fighting ability…or…martial art*, he thought to himself. It had been as simple as breathing, no thought, purely instinctive, simple fluid motion. He continued to think about his training, unconsciously wiping the remnants of mud from his hands to the blanket covering his lower body. As complete as the ability "felt," the old lady and the young girl had managed to avoid his awareness, an occurrence that annoyed him. His "art" had either not included being fully aware of his surroundings or he was out of practice. "Practice?" he mumbled, pushing another branch from his face. "I don't even know what I know, and I'm thinking about practice! Maybe it's a version of the tango." He laughed. "Whatever in the hell the tango is!" Shaking his head, Zen continued forward, searching for an opening. *This will never do*, he thought. After a brief survey of the trees close by, he selected and climbed an unusually tall birch tree.

"Unbelievable," he offered quietly, taking in the view. The forest seemed to stretch for miles, bordered by rolling hills, high bluffs, and a distant but recognizable mountain range. The mountains stood tall, an illusion of jagged onyx crowned in opals and finely cut glass, shimmering in the sunlight. Clouds cascading the peaks and valleys like a shawl of pristine colors. One mountain seemed to stand separate, eremitic, transcending the range, a vanguard casting its influence and shadow as far as the sun would allow. Its peak and crest shrouded by mists made possible only by an eternity of weathering, watching, waiting for some rare event known only to it yet linked to all that made this picture-perfect—a masterpiece in its own right. The forest, a carpet of greens, magnificent in its splendor, made unique by its imperfections, ebbed and flowed to the rhythm and command of a gentle breeze winding, skipping, twirling its way from the south to the northwest. Standing tall, the forest masked the olive and turquoise ugliness of decaying undergrowth. Like ancient watchers, the wooden kind, stood motionless through the years, in detached observation of a world growing darker with each passing of the sun. The emerald richness dwindled into a sparseness of tree line and boulder rock that stood out like whisker stubble on the face of Father Nature. Zen smiled at the mental picture. *Mother Nature is truly beautiful.* A distant bluff challenged the dominance of the forest, denying flora from invading its territories, the base of which appeared to deepen noticeably.

Shaking himself from a glamour that only nature could produce, he returned to his task. The forest near his perch presented a different picture. All sorts of trees existed in harmony. Meadows, or natural clearings, it was difficult to tell from this vantage point, dotted the landscape. A very long and winding creek emerged from the glen, not more than a few hours' walk from his current position. The bards among the wildlife chimed their soliloquies, songs from creatures known and unknown, all sizes and all shapes.

"There!" Zen spoke aloud, disturbing the natural harmony, silencing woodland. He identified a clearing about two hundred yards to the west, much closer than he'd expected given the terrain he'd been traveling. He took a deep breath, not wanting to let go of the vision. *There is an undeniable beauty here,* he thought to himself, *and the illusion of peace.* He smiled to himself. With regret, he slid soundlessly through the limbs, down the tree bark, finally stepping away from the tree. After quickly glancing down the trail he'd created, he bowed a silent apology for imposing his presence upon this pristine surrounding, then proceeded to the clearing.

Though weary, Zen instinctively hesitated, crouched at the clearing's edge just far enough in the wood to remain hidden yet having a clear view. He took several minutes to scan the area, watching and listening closely. Once satisfied he was alone, Zen stepped to the edge of the clearing, hesitated a moment, then stepped out of the woodland camouflage fully alert. "A perfect place for an ambush," he whispered to himself. No ambush came. He relaxed a bit while he examined his surroundings. The shadows had shortened, and the sun was near the right eyebrow position. Zen laughed at himself. He'd developed a very strange way of keeping time as an amusement. He was aware there were other more dependable methods, but they were not "his" methods. He considered midday when the sun was atop his head and sundown when the sun reached his chin. Quarter days were measured by his ears, left ear in the morning right ear in the afternoon, depending on whether he was facing north or south.

"I still have an ear and a chin's worth daylight. I guess it's time to practice."

He stepped into a more open section of the clearing as if expecting opposition, then launched himself whirling the staff in the design of figure eights. *Whoa!* he thought. *Just go with it and see what you can do.* He smiled. *Only don't forget what you are remembering.* He laughed out loud at his instruction. *I might be a bit rusty. This... um...rooted stance*—glancing down—"doesn't feel comfortable," he whispered to himself. The staff split the air, whistling its presence and authority. With near blinding speed the staff arced, a blur against the backdrop, one 360 degrees attack after another, the whistle, again and again, marking its presence and lethality to the woodland. As sweat began to bead, Zen's movements flowed more precisely, smoothly. The patterns made by the arcing of the staff were complemented by the strength of each stance the combination of which produced a beautiful yet eerily deadly dance. Zen finished the jump spin side-kick, tucking his feet, anticipating a measured landing, relaxing then tensing muscles, then with a second flex and turn, the staff whirled very closely to Zen's body, through the imaginary foe, then stopped with an abruptness that surprised even Zen. He stood very still for a moment, nearly frozen in a horseriding stance.

The breeze created by the speed of the staff still spinning eddies across the dampness of Zen's face. He bowed his head slightly as if anticipating first an attacker from the front, then attackers from behind. He carefully slid his right foot, angling the toe from a parallel position to his attacker to a modified Korean fighting stance. Suddenly stepping his left leg forward and bringing the arcing the staff from the upward with the left hand, the staff struck the imaginary foe in the chin, Zen immediately pulled the staff downward with his left hand and upward with his right striking the imaginary foe a second time on the forehead. He and the staff were one, and they danced feverishly. Zen led. The staff followed. They moved in unison, one an extension of the other, synchronized, lethal, graceful, and deadly. The precision was unmistakable. Zen performed more and more complex movements increasing the speed and the difficulty of the dance. Each movement was fluid and precise, vigorous yet balanced. Zen's body became more defined as the reunion continued, each muscle pressing for more energy, extending and retracting with an undeniable precision and agility that most would not expect from a man of Zen's build.

Zen smiled inwardly. "Lord…I love the staff… I'm a bit rusty," he whispered. Instantaneously, the movement stopped. The abruptness silenced every living creature for fifty yards. "Not that rusty." He relaxed, patting the staff in appreciation. Zen noted the dark creature frozen by the abruptness of the dance's end. An onlooking raven blinked, its neck crooked so far that Zen was sure it would permanently be bent. "What are you looking at beady eye?" As he commented, an owl hooted. "Must be at you, banjo eyes." He smiled. "Whatever a banjo is." He laughed. "Ya, I remember what a banjo is, but why I remember what a banjo is is still the unanswered question." Zen took a deep breath, deciding to return to practice. He pulled off the woolen poncho that he'd handily converted from the blanket, to shirt, exposing his torso to the elements. One throwing knife, slightly exposed, rode comfortably in his right boot. The second knife, elevated for quick access, was nestled in the small of his back. Instinctively, he reconsidered removing them during the practice.

Front stance, back stance, fighting stance *Korean*, he thought. "What is Korean?" *Sanchin dachi. Japanese*, he thought. *What is Japanese?* Round kick, spin sidekick, jump spin sidekick. After thirty minutes of rigorous kick, block, and sweeping combinations, Zen smiled in exaltation, blinking salt from his eyes. "Time for punching and striking combinations." Zen continued, completely absorbed by the need to be precise in the patterns. Reverse punch, knife hand strike, leg sweep, elbow, back fist, middle finger knuckle fist, butterfly punch, dropkick, jump spin sidekick, lateral block, rising block, front kick forward, jump spin crescent kick backward, two-finger spear left, tiger mouth right, neck break. *Twing.* He lurched forward, ducking his head turning slightly to the right.

The left hand shot forward, stopping ear level while the right hand clasped the knife in the right boot. The left hand clutched, burning from stopping the arrow mid-flight. The arrow's impact carried the left hand forward, causing Zen's body to rotate to the right. Zen, taking advantage of the rotation right, pulled the knife from the boot, raised it to the tip of his nose, and fired at the assailant. Miraculously, he managed to alter the angle of release, the last inch of his fingertips. The projectile sped forward altered away from the young boy's face. The knife struck the canine instead. The force carried the dagger through the base of the canine's throat just above the breastplate then disappeared. The dog dropped immediately, with no sound but a gurgle of air escaping from the lungs. The second knife poised ready.

Zen screamed, "What the hell are you trying to do?"

The boy stepped back, tripping, and fell to his rump. Too frightened to cry out, he trembled, wide-eyed and speechless. Zen stepped forward and snatched the boy to his feet.

"Why did you try to kill me, boy?" Zen's voice was quiet and much calmer than the boy anticipated.

Only Zen could hear the slight twinge of guilt edging his voice and dampening both the anger and the adrenaline that pumped through his body. Though he was calming, the incident continued to cause muscles to tremble.

"I'm sorry I hurt your grandmother, boy. She shouldn't have been so bent on having me beaten."

The boy's eyes widened further, yet his fear began to dissipate. "Gramma? I ain't got no Gramma."

Zen frowned. "No grandmother, then where are you from? Why are you here?" Zen released the boy's topcoat.

"I'm Frankey's little knave," the boy offered sarcastically, straightening the coat and kicking a small piece of wood to the side. Not a trace of the fear that had been apparent only moments before.

Zen smiled, stepping back, eyebrow cocked looking curiously. "You say you have no grandmother?"

"That's right," the boy replied, "I ain't got no Gramma and my mother ain't returned home from Battersea for a week."

"Then who did I nearly kill?"

"Black jaw, my sister's dog," the boy responded. "But you didn't nearly kill her, you did kill her." Zen noticed the boy's eyes mist at the same time the boy's fists clenched. "Lyra's mine." The boy glanced at the dog lying silently beside him. Zen reached in and pulled the knife free.

"This one's dead too"—turning to face the boy—"it was damn near you!"

The boy nodded, still looking at his dog. "You should have killed me," he said as he knelt to hug his pet.

Zen's eyes widened. "Why is that, laddie?" Zen resisted the urge to rest his hand on the boy's shoulder.

"Frankey'll be beatin' me till he breaks somethin' when I get home. I knew he'd beat my ma and I'd have to fight him." The boy wiped tears from his eyes. "I thought if I killed you, he'd let us off. Now Lyra's dead cause of me." The boy hugged Lyra's limp body.

"Let you off for what?" Zen asked.

"For your beatin' him and our not helpin' him out!" the boy's voice and chin raised angrily, tears still present but ebbing. The boy stood, pushed his chest out, elbows slightly back standing with heels shoulder length apart in obvious defiance.

"Oh," Zen replied, nodding and scratching his chin, smiling inwardly at the boy's defiance. "Well, that's no concern of mine." Zen straightened, as to not tower over the boy, and assumed a less threatening but no less ready stance. "I'll let you go with your life, but don't try to stick me again. You were lucky this time. I'm rusty, and the next time, my knife may not be so forgiving. Tell your father that you talked to his friend with the big feet." Zen grinned. "That'll shake him up. Now move your butt out of here, and I don't expect you back."

The boy nodded then turned and said, "Frankey's not my father. He killed my father."

Zen stopped. "Then you should return the favor." He realized too late that his response was too quick with a bit more fervor than he'd intended.

"I know! I'm sure I can do it with all four feet of me!" the boy replied "And you don't owe anyone nothing, do you! You just go along your stupid way, not carin' about what you might mess up for anyone else. Long as it don't hurt you, then it don't matter." The boy picked up the dog, which was nearly his same size, and slung it over his shoulder.

Zen started to help, but the boy frowned and backed away. Zen dropped the arrow he'd been holding near the boy's boot.

The boy kicked the arrow aside. "Well, you don't owe me nothin' for the beating I'm gonna get either way, but don't worry, it is not your doin'… It's mine, and I'm not like you. I'll take the beating." The boy ran for the woods, stopping momentarily before vanishing in the foliage. "But by tomorrow, we'll be even for your killin' my dog!"

All that from such a little bugger. It's no concern of yours, Zen thought to himself as he pulled the shirt back on, shaking his head. On one hand, Zen guessed the boy must have been much like he was as a child, though he did not remember his childhood. On the other hand, his cold logical side insisted he not get involved in something that would only slow his travel northward. *I'll not be part of a family's feud.* He bit off a chunk of jerky. "Besides, that little tike looks to be able to take care of himself… All four feet of him… A damn good shot with a bow for his age." Zen gathered his poncho and the few scatterings of belongings that graced the practice area. Staff in hand, Zen resumed the trip northward chastising and denying that small part of his spirit that reached out to the boy. *I said it's no concern of yours!*

The forest dampened at dusk. Zen gathered grass, small twigs, bark, and larger pieces of wood for a small fire. He combined them and placed the combustibles in a small hole freshly dug. After filling the hole, he piled rocks, forming a dome over the fire trap. The makeshift oven was built in an oval shape, appearing as if one end had been severed exposing the hollow end to the elements. Confident the dome was balanced sufficiently to resist fluctuations in heat, Zen used the flint to ignite the grass. In no time, the sparks from the flint sparked the kindling to flame and the fire was crackling. The majority of light reflected out of the oven's open east end. *That should keep the coals till mornin'*, he thought, *then it's a partridge hunt and hopefully roast partridge time in the mornin'!* Zen rubbed his hands over the fire then removed his shirt. After putting the poncho back on, he placed two sticks inside the shirt's sleeves supporting the shoulders then leaned it on the tree receiving most of the light. He placed a chunk of maple upright then topped it with the scarf taken from Frankey's place.

"That should keep me safe." Zen scanned the area a final time. "And if I'm lucky"—noticing a mound of earth strategically placed in a nearby thicket—"I'll have a boot liner donated by my neighbor." He smiled to himself. "I wonder if I know how to skin and treat a pelt…if a fox or coyote decides to visit?" He climbed the large oak opposite the effigy. Looking back one last time at his makeshift lookalike, Zen winked. "You sure are ugly."

The night was warm enough that Zen did not need any more insulation than his suit of clothes provided. Zen relaxed, looked at the stars, and pulled his uniquely designed poncho close to his throat. "Not as comfortable as I'd like, but it'll do." Zen began to dream, the same dream: chains and darkness, plates filled with slugs, a strangely familiar face. He unconsciously adjusted his body to alleviate the pain from bark pressing into his hip. The dream had been so repetitious he found himself narrating and laughing silently to himself. Again, Zen felt the tree bark biting his backside. He shifted to relieve the biting. Zen's dream shifted as well. He began reliving the altercation with Frankey and the boy. "Pooooor dogs," the narrator mumbled.

"*Z-E-N…*," a voice came.

Startled, Zen opened his eyes. "That's never been part of the dream." Shaking his head and licking his lips, thinking how nice it would be to have a cup of water, Zen settled back into the tree. Just as the narrator began, Zen heard a twig pop and a boot heel slide. Without moving from his position, Zen looked first to the effigy then intensely examined the area. *Pop!* Another twig sounded, not loud enough to silence the wood, but loud enough to stir Zen into action. The distance and positioning of the two twig breaks made it plain that someone or something large was circling closer to Zen's position attempting to quietly position to ambush. Without hesitation, Zen released the throwing knife and launched himself out of the tree cat rolling into an upright position shadowed by an adjacent tree next to the fire. Zen could not reach his staff, but the second knife poised in readiness.

"Thank you," a small voice drifted from the wood. Zen tensed but did not release the dagger. He remained silent, barely hearing the young boy's departure. *Amazing little beggar*, Zen thought. *I wonder what he's thanking me for?* Zen tracked a small animal scurrying in a zigzag pattern through the underbrush. The little beast was no threat, yet Zen's tenseness remained. Zen strained eyes and ears but heard no other suspicious sounds. Slowly and silently, Zen moved back to the original tree. After hours of watching, Zen climbed the tree, carefully assuring his back and sides were protected by the tree's largest branches as he climbed. Zen eyeballed the area, forcing himself to remain awake and await daybreak.

Dawn's light very gradually made its way past twig, leaf, and branch. Ever so slowly, shadows formed and shifted. The sun pushed its way through the layers of morning cloud cover, cascading streamers of light in golden hues through the treetops as it crept above the horizon. Light beams multiplied by thousands of tiny water diamonds glistened as the sun efficiently converted drops of dew to a mist that steamed its way above the trees, a routine it had repeated a million mornings before. The sun's light, though partially blocked by the forest, continued to work its way toward illuminating the undergrowth. Zen continued to examine every shadow, odd silhouette, and shape until he was eventually able to determine the source of the disturbance from the night before. Through the dissipating dimness, Zen could make clear a large silhouette. It appeared to be human, and it was standing looking in his direction. Zen stiffened but managed to remain silent and hidden. The large shape, standing motionless near a tree approximately thirty yards from Zen's perch, had not moved for several moments. Zen continued the surveillance. His eyes hurt from the strain of watching intently for the source of the intrusion through the night, each blink a fresh abrasion from what felt to Zen to be bits of sand and gravel, unwelcome residue from a nearly sleepless night, attached to the inside of his eyelid. He rubbed his eyes trying to pick out the aggravating substance while he waited for enough brightness to identify the silhouette. Zen's mind played tricks amidst the eye strain—it looked human, but was it human?

The dimness lifted. Zen rubbed his eyes once more, unsure he was seeing what he believed he was seeing. A large human shape, motionless and rigid, had been transfixed to the oak. Zen identified the figure, shaking his head in both amazement and begrudging approval. Zen thought through the past evening's events. Within a few moments, he believed he'd pieced together the past evening's happenings and understood why this large human lost his life. Frankey stood, like an effigy of what formerly lived, nailed to a six-foot branch by Zen's twelve-inch dagger. Zen dropped from the tree, proceeded to Frank's body, then up the tree and out upon the limb where could reach and removed the dagger from Frank's throat. Frank fell forward like the giant he was. His body bounced stiffly in the undergrowth. Rigor Mortis had already set in. "The little beggar!" Zen said aloud, shaking his head and scanning the woods for any sign of the boy. "Laddie, you'll surely live to a ripe old age."

Zen scanned the area for signs of any accomplices. After being satisfied that no one of threatening size had been near, he bent down and removed Frank's coat, bow, a quiver of arrows, and a large parcel hooked to the belt. *I can use some of this*, Zen thought, gathering in Franky's donations as he opened the hidebound parcel. Ten gold pieces, two silver, and a small map with "instructions for collection." "Collection? This should be interesting," Zen said aloud.

Bounty for Collection

A bounty is offered and will be paid upon the collection for the killing or the bringing of a stranger to these parts to my inn. Five feet eight inches tall, two hundred pounds, and balding.

If killing be the choice of the collector, proof of kill required. Bounty paid at John Rippion's Inn. Bounty must be collected in person by the collector.

John Rippion, Esq.

"What!" Zen hissed. "They know who I am, they know I'm nearby, and they want me dead." Zen stood up looking in all directions. For no apparent reason, Zen began chuckling. "They know more about me than I do! Then again, might be some other idiot that has the misfortune of looking like me." He folded the paper neatly and sat, contemplating his next move. He scratched his chin. "Not likely though…or you wouldn't have come back after me now, would you have, Frankey?" Zen shook his head at Frankey. "I'd express my apologies, but I have none to make…and I'll not bury you, Frankey. If something is desperate enough to eat the likes of you, it is welcome to you, but…I will take your clothes. What I can't make fit, I'll strip and use for other things."

* * *

Abkhas felt the death of Frankey. "I should have known better. Release him from the fetter." Abkhas peeled the flesh from an atrophied tendon and grinned as only It could grin. "No matter this time." It noted the subtle glow from its belt. "His soul was donated in kind." Abkhas looked on dispassionately, then suddenly frowned. "And where did that boy come from?" A second shape shimmered momentarily, ocean-blue eyes, that which had been the boy vanished. "Messmor!" Abkhas bellowed in its usual way. "You've interfered!"

"Not so," a distant whisper lilted. "Frank was not under my compulsion. He entered the wood either of his own volition or by your command. Zen did the killing, not I." The specter vanished as did the anomaly. The latter's rage was so intense prairie grass ignited, which, of course, required Abkhas to return and extinguish as not to violate the game. "Play as you may, Messmor. In the end, I will rend your spirit and imprison your soul." Abkhas hissed.

Blue eyes returned for a moment. "Our time will come as the council commands. Your arrogance is only surpassed by the ugliness of your pock-ridden carcass." Messmor accented the last syllable quite pointedly, his chuckle faded as his visage vanished once again.

* * *

Wigan blinked and rubbed her temples. She'd attempted several times to contact Zen without success. This time, there was a contact of sorts. *I touched something! I wonder if it was him?* She thought further, *So cold and callous…such loneliness and resolution.* Shaking her head, she concluded, *Must have been the wrong one. He couldn't be Zen.* Her eyes squinted the pain away. *Oh well,* she mused as she pulled the blanket closer to the pillow. "I love you, Mother," she suddenly exclaimed and smiled. "I'll try again tomorrow night." She dozed off. Relishing the quiet of the night and the memory of her mother, she was finally able to push away the voice of those blue eyes. Her bubble had attached itself to a small bluff. Hovering invisibly, the bubbled provided a shelter and protection that Wigan would soon come to miss.

* * *

Omurcada placed both palms flat, lifting himself to his knees. He'd fallen directly on his face. *My head,* he thought as he spit a bit of leftover food and moss from his mouth. "I'm still here and alive," he muttered, still picking bits of dirt from his beard and face, again, spitting minute particles from the tip of his tongue while mentally evaluating his body parts for additional injury. The pain seemed to be receding, yet each throb of the heart pulsed pain deep within his skull. *I can't seem to breathe,* Omurcada thought as his mind raced, quickly repeating the mental assessment for damages.

"My nose is broken! What next?" Omurcada's stomach churned as he contemplated the remedy. He could feel the tip of his nose touching his left cheekbone. "There is no way I'll go through life looking like what I think this looks like!" Omurcada placed the curled pointer finger of his right hand under the tip of the nose while positioning his thumb on the opposite side. "Please don't heal before I get this straightened!" he muttered.

In a single motion, Omurcada swept the tip of his nose to its original position then slammed both palm heels simultaneously together, bracing each side of the nose. He pulled the flesh straight toward the tip of his nose. He heard the sound of readjustment, like a boot-crunching Styrofoam as the cartilage of his nose pressed into place. "My god, that hurt," he mumbled as he staggered, shoulder against the wall. The pain caused Omurcada significant disorientation. He could not see but felt his vision narrow as his knees wobbled. He reached his left hand out to balance against the wall. The pain throbbed intensely. He could feel his pulse in his temples. His knees began to buckle, but the wall provided just enough stability to keep balance. He patted the wall. "Let's not do that again." Omurcada turned, pressed his back against the wall, and slid to a sitting position. "I can't believe that I just did that," he offered to the darkness. "Straightened my nose...unbelievable." He scratched his chin then carefully felt his nose. "My synapse must have been on fire to cause such a rash decision and act upon it at light speed."

He laughed, still not believing he actually had straightened his own nose. He began to stand as his mind began to clear. Just as quickly as he began to rise, he felt himself fall forward and could not stop the momentum. Dizzily with palms flat, Omurcada caught himself inches from the floor. Sweat trickled down his somewhat-swollen nose. "A bit too close," he muttered, shaking his head. "Just what I'd need...to go through that again." Omurcada placed his thumb against his right nostril, hesitated, and pressed slightly. "Feels straight." After thoroughly checking both sides of the nose, he again placed the thumb next to the right nostril and cleared the left of blood and snot. Just as quickly as the nostril cleared it healed, he thought, *That was close!* The pain throbbed, receded, then ever so slowly disappeared. "Glad the right side was already clear," he offered the emptiness as he once again slid down the wall to a sitting position.

Omurcada contemplated his existence. "If that glitch was Zen, I don't think I'll survive two more," he breathed out slowly. Sitting, elbows braced on the inside of his knees, chin resting in palms, Omurcada reprocessed what had happened. "That...that glitch seemed to come from my unconscious. I must be insane... That must be it." (*Hysterical neurosis dissociative type... Well, maybe conversion if you believe that orb was a physical manifestation of a neurotic or psychotic form of self.*) "I guess I can't be that because they changed the book. It's no longer DSM III." (*Besides there is nothing in the DSM's latest version that describes this.*) He laughed aloud, realizing he was talking to himself and answering again. (*You've been through all this before, buddy, whether you're insane or not is not relevant because this is your current reality!*)

"Getting pretty heady, aren't we?"

Again, he laughed at himself. "If this is real and that glitch came from my subconscious, how am I supposed to duplicate it two more times!" Omurcada painstakingly reviewed the events working back through the process. "I was frightened, panicked, desperate...angry, hopeless, then I...it...yes, it took over."

(*It forestalled our extinction...*)

"How can that be? Abkhas said I could not die. That it would be prevented...until when..."

(*Until the game's conclusion!*)

"That's when!"

(*Damn, Abkhas, you're a devious bastard...*)

"Yes, devious bas—that's what I'll do!" Omurcada hesitated, "If I can," he offered second-guessing himself.

Omurcada wondered whether he could recreate the process. If he could control the outcome, Camen the Chameleon could be devious and manipulative as well as resourceful. Omurcada had only a vague notion of Zen. It had happened so quickly that there was no time to assimilate the event or analyze Zen's personality. He could only guess that the rage he'd lived with had been personified. *Does it have a conscience, I mean, a sense of right or wrong?* he wondered. "That complicates things. Camen will truly require cunning instead of courage to deal with Zen effectively, let alone Abkhas." Omurcada began to intuit what was happening. "My rage is gone... I can't explain it, but it's gone... It's been replaced by a...a...a preoccupation with calculating every angle of everything.

(*I'm overly meticulous and analytical...hypervigilant and anxious...*)

"THERE I GO AGAIN! My psyche seems to be changing. Without the rage, I feel unencumbered. That must be Zen... Zen was my rage. Camen must be my..."

(*Our more devious analytical, self-manifesting...*)

"Well, Camen, not much point in attempting to duplicate the process. It's happening unconsciously and automatically. Just as Abkhas planned it..."

(*Maybe, on the other hand...*)

"He didn't plan it. Maybe, he was only aware it would take place, but he can't control the process.

(*That would make sense.*)

"In any case, it would require a good deal of planning to put Camen's character together."

(*And even more discipline to hold it all in our mind...*)

"At the time of the birthing—STOP THAT!"

(*Okay...I suppose I will...for the time being.*)

Omurcada, task in hand, paced back and forth, analyzing himself, categorizing, cataloging every character trait, and the associated thinking process. He stood a moment. "Three domains, three domains to his personality. A remarkable capacity for deviance, extremely resourceful, and...and charismatic." He smiled and began pacing once more. "He will be intelligent without question. He will have to be to use all three domains effectively." He'd strained himself, trying to remember all the variance in his life experience sorting through character strengths, defects, and thinking patterns. Omurcada settled for mentally listing the most prevalent and identifiable. He surmised the aspects he sorted into domains were also the most apparent. He smiled, as he contributed the insight and apparency to the nature of his situation and the need for the game to progress, rather than his brilliance. He laughed aloud, thinking the thought was as arrogant as it was sarcastic. That said, he understood he had an obligation.

"I must choose wisely," he muttered. "Camen must survive the meeting with Zen."

(*That means approach what may be unapproachable.*)

"How the hell can they be a team?" Omurcada scratched the end of his freshly healed nose, attempting to ignore the voice inside his head. "Well, if he's good in the resource department, he'll manage. I wonder what else Zen might have taken with my..." (*our*) "rage? Camen will need a flexible code of ethics." Omurcada laughed aloud. "That's a nice way saying he'll need to take advantage of the moment without much concern for what others might think, except in how they may help or hinder his goals."

(*Almost but not quite a sociopath... I wonder if they have addictive drugs here...?*)

They laughed again. "Camen, my boy, you'll need to stay away from those. You'll need to be sociopathy at its best! Hmm, that means Zen—no, Abkhas wouldn't. If the two of them survive each other, they could be quite an adversary for Abkhas."

(*A balancing force.*)

"Yes! That they shall be!"

(*Better add a little conscience... Not much but a little.*)

"Shut up, I said! Now where was I...? Uh, yes...better add a little conscience... Not much but a little. I'll worry about Camen when the time comes."

Omurcada began to form, shape, and mold what he hoped to be Camen's persona. Unconsciously, Omurcada instilled a separate set of traits for Camen. Despite his effort to remain calm and collected, an underlying impatience and disdain for human emotion coalesced. Without thought or precaution to remedy this new dimension, Omurcada focused his energy on the development of Camen. The process would take days. He smiled once more. Time was a commodity in excess.

CHAPTER 6

Entrapment

Zen pocketed the gold and silver pieces then shouldered the quiver of arrows, wishing Frank would have packed a canteen or water bag. "Well, can't have it all." After a cursory review, Zen removed the long leather strap that had been tucked in Frank's boot, tied a loop, and circled the strap around his waist. Within moments, Zen had the equipment evenly distributed. The unstrung bow held close to his body by the leather strap, the throwing knives nestled comfortably in their hiding places.

"I'm beginning to feel like a pack mule," Zen muttered while biting off a piece of jerky. "I guess I'll have to visit this village and collect my bounty," picking a piece of gristle from between molars. "Yes, that's just what I'll do."

Zen stepped forward, stopped, turned, ignoring his uncaring side, removed two silver pieces from his pocket.

"For the boy." He smiled and dropped them carelessly atop Frank's chest. "He might bury you after all."

Zen unfolded the map as he walked from Frank's body. *Battersea…an odd name for a village. Two miles due east from Ablis Rock… Join Oxbow Road three miles north to Battersea. Meet the keeper of John Rippions Inn. Proof of kill required.*

"PROOF OF KILL REQUIRED! That'll be something to manage."
For a moment, Zen thought about Frank's ear. *No.* He grimaced.
There are some limits even for me. "We'll see what kind of arrangement
this innkeeper will make after I cut…um…negotiate a settlement.
Then it's north again"—glancing back at the map—"at least it's only
three miles or so." Zen glanced overhead, checking the angle of the
sun.

"Ablis Rock, huh." Zen searched out the largest tree in the area,
climbed up far enough to survey the landscape. "Probably obvious,
a large rock, but who knows." Zen situated himself near the top of
the tree, and immediately, he spotted what he believed to be Ablis
Rock, a monumental chunk of granite close to the size of a small
house. Squinting further, he managed to identify a minuscule line, an
indentation in the trees. *That must be the road*, he thought. *I should
be able to cover that ground in less than one ear's movement of the sun.*
He chuckled to himself. "No one is going to understand how I keep
time"—he patted the tree—"not even you, my friend." Thinking it
wise to arrive just before dusk, Zen shinnied down the tree and went
hunting for breakfast. Within a fairly short time, less than one ear's
movement, the partridge was field dressed, stuffed, and skewered.
The small fire crackled as the bird roasted. Zen inhaled the smell of
the roasting bird.

"Aaaahhh, a feast in the making!" Stuffed with wild onions,
mushrooms, and asparagus shoots turned slowly, the bird produced
the enticing smell of meat well done. Using a stump top for a plate,
Zen carved the first bird. "What I'd give for a pinch of salt." He
smiled then ate. Stomach full, he leaned against the perch that had
served as a sanctuary the night before and snoozed.

About one ear's movement before dusk, he awoke, climbed
down the tree, stretched vigorously, joints popped into place. Zen
vaguely felt the compulsion to go north. He remained intent on
practicing his basic patterns. First breathing exercises, then isometrics, and finally finishing with balancing exercises. Sweat oozed read-
ily from Zen's skin. Trickles collected and ran down the middle of
his back, predictably soaked up by the blanket that remained around
his waist. Zen's movements formed a complex yet graceful pattern

of lethal intricacies. His squat body masked his inherent potential, but more so, the dancer's precise choreography masked the lethality of the dance's intent. What Zen enjoyed the most about this pattern was his ability to traverse the physical challenges and, at the same time, find a calm and contemplate his journey. He still regretted killing the dogs but not Frankey. The events of the shack, Frankey, the old woman, the children, and the dogs were unsettling, yet somehow finding the note about the bounty and John Rippion's seemed to bring a purpose to whatever his life was destined to be.

He dipped his left shoulder slightly, shifting his lean and associated stance to balance at a sixty-degree angle from his shoulder, Zen dipped slightly left then shifted the tip of his shoulder back right and launched left, palm up spear hand to the right side of his imaginary opponent's neck halfway between the back of the right ear and the base of the neck as he pivoted his right knee forward, bringing through a powered ridge hand to the Adam's apple. Zen followed with a left to the exposed rib beneath the opponent's right arm and a final right palm heel to the imaginary opponent's chin. The final punch was underscored by a deep guttural release that sounded more like a growl than a yell. Zen was aware he could be seen as slightly overweight and easily defeated by others at first glance. Zen enjoyed the thought of being underestimated almost as much as the thought of the repercussions of making that mistake with him. The dance progressed to a near-frightening pitch, culminating in a final knife hand strike and a guttural emission that could only be described as primal. The dance ceased with a suddenness that exclaimed precision to any who might have observed. Shaking himself free from the pattern, Zen contemplated his next action. He wiped the sweat from his brow with his left hand, now a bit more aware of the compulsion to go northward. "Hmmm, the sun's moving…not long till dusk. Time to move."

Zen wiped himself down with the extra blanket, wishing for a bath or at least to be closer to the creek or the stream he'd noted far ahead. Disguising camp, Zen prepared to move onward. All gear was comfortably placed. The camp was obscured, except for Frank of course, who was making his presence known. Zen moved quickly through the woods. The fragrance floated downwind; unfortunately, the direction Zen was traveling. Zen inhaled, then grimaced. "Is it a bit too warm for you, Frank? I guess you're gettin' even with me after all."

Zen recounted the day's events while trudging toward Ablis Rock. Travel was much less difficult, though the countryside was more peculiar than he'd anticipated. The wood was very dense, but curiously, a noticeable lack of undergrowth existed. *Must be because the wood is so dense,* Zen thought. *Not enough light.* Zen pushed leaves from his face. Listening to the recoil disturb, its fellow limbs half expecting ticks or mites to be shaken loose from their lodging only to land and invade the ridges of the hairline that remained on his balding head.

The wood, dim, practically absent of light, was naturally high in humidity but even more so this day. The sun's heat turned the dampness from clammy to near stifling, a thickness that made walking feel like swimming. Mushrooms of several varieties thrived forming clusters of curious patterns, filling the air thickly with their odor, silently shouting claim to the misty universe. *What a day,* Zen reflected. *First, no sleep... That damn dream...then the boy and Frank. I hope things ease up long enough to solve this riddle of mine. Like, why am I compelled to travel north? Why do I remember only darkness and pain? Why am I instantly filled with rage when even the slightest threat exists? Why am I here, wherever here is? And why do these mushrooms smell like moldy socks?* He chuckled out loud. Zen trudged forward, losing himself in the contemplation of existence and what seemed a new and mysterious world of foliage and forest.

He wiped a combination of sweat and mist from above his brows with a forefinger. He looked above through the more and more infrequent gaps in the forests canopy, hoping to discover clues about his location as well as determine the amount of daylight remaining. Finding no clue in the infinity of green and occasional sunbeam, he scanned the area ahead for an indication of his nearness to Ablis Rock. He knew he would need some sort of shelter for the night in this odd place. The light seemed to form spokes in the distance, through the treetops, illuminating spores, insects, the occasional falling leaf, randomly spotlighting patches of bark and stands of mushrooms. *Harp strings, they look like golden harp strings held rigid yet not attached at top or bottom to anything,* he smiled to himself. Harp stings slowly dimming their way to narrow lengths and eventual nonexistence until the sun weaves its strings on a new day. The slow-moving light occasionally flickered with the passing bird or intruding cloud but remained steady, for the most part, caressing the inhabitants of the wood with its grace, warmth, and sustenance. Zen stopped for a moment to take in the totality of what the woodland presented. Both awed and gratified by the vision, he grinned and, for once, did not question why this would be the case. He simply took in the moment. Zen could see the extent to which nature worked its miracles. In all of its complexity, there was still a balance—just enough light, just enough moisture on the forest floor, the right combinations and specificity of flora, light and moisture to sustain the cycles of life.

Those who failed to accommodate the mother trees also failed to exist. In the balance of things, however bleak the picture may be for those who did not survive, the canvass here was incredible. Zen remained, distracted by the peacefulness and beauty of this curious woodland—majestic, pristine, and oddly abiding. There was as much mystery in this woodland's existence as in his, Zen traveled a good distance before noting subtle changes in his new environment. He was not surprised that the forest floor's dampness muffled the sounds of his step, but things were different. Zen slowed his pace to observe those differences. He knelt, scooping a handful of flora, and squeezed. The dampness turned to droplets and trickled momentarily into a small stream that curved around the heel of his palm to his wrist then back to the forest floor. *Smell sweet and musty… decaying,* Zen thought to himself. He dropped the remnants back to their natural resting place and straightened to a standing position. Zen wiped his hands on the poncho while adjusting and snugging it to his body. He was a bit uncomfortable from the dampness but shook it off. Zen continued to work martial art patterns in his head while contemplating the light permeating this portion of the wood. He realized it could not be emanating from the sun. The light was much too soft—much too unfragmented to be coming through the trees from the horizon. Zen slowed, tensing slightly.

"I have a feeling I won't make it to Battersea by dusk," he offered quietly to the wood, automatically making a quick visual sweep to all sides. The surface of the forest floor softened, even more, becoming spongy and feeling mushier with every step. Zen's step pressed inches into the forest floor's decayed mat of moss. Moisture gathered, pooled atop, then down the sides of Zen's boot. He hesitated, thinking he might be in danger of falling through the matting or being pulled into a suck hole, he tested the surface cautiously with every step. After several steps, Zen barely trusted the bog-like surface to support his weight long enough to give warning before breaking through. Even with confidence in his ability to spring quickly, he slowed, stepping lightly, conscious of the weight of each step.

The mist and early-evening air coalesced into a mild fog suspending just below the knee, forming a blanket that obscured the forest's floor. Zen could sense something—critters running to and fro concealed within its protective cover. If he concentrated, he could pick out an occasional swirl, the only telltale sign of their existence. Zen sensed their awareness of his presence. He felt their eyes upon him, analyzing and assessing his strengths searching for weaknesses. Though he could not see the beings, their mental presence was noticeable to an amazing extent—almost physical. Though there were no sounds, the psychic energy was nearly deafening.

"Silence!" he bellowed. "Stop pressing me with your minds!"

The sense of kinetic pressure stopped for an instant then began to build its way to the previous pitch. The critters pressed more diligently continuing in unison, seemingly purposefully ignoring Zen's objections. Zen realized the psychic pressure was merely a diversion to conceal their edging closer to him. *Two can play that game,* he thought. He stared straight ahead, directly at the glowing area emanating soft light and fog. *Where did that come from?* he wondered. *How did I miss it before?* he thought all the while conscious of the critter's surveillance. He covered his ears first, feigning distress while keeping his eyes open and all senses actively awaiting any noticeable change in the fog, the light, and his surroundings. Zen proceeded forward maintaining the facade of distress as if occupied somewhat immobilized by the psychic press appearing to ignore the critters completely. *They seemed to be grouped in large numbers just at the mouth of the fog*, Zen speculated, shaking his head as a necessary part of the charade.

Just then, the fog swirled approximately four inches from Zen's foot. In a single blinding motion, Zen swept the creature into the air catching a good look just before wrapping it in his poncho. The glance was all Zen needed to realize he'd wandered into something much more difficult to wander out of. The creature was just over thirteen inches in length. It resembled a lizard with an armored rib cage, razorback, and eight legs. Each foot resembled a human hand, except there were six digits instead of five. All forty-eight were clawed. The head, however, looked strangely human in the face. The eyes were purple. Armor covered the skull in place of hair. The teeth, disproportionately long and pointed, jutted forward. The little beast screamed and wailed in an attempt to writhe free. When the first line of defensive attempts were unsuccessful, it bit, chewed, and emitted an odor that gagged Zen, making his eyes water.

Zen pitched the critter, exclaiming, "I wasn't going to hurt you. I just wanted to see what the hell you were!" He laughed, holding the rage in check, only a momentary occurrence. Zen's mood abruptly changed. "LEAVE ME ALONE!" he bellowed. The staff whistled quietly as Zen wield it through the air in a perfect half-moon. The critter that had been released ran up the side of an oak, stood horizontally, then began bobbing.

"Schoom Chaka Chucka Schoom Chacka Chucka," it chanted.

One by one, each critter in the group picked up the chant. Zen stopped the staff abruptly and stared at the lead critter. It was grinning at him. The chant was absolutely deafening, threatening to a point that covering his ears provided no relief. *Only one way out*, Zen thought. *Go to the source.* Zen headed toward the mouth of the fog, the center of the light. With each step, the chant became more incapacitating, more pressing. Zen struggled, face contorting, muscles flexed, yet more determined to reach the source of the light. The critters seemed to delight in his discomfort, pressing more and more vigorously. Zen stepped forward, sighing relief as his left foot met the source of the light—Ablis Rock. As if satisfied with the outcome of Zen's struggle, the lead critter chirped and darted into the underbrush, ending the chant as abruptly as it had been initiated leaving the forest without sound and Zen with an uncanny irresistible compulsion to walk face-first into the shimmering rock.

Zen watched with amazement as his hands lifted involuntarily stretching out before him. On one hand, mentally examining the compulsion to step into the rock and, on the other, analyzing options. Zen managed to slowly return his arms to their original positions. "It's strange. I feel as if my flesh will be pulled from the bone if I don't walk into that rock but my mind is calm"—he paused—"curious but calm." Zen noted a critter had returned to the scene. Though he could not determine its exact location because of the compulsion, he sensed it as somewhere behind him, watching closely. Each moment Zen resisted, the compulsion grew and the light intensified, both pulsing in syncopation, seemingly attempting to break Zen's concentration. The rock arced electrically. Magically charged impulses, resembling very small but powerful storms, covered the face of the rock and obscured vision beyond its surface. Suddenly, Zen was not calm. His hair stood on end, writhing and pulsing with Ablis Rock. The compulsion tripled in intensity. The face of the rock cleared, revealing a door of granite and diamond—a very large door. The ground trembled as the door slid open. Winds burst forth, the air seemed charged and shimmered as the witching reached its peak. Zen's body felt as if every molecule had been ignited, yet he resisted the compulsion to enter. "I will not relinquish my position despite the melodramatics," Zen stated decisively yet remarkably without malice.

"As you wish," chuckled a mesmerizing distinctly female voice. All but an octagon of light vanished.

Zen maintained a facade of unrelenting, steeled courage. *Holy shit!* he thought. His face remained sturdy and analytical. *I can't move a muscle.* He strained.

Commented to his thought, the female voice responded, "It's like being bathed in iron. The spell's a fine one, isn't it?" Her voice lilted gently throughout the prism.

Zen said nothing but thought, *I'll bet she's smiling*, wanting to scratch his head but unable. *That is if she is a she.*

"I am...and I am to answer your question."

Zen startled. *Damn, she can read minds!*

"You certainly have a knack for the obvious." She laughed aloud.

"I don't have time for games, woman!" Zen bellowed angrily.

My, my, she transmitted, *not only do you have time, but you'll stay where you are until I deem otherwise. Your manners are atrocious... You'll stay at least until they improve!* She ended sternly with an air of absoluteness.

"You'll not intimidate me." His rage built to no avail. He could not move.

"Intimidation is only necessary if you don't believe you can win. You flatter yourself to think it necessary in your case. You're in check"—she smiled mischievously—"though not mated."

Zen sensed the smile and responded with irritation. "At least show yourself."

"In time," she asserted, "but I have more to do than sit and chat. I hope you enjoy your predicament."

Zen responded immediately, "You can't leave me to the elements!"

She turned back. "I thought you were a warrior, afraid of nothing." She chuckled.

He responded, "I' am no warrior. I pledge no allegiances. I—"

She cut him off abruptly, "Yes, yes, I know. You have no enemies...living." She smirked. "I must be a friend," laughing loudly for more than a moment.

"Damn you, you leave me to die without even letting me know your name!" Zen retorted, still unable to move a muscle.

"If you die, it will be as much to do with your bad manners as with your lack of sense. My name is Ablis. I am the vanguard of Brackland and the Land of Three Wards...and your name is?" Ablis requested.

"What, you can't read my mind?" Zen's rage nearly disabled his ability to speak.

"Your name?" Ablis responded a second time.

"Zen is my name," he retorted. "And you'll get no more from me."

"Fair enough." Ablis's voice, though a bit irritated, sounded more resigned to her mission and less interested in taunting her captive.

"What do you want from me?" Zen inquired.

"Nothing," Ablis responded, "You're the one who came to me, I not to you. You are wearing my patience, Zen, a mistake not rewarding to either of us. I'll be back in a week to see if your manner has changed." The voice ceased. Ablis Rock returned to its previous form, an ordinary yet monumental piece of granite.

"A WEEK!" Zen screamed. About to panic, he realized he could move his body. The woman was gone, but the octagon remained.

"Hello? Helloooooooo?" he offered the air, turning in all directions. "A week? I am here for what purpose?" Zen waited several minutes before concluding the woman was gone. He turned to leave, hitting his shoulder on an invisible wall. Zen grimaced. "What the..." He reached his hand out to feel the wall. The boundaries were only recognizable by touch. He'd been caged in an invisible clear prison. Though not one to dwell much on what could not be changed, Zen did not accept hopelessness or believe that he was without a solution. He simply believed he had not discovered the key to the current puzzle. Zen scanned the area. "No food, no water, what now?" Zen, attempting to make the burden of imprisonment a bit less disheartening, reached into a pocket he'd cut in the makeshift poncho. "I won't starve after all. Four pieces of jerky should keep me for a week." He picked a bug that had been crawling up his neck and flicked it off to his right while contemplating his situation. He concluded though the food would last a week. He would die at the end of six days if he did not obtain water. "Well"—shaking off the gloominess—"I needed time to think anyway!" He grinned.

And think Zen did. He wondered how he would last seven days. He wondered what the limits of his cage were. He wondered about the woman. Over time, he scratched his head, rubbed his chin, picked at his nails, glanced in all directions, took deep breaths, and shifted positions from standing to sitting to lying prone to standing again. Finally, Zen began examining the cage. He tested every inch of the octagon. Push, gouge, punch, kick, ream, scream, glare, mesmerize, and will...he tried them all with no consequence. The walls of his prison remained unscathed—no weakness could be detected before he assaulted the structure, and though he was drenched with sweat, there were no signs of weakening. He could not get out—it would not budge. He could not escape physically.

Zen repeatedly attempted to magically project himself outside the octagon with equally disappointing results. He could not surmise whether the results stemmed from lack of focus or simply not knowing what he was doing, but it was obvious, in either case, he was not going to be successful. Despite the wall being impervious to his attempts, he was surprised that he experienced some relief by diverting energy from frustration, and at times rage, to focusing on projecting his spirit from his body. He gained a deeper understanding of the communion between body and spirit as well as an appreciation for Ablis's creation.

Zen did not despair in captivity. He vacillated between rage and hope that a solution to the dilemma would appear if he diligently applied himself. During the raging periods, he wasted energy screaming and banging on the octagon's surface. When not raging, he spent a good deal of time intensely contemplating his entrapment. Even after attempting a multitude of approaches to escape, some of which he believed were ingenious, he was unable to find a weakness. Despite the bleakness of captivity, the periods of rage, and frustration there were still times where he was forced, by lack of other pursuits, to contemplate himself and his existence. Zen began to realize the extent to which rage inhibited clear thought and likely had consequences that would be far-reaching. On the other hand, Zen became more convinced that though the decisions were not always appropriate, the increase of energy and the absolute focus of the energy that accompanied the rage could be put to good use. He believed, if harnessed, he might be able to turn those rage-fueled bursts of energy into productive creative moments of spontaneity with practice. Zen believed, after considerable thought, that his apparent history of martial arts training, would be an asset in harnessing that energy...as long as he didn't kill something between the time the rage began and he was able to successfully harness it.

Days passed slowly. Zen attempted to use the circumstance to his advantage. During the day, Zen practiced Japanese katas as well as Korean Poomse or patterns and performed isometrics, carefully recalling each moment in his encounter with Frankey, the old woman, and the canines. He could marshal an intensity and at some points experience a surge of anger, but he could not recall the rage. Zen balanced his mental exercises by taking the time to embrace his surrounding, examining, closing his eyes, and recalling minuscule changes in his environment. He listened and observed his environment with a fresh eye and an increasingly discriminating awareness. He found and embraced peace in contemplation and serenity in meditation. Each time he emerged from meditation, he seemed to see the world differently, though for just a short time. He experienced disappointment when things seemed to return to normal. In those times, he would lie on his back, staring up at the trees, listen, feel, smell, and attempt to be one with the forest. It was an intensely complicated process of letting go on one hand and fully sensing the intricacies of his environment on the other. Zen believed he'd always been that way though. Whoever he was, wherever he was from, he was convinced he approached life in an all-or-nothing sort of way, and when he needed to shift away from one obsession, it required becoming equally immersed in another to find freedom from the first. Unfortunately, that meant being entrapped by the next...and so the cycle would continue much in the same way it was occurring in his newfound home.

Each night at moon peak, the critters marched, as a regiment, to observe Zen. In a well-ordered military parade, they maintained "eyes right" while passing Zen. Step, step, bob, bob, step, step, they marched to that peculiar cadence. Their chant hummed harmoniously orchestrated with the step—Schoom, step, step, Chucka, bob, Schoom, step, Chucka, Chack, bob, bob, with every pass the cadence grew slightly in volume. In its culmination, the chant was deafening yet somber and beautiful in its own right. By the third night, Zen was disappointed when the regiment's song concluded. Their discipline in synchronistic marching, which at times appeared to be an odd sort of jig due to the number of legs, was amazing to Zen. After marching past the prisoner, several critters individually visited Zen. Some growled, some smiled if that is what it could be called, some just gazed curiously but all made way when the lead critter arrived. Zen nicknamed him Guts and Glory, G. G. for short. G. G. was quite a performer.

Before dividing the ranks to observe Zen, G. G. would climb the nearest stump like an orator of old and demonstrate through chirps and physical prowess his rights to leadership. His monologue always included a challenge to the ranks, standing upright on his hind legs, a moment of silence while awaiting a response, arms or feet, depending which they were being used for, crossed, and a wide grin. The entire event concluded with chirps, bobs, and a barrage of audible commands culminating in G. G. leaping into the air and landing crisply in front of his purple-eyed battalion, a grand flourish and a bow in conclusion The battalion would respond with an excited flurry of chirps, bobs, and demonstrations of agility, each ending as abruptly and crisply as G. G.'s.

The synchronicity was extraordinary as they, in military fashion, concluded with all the entire troop of critters perfectly lined and perfectly balanced. Each movement, each turn, each step choreographed with the precision necessary to make each step sound like one, and each sound multiplied by the number of heals landing or scraping at the same time. The total display demonstrated this troop was more than battle-ready. They were a single organism...trained and honed to respond without thinking should the occasion call for such.

On the third night, G. G. climbed the stump then proceeded to the edge nearest the audience. The regiment responded with chirps and grunts. G. G. rippled muscle beneath armor and scale beginning with shoulders and ending at his tail. He stomped all eight feet while flicking his tongue, piercing holes in the stump. Stopping suddenly, he grinned and bit off a chunk of stump practically equal to his size, lifted the projectile several inches above his head with the tongue, then flipped it several feet to the center of the regiment ending the display of grandeur and audacity challenging the other critters for leadership in his usual way. This night, however, something unusual occurred—one of the critters accepted the challenge by launching himself to the top of the stump.

Scraping his claws in an arc around G. G.'s feet and growling gutturally, the challenger made it known his intent was a serious one. The challenger backed away to the left and appeared to ready himself for combat. G. G.'s expression did not change. He stood very still, tilting his head slightly to his right, eyeballing the challenger. G. G. turned very slowly until he faced the opponent, eyes of each growing a deeper shade of purple, the very small bright red circle around the pupil enlarged and brightened contrasting the purple in a very ominous way, teeth barred both critters salivating. The challenger attacked first with a flick of the tongue directly at G. G.'s face. G. G. parried, dodging left and blocking the tongue outward with his rear right foot. G. G. shot a short flick at the challenger's lead foot just far enough to cause the opponent to move the foot and look down.

In mid-air, the tongue shifted trajectory and pierced first the opponent's right eye then throat with incredible precision, which could only be achieved by a veteran of years of combat. *Well done*, Zen thought. The opponent's expression was frozen in surprise, his body quaked, and his life passed. G. G. backed up and looked sadly at the opponent's corpse. The challenger's death had occurred quickly. The troop watched silently as the challenger's death spasm concluded. G. G. lifted the challenger with the first four feet and faced a silent regiment. Both eyes oozing, G. G. slowly raised the challenger to his chest, hugging him. *He's crying!* Zen thought. *Tears? What? What the hell for?* G. G. cautiously lowered the challenger, hauling him down the stump then carried him to a barren patch of ground between two mushrooms. He gently placed his once comrade next to the largest mushroom. The entire regiment surrounded the gladiators, silently mourning the death of a compatriot while G. G. dug the opponent a temporary grave. Zen was taken back by the obvious compassion or love G. G. displayed for the critter that had just attempted to take his life. The regiment parted. G. G. slowly tramped up to Zen's prison, smiled, then walked off, the entire regiment following. Zen could sense G. G.'s agony, the weight of kinship, and a curious absence of victory. "I'll be damned," he mumbled aloud.

Four more days passed. Zen still mulling the event over in his mind, had not recovered from G. G.'s combat or G. G.'s manner. He sat as if transfixed to the center of the octagon. His entrapment by Ablis, G. G.'s behavior, the military design of the regiment all suggested a clear-minded dedication to achieving whatever goal was in mind. He had not anticipated the depth of feeling or attachment G. G. and his troop had for one another. The meeting with Ablis was equally odd in a different sort of way, but both circumstances seemed fairly unencumbered by emotions, at least initially. The fact that emotions entered into it caused Zen to rethink the times emotions seemed to surface amidst or after his rage.

Zen, though deep in thought, realized his tongue was so dry it no longer felt real. He attempted to ignore the thirst by clearing his mind, but each time he attempted to clear his mind, his concentration was interrupted. He could not shake the vision of G. G.'s demonstration of kinship or love or respect or whatever it was that G. G. clearly felt toward his dead opponent. The response was so foreign to his experience that the retrospective analysis literally interrupted the normal sensitivity to his environment and hypervigilance related to safety, both were integrated subconsciously trained aspects of Zen's persona yet were overshadowed by the mental energy expended in the retrospective analysis of the events. Deep in thought, he failed to notice Ablis appearing behind him.

Ablis shimmered into existence through the octagon's wall. She immediately realized Zen was in deep thought, and rather than disturb him, she chose to stand and observe this time with more than casual interest. Outfitted in tight brown rough leather, her shoulders supported a bearskin and leaf cloak, ankle-length, shifting, turning, blending with the environment, making detection next to impossible for all but the most intent observer. An elegantly crafted, obviously lethal sword rocked in the brown and swirling forest green sheath that matched the coat's design and obscuring qualities, making the sword/hilt combination equally near impossible to focus upon. The sword hilt protruded slightly and, though resting comfortably on her hip, seemed to express ambivalence about patiently waiting its time for service. Zen lifted his eyes, turning suddenly.

"God," he murmured, eyes wide. Zen sprang to his feet, careful to spring away from Ablis, into a casual fighting stance with his hands to his side. With unusual perception, Zen beheld Ablis for what seemed the first time. The shape of her lips, the sharpness of her features, the nobility, and confidence in her stance—the absolute dedication to her mission, no matter what that might be. His eyes filled as his throat thickened. Zen's heart responded unexpectedly. She was an uncanny blend of beauty and competence, a queen in spirit. Her eyes were black as coal. Hair deep brown waist length in an efficient yet magnificent single braid. She stood five feet five inches and was light-brown-skinned looking a bit curious.

"I suppose you're in love."

Zen's heart flickered while his eyes steeled, instinctively removing any sign of vulnerability.

"Love?" he retorted. "And you said I was the one who flattered himself." He smirked. Suddenly, becoming serious, Zen turned his head from Ablis. "Love is something I've not experienced, only contemplated and, in very rare instances considered. In all that, I have no time for something as, evidently, incapacitating as it would appear to be. We're much alike, my lady. You have a heart without passion, an eye without tears."

Startled by the quick recovery and the directness of Zen's response, taken back by the accuracy of his disclosure, Ablis pulled her coat more tightly to her throat. "Who the hell are you to say such things to ME?" she exclaimed, momentarily losing composure. In a blink, Ablis regained control and continued. "I see, however, the warrior breaks." Her arms crossed while she shifted her weight to back leg and hip.

"I said I am no warrior! I have no allegiance! I am in no one's employ, and I am certainly not yielding to you." Zen asserted while turning to face Ablis and holding the rage that was building in check.

Having reestablished communication on a plane Ablis was familiar with, her confidence returned. "Such manners…tsk, tsk." She picked a fingernail, looking down, her expression somewhat matter-of-fact. "Have you learned nothing from your captivity?" she asked.

Zen responded immediately, and unfortunately without much forethought, "Nothing that could interest a callous bitch such as you!" He growled as he stepped toward Ablis.

"Again, my friend, you know nothing of me except your prison," she replied calmly. "You've proven your ignorance, and your manners continue to annoy me. How you've managed seven days without losing sanity, considering your lack of discipline, is beyond me."

"Lack of discipline!" Zen screamed, spit flying in all directions. "I'm not your guinea pig. What the hell does my discipline have to do with this?"

Ablis smiled, her next sentence absent of passion, "Fourteen more days," and vanished.

"Fourteen more days! FOURTEEN MORE DAYS! Damn you, wench! Damn you!" Zen's muscles strained to hold the rage back. Maintaining the fighting stance he'd unconsciously shifted to, Zen inhaled deeply then exhaled slowly, forcing the rage to ebb away.

Ablis had departed, but in her departure, she felt a pang from the accuracy of his earlier statements. "Eight thousand previous and none suited to the task…and now I decide to get weak?" Ablis shook her head. "Oh, Father, don't let me falter in my task. I shall find one truly capable to assist without being a perpetual hindrance, and we will find you. I know I cannot do this alone, but the longer you're missing, the more pressed I am to find one at least capable. This one is unique in perception, but I doubt prepared for such a task. I cannot allow his ramblings to dissuade my position or delay my quest."

Zen stared at the space previously occupied by Ablis, rage subsiding. "To think I was enthralled with a female the likes of her." Behind a pretense of anger, despite a natural and considerable resistance, Zen's hurt survived. On impulse, Zen leaped into the air jump spin side-kicking. The grace and elegance of the kick, unusual for a short two-hundred-pound man, though magnificent, turned into an entanglement, when the target offered no resistance. Zen landed on his leg and left forearm.

Shocked, Zen exclaimed, "No WALL!"

Lifting the staff, he hurled it like a javelin. The staff carried several feet into the wood. Zen tilted his head back and shouted to the world, "Good god, I'm free!" and dashed forward. In full stride, he crashed knee then the forearm and head into the invisible confine. Zen's muscles rippled forward to add to the impact, and as quickly as he arrived, his body rebounded, sending Zen to his rump then onto his back. Zen shook his head, blood trickled over the right eye. His knee ached violently. He slowly rolled to his side and leaned up on his elbow. He spent a few moments looking over the aching knee and attempting to get to his feet. His knee shook, and the muscles supporting it expressed their desire to have him remain sitting sending pain in all directions. Rage began to build. Zen closed his eyes.

"*STOP!*" he commanded himself.

The rage held but did not progress. Zen glanced at the wood, angry at himself and his rage. "My favorite weapon, gone, and I'm still within the wall," he mumbled as he pressed against the wall and initiated a limping search for weaknesses in the octagon. Zen's knee gave way. He acrobatically caught himself and slid down the octagon's wall. Zen sat for a moment, knowing that he'd survived without water because he'd rationed the apples he'd taken from the cottage, but the apples were no more. Thinking this was the final day of his captivity, he'd eaten the remainder a few hours before Ablis's arrival. Zen pushed the feeling of panic away. He looked skyward. "Fourteen more days, huh. Well, fourteen more days it is," he offered the treetops. Zen, utilizing the wall as a brace, levered himself back to his feet. He grimaced, rubbing his right knee. *I still have arrows,* he thought. *If this prison is to keep me in but allows projectiles out, the arrows will provide an excellent defense.* Zen smiled to himself. *A surprise for my captor.*

Zen strung the bow then lifted the quiver. Twenty-eight finely crafted arrows, balanced and expertly feathered stood in readiness. *Exquisite workmanship,* Zen thought. *I hate to lose them.* Placing an arrow in the bow, Zen drew back and released. *Zzzzing!* The shaft flew straight above his head, disappearing for several seconds. It reappeared a considerable distance above Zen's head, descending rapidly toward its mark. *THUD*! The arrow arrived burying itself to the feathers. "EXCELLENT," Zen remarked aloud. *Maybe not so excellent.* Zen's smile was interrupted by the thought. *That means I CAN BE SHOT AT*! Zen lifted the arrow cautiously from the earth, ensuring its original workmanship held true. Zen examined every inch to ensure the shaft remained viable. Nodding in satisfaction, he replaced the arrow in the quiver with the rest of its fellowship. *Twenty-eight arrows, two throwing knives, and my body against no food, no water, and the elements...* Zen scratched his beard, *first, I pray for rain.* If it rains, *odds remain in my favor. Then we'll see what she has to say.*

Zen walked the perimeter of the prison touching the walls with fingers and marking the corners by pulling up grass and sod. "At least I'll be able to stretch," he offered to the open air, hands wide apart above his head. The prison was twenty-four feet at its widest diameter. Zen stared out into the wood, noting the staff's location. "I feel like I've lost an arm without that staff," Zen chastised himself as he leaned his face against the wall of his captivity. He shook his head a final time then stepped away from the octagon's edge. Resigned to captivity, Zen walked to his favorite corner, now expanded a few feet, and prepared to meditate. Zen decided to sleep by day and watch by night would be the surest way to survive the wood. The bulk of activity had always been at night. The wood had been calm in the sunlight, except when disturbed by Ablis. *A strange woman, Ablis,* Zen thought, his eyes narrowed. *Definitely a royal and arrogant but a queen? The vanguard of Brackland or the Land of Three Wards?* His anger seethed as he contemplated further. *I'll find that out...in fourteen days.* Zen pulled his left knee close. *I wonder if the arrogance comes from the advantages she has with magic or other skill. I don't know the extent of either.* He tilted his head back against the octagon, unconsciously clenched his teeth. He leaned back against the wall. "Time to get comfortable. Five hours until wake up."

Zen slept longer than he'd intended. A familiar chant invaded his dreams. *Schoom chucka chaka, schoom chucka chacka.* Zen opened one eye, noticing the spittle in his beard. *Drooling, huh?* he commented silently. *Don't need to waste water this way! Wouldn't that please her.* He smiled, sat up straight, and stretched. The critters marched eyes right, step, step, bob, step, bob, bob, step, step. Zen tapped his fingers, watching with genuine interest. "Damn well-trained regiment, G. G.," he commented. The regiment halted and in unison turned to face Zen. The scoot and scrape of the turn was as sharp as the halt was distinct. "Well done, G. G.," Zen offered in admiration.

G. G. chirped. In immediate response to the command, an aisle within the battalion formed. G. G. strolled down the center, two legs on each of his sides up and crossed. The remaining four legs were used for propulsion. Three quarters the way down the aisle, G. G. signaled four lieutenants. They immediately fell in behind him. G. G. and escort proceeded to the wall closest to Zen, sat, and observed.

"What are you looking at?" Zen said directly to G. G. then smiled. "I guess I shouldn't bitch at company."

G. G. stared at Zen, curiously turning his head to and fro as if not quite completely satisfied with the angle. Zen jumped face-first to the edge of the invisible wall, staring ominously at the critters. G. G. did not flinch though the lieutenants backed up two to three steps. Zen laughed and saluted G. G. "I sure named you right, Guts and Glory you are!"

G. G. mimicked Zen's laugh then chirped, lifting a pebble with his tongue. Balancing the pebble carefully on the tip of his tongue, G. G. fired the pebble at Zen with amazing speed. Just before impact, Zen snatched the projectile from the air. His palm stung from the missile's impact. "Mean little bugger, aren't you!" he whispered to himself. Placing the pebble on the tip of his middle finger, using the thumb to generate a powerful torque, Zen released the pebble. It sizzled directly at G. G.'s face. In a single motion, G. G. deflected the pebble with the lead foot. Rather than stopping the pebble, he added force, angling the stone directly toward the trailing lieutenant who had not been paying attention. The projectile nicked the lieutenant's chin with enough force to fiercely vibrate the little critter's skull. Zen laughed aloud.

"You are a skillful little bugger, aren't you! That rock must have seemed slow after the battle of tongues, eh, G. G.?"

G. G.'s expression changed suddenly. In an instant, he spun 180 degrees, chirped distinctly three times. The regiment scattered in every direction. Zen, startled, lifted the bow and readied himself for an unexpected intruder. Zen scanned the area nearest his prison, all senses perked. His hypervigilance, in full swing, his sensorium took in every movement, smell, and sound. Rage sitting in readiness, below his conscious awareness, pressed by the adrenaline that pulsed through his system, would spring at its earliest opportunity. "If it's you, G. G., you'll find the arrow much more difficult to deal with than the pebble," he mumbled. The forest went silent. It was as if all life existing in his surroundings was waiting, without breathing for an event that was hidden. Zen's keen eye picked out several small groups of critters deployed in trees, on rocks, and behind mushrooms silently blending into the landscape.

The wolf pack was barely visible, sniffing the air sensing Zen's presence. His stomach tightened as a prelude to combat. Even so, Zen believed himself safe from physical attack inside the octagon. *I have nothing to worry about. They can't enter this prison any more than I can leave it. Pebbles are one thing. Bodies are another.* Zen's mind wandered. *Though I'd like company, I'll pass on these.* Zen sat the bow in the corner.

"Well, G. G., you're on your own." Zen peered through the moonlight, realizing the denizen were much larger than he'd originally surmised. The lead wolf snorted. Drooling, it surveyed its perimeter. Spotting Zen, the wolf bristled then trotted up to Zen's prison, bearing teeth, streaming spittle and growling viciously. Zen's laugh was cut short when he realized the wolf was coming through! He sidestepped just a moment before jaws that would have had his throat snapped shut. The wolf carried forward. Zen stared coldly at the beast while drawing the knife from the small of his back. *A quick arrow would be better*, he thought, but the bow and quiver were not within arm's reach, and there was no time to get to them.

The wolf squatted as if preparing to lunge then hesitated in anticipation. Zen sensed something was wrong. Why wasn't it attacking? Then he realized, "You never attack alone," he offered, ducking, and turning instinctively. He evaded the second attacker. The she-wolf flew over his head, narrowly missing the back of his neck. Her rear leg caught his poncho, pulling it over Zen's head and, thankfully, off.

"Damn!" Zen exclaimed, kicking the second beast firmly in the ribs from the back side, sending it to the perimeter of the octagon. The first wolf sprang as the second wolf rolled sideways in response to Zen's kick. The angle of attack taken by she-wolf deprived Zen of a way out or a way to avoid a face-on encounter with the first wolf, now pressing with determination. Zen shifted from horse rider to rooted stance. Steeling for the impact, he ripped forward with the dagger. In a single slash, Zen severed the animal's juggler, burying his knife and fist deep in the animal's throat. The impact was substantial but failed to stop the attacker's forward motion. The she-wolf sensed Zen's subsequent vulnerability and was immediately upon him. Half of his mind pressed limbs forward in avoidance of teeth and claw while the other listened to the cracking bone and screaming critters. The she-wolf clamped jaws on Zen's thick burlap outer garment grazing the forearm. Zen lifted the arm with the she-wolf attached and gutted the wolf. The attacker released the arm and without hesitation lunged for Zen's throat. Dragging entrails, powered by savage instinct, and what only could be described as animal rage, the wolf rushed forward. Rage upon rage, the two danced a duet of lethality. Zen, instinctively, gouged the wolf's lungs and, just before the wolf's anticipated impact redirected the wolf, open jaws and all, by striking its skull with a left palm heel to the temple. The blow caused the wolf to carry forward to Zen's right. Zen turned right. Continuing to assure that the wolf remained directly in front, Zen stepped forward and, with near inhuman quickness, landed a right-handed bottom fist forcefully through the top of the wolf's skull. Staggering backward, Zen was aware that the dagger, hilt protruding from the bottom of his right hand, had caused the final damage. Without it, he would not be alive to analyze what had happened. The wolf bounced and rolled in unconscious near-death muscle reflex until it lay silent, lifeless. Zen kicked it one time to the prison's edge, assuring himself that the she-wolf was indeed dead. Free from danger for the moment,

Zen grabbed his bow and returned the fallen knife to the scabbard in the small of his back.

"Bejeebus!" Zen exclaimed, sucking in air, wiping blood from his face. He turned to G. G.'s troop. The wolves had successfully killed several of G. G.'s troops but had not routed the little critters. The fact that six denizens lay incapacitated after being swarmed by the battalion served as a testament to their tenacity. It also caused the remaining wolf pack to frenzy. Their eyes pulsed red, tongues hung out, panting, and ears flickered nervously. The wolves were completely bent on annihilating the remaining critters. One of the nine remaining canines veered off and galloped toward Zen. While drawing down, Zen noted two wolves had cornered G. G. and twenty critters at the base of a tree. Zen realized that, as skilled as the critters had proven themselves to be, without assistance, G. G. and troop were doomed. Back and forth, Zen's eyes traveled to the oncoming wolf and G. G.'s doomed troop. Zen's mind battled too and fro. "Dammit, G. G., what are you doing to me?" he mumbled.

Time seemed to slow and to suspend as the adrenaline pumped through Zen's body. His speed of thought accelerated. "I stand a good chance of being killed if I don't defend myself," he mumbled aloud, but the bow did not move. Zen's ambivalence was as puzzling as the feelings that had arisen the first time he'd seen Ablis. Something was happening to him. He could not understand why he was "caring." Ablis, he could rationalize because of her attractiveness but G. G. *Why should he give a damn about a lizard?* he thought. The bowstring hummed from the strain of an extended pull. He pushed the concern for anything but himself as far away from consciousness as he could, but it was to no avail. A new code of honor was developing, and Zen could not prevent its birth. He did not want the responsibility or the entanglements of others, but it pressed forth. From deep within, like a gusher of ice water, his conscience flooded with clarity and panic, sheer desperation to help G. G. despite the deadly force approaching.

The arrow slid neatly behind the jawbone through the wolf's brain, bursting the skull, sending fragments into the companion standing closest to G. G. Startled by its partner's death, the second wolf sprang backward, every hair on end, growling and shifting from side to side attempting to locate the latest threat. The second arrow struck the companion just behind the left foreleg piercing the heart. The wolf dropped instantly. Before the wolf could realize the arrow had penetrated, the wolf died. Zen did not see the arrow reach its mark, his wolf was upon him teeth gnashing, signaling its determination—there would be no reprieve. His left arm ached and was bleeding profusely from a deep gash after the wolf's first strike.

Zen, knocked to his back, rolled the wolf off to his side while grasping its throat. Wolf spittle and froth covered Zen's face and chest. The animal was ferocious, much stronger than Zen had anticipated. Zen gripped with all his strength. The wolf was unrelenting. The animal had not been allowed to inhale for several seconds yet seemed to grow in strength. Zen's strength, on the other hand, diminished, his lungs burned and rasped with every rapid intake of air. He could not risk reaching for the other knife. If the animal continued to press, he would not be able to withstand it. Closing his eyes, Zen summoned all his strength, letting the rage loose. The wolf sensing Zen's desperation and the finality of Zen's struggle pressed with all its might. For a brief instant, the wolf and Zen seemed to become one beast. A contorted and blurring embodiment of human flesh and wolf skin.

Zen's rage surged as he roared gutturally, "I will not die!"

Zen felt the wolf's press recede then desist altogether. He opened his eyes. His arms and chest were covered with blood, partly from his arm but primarily from the wolf's throat and chest cavity. Zen held his foe above his head. Both hands had penetrated and disappeared within the wolf's throat. He'd pressed his fingers through the wolf's hide, flesh, and broken the neck. Several seconds passed before Zen realized what had happened or that the wood was silent. Zen dropped the wolf, slowly rolled on his side, and gazed in amazement. Fourteen wolves were dead. He'd killed five. The critters killed nine! He smiled, in exhaustion and gratitude for life, sinking to his knees, Zen passed out thinking *I hope G. G. survived. The little bugger got more guts than brains.*

G. G. scurried out from under the mushroom paused, then vaulted to the largest of tree roots. Within seconds, G. G. assessed the damages. His troop had devastated six attackers and were well on the way to killing two more when the first of Zen's arrows struck. Startled by the arrow's impact, G. G. crouched, widened his lips to eyes, bearing teeth and flicking his tongue rapidly. The first wolf dropped thrashing madly. The second sprang backward then drew a bead on G. G. As if realizing he would die alone against the wolf, G. G. tossed caution to the forest, leaping directly at the wolf's forehead. The wolf's eyes gleamed, saliva drooled and foamed. The jaws of death opened wide in anticipation. G. G. descended, balling himself in a manner that allowed his armor to cover the softness of his belly and face. The armored razor backbone protracted and stood out exposed. Gnashing teeth surrounded G. G.'s entirety. G. G. hunched his back, spiked the inside roof of the wolf's mouth, then bit off a chunk of the tongue. The wolf shook G. G. loose. As quickly as G. G. hit the dirt, he sprang to the wolf's throat. The canine's eyes bulged, body convulsed, then dropped to its knees. G. G. had only slightly penetrated the hide when the canine died.

G. G. clung with all his might, fearing the animal was only feigning death. G. G. held fast until he was sure the animal would not make a sudden and lethal move. He very gradually released pressure. First, his teeth then each of his feet, one digit at a time. Once completely free, G. G. scampered backward, eyeballing the canine meticulously from head to toe. Suddenly, in a blaze of speed, G. G. covered the distance to the attacker, bounced up the shoulder blade, chirped triumphantly, then discovered the arrow. As if oblivious to the trauma surrounding him, G. G. sat down, scratching his head with all six digits of the right foot. Eyeballing the arrow, the little critter's face lit up, then frowned. Tilting his head, he watched Zen strangle the canine within the octagon.

G. G. grinned to the point of contorting his face inverting his lips. As if inspired, G. G. stood upon the hind legs and barked a command. All critters withdrew from the attack, then reformed into a single large ball of armor between G. G. and the five remaining wolves. Two of the five were severely beaten, gouged, and abraided but standing. Both were ready to withdraw, but their counterparts were enraged beyond retreat. The largest wolf lunged first, closely followed by two healthy wolves. G. G. jumped bobbed and chirped gleefully. The armored ball split into hinged but equal halves, allowing the lead wolf to enter precisely centered within newly created divisions. Just as the wolf lunged to attack the left half, the halves slammed shut, reforming the ball and engulfing the wolf. The remaining healthy wolves relentlessly skidded fangs against the ball's exterior, biting, snarling, and drooling in an attempt to locate a weakness. The engulfed wolf fought frantically to no avail. Within seconds, the engulfed wolf was disemboweled and devoured. An aperture appeared, deposited the unrecognizable remains, then slammed shut.

The lead wolf's brutal end failed to detour his counterparts. The aperture reappeared as one of the wolves lunged, allowing the head in before closing. The wolf's scream muffled, faded, and was gone. The wood hushed, entirely soundless, except for the fading rustle of leaves as the three survivors retreated. The retreat was resolute. G. G. grinned knowing the marauders would never return to antagonize his troop or the newfound human friend. With a single bark, the troop unraveled and regrouped in front of G. G. The troop members exclaimed victory to their compatriots in jubilation. As if a silent command had been issued the troop, in harmony, began to chant that familiar chant. *Schoom chaka chucka schoom chaka chucka.*

The troop rejoiced in their survival. G. G. surveyed their dead. His expression changed from triumph to sorrow. Dropping to all eight, G. G. commanded the ranks to gather wounded and dead. Once gathered, the chant changed as G. G. intoned, "*Looo Ray Rooaaauuummmm.*" Tears of goo streamed from the living critter's eyes. A column formed. Five thousand critters carried their eighteen hundred dead. G. G. and lieutenants took outrider positions, head high, face filled with sorrow yet pride for the companion's valiant fight. The moonlight flickered eerily amongst the swirls and eddies of rising fog—purple eyes, veiled in mist, glowed ominously as the critters marched to their burial ground. Their sorrow-filled hymn stirred every living creature to take notice. Their loss was great, and none evidenced their despair more than G. G.

He honored the dead as all great leaders do—standing tall, making valiant their sacrifice, elevating their feats, unforgettably etching their nearly magical contribution to the survival of the living.

He continued to communicate his indebtedness through chirps and grunts that were unmistakable demonstrations of honor—honor that assured their memories would live on in the minds and myths of their fellows. G. G. seemed to gather himself in as if to say though they deserve the honor and the gratitude their deaths should have been unnecessary. Their world should have been a better place. Dedication to duty and altruism did not erase the agony or bring back the dead. He would not address, challenge, spare, or share fellowship with those who were being carried. Death loss outweighed valor. A dead hero is still dead…and a living enemy a constant reminder of senseless death—past, present, and future. The hymn echoed their sorrow, their pride, their disdain of death, and their peculiar fellowship as the columns of critters marched under G. G.'s command.

The sun rose high in the sky, radiating energy that nurtured the forest beyond its usual muggy self. Zen awoke, bruised, weak from loss of blood, squinting and blinking sunlight, attempting to minimize the peculiar effect of bright sunlight on aching heads. Despite the humidity, Zen's lips cracked from lack of water. Leaning on one elbow, rubbing his head with the opposite hand, Zen smacked his lips. "My tongue feels like pine board," he remarked. Zen pushed himself to a sitting position, back against the wall, and examined his surroundings while picking dry cracked skin from the edges of his lower lip. He could not help noticing the victims from the foray the night before. Glancing at the sun, he calculated he would not have much time before the meat would spoil.

"Well"—wrinkling his nose at the smell of fresh but dead wolf—"I guess I won't starve." Catching a deeper whiff, Zen shook his head. "What a starving man will do to survive." He cut several strips of raw meat then skinned one of the three animals. Digging a hole and lining it with wolf's skin, Zen drained as much of the uncoagulated blood, of the remaining denizen, into the hole. The task's tediousness was only transcended by the effort to withstand the stench that erupted from the carcass. As much as he wiped his hands on the grass near the carcasses, he knew he would not be able to remove the smell anytime soon. His left arm throbbed from the wolf's bite.

Both legs hurt. He became light-headed whenever moving too quickly, which was much more often than Zen cared to experience. Zen persisted, understanding that butchering the animals would be his only means of surviving until and if the woman returned. After the three animals were skinned, Zen estimated he had about six quarts of liquid. Zen's stomach clenched, thinking about what he would have to do to survive. Bracing himself for the first drink, Zen muttered, "Think water, water, water"—dipping his head, *gulp*—damn! WATER! WATER! WATER!" Two gulps were all Zen could manage. "I'll have to be much closer to death than this to drink that suet," he offered to the air, stifling the urge to vomit what he'd just consumed. Chewing on a strip of raw meat, which was much less difficult to deal with, Zen stumbled back to a sitting position, inhaling deeply through his nose, exhaling ever so slowly attempting to relax aching muscles. "What I'd do for some wood and a fire!" Dizzily, Zen leaned back against the translucent wall. "It'll only keep for a few hours so…" He stuffed himself, an ordeal in its own right. When he'd eaten his fill and then some, Zen rolled onto his side and slept.

Six days had passed with no sign of G. G. or the regiment. The food and makeshift water spoiled. Zen was growing weaker by the day. He'd consumed enough nutrients but not enough fluid. Dehydration was becoming a serious threat to his existence. Sitting in the corner of the octagon, scraping hide with one of the daggers, he muttered, "I may die of thirst, but I'll not give her the satisfaction of yielding." He laughed. "G. G. will be calling me Ole Blood and Guts pretty soon." Zen raised the hide to eye level, stretching the hide as far as his arms would go apart. "Will you catch the dew and share it with me or drink it all yourself?" Zen returned the hide to the hole in the ground, hoping that a drop or two of precious water would be captured overnight or that it would rain. Too weak to do much more, Zen dropped to his stomach. He placed his head to the ground, face next to the wall, and slept.

On the evening of the seventh night, G. G.'s regiment returned from their mourning to find Zen practically dead from dehydration. The carcasses of both wolves fallen by Zen's arrows remained. G. G. stared curiously at Zen then the two fallen wolves. G. G. eyeballed his ranks, still milling around, then returned his attention to recalling what had happened during the battle. G. G. proceeded slowly to the large root next to the wolf carcass. Climbing first the carcass, he stared momentarily at the shattered skull, then hopped to the root. He turned to the troop, silently engaging the attention of his kinsmen. Smiling sadly at Zen, G. G. psychically recalled and transmitted the events and behavior leading to Zen's current condition. At the conclusion, G. G. turned toward Zen, conveying gratitude and kinship. G. G.'s sentiment and sadness were echoed throughout the troop. One of G. G.'s lieutenants approached. Startled by the report, G. G. organized the troop, commanding then to set off for an unknown destination.

Zen dreamed the same dream as always—darkness, chains, confinement, and rage.

Zzzeeennn... a voice lilted from an extraordinary distance. Zen fidgeted. *Zzzeeeeennnnn...*, the voice called.

"Ablis?" Zen called through the haze of sleep.

No, I'm not Ablis. I'm—

Zen's face felt as if a mountain spring flowed across it. His concentration broke. He drank deeply. *Damn good dream*, he thought. *Too bad it isn't real.* His head lifted just before he thought he would drown then back again into the pool. *This is heaven...a beautiful heavenly dream.* His head lifted then dropped without effort for hours. His thirst fully quenched, strength was returning. "This is the damnedest dream. I hate to leave it," he mumbled, still sleeping. Zen's jaw felt as if a log had been rammed through it. His entire sensorium throbbed. "My head," he muttered as each eye opened slowly. Just as they focused, his face was submerged. Zen exerted a great deal of effort but managed to bring his head up, squinting through streams and droplets of water running over his eyes, nose, and lips through his beard and back into the small pool below his chin. "WATER!" he exclaimed hoarsely.

The familiar chant filled the air: *Schoom Chacka Chucka Schoom Chacka Chucka.*

"G. G.?" Zen sat up despite the pain. Two trenches filled with flowing water extended as far as Zen could see. The trenches protruded eighteen inches into the prison, forming a point under Zen's head. A bend of sorts formed, causing the water to slow and pool at the junction. Water entered the pool through the first trench, circled, then exited the second trench. The canal stretched as far as the eye could see. Zen's staff lay perpendicular to the prison, one end in the pool and one end four inches in the air. The center was supported by a small stick for a fulcrum. Zen could hardly believe G. G.'s ingenuity.

"I can't believe this, you magnificent little bugger!" Zen whispered euphorically. Zen was awed at the feat the critters had accomplished. It was obvious the critter used the staff to dig a hole under his head. G. G. and associates had gone on to lift and brace his head up with the staff while the pool refilled after each dunking! Rubbing his jaw, he said, "That's why my jaw feels like it's been rammed with a yule log! It has been!" Zen laughed aloud. Zen, though very weak, managed to get to his knees and scoop water, splashing it over his arms and chest, finally scooping the water and flinging it into the air. G. G. watched, expression unchanged, the twinkle in eye withstanding, then chirped to the regiment. Dawn was breaking, and debt had been repaid. The regiment formed parallel ranks then marched off into the trees humming their uncanny song *Schoom chacka chucka, schoom chacka chucka…* Zen watched their retreat silently and gratefully. "I wonder if I would have done as much for you," Zen offered as he bent down for another mouthful of water. Zen drank deeply without realizing he'd already done as much for G. G.

Thirteen days had passed. Zen's recovery was complete though hunger remained. Grass, mushrooms, and worms were enough nutrients to maintain strength. The critter's water flowed consistently, providing the liquid necessary to round off the monotonous yet adequate diet. Zen practiced his art and meditated to free his mind from the oppression of captivity. He took the time to analyze himself and his newly found friends. He and G. G. were getting along famously. Each night since the trench had been completed, they would stare at each other for hours, making faces, grunting, bobbing, and chanting, only occasionally realizing how ridiculous they would look to their own kind. Neither understood the other's language but each, without a doubt, had established a kinship, a bond between combatants.

Sweat rolled over Zen's brow, salting his eyes. The salt caused little irritation, a benefit from discipline and dedication to the art. Zen did not flinch from the irritation. He was only vaguely conscious of the sting as he stretched and suspended his sidekick shoulder level, slightly above his head then caught the droplet of sweat and licked it,

Salt...such a sweet luxury, he thought. G. G. grunted, shaking his head as if to say "You're nuts!" Zen's concentration broke, laughing at G. G.'s opinion of the isometric. "I wish you could talk," Zen sputtered as he hopped on one leg, trying to maintain balance and keep the leg extended.

"He can" came a distinctly female voice.

Zen clenched his jaw, carefully masking his thoughts. Paying little attention to the intruder, he slowly lowered his leg. Taking a deep breath, he exhaled and turned toward Ablis.

"My lady," Zen spoke without emotion, eyes lowered, wiping sweaty hands on his trousers.

"You smell like a bathhouse...without a bath," Ablis commented, raising an eyebrow.

"And what do you know of bathhouses?" Zen responded with only a hint of humor.

Ablis's eyes twinkled. "I guess I deserved that."

Zen picked up the staff, lovingly twirled it. Lifting the staff eye level, Zen winked at G. G. "Thank you. I missed her while she was gone."

G. G. stared ominously at Zen then at Ablis. With a chirp, he vanished.

"Not Ablis, you buzzard, the staff!" Zen yelled after G. G. As Zen expected, G. G. did not respond. Zen set the staff next to the poncho then sat back to the wall and began to meditate.

Ablis, a bit annoyed by Zen's manner, said, "Ignoring me now?"

Zen smiled thinly. "I wouldn't want you to get the wrong impression. I'm not exactly ignoring you, but I'm not nearly as swept up by your charm as you think."

"That certainly simplifies things," Ablis retorted.

"Get to the point." Zen's voice hinting at his impatience with the bantering. "Are you going to let me go or toy with me a bit longer?"

Ablis's brows narrowed sternly. "This is not a whim of mine. I did not request your presence. You came of your own free will as many have before you."

Zen perked. "Many before me? You make it sound like I've planned this meeting. I not only am without a clue about you or my imprisonment, but I also don't know where I am. I didn't come here any more of my free will than G. G.'s troop died of free will," Zen barked angrily.

Ablis cocked her brows further, hands on hip, attempting to regain control and sustain an aloofness. "What's this warrior? Compassion? You feel sorry for the lizards?"

Zen sprang to his feet. "Don't fiddle with me, woman. Get to your point!"

Ablis glared ominously. "The point is not a point. It is a choice. You either choose to live as my instrument until such time as I release you, or you join G. G."

Zen stared in horror, stumbling backward, understanding almost instantly what happened. "No wonder he ran, you ruthless witch! He was here before me, wasn't he? WASN'T HE? HE WAS HUMAN!"

Ablis turned from Zen, quickly putting a safe distance between them before turning back. "I thought he would have survived." Her answer, obviously painful, was accented by a single tear drifting slowly down her cheek.

Zen was taken back a bit yet undaunted by the tear. He pressed the conversation forward, "Survived? Survived what?"

Ablis turned back completely composed and austere. "Your CHOICE, ZEN, MAKE IT!"

Zen's eyes hardened. "It's death in either case… Being your instrument means servitude until you are satisfied with me. Joining G. G.'s troop means never to know humanness."

Zen's voice quieted to a strained whisper. His eyes locked with Ablis, both realizing this was a final confrontation. "What if I choose to remain where I am?" Zen finished.

Ablis answered flatly, without emotion, "The octagon is an oscillator that causes the metamorphosis. If I leave without your agreement, the transformation will begin. In your terms, 'quit fiddling,' Zen. I've waited a long time for the one equipped to help me. You may or may not be the one..." Ablis's eyes did not waver.

"If I am the one, what happens?" Zen demanded.

"I don't know," Ablis responded impatiently.

"YOU DON'T KNOW! You mean you won't tell me!" Zen stepped forward.

Ablis did not move, her stance, an unyielding determination. Zen was certain Ablis could and would do whatever she believed she must, including transforming him into something less than G. G. Ablis paused momentarily. "I mean I can not predict the future, and given your current skill, you couldn't comprehend if I could."

"What's in it for me?" Zen asked, moving ever so slowly closer to Ablis.

"Life," Ablis responded.

"Is that it?" Zen retorted.

"Is that not enough?" Ablis finished stepping again out of Zen's range.

Zen lifted his staff, twirling it mischievously. The knife slid nonchalantly from in the small of his back as the staff twirled around his waist into a vertical stroke. Time suspended, Zen's eyes misted a millisecond before the knife slipped from the fingertips and the staff slid to the ground.

Ablis smiled, eyes twinkling, as the knife stopped just before sinking into her breast. The projectile hovered in front of her chest, vibrating and turning slowly toward Zen. The dagger took on a life of its own, darting, with amazing speed, toward Zen. Startled by the failed kill as much as Ablis's response, Zen barely caught the knife, rewarded by the edge cutting his palm. Ablis raised her hands above her head, spreading her legs should length.

"Your choice has been made."

Twin beams struck Zen flush in the chest. The impact lifted Zen from his feet and cast him backward to the octagon's wall. His body struck the wall with a force he knew he would not survive. He slid limply to his rump then to his face, muttering something about "You and I, G. G." Ablis shook her head in near apathy. "I would have made the same choice…but I would not have been defeated."

Zen's mind called from his devastated practically lifeless body. *How long does the transformation take?*

Ablis smiled, then laughed. "In your case, probably years, you idiot."

Attempting to open one eye and failing, he said, "*Years?*"

"You chose life, mage born, a necessity in our line and a must for our survival. Had you simply chosen servitude, I'd have accepted you just long enough to arrange your recruitment to G. G.'s regiment." Her eyes enveloped Zen's mind.

They both shimmered broken, body and all, into elsewhere.

CHAPTER 7

---✤---

Woman-Child

Wigan massaged her temples. *So close, but I'm not strong enough.* Wigan had attempted contact with Zen for several days with little success. *Only one sure contact,* she thought. *It nearly destroyed me.* Wigan's assessment was correct. Though very aware of her surroundings, each attempt to contact had not only depleted mental energy, but her physical strength ebbed as well. The last attempt would require several days of rest to recuperate. Time moved quickly within the protective environment of the bubble. Wigan stretched, blinking and squinting while removing remnants of a fitful sleep from the corners of each eye. She'd recuperated much quicker than she'd expected. *What now?* she wondered. *Mother will know.* She smiled, eyes twinkling. Contacting her mother did not require near as much strength—maybe she could. "Mother? Mother... MOTHER," she called psychically.

Peace sat up, senses on edge, straining to determine whether the voice was actually Wigan's rather than the voice of her dreams. "*Wigan?*" she offered tentatively.

"Yes, Mother, it's—"

"*Speak up, girl! I haven't heard from you in days!*"

"I know, Mother. I'm sorry. I was trying to contact Zen, but I couldn't reach him. For some reason, I can barely lift my head when I'm finished. I'm not strong enough to reach him." Wigan's chin sagged between her palms, bangs dropping across her forehead in exasperation. "What should I do, Mother?"

"I don't even know how you can do the things you do, girl. How am I supposed to know how you are to contact this…this Zen?"

"You're *supposed* to know how, Mother. I *need* you to teach me." Wigan stood up in the protective bubble, pleading to the point of whining.

"Some things I can teach, that's true enough, but I know practically nothing of your abilities… They're paranormal, Wigan." Peace paced back and forth, rubbing the back of her neck. *"Your abilities could not have come from me…"* Peace transmitted puzzlement. *"Yet…they must have originated from somewhere within me. I don't have an answer for you yet, Wigan, but don't fret."* Peace took in her surroundings. *"I have all the time in the world to think about it."*

"What would you do in my position?" Wigan frowned.

Peace laughed. *"Why, I'd rejoice! Wigan, you're young and beautiful, and neither of us knows the extent of your powers or talents for that matter."*

"You think this is FUNNY!" Wigan blurted out.

Though Peace could not see Wigan, she knew her daughter was on the verge of a tantrum. *"Yes and no… Yes, there are times I think it's hilarious… Maybe an irony that I can't help but laugh at is a better way to describe it. To find myself in this position in the first place Wigan is almost unimaginable. I can't tell you what a mind-bending experience it is for me to accept this situation, even our discussion, as a reality. I keep thinking I'm going to wake up to a bright light and a stethoscope. And no, to explain the other part of my answer, I don't think this is funny. If I accept this situation as real, which I have, I must accept both of our limitations… I don't know much about our enemy, but I do know you'll never survive a true confrontation with Abkhas in the condition you're in or with the skills you possess."*

"What's Abkhas have to with us?" Wigan shuttered.

"*Everything,*" Peace muttered. "*I really don't know what this is all about, Wigan, but I have a feeling I'll find out soon. Abkhas called me the **seed**, the **medium**, the **counterpart**. I'm guessing that medium is being able to communicate with you the way we do. What else I don't know, maybe I'm the counterpart of this Zen... I truly do not know, Wigan.*"

"What's a stethoscope, Mother?" Wigan interrupted.

Peace stood, hands quickly traveling to hips, flabbergasted at Wigan's question. Before she could respond, Wigan asked, "And why can I talk to you without getting tired," drifting further from the course of the conversation.

"*Wigan! Haven't you heard what I've been saying?*" Wigan frowned. Peace waited for a response. Wigan remained silent, seemingly, more attentive. Peace dropped her hands to her side and continued, "*In any case, it's too dangerous for you to stay in one place. When you probed me before, you chose only the loving things about me. It's time you read me deeply and take whatever experience you can use. You'll need every trick you can find, Wigan.*"

"Mother, why am I out here and you're in there? It seems to me you're better at this than I am...and you already know Abkhas."

"*Don't you think that I would change places if I could! Enough questions! Probe!*" Peace demanded. She shook her head, struck by humor and frustration at the same time. "*I mean it, Wigan! No more whining and no more questions! Abkhas is sure to be searching for you if or when he realizes you live.*"

"You're frightening me, Mother." Wigan glanced over both shoulders.

"*GOOD!*" Peace retorted sternly.

Just as Wigan pressed past the initial barriers to the more private reaches of Peace's mind, Peace caught Wigan's whisperings of fright and disapproval. "You're sounding just like Abkhas, Mother."

Peace smiled, knowing that frightful information might cause just enough fear and awareness to keep her daughter alive one more day.

Peace opened her mind. Wigan plunged forward. "*CAREFUL, GIRL! You'll knock me cold!*" Peace grimaced, temples throbbed.

Wigan slowed her journey yet continually delved forward, "Sorry, Mother." Wigan probed for several hours. Smiling, giggling, gasping, and grimacing, Wigan took in Peace's memories. Wigan sorted through concepts, experiences, and behaviors attempting to memorize those that seemed useful as well as those specifically ordered by Peace. Peace sat in wonderment re-experiencing moments of the past as if they were the present each time Wigan opened another corridor. "Mother! You didn't!" Wigan exclaimed, unconsciously moving her hand over her mouth, hiding her grin.

"*GET OUT OF THERE!*" Peace demanded, literally pitching Wigan's mind from the memory. "*You'll learn that soon enough,*" Peace offered, shaking her head.

"I didn't see anything I didn't understand, Mother." Wigan smiled.

"*Some memories are sacred,*" Peace retorted.

"I want to know more about John Mason, Mother."

Peace's face reddened. "*He was a very determined and persuasive young man, Wigan. I don't really—*"

"I need to look at everything I can, Mother. Neither of us knows what might be useful."

Peace grimaced. "*You're really stretching this, Wigan.*"

"I love you, Mother."

Peace smiled to herself, sitting down in her favorite chair. "*Lord, help me... Go ahead, Wigan. Probe away. Ask all the most invasive questions you can imagine.*"

"Tell me more about John Mason."

"*Wigan!*" Peace retorted.

"Mother!" Wigan held her ground.

"*John was the first boy to get by my defenses.*"

"How did he do that?"

Peace remembered with greater clarity than she had anticipated. Wigan shared the vividness without the emotional repercussions. "I guueeeess he got by your defenses...on the kitchen floor, Mother!"

Peace laughed in spite of herself. "*Believe me, I was as shocked as you are!*"

"Did you love him, Mother?"

"*No...I don't think I would call it love...or even puppy love. He was very handsome, and I was very curious. If you add handsome to curious, multiply them by sixteen, then pour on a half-pint of apricot brandy...you'd have me that night.*" Peace stared without seeing. "*A girl who believed she could stop a freight train by herself...with her will-power subdued, was it the cosmic universe or karma that provided no choice but to experience the boy, the brandy, and the kitchen floor.*"

"It was hormones, Mother! What did you think afterward?" Wigan asked.

Peace laughed. "*I tried not to think! I tried to pretend it didn't happen...at first anyway. Then I tried to convince myself I was in love and this was the only boy for me.*"

"What?" Wigan could not comprehend the thought.

"*I know it sounds a little hard to believe, but I was raised to keep myself for the man I was going to marry. I sincerely meant to do that. I didn't expect that brandy and a boy's cologne would be such a strong combination. I regretted doing it, so I tried to make it better by convincing myself I was passionately in love.*" Peace admonished herself. "*Rather than realizing I was just a kid experiencing—*"

"Hormones?"

"*Yes, Wigan, hormones and a need to know about sex.*" Peace hesitated while recalling the memory. "*Maybe there was also a need just to be needed by someone...who knows?*"

"Have you been in love, Mother."

"*Yes, Wigan, I was in love once.*"

"How could you tell the difference?"

"*The difference between what, Wigan?*"

"The difference between love and...and just being needed?"

"*Can't you think of an easier question, Wigan? Don't answer that! Love was much more desperate and wonderful than the curiosity that led me to the kitchen floor. It was a total and compelling preoccupation that could not be ignored. It redefined the meaning of companionship...and touch. It's a completeness that just does not exist without the other person's presence, yet it is unselfish in the sense that you take joy in knowing your partner is happy and that you are a part of that happiness. It is not physical, yet it truly changes sex to making love.*" Peace hesitated, realizing she was heading in a direction that would increase the agony of being imprisoned. Peace abruptly attempted to change the subject. "*Let's talk about that at a different time, shall we?*"

"Who's Greyson Mirphey?" Wigan asked.

"*Who?*"

"Greyson Mirphey."

"*Greyson Mirphey? I don't know a Greyson Mirphey.*"

"I suppose you don't remember him, Mother," Wigan offered sarcastically. "It is, after all, your memories that bring his name to me. You only saw him briefly. He was the last man you talked to before your interview for this job."

"*I don't remember anything about him.*" Peace went on, "*Aren't there more important things for you to attend to than looking at all the men I've ever met and remembered in my life?*"

"Probably, but I think he was cute. I know you remember, Mother. You're just avoiding." Wigan smiled. "You couldn't decide whether you like him or not and could not understand why both of you were being interviewed for the same job."

"*Get off it, Wigan!*" Peace demanded, losing her patience. "*You need to get this probe over with. You and I can talk about the rest of this some other time.*" Wigan crossed her arms in perfect emulation of her mother in a determined mindset.

"Promise me, Mother, and no backing out of it?"

Peace sucked in air. "*Yes, I promise. NOW GET ON WITH IT!*"

"Okay, I am, I am!" Wigan loved winning almost as much as she loved her mother.

Wigan probed on into the night finally stopping, head reeling with memories of her mother. Wigan tried to make sense of several memories without success. The difference between what Wigan had experienced and the memories of her mother was almost too much to entertain simultaneously. Wigan's head throbbed as she agonized, adjusting to hosting the foreign memories.

Peace interrupted, urging Wigan to conclude and safely depart from this conversation. "*You must leave, Wigan.*"

"LEAVE, what do you mean 'leave,' Mother?"

"*You need to leave my mind and move from wherever you are. It's no longer safe for us to be in contact.*"

"But I don't know where to go or what to do. I don't know where I am, and I'm completely alone! Mother…," Wigan hesitated, "don't you want me with you anymore?"

"*Wigan, what kind of question is that? Of course, I want you with me. That's just it. I love you too much to have you hurt, and the longer you linger, in whatever form, the more you're in danger. I don't want Abkhas to find you, and he will if we continue this conversation… YOU NEED TO LEAVE, WIGAN!*"

"But where do I go, and what about my sisters?"

"*Your sisters will be fine. I don't know which way you should go.*" Peace struggled momentarily. "*Go south.*"

"Why south?" Wigan responded.

"*I don't know 'why south.' Just go…*" Peace's exasperation with Wigan's resistance bled through the psychic discussion. "*Maybe you'll find someone else who has similar powers. Maybe you'll find others who can help you. All I know is that you'll only find Abkhas here! Our hopes, whatever they may be, will be dashed if you don't leave.*"

"How will I know if others know magic? How will I judge if they will help me?"

Peace inhaled deeply then exhaled through her nose. "*You'll just have to be curious but not obvious. Look vulnerable but not too vulnerable… Damn it, Wigan, you'll just have to fend for yourself!*"

"So you want me to act as you did with Greyson?"

Peace suddenly remembered Greyson and smiled. "Of all the memories she would cling to, why a ten-minute acquaintance of no consequence…someone I should not have had any interest in," she wondered out loud, unconsciously shielding her thoughts from Wigan. She lied, managing to shield her actual thoughts. "*I don't remember Greyson. Will you please follow my instructions?*" Peace added wearily.

"Okay, Mother, I guess I'll go south as you said. I don't like it. I'll miss you, Mother."

"*I'll miss you as well, Wigan. Wait! Call for me at least once a week… Now go!*"

"I don't know if I can contact you at a distance," Wigan fretted.

"*We'll worry about that when the time comes.*"

Wigan smiled. "You're a sneaky woman, Mother…and not a very good liar."

"*You'll be a sneaky woman yourself before this is done.*" Peace smiled though annoyed at Wigan's consistent delay. "*One more thing, Wigan, NO MORE PLAYING WIZARD! Especially where people can see you! And tell no one about yourself without talking to me first!*"

"Okay, Mother." Wigan began to fade, enjoying Peace's concern.

Peace continued, "*No matter what happens, remember my advice or you'll lose your life and probably more than either of us realize…and, Wigan?*"

"Yes, Mother?"

"*You need to start acting more mature. Quit being such a little girl… You sound like a ninny!*"

"Just practicing, Mother. Seems to me you accomplished a great deal acting like one!" Wigan's eyes twinkled mischievously as she smiled wide.

Peace laughed. "*You are a little stinker, but maybe you're not such a little girl after all.*"

"I'll try to stay away from the apricot brandy too, Mother!"

Wigan and Peace laughed simultaneously.

Peace transmitted a farewell to Wigan then broke contact. *These damn chains!* Peace thought as she glanced about the room. *At least I can move.* Peace sank in the feather-filled cushioned chair, hand bracing chin as she stared at the floor. *I wonder whether Wigan's magic comes from me? It must come from me, but why haven't I been able to sense it within me? Definitely a conundrum.* She twisted a bit of her hair. *It must come from within me, but…I've not ever tried to sense it. For most of my life, I believed magic to be nothing more than nonsense. Good old sensible, Miry.* She realigned her weight to get more comfortable while she contemplated, *Well, Miry, you are no longer you. You are Peace, a different person with different skills.* Peace glanced at the shackles, wondering whether she could break them with willpower alone. She inhaled deeply, closed her eyes, and strained her mind. Try as she might, she was not disciplined sufficient to keep her mind from wandering to other thoughts.

Frustrated with the lack of discipline, she tapped her head against the back of the chair. *I don't know why I keep trying the impossible.* Peace abandoned mind-melting the chains. There were simply too many sensible arguments against the power she knew she must have. Unconsciously, she fingered the cup Wigan had given her. Water spilled, trickling across the tabletop to the table edge, pooling until amassing a quantity too much to contain. The water began cascading down the table leg, puddling next to Peace's right foot. "It can't be possible," Peace muttered out loud. "It must be imagination or delirium... Delirium makes more sense."

Blip, blip, blip, the droplets echoed into the pool near Peace's foot. "There is a logical explanation somewhere amidst this insanity. That's it...," she told herself, "just relax and let the logic seep in." Peace stretched arms and legs in unison, attempting to release tension physically as well as calm herself emotionally. She began by exhaling enough air to cause her bangs to lift. The stretch felt extraordinary. Dropping her arms on either side of the chair, she let her legs go limp. Peace attempted to clear her mind of all distraction only to be startled by a coolness enveloping her right foot. Peace lifted the foot, touching the heel with her fingertips while staring at the source of irritation. *Water?* Peace touched the small puddle of water following the steady drip, drip, drip to the pool on the tabletop and the small but steady stream of water erupting from the cup now lying on its side. Peace automatically reached for the cup intending to return it upright when the engraving caught her eye. "Forever Full" was engraved, by a skilled craftsman, on each side of the cup.

"Forever Full," Peace mumbled as she set the cup upright. *So much for logic,* she thought as she observed the cup replenish itself with sustenance. She emptied the cup several times, only to repeatedly observe it replenish with water. The cup consistently filled to just below the rim, stopping precisely the same place each time. Peace repeated the ritual. She was continually amazed at the magical cup's persistence and precision. Peace found herself smiling, swirling circles in the water with her fingertips while tracing figures in the mud with her toes for the few moments it took for the floor to completely absorb the water. Suddenly, Peace laughed aloud. "Now who's the ninny, Wigan!" She giggled, drank deeply of the water, and relaxed back into the chair. Without attempting, Peace's mind slipped into emptiness and a deep yet welcomed sleep.

Wigan dissolved the bubble of protection then returned the stump to its original form. She sat down determines to test her magical abilities. She had no idea what she could or could not do, how powerful or weak she might be. She recalled the creation of the gown, the bubble, and the stumps transformation. It had all been instinctive automatic as if an innate ability. She seemed to cause the metamorphosis without thought.

Despite understanding the metamorphosis had been successful, she still had very little understanding of what had occurred or the origin of the power. *What if it's an illusion?* she thought. *The gown feels real but the stump certainly didn't look like a stump. My communication with Mother has been real.* Wigan realized she'd expended a great deal of energy talking to her mother. She would likely have to expend more to bring her magic to bear, but she needed to know whether her power was just to create illusions or something of permanence. Wigan began to draw energy, watching her surroundings closely. She noticed she was very exposed to observation by anything or anyone. Wigan second-guessed the drawing of energy, deciding Peace was right about showing her power. *None must know,* she thought, gradually letting go of the energy that had been building. She delayed her plan to test her powers, understanding she would need to find a safe place to resume that test. She was disappointed with the delay but knew it was the right decision. She would require a safe obscured place to learn about herself. Wigan understood she could not put off the need to understand her abilities before facing whatever was to be faced, particularly if she were to face it by herself. Wigan knew Peace could guarantee neither advice nor assistance at long distances.

Wigan stood up, stretched backward, then leaned against a large conifer. She considered the surrounding at length. The air was pure and crisp with an added fragrance of pine that lifted Wigan's spirits. She smiled to herself. "I love that smell!" she offered the woods, arms wide she pirouetted taking in the smells of nature nearby. It was late summer in the mountainous region. Seed pouches and pods retained some freshness but were fading in preparation for autumn. Honeybees worked diligently guided to gold by the sweet fragrance of ripened fruit and late-blooming flowers. Wigan listened to their buzz as they continued searching for pollen to feed their fellows and increase the supply of honey.

Though far into the highlands, Wigan was not alone. She noticed smoke streaming from dwellings in a village two to three miles below. The village appeared meagerly populated judging by the number of smokestacks but large enough to threaten intrusions by villagers wandering or attending to gathering herbs and fruit growing near her location. Her caution was warranted. Turning toward higher elevations, Wigan wordlessly set foot deeper into the forest.

The woodland, a magnificent visage, an artist's dream, canvassed in a multitude of colors against lime rock bluffs stretching in splendor to the base of an equally extraordinary mountain peak. The peak, elevated high into the sky, snow-capped and obscured to a degree by the dense mist forming as a result of the sun's heat against the ice and snow. The mountain, a vanguard to the woodland and adjoining ridgelines. Majestic against the blue sky yet ominous in the degree to which it towered over the landscape casting an enormous shadow that grew as the sun traveled closer to the horizon. Snow crested, shouldered in mist, the east face of the peak seemed to brighten in the sunlight as the red sun descended to the west. *A perfect union*, Wigan thought, *and I'm somehow part of it.* Her eyes twinkled in appreciation and recognition of a different sort of kinship. She inhaled deeply, her heart pulled by this newly experienced fellowship. She felt without saying, some sort of spiritual bond had occurred with nature she'd observed. As if in response to her thoughts, a gentle breeze lilted through lifting Wigan's auburn hair and gently caressing as if to say, "Welcome, sister. You are among us. Our bond is your bond." Wigan breathed in the clear clean air, enthralled and mystified yet deeply moved by the communion in spirit. "This is being alive." She smiled.

Discovering several minutes had passed, Wigan regretfully returned to the task of selecting a sight that would provide security and secrecy. Three hundred yards upland, toward the base of the mountain peak, she noticed an obscured indentation. She shielded her eyes from the sun with her left hand. With closer scrutiny, the cave became more and more distinguishable. "PERFECT!" she exclaimed. Glancing at both gown and bare feet, she realized she was poorly equipped for the climb and the climate. Wigan took a deep breath. "Either I can do this, or I can not do this," she mumbled recalling the conversation with the intruder the night before.

She closed her eyes and sat, clearing her mind as much as she could of all distractions and pictured the dress she was wearing. She embraced the dress, smelled the fabric, pressed her mind against each fiber, caressing, spinning, wishing a transformation to occur. She imagined herself at a sewing station blending strands of fabric… tweed? No…burlap? No…cotton and silk… Yes…cotton and silk. She imagined the softness of cotton for undergarments, shirt, and trousers. Silk jacket and scarf to pull her hair up. She smiled inwardly as she felt the chill of the breeze upon her back. Startled, Wigan opened her eyes nearly coming to tears as she beheld the jumbled pieces of cloth that once combined to be her very, very beautiful dress. She quickly grabbed the larger pieces and covered herself, wondering what to do next. She knew that she could transform the gown into a durable jacket and trousers. She had pictured both in a weave, resembling deer hide and a weave resembling cotton and a weave resembling silk. She laughed at herself. Though exhausted from the first experiment, she realized that pieces of cloth were representations of the different weaves she'd imagined. She could not, however, imagine how she was going to piece the would-be makings of a meager wardrobe together. "Here." A gray-haired blue-eyed wizardly gentleman offered, stepping forward.

Wigan turned quickly stepping backward nearly stumbling to her rump, startled by the presents of the gentleman. Messmor laughed. "I'm not going to hurt you, girl. I provided you with some clothing that actually might be of use to you."

Wigan frowned. "I'll not accept gifts from you. I didn't give you permission to sneak up on me or talk to me, let alone bring me gifts."

Messmor laughed and coughed smoke through his nose, simultaneously trying to exhale the offerings of the Wizard's blend.

"Um...permission to sneak up on you? Why, girl...if one sneaks, one is obviously doing so without the other's permission, or it wouldn't be sneaking. Besides, I simply arrived to offer you meager coverings. I do not intend to do more than wish you well and then, with or without your permission, take my leave."

Wigan's brow narrowed. "Why would you want to wish me well?"

Messmor's patience dwindled, not being one to tarry for a moment longer than he believed necessary, but before he could respond, Jeb blinked in. Wigan leaped backward, falling to her rump, nearly losing the cloth that covered her private parts. "WHAT IS THAT!"

Messmor pulled his pipe from his lips, puffing smoke rings and winking at Jeb. "This...young lady...is a scoundrel...a vagabond of vagabonds. A winged Gypsy with a beak and a mind of his own." Messmor laughed.

Jeb bulged an eyeball toward Messmor and squawked his disdain at Messmor's depiction. The exchange was so hilarious Wigan caught herself giggling. "It's a bird without feathers or hair?"

Messmor chuckled. "How old are you supposed to be, girl? Six or sixteen or twenty years? You seem all three at once."

Wigan frowned. "I think I'm supposed to be seventeen if it is any of your business, but I don't know for sure how old I am... Maybe just a day or two old," she concluded.

Messmor scratched his chin. "Well, it makes no difference. Those clothes are yours. I took the liberty of putting a small pouch of silver in the trouser pocket in case you need it."

Wigan stared at the trousers then back to Messmor. "What exactly are your interests here?"

Messmor brushed Jeb off his shoulder to the ground. "Just to make sure you begin your journey safely...that's all. I bid you farewell." Messmor bowed, stamped his staff one time, and vanished.

Jeb spun, squawked, both eyes bulging, expressing more than a bit of aggravation at being left behind, flapped his wings toward Wigan while standing stationary. Wigan clapped her hands in appreciation for the wyvern's attention. Jeb stopped flapping, stepped one step toward Wigan, then seemed to think better of his decision and launched himself into the air. Mid-flight, Jeb vanished. Wigan squealed in delight in seeing such a creature.

"A MAGICAL BIRD! Or...um...LIZARD." Catching herself mid-sentence, Wigan laughed at herself.

"You are a ninny, and you sound like you're six."

She walked toward the garments and picked up the jacket and trousers. Wigan had no idea what the material was made of or how it came into being but she was grateful nonetheless. She stared at her bare feet. "Well...if he can do it, so can I." Wigan covered both feet with moss, focused her mind on the material the trousers were made of. Stood very still with her eyes closed as she gathered in as much energy as she could. Wigan tried to merge external energy with innate energy that seemed to rise from within. Wigan imagined the moss reforming into a leatherlike durable substance. She lost track of her surroundings, deep in concentration, her fingers twitched between rhythmic motions, hand movements choreographed to the draw of energy.

Suddenly, she felt herself falling backward. Light-headed and panting from the strain, she landed firmly on her rump. She looked down and could not help but smile, both feet were surrounded by a soft leatherlike cloth, smooth on the outside and moss soft on the inside. For a moment, she believed the moccasins were attached to her flesh, but she realized with a brief inspection that they were not only independent of her feet they were a perfectly matched pair. The transformation depleted her physical strength. "Maybe a magic carpet next." Wigan laughed, light-headed, knowing that even as exhausting as transmuting the moss to moccasins was, she'd accomplished a very, very small feat in the world of magic. Pleased with herself yet sad that she was not as accomplished as she'd originally believed and the stranger had been right. Suddenly, she felt more fearful than before, unsettled by the discovery that she was not as powerful as she once thought. "Just have to be careful," she instructed herself. "Rest another day and move on." She stood, contemplating what to do next while clearing her mind and changing her mood.

Wigan decided to make the journey toward the cave she'd seen as soon as she gained enough strength to do so without risk. She leaned against a large oak tree, taking in the view, still, a bit light-headed, and breathing deeply. The gentle breeze returned ever so slightly, lifting her spirits. Wigan, though mystified by the breeze's lifelike feel, rejoiced in the subtle but evident gift of strength.

"Thank you," Wigan whispered, "who or whatever you are."

The breeze stilled. Wigan hummed a tune of an origin she could not recall, contemplating the world around her as she pushed herself away from the oak and began her journey once more. She noted the breeze that had been with her since she'd been resting but was no longer present. "Are you real or just a figment of my imagination?" she mused aloud. The breeze failed to return. She laughed, humming and talking aloud but to herself. "Maybe you're just a fickle memory of my mother's." She offered to whatever may be there. The breeze returned a bit brisker than before. Wigan stopped, faced the breeze, not expecting a response but curious that the breeze had picked up intensity. "Well, you're not my imagination, but you're not likely more than what you appear." She resumed her journey pushing away the thoughts, strange feelings, she was beginning to experience about this woodland. She skipped along the low grass, humming and chiding her imaginary friend. The breeze, as if taking offense, intensified the force pushing and pressing Wigan against her will back in the direction she'd traveled from. "Okay! Okay! You're real! Whatever you are!" The breeze sustained its intensity. Wigan glanced to all sides, attempting to determine the source of the breeze. "How was I supposed to know you're more than a simple breeze?" she offered while attempting to resist the push. Wigan was standing at nearly a forty-five-degree angle from the ground, into the wind when the breeze stopped. She immediately fell forward.

Wigan's reflex was quick but not quick enough to prevent a nose full of moss and a mouth full of the forest floor. Wigan's temper flared. "I guess you like bullying defenseless humans." She spit the dirt from her mouth, picking pieces of leaf from her tongue, then rolled to her rump, sitting up. The breeze remained silent. "Or is it you just like pushing me around?" Though miffed at the breeze, Wigan realized she felt replenished and completely fit for travel. Her anger quickly abated. "Who are you? Can you speak? Do you have a name?" she offered as she continued her trek to the south. The breeze resumed its gentle caress.

Breeze is my name, daughter of the same, the wind whispered gently against the conifers. Wigan froze, her reaction an ambivalent mix of fear and wonder. The resonance, both heard and psychically perceived, was remarkably unsettling. She had not expected a response and was unclear how to proceed. The breeze continued to gently press Wigan in the direction she'd been traveling. Wigan could not see the cave but knew it was within a mile of her current position. She silently attempted to maintain contact with Breeze while deciphering the most direct course to the cave. The breeze continued to guide, nudging her consistently on a course that appeared most direct to her destination. Wigan traveled through briars, bushes, and conifer needles, ducking, weaving, snagging, and complaining about every obstacle. Wigan was still swinging at imaginary branches when she entered the clearing contingent to the cave and noted the breeze was no longer present.

Wigan looked in all directions before concluding the breeze was gone. She could not help but try to explain away the conversation with the breeze as a result of her exhaustion, but she could not explain how her strength had been replenished. Despite how absurd it seemed to do so, she thanked the breeze for her assistance, looked about, deciding ultimately to enter the cave and seek shelter for the night.

Wigan was surprised by the brightness within the immensity of the cave. The cave light undulated ever so slightly, as iridescent stalagmites and stalactites sparkled light throughout the enclosure. Wigan suddenly felt alone and insecure. Breeze was no longer in her company, but something else was. She sensed a different almost opposite presence, silent, strong, and self-assured.

"Anyone here?"

Here, here, here…

Wigan met her own voice echoing and rebounding from wall to wall. "Some kind of acoustics," *acoustics, acoustics,* Wigan muttered, crossing her arms and rubbing her shoulders for warmth. "Must be just me," she offered aloud, "and 'just me' better get started." *Get started, started.* Wigan selected a tight grouping of stalagmites. *Nice place for a bed,* she thought to herself, not wanting to hear her voice's repetition. Smiling, she placed her hands on the tips of the foremost stalagmites, closed her eyes, and began willing a transformation. Something shifted, her spell went awry, rebounding with even more energy than she'd expelled in return striking a sharp mental blow. Shaken by the unexpected turn of events and the assault of her own magic, Wigan staggered and caught herself barely able to stand, her eyes burned, temples throbbed. She braced herself against the stalagmites.

"Mother!" *Mother! Mother!* she screamed, expelling more energy, nothing happened except the repetitive return of her voice. Wigan started to lose vision, to blackout falling to her knees. Unconsciously digging nails into the cave floor, she struggled to gather her senses as well as her strength. "I mustn't pass out. I must not pass out. I must not pass out," repeated endlessly as she crawled toward the cave opening. Shaking her head it began to clear. "God, I'm weak," she squeaked so low that the echo could not form. Crawling on all fours, Wigan inched her way toward freedom. She felt as if she were swimming in syrup. Limbs heavy ached with exertion against the force within the cave. Her strength ebbed. Wigan was nearly unable to reach the doorway. The concentration and strength required to push aside the psychic fog had zapped her strength and nearly ended her life. Finally reaching the doorway, she pushed herself through, first her head, then chest, finally dragging her feet forward and collapsing outside. Wigan whimpered, momentarily losing control to the relief of being outside the cave and the pain of utterly depleted strength. "Darn!" she slammed her palm in the moss. *Pull yourself together,* she thought. *That's what your mother would say…and do. Quit acting like a ninny,* she thought.

Wigan contemplated the experience for several minutes before remembering the earlier exchange with Breeze and the seemingly miraculous return of strength. *I wonder*, she thought. "Breeze… Breeze, are you there?" The conifers stirred ever so slightly. "Please, Breeze." The wind lilted through the wood touching Wigan's face.

Strength began to return. "Thank you, Breeze." Wigan could not contain the tears while she pulled herself further away from the cave. *I'm still such a ninny, such a little girl.* She wiped her nose on the sleeve of her jacket. *You have to grow up, darn it!* Breeze's wind continued to give strength, pushing away despair, replacing an earlier hope. "Can you talk to me?" Wigan asked. No answer returned. "Will you talk to me?" Wigan offered more assertively while struggling to her feet.

Yes, Breeze whispered with the assistance of the trees.

"What did this to me?" Wigan slid down, bracing her back against a tree trunk parallel to the cave's opening.

Stoneguard, the spirit of the rock, Breeze answered matter-of-factly.

"Why?" Wigan inquired.

You insulted him.

"How could I have insulted him?" Wigan shook her head doubtfully.

By assaulting his domain with your will. By entering his domain without gaining his permission.

"I needed PERMISSION TO GO INTO A CAVE?" Wigan asked incredulously.

Unless you are strong enough to command.

"And I'm not?"

You've answered your own question…and you have too many questions. I must leave you here… I am a spirit of this world, and you are a voyager of two worlds…a child in each… Breeze's psychic persona faded into the wood.

"Wait, Breeze!" Wigan stood as quickly as she could. "What do you mean? I need help! Where can I get it if you just abandon me here!"

Breeze's voice lilted faintly through the trees. *Too many questions for one so young, but I will answer your final one. Search out the*

Apotheosis. He will give you strength and more if you are worthy…but only if you are worthy.

"The Apotheosis? Where do I find the Apotheosis?" Wigan stood exasperated on the verge of kicking the tree trunk when winds turned her 180 degrees, forcing her to stare at the mountain peak.

THERE…, Breeze's voice moaned. *Many have gone before you. None have returned…in human form. Your life is your own*, Breeze added then vanished.

Wigan felt chills dance up her spine and across her face, but she could not tear herself away from the mountain peak.

"My life is mine…but it is meaningless without knowing what is meant for me or how to use this magical energy…or finding some answers to what caused my life. I'll go… Sorry, Zen, we'll meet some-day." Wigan set out for what she believed to be the Apotheosis, a mountain peak hidden deep within the misty sky obscured by the darkness of dusk, eclipsed by a rising moon.

The bluff acted as a monumental hedge, separating the lower wood from the mountainside. The rock face looked almost man-made in the manner in which it wreathed and girded the moun-tain's base—a quiet yet ominous crag. *It must twist for miles*, Wigan thought. Shading her eyes from the sun, Wigan examined the face of the bluff. "It reaches upward to nearly nine hundred feet!" Wigan decided to follow the bluff southward to find a break, crevasse, or a manner of passage to higher elevations.

The night began to fall, and she had not found a passage or method of traversing the bluff safely. Wigan sat with her back against the bluff. Just as she relaxed, she found herself separated from the bluff by several inches. "That's curious," she muttered putting her back against the bluff. Wigan nestled tightly between two boulders. Again, she realized and found herself being moved so slightly it was barely noticeable. She smiled. *Stoneguard*, she thought. "Why would you push me away, Stoneguard?" Wigan asked flatly as she asserted her back firmly against the bluff.

The lime rock began to warm then sizzle. Steam gushed for-ward. Wigan gritted her teeth attempting to ignore the heat and the pain. "Please stop," Wigan pleaded.

The heat quickened, rock began to glow. Wigan found herself cringing from the heat. As she moved from the bluff, the lime rock began to cool. Wigan smiled mischievously. She moved back toward the rock, and it warmed. "Is it that you care so much about me, Stoneguard, that your heart warms at my touch?" The bluff rumbled. "Is it that your body quivers from my presence?" *Those are some great memories, Mother*! She giggled to herself, planning the next verbal assault on Stoneguard. The bluff hardened to the point of cracking. "Is it that I move you so much you lose composure around me?" Wigan laughed fully.

WENCH! Stoneguard bellowed, rocks reverberating.

The wind stirred. *You speak*, Breeze whispered.

Stay out of this! Stoneguard reprimanded.

Breeze retorted calmly, *You have no power over me. I do as I please*!

"Breeze?" Wigan stood, glancing in all directions.

Yes, Breeze responded.

"What are you doing here?"

HEEE called, Breeze answered.

"He was speaking to me," Wigan explained.

Breeze's warmth radiated the wind. *You've progressed more quickly than you know.*

"Progressed, I've barely begun this journey, and I can't even get past this bluff!" Wigan paced back and forth.

You have not progressed far in your journey, but you have progressed in your relationship with Stoneguard. He must respect you.

"Respect me!" Wigan laughed. "You can't be serious."

Breeze's giggle undulated oddly through the trees, bouncing off the bluff. *He only speaks to peers.* Breeze could hardly contain herself.

HUSH! Stoneguard exclaimed.

Breeze laughed. *He only speaks to his peers.*

"You mean an EQUAL?" Wigan looked puzzled.

Not equal, but being "not ignorable" is very close to being equal, Breeze offered. Lime rock turned red then yellow, then white. Wigan stepped away from the heat. *See what I mean.* Breeze pushed the heat upward and away from Wigan.

Stop interfering bag of wind! Stoneguard rumbled.

Wigan's eyes twinkled, delighting in Breeze's female company and in antagonizing Stoneguard when there was an audience.

"He certainly has a temper...sort of goes off his 'rock'...er! If you know what I mean!" Wigan and Breeze giggled in conspiratory unison. "Makes me want to call his 'bluff'!" Wigan could not contain herself holding her sides. "I wouldn't taunt him if he were a little 'boulder'!" Wigan fell to the ground, pounding her heels and hands alternately out of control. "What's your first name? CLIFF?" Wigan offered out of breath.

Stoneguard's rumble echoed through the length of the bluff. *Taunt me not, woman-child. You have the advantage only because I cannot move, but you will not go over me.*

"I may not be able to go over you, but we sure can get over on you! I'll bet you get tired of being taken for GRANITE! Hahaha!"

Stoneguard shook yet did not respond. Breeze began to withdraw. Wigan sensed that Breeze did not want to take unfair advantage of Stoneguard. Wigan could not resist gloating. She believed she'd won this battle of wits and was more than a match for Stoneguard. She still resented what he'd done to her in the cave and could not help believing that revenge would be sweet.

"What's the matter? Can't think of anything to say?" Wigan picked up several large rocks and began throwing them at the bluff. As each rock struck the bluff, Wigan could sense more irritation than pain and an anger building. The air chilled. Wigan stepped forward in a show of excessive self-concept. "You're right. I am not your peer." Wigan slammed another rock on what she believed to be the face of Stoneguard. Stoneguard's helplessness was apparent. He could not move. He only could endure the punishment. The air chilled further. "I've won this battle! You're nothing but a little boy," she sneered. "You admit it by your silence. You just sit there being your miserable self. You can't even do anything about what I'm doing to you." Wigan slammed the final rock.

Stoneguard steeled against the emotional and physical onslaught. His only defense, the one he'd developed over several years of torment, accepting reality, was the most difficult aspect of his existence, but accept it he must. He could not argue with her comments.

Wigan continued, "I am more than your peer. I'm your better." The air chilled further and misted. "It's obvious to all that I've beaten you. I've won!" It began to snow. Wigan felt Breeze's presence.

Won…? Won what? Breeze inquired.

"I've beaten him. Now *'I'* command." Standing, chin up and forward, arms crossed, Wigan emphasized the "I" in a way no one could escape the arrogance. The air iced. Wigan startled.

You've won? Breeze's presence was even more unmistakable. *You've won nothing but the attention of this rock pile. You command nothing including yourself. You are no one's champion here. Where I teased, you intended hurt. I need not be in the sight of you.* Breeze vanished.

Wigan stepped back, dismayed shaken, and hurt by Breeze's sudden negative observation about her behavior. "I didn't intend to hurt anyone! He was the one who interfered with me! What do you want from me anyway?" Wigan chewed her lip, fists on hips. Red-faced, Wigan added, "I don't owe you anything, and I didn't ask you to follow me around. I…" Wigan stopped. Realizing the last remark was meant only to hurt and was largely untrue, she turned and kicked the bluff. "I'm sorry, Breeze," she offered quietly. Stoneguard rumbled. Wigan turned, "Stoneguard, you're an ass!"

Stoneguard's chuckle, neither friendly nor threatening, caused small rocks and pebbles to cascade down the bluff's face. *I guess that really does make us peers.* Stoneguard managed to sound very much like a young boy rejoicing in knowing for the first time he was someone's equal. Wigan opened her mouth, intending to provide an acerbic response but smiled instead. Stoneguard had a point after all.

"I hope you know neither one of us should be proud of it." Wigan shook her head and searched for a likely place to rest for the night. Very near were two moss-covered boulders. Wigan discarded the thought to attempt a magical metamorphosis to form a blanket from the moss, remembering both her mother's advice and her experience in the cave. Wigan plopped her rump between the two boulders nearest the bluff. "Truce for the night, Stoneguard?"

Wigan received no answer, but as she nestled closer to the bluff, in the shelter of the boulders, she was well aware that Stoneguard had not pushed her away. "Truce for the night then" were the last words she mumbled as sleep swept her away.

Wigan slept soundly through the night. Dawn broke to the serenade of meadowlarks and the call blue jays. Wigan gradually rose to her elbow, digging the matting from her eyes, and yawning. She stretched her arms and back as she sat up. Wigan smiled, patting the boulders at each of her sides. "Morning, brother of the rocks." Wigan half expected some sign of presence. None came. "I'm famished," she muttered, rising to her feet, stumbling slightly then balancing against the bolder. The boulder rolled on its own accord, causing Wigan to drop to her side. "I get it." Wigan pushed herself to her knees then stood up. "A truce only for the night, right?" Wigan eyeballed the crag, and as expected, no response was offered. Wigan resisted the smart remark that tickled the tip of her tongue. "If you sleep, I hope you slept well." One more stretch and Wigan set out to find breakfast never losing track of her goal…finding a way around or over the bluff.

Wigan continued the trek, never wandering too far from the bluff. After a few hours of rummaging through bushes, flowers, weeds of a wide variety, Wigan's stomach began to growl. "Annoying," she muttered, realizing the hunger as well as knowing she was no closer to determining what was edible and what was not. Before long, sweat dampened her hairline. The moist hair clung to her temples, another sign of exertion that was not celebrated. Wigan was frustrated from the lack of success finding a pass around Stoneguard as well as at least some fruit to eat. "Why can't there berries…or onions…or carrots or something," she announced to the sky above in exasperation. Wigan had traveled a considerable distance following the base of the bluff and still had not identified a reasonable place to negotiate its heights. "All I need is a crack or crevasse…even vines would do." Her voice echoed off the bluff which, now, nearly obscured her destination—the mountain's peak. While looking skyward, she stumbled onward, briars catching, pulling, and clinging to all parts. Wigan looked down in genuine consternation, tired of continual snags, to be delighted by the sight of berries. "Raspberries!" Wigan spent the next hour gorging herself on berries, smiling in the wake of their tartness. She licked her fingers often in an attempt to minimize the stain, knowing no matter how diligent she might be, the purple coloring on her fingertips was a fairly insignificant consequence to enjoying the fruit.

Replenished, Wigan continued forward. Though several hours passed without finding a way around the bluff, Wigan found the journey to be rewarding in other ways. She located two apple trees, several different types of berries, and a variety of wild nuts. She gathered a moderate supply to eat later, jammed all she could carry into her pockets then sat to have a late afternoon meal. She selected a golden delicious apple, shined it on her shirt, then took a large bite. Juice flew in all directions, she laughed aloud, savoring the flavor, enjoying the crispness and the sound as it snapped and crunched. She stood, smiling at the world, deciding to continue her trek. Wigan's luck continued. She examined the bluff closely where she discovered a lengthy, wrist-sized limb, lying a short distance from the bluff.

The limb was large but not so large it could not be managed. Wigan grasped the limb concentrated and, after a good deal of panting and exertion of mental energy, changed it slightly. "A little shorter and a little fancier." She admired the newly formed walking stick, as she wobbled from the exertion nearly losing balance. She grinned, holding the large stick above her head as she announced to the wood, "This is my staff," in a reverent tone much lower than her normal lilt as she brought the staff close to her side. "By the power of gray skull!" she shouted, lifting the staff with one hand in front and above her head, laughing heartily, head tilted back.

Almost shocked at what she'd said, Wigan quickly brought the staff to its proper position. She checked over both shoulders to make sure she had not been observed by anyone. "Where in the world was that memory from, Mother!" she asked aloud while looking back and forth for anyone or anything that might be observing her movements. Knowing there would be no answer, Wigan resumed her search for a passage. Before stepping forward, the second memory of her mother's invaded her awareness. She grinned. "I know, Mother, I am not

'He-man' and I do not have the power of Greyskull." She chuckled. "Maybe I should call myself Merlin'da! Sorceress of the Bubble and Crag!" She smirked as she skipped along. "Yes, I am Merlin'da Sorcerous of the Court of… Let's see…" Wigan thought about a proper name for her kingdom, her court. "That's it! Campalot!" Wigan laughed out loud, grabbing her sides, tickled with the word-play. She continued play-acting while she walked. Wigan swept a royal bow toward the oak to her left. In a deeply rich yet feminine voice, she addressed the oak. "Welcome to Campalot, your oakness!" She laughed fully, always enjoying her mother's sense of humor and not realizing she was beginning to develop a similar one. Wigan, a bit less exuberant about play-acting yet joyfully reveling in her surrounding, continued in search of a passage to the mountain beyond. "Onward, staff in hand, and apple in mouth, onward! Your quest begins, Merlin'da."

Wigan traveled forward, talking to herself and a host of imaginary companions. "I'm truly fortunate to have been blessed with such an ability…don't you think?" Wigan pirouetted, arms extended enjoying the warmth of the day and the bond with the forest. The bluff vibrated a very low-resounding sneer. Wigan stopped walking, turned, and looked directly to the crag lifting her right eyebrow. In the best imitation of her mother, Wigan commented, "You certainly are an indignant oaf, aren't you?" She tried successfully not to giggle, maintaining a false air of aloofness, thinking to herself, *That's you at your best, Mother.* The bluff was silenced by Wigan's comment. She added, "Your timings right though, dear hardheaded Stoneguard. I have much to do, and I appreciate your attempt to keep me on track."

Wigan traversed for several more hours, discovering no sign of weakness, not a broken branch, a crushed blade of grass, or a worn trail from a past negotiation. Frustrated and tiring, she faced the bluff. Fists on hips and staring upward, Wigan blew a lock of hair from in front of her eyes in exasperation no longer content in merriment. "Well, Stoneguard, you win. I can't find a way around you, and you have no openings large enough to walk through."

The rocks radiated warmth. Appearing to more than agree with Wigan's assessment, Stoneguard emitted an air of superiority.

Wigan sneered, childishly sticking out her tongue, bending forward at a forty-five-degree angle. "You think you're hot stuff, don't you!" Stoneguard appeared to pay no attention. "Well, I'm going to have to climb you!" The bluff shook at the thought.

Wigan stood, most of her weight tilted to her right foot. The fingertips of her right hand drummed her chin as she contemplated the climb. *He surely won't cooperate*, she thought. She surveyed the area around herself for something, anything that could assist in the climb. "But..." Wigan pulled loose a long length of vine that had been lodged in the junction of two boulders. "He won't have to worry about it once I'm over him and on my way." She located and pulled free a second vine that had been dangling very loosely from several feet above her. She was surprised that a vine that had rested so loosely hadn't been dislodged previously by the wind. She smiled to herself, realizing that any vine that would have been secure enough to use to support her weight would be dislodged by Stoneguard to prevent Wigan's climb. Determined to not allow Stoneguard to "win," she focused on combining the two vines into a makeshift rope of sorts. The project took a bit longer than she would have preferred, but nonetheless, in the conclusion, Wigan believed she'd figured a way to merge the two. After inspecting the vines, she began pruning and twisting them together as tightly as she could. She continued to glance up from tying the two, hoping to spot a third vine that, in her mind, would be the final and ideal addition for a sturdy rope. She finished spinning the two vines tightly together, then lifted and pulled the length through her hands, checking for weak points or places the weave was not tight. Once satisfied with the length of the rope, she double-checked the knot strength where they were connected. Three very sharp tugs, "There," she mumbled out loud, "that should do it." Wigan curled the vine around her left shoulder and proceeded to the face of the bluff. *I'll start here*, she thought, standing next to a very large oak tree, carefully sizing up the area of the cliff she believed might allow passage.

Wigan tied the vine to her walking stick and tossed the vine over the first branch some twenty feet in the air. The staff successfully made its journey over the limb with a few feet to spare. Wigan waved the vine, sending large ripples up to the branch the vine had been thrown over. With each ripple, she added slack and advancing bits of vine forward until she was able to work the staff back to the ground. She smiled as the hope of finally making her way past Stoneguard grew. Wigan made a large loop at one end of the vine then slipped the other end through it. She worked the loop back to the top of the limb by rippling the vine and pulling until the loop and makeshift slip knot were secure against the bottom of the limb. Wigan climbed the rope, wrapping one leg in the rope and stepping her foot against the vine with the opposite foot for leverage. In a surprisingly short time, Wigan was negotiating the branch and attempting to pull herself to the top. Her muscles ached from the exertion, yet she smiled at the accomplishment and thanked her mother for the strength she'd inherited. The limb she'd chosen as a platform was very large and broad, making the final move from the rope to the limb difficult but not impossible.

Wigan felt the sweat trickle down the sides of her temples as she finally pulled herself atop the limb. She settled on the perch and retrieved the vine, now rope, all the while catching her breath. She wiped the sweat from her forehead and cheeks with her hand and a set of large leaves. Wigan stared at the crag, thinking it had been lower when she initially surveyed the area. She calculated the ledge distance from her new vantage point. She concluded that the small flat area that would be her destination was about five feet above her and ten to twelve feet away. Wigan, after a moment more calculation, decided that another tree limb about eight feet above her would have to serve as the brace for a swing of sorts.

She took her staff and launched it a second time over the branch above her with sufficient slack to reach the staff as it came to rest about nine inches above her head. She looped and knotted both ends of the staff with her makeshift rope, forming a seat for the newly formed swing.

"If I pump and swing, I should be able to reach that ledge. I'll lose the rope, and likely the staff, but I can climb the rest of the way from there."

Wigan rechecked the connection of the rope to the limb, tugging on it firmly. After being satisfied it continued to be securely fastened, she shinnied up the rope then slid back down into the seat. Within a few minutes, Wigan was pumping and swinging level to the ledge. *Just a few more feet*, Wigan thought, knees bending and extending rhythmically. Sweat rolled down her forehead and stinging her eyes. She pumped one, two, three, four more times then released the vine. Her arc culminated four feet higher than the ledge. Screaming at the top of her lungs, Wigan flew feet first to the cliff's edge. Wigan slid onto the ledge in the last moments, arching forward, barely balancing to keep from falling. "Heck of a way to land," she mumbled to herself, rubbing and wiping the dust from her rump. Standing back from the edge, Wigan relaxed preparing to sit but found herself suddenly without balance, in mid-air, plunging toward the ground at an amazing pace. Wigan was almost totally immobilized by the suddenness of the plunge, screamed for assistance, and flailed the air. Just before landing, the fall slowed but not enough to prevent the severe bone-jarring impact. Wigan thumped the Alluvian soil bouncing to the base of the oak tree.

She winced, unable to breathe for a moment, having the wind knocked out of her. It was difficult to breathe, but she did not lose consciousness. Too shaken to cry, she pushed herself to a sitting position, looking at elbows and hands for scrapes and bruises that might need tending. In a few moments, she was able to get air back into her lungs. Her palms and elbows stung, but no broken bones or ruined clothing. Finally, she stood, balancing herself against the oak tree. She rubbed the soreness out of the hip she landed on and glanced back to the bluff. "It's completely smooth," she whispered. "The ledge is gone!"

Wigan's head had not cleared when Breeze's comment scalded Stoneguard. *You numskull! You could have killed her!* Stoneguard rumbled. *Would serve her right! She HAD NO RIGHT!* he bellowed.

No right! Breeze challenged. *She has every right to seek Apotheosis! You and I did, and no one tried to purposely kill us!*

The crag responded, *No…they only wanted to change us into slaves! She has no sense, no respect…NO RIGHT!*

Breeze quieted, *What if you'd killed her? What then, Stoneguard? Would you face Apotheosis?*

Wigan began to realize Stoneguard had indeed attempted to kill her. *Kill me!* she thought. *KILL ME...you tried to KILL ME!* Wigan's head cleared completely. She stood beneath the oak tree, staring ominously. Neither Breeze nor Stoneguard realized Wigan's pose or the intensity of her anger. Raw and untrained, Wigan stood firm, radiating power. Breeze gasped and turned, Stoneguard was suddenly quiet.

"Yoouu," Wigan's voice reverberated and echoed off the face of Stoneguard. "YOOUU!" she screamed, pointing at the bluff. Lifting hand, palm open directly in front of her face, palm heel toward the bluff, "Receive your reward!"

Nnnoooo! Breeze screamed as the ball of energy sped over her head, searing the oak's branches. Breeze attempted to alter the trajectory to no avail. Stoneguard braced for the impact, sneering with low-resounding vibration. The explosion shattered rock and ledge, searing a crevasse several feet long, fifteen feet wide, directly in front of her. Chunks of lime rock, boulder, and miscellaneous debris sizzled through the wood, causing trees to buckle and earth to tear. Smoke rose from the bluff's face. Breeze stood in shock. Wigan's pose had not changed.

Woozy from the expelling of such a large amount of energy, and already was regretting the loss of temper, Wigan did not unclench her jaw but dropped to her knees nearly blacking out from weakness. Stoneguard moaned. Wigan had not fully comprehended what had taken place, but she knew she had been determined to kill Stoneguard. She knew in the recesses of her mind that she should not have expended the power. She should not have lashed out so vehemently no matter what he'd done in irritation. She knew she need not kill him for it. Wigan, pale with regret, finally focused on the aftermath. She stood determined to not show weakness yet express her regret. She faced Stoneguard. Stepping forward, Wigan hesitated, seeing blood on her shirt. She quickly inventoried herself discovering it was not her blood. Wigan looked toward Stoneguard and panicked.

"The rock...it's...it's...BLEEDING!" Wigan screamed, clutching her cheeks rushing to the bluff.

No! Breeze warned. *He'll try to kill you again!*

"But he's DYING!"

Wigan lunged into the crevasse. Despite her weakness, she brought energy forward, touching and cauterizing wherever the rock bled. She was oblivious to Breeze's warning. She knew that she caused this and knew it was her responsibility to fix this. Her initial regret was replaced with anxious despair, fearing she would not be quick enough to stop the bleeding. The bluff reverberated for miles with Stoneguard's pain. Wigan worked frantically to repair the damage she'd done. The vibration ceased, the rock no longer seeped blood. Wigan felt no sign of Stoneguard.

"Have...have I destroyed him, Breeze?" Tears began to form and trickle down Wigan's nose.

I do not know, Breeze moaned. *Apotheosis will decide... You may die, Wigan.*

"I cannot!" Wigan screamed, launching herself to her feet. "It will be the death of my mother. She warned me not to do this."

Breeze hesitated, *She warned you?*

Wigan nodded. "Yes, she warned me not to demonstrate my power to anyone, or Abkhas would find me."

Abkhas! Breeze shivered.

"You know of Abkhas?" Wigan asked.

One of the devil's own, Breeze moaned. *Death is its mistress, a demon of great malaise, maelstrom personified. Its coming is prophesied. The outcome has never been foretold, but the greatest of evil is its quest. Why does Ab_we should not mention its name ever again! Why does or what does the demon have to do with you?* Breeze asserted.

Wigan shrugged her shoulders. "I don't know. My mother only told me he was my enemy."

What makes you believe that it is a "he"? Breeze asked.

Wigan rubbed her cheek, removing specks of Stoneguard's blood. "Again, I don't know... That's how my mother referred to it or him. I am only to fear him," Wigan offered cautiously.

A wise stand for all, Breeze responded, not fully understanding but relieved Wigan was Abkhas's enemy.

The sky clouded, grayed, then blackened. *He comes*, Breeze whispered shakily.

Wigan strained her senses, attempting to isolate the "he" Breeze had referenced. "I don't see anything," Wigan offered Breeze.

"You must be blind" the voice emanated, shattering silence.

Wigan stumbled forward, taken off balance by the nearness of the voice. "Who is this? Who causes Stoneguard pain?" the introducer's voice cut the air.

"Wi...Wigan...Wigan is my name," she squeaked, still unable to isolate the voice's origin.

"I'm sorry, I didn't mean—well, I did mean to hurt him...but only after he tried to kill me."

Apotheosis tilted an eyebrow. "You did this?"

Wigan turned to see an elderly bearded man unusually supple for the years he projected. "Yes," Wigan replied.

"Why are you here?" Apotheosis queried.

"I really don't know why, only that I needed a place to find the true nature of my gift," Wigan offered.

"How did you do this?" Apotheosis gently continued his questioning.

"I became angry and wanted to hurt Stoneguard. The rest just... just happened," Wigan whimpered.

"Stop sniveling," Apotheosis directed impatiently, "and tell me exactly what did you do?"

Wigan started to answer when Breeze interrupted, *She hurled a ball of energy.*

"Silence!" Apotheosis voice reverberated, startling Wigan to tears. "She is to speak for herself."

Turning back to Wigan, Apotheosis mellowed, "Go on, Wigan."

"I...I...I raised my hands above my head and gave him what I thought he deserved."

Wigan lifted her head, feeling more in control of her emotions and confident in her memory of the incident.

Apotheosis smiled. "And what did he deserve?"

"My anger," Wigan stated flatly.

An aura of wisdom emanated from Apotheosis. His soft yet penetrating expression caused Wigan to examine her statement. "Do you think you are Stoneguard's better?" Apotheosis queried.

"Well...yes," Wigan replied. "He challenged me, I won, and that's that," Wigan concluded.

"And that's that?" Apotheosis asserted, eyebrows knitting slightly.

"Yes!" Wigan snapped, flinging her hair and lifting her chin. "That's that!"

Apotheosis frowned, turned, and began walking toward the mountain.

"Wait!" Wigan cried, a bit more panicked than even she'd realized. "I need your advice to...to learn from you my true capability to...to find my destiny!"

Apotheosis slowed, stopped, then half-turned gazing over his left shoulder, eyes penetrating. "You have not conquered Stoneguard, the least of your enemies... You have not conquered yourself...the most undisciplined of your enemies, and you have not and will not conquer me. You are no better than Stoneguard, much less skilled I might add." Apotheosis turned slightly toward the mountain silhouetted by the dusk's sun, faded to translucence.

Wigan stepped forward, trembling in near hopelessness. "Please, Apotheosis...please help me..."

He's gone, Breeze whispered.

"No... No, somehow, he's still here," Wigan mumbled as if to barely notice Breeze.

"Please, Apotheosis, please help me," Wigan asked quietly.

Her courage and genuineness were unmistakable. Apotheosis's aura coruscated phosphorescently. His shimmering presence remained translucent. "You need not a mentor, girl. You need a guide. Your powers are strong in the measure, undisciplined, but uniquely your own. I cannot provide you with what you already possess." Apotheosis aura faded.

"Wait! If you cannot help, you must know something. Give me something! Anything," Wigan pleaded.

"Something then…" Apotheosis riddle lilted for a moment that diminished into nothingness.

> *This questor's quest has failed to cease dependent on mourning's breeze will move no further yet not retract until the day of the guardian's pact. Their secrets shared their spirits free will set you forth toward destiny.*

Wigan stood motionlessly, setting the verse to memory. Concentrating with every particle of her consciousness, Wigan repeated the verse. Wigan persisted in reciting, turning, twisting, and reversing the riddle, attempting to decipher its meaning. She unconsciously snuggled next to the boulders rubbing her arms to maintain warmth. "This questor's quest has failed to cease… That's obvious enough. I'm still here. Dependent on morning's breeze… Morning's breeze. This morning, tomorrow, yesterday, or most morning breezes? Until the day of guardian's pact… What guardian? Who is the guardian? And what pact?" Wigan closed her eyes and focused all her energy. "Mother… Mother…" From a great distance, a vaguely perceivable voice hummed through Wigan's mind.

"*Hello, birthing… My little princess, I am your brood mother's nemesis!*"

Wigan cringed as the specter's face took shape in her mind, eyes of ember dipped in carnal fire, lips stretched agonizingly over broken yellow teeth.

"Get out of my mind" Wigan hissed covering her ears.

"*I shall leave of my own accord. Your weakness now you can't afford. Your destiny rises full of fright my minion return to test your might until the time we next do meet, I leave you with my favorite treats.*"

"Treats?" Wigan frowned, watching the apparition in her mind. Abkhas's grin widened sardonically as he raised an open remnant of a hand. Wigan watched curiously. Abkhas faced the palm directly at Wigan, obscuring his face then slowly clutched. As fingers retracted, the pain seared through Wigan's temples. Wigan screamed and stood stooped, leaning left shoulder against the bolder. Abkhas's laugh resounded throughout Wigan's mind then vanished. Wigan dropped to her knees, tears running. She could not see. The pain slowly receded, but Wigan's blindness remained.

CHAPTER 8

———————— ❧ ————————

The Tempering

Zen squinted in the candlelight. Every muscle ached, sweat dripping. "Again," Ablis murmured, "how long must I continue this?"

Zen responded, wiping the sweat from his forehead and temples, "Until I tell you to stop!"

Ablis instructed sternly, motioning Zen to continue. "You must develop the physical discipline if you ever hope to master the powers I will enhance in you. We've been over this a hundred times! Now concentrate."

Zen grinned, shaking his head as he readied himself in a lackadaisical horse rider stance. "I don't have any magical powers. I hope you find this amusing."

"Shut up!" Ablis commanded. "It comes..."

The conjured adversary, Zen had come to know as Grink, shimmered into being. "How many times do I have to kill this thing before we move on?" Zen inquired as he circled left then right, carefully analyzing Grink's movement. Ablis remained silently locked in meditation. Grink stepped forward, growling.

Though purely Ablis's creation, Zen understood only too well the apparition's danger. Grink was humanoid, well-muscled, and extremely strong. He stood seven feet tall and weighed close to four hundred pounds. Grink's physique, remarkable in size, was unusual in other ways. He possessed two very dangerous appendages—tentacles. Each tentacle was connected just below the clavicle, symmetrically balanced, on each side of his neck. Alive in their perpetual undulations, the tentacles were multipurpose, resembling bullwhips, very leathery and pointed. Zen resisted an impulse to rub the large welt on his rib, remembering that the tentacles could not only slash and pierce, but these extensions could also grip the prey tightly in tandem or singularly. Grink's eyes were radiant, his teeth canine, and his tentacles in constant motion. Grink was quick for a humanoid and amazingly adept with his natural flails. He was not, however, invincible. Grink could be killed, dematerialized, by inflicting an extensive amount of injury, or, as Zen had discovered in an earlier contest, he could be defeated rapidly if Zen could locate and crush a very small and unusual abnormality.

Grink's conjured existence was dependent upon a mind link from Ablis. The physical manifestation of the link was a coin size indentation located in a different spot each time Grink was recreated. During the third battle, Zen noticed the pockmark moved to different parts of Grink's body on each manifestation. Zen surmised the mark was part of a conduit that allowed Ablis to manipulate Grink's movements. Zen surmised the incongruity during the third battle. He'd managed to reverse punch Grink directly in the weak point, causing the conjuration to turn nearly holographic then dissipate. Zen kept the observation to himself though each victory made it more difficult to conceal his discovery. He was well aware that at any time, Ablis could discover what he'd managed to conceal from her awareness. Zen smiled to himself while preparing for Grink's attack. *It's a small victory but a victory just the same*, he thought. Each bout progressed in tenacity, making victory increasingly more difficult. Zen discovered in an earlier bout to not be cornered by Grink unless he was willing to pay a severe penalty. Zen's chest still itched where the welts from Grink's tentacles served as a fading reminder. Zen had also surmised Grink could remember the moves of earlier battles and was not nearly as easily fooled by feints and dodges. Ablis assured Zen his games were foolish. *Always trying to build my confidence*, Zen thought. Only one loss was required—not only the bout, but Zen as well would be ended. Zen understood this part of the game unconsciously, automatically, like breathing. He understood that the dance, the dodges, and feints were a necessary part of staying alive and of delivering death. He moved close to the room's center.

While circling, Zen examined Grink carefully making certain even Grink's most minute movements were assessed, analyzed, and cataloged for future reference. Zen noted Grink's changes in posture and stance, the subtle shifts when preparing to attack, as well as a variety of combinations available with each movement. Grink was not entirely predictable, but he favored and telegraphed certain attacks that allowed Zen to pattern an aggressive defense. He consistently managed to dominate Grink with counterstrikes and counter combinations. He rarely risked fully offensive aggressive combinations outside the defensive response to Grink's aggression. Though the entirety of his martial art was instinctive and reactionary, he couldn't help but think he'd been trained in a defensive style that depended on the opponent to create vulnerability by exposing openings to the adversaries body that occurred as a natural part of the process. Grink was very efficient. When he attacked, not many weaknesses were apparent and, if apparent, not for long.

As Zen circled, he focused on each opening and closure. The slightest shift of weight, the tiniest flex in muscle gave Zen clues to when to strike and the timing of movement, especially when Grink fell into a rhythmic cadence. It was at that point Grink became most predictable. Zen circled, constantly lulling Grink into a rhythmically predictable pattern of movement. Ablis, looking through the eyes of Grink, could see the extreme martial skill. She surmised that this was Zen's world—the dance of death, combat to combatant. He must have lived to fight and fought to live to be this accomplished.

Zen continued to circle. The contest was truly his only reality while engaged with Grink. The single aspect of his life he completely understood and felt at ease with. His entire being responded to the challenge. He was one with the dance. *There!* Zen's eye's squinted ever so slightly in an attempt to shield his mind and nonverbal reactions from giving any clue to Ablis. He was well aware of her propensity for picking off his thoughts. He continued the dance carefully, remaining focused and directing his mind inward to avoid Ablis's attention. *Just below Grink's Adam's apple.* Zen stopped abruptly.

"Ablis, I'm sick of this," Zen offered in a whisper.

Ablis did not respond. Grink attacked full speed. With a deafening scream, Zen launched, defending as well as attacking, with a jump spin sidekick as he'd predicted Ablis's reaction and Grink's attack. Zen's body responded without thought, effortlessly spinning one hundred and eighty degrees reaching a height of six feet. Zen's right heel struck Grink flush in the throat. The impact lifted Grink from the floor, crushing windpipe and breaking his neck. The mind link was simultaneously destroyed. Grink's shimmering body bounced on the sanctuary floor just a moment after Zen had landed comfortably.

"I said I've had enough…"

Zen turned his back to Ablis and walked to the corner picking up his staff. "I'm hungry, tired, and need to practice my patterns. I must have time for myself, or I will not serve you."

Ablis raised an eyelid. "Don't tempt me, Zen."

Zen laughed. "Do what you will," he added as he sat back to the corner pulling a piece of venison jerky from his pocket.

"I shall…," she muttered while stretching out of the meditative position.

Ablis finished stretching, stood, and tossed Zen a winter apple. "That should taste better than the jerky."

Ablis rubbed her temple. "We'll have stew for supper. It's time you learn to cook, and you'll need your strength."

Ablis smiled in a show of feigned domestication, causing Zen to choke. He eyeballed the apple suspiciously. Ablis laughed. "Why would I poison you when I could kill you outright?"

"I suppose you're right." Zen bit a small piece of apple slipping it beneath his tongue. After waiting for a soul-satisfying moment, Zen was convinced the apple was neither poison nor drugged. Zen devoured the apple core and all. Plopping the last bit of apple in his mouth, he relaxed and leaned snugly against the wall. Grink shimmered back into form. "More games, Ablis?" Zen snorted as he quickly got to his feet. "I am really getting sick of this. You're pressing me beyond reason."

Grink did not hesitate despite Zen's comments.

Zen's movement to the center of the room had become a ritual. First, he would stand motionless, assessing Grink's strengths as well as weaknesses. Finally, he would circle and attack or defend. This meeting was no different from the previous one. *Where is it?* he wondered while as he had so many times before. *There! Just under the armpit.* Zen smiled, circling, circling, feigning, weaving in and out. He played with Grink as he circled. Jab to Grink's nose with his right. Rear leg round kick to Grink's thigh while he avoided the combination of punches that resulted. Shifting from southpaw to right side, left leg leading moving fighting stance. Zen knew that his left leg gained power from blazing speed. He could implement combination kicks with his left leg alone, devastating his opponent. His right leg was extraordinarily powerful with or without speed. Zen favored the left leg lead but was not opposed to using any angle or stance to achieve victory. Zen slid then side kicked with limp extension as a feint, Grink swept his left arm to block and leaned forward to punch as Zen's round kick, same leg, struck Grink with considerable impact to the right eye. Grink, still traveling slightly forward, reached his left hand up to protect his left eye, not anticipating the hook kick, from the same leg to his knowledge knot. The heel landed firmly, sending Grink several feet stumbling to the wall. Zen understood that Grink had great difficulty defending several high-speed kicks from the same leg, which Zen did not bring down until the hook kick sent Grink across the room. His left foot returned to the floor, again in a Korean fighting stance. The combinations would have continued had Grink remained in range.

Grink returned. He circled, agitation apparent, in unison with Zen, flicking tentacles in an attempt to distract and gain an advantage. Zen guessed that Ablis was analyzing his moves as thoroughly as he scrutinized Grink's. *I must be careful enough to not show her everything.* Zen's concentration lapsed with the thought of Ablis analyzing all his moves. *CRACK!* Grink slapped Zen directly in the face with his left hand. Both were stunned by the contact. Grink had initially reached out as a lure to bait Zen for a much stronger punch. Zen had never remained in one position long enough to be punched firmly before. Zen was as much astonished by Grink's power as being hit. Grink quickly realized the advantage. He swung a back fist with the left hand before it had traveled full circle from the first punch. The back fist struck Zen's left shoulder just missing his temple as it ricocheted. The force tumbled Zen across the floor. Zen cat rolled bouncing quickly to his feet. He growled a low ominous growl that gained in intensity while gradually increasing volume. Zen's lethality was evident while he searched for a weakness. Rage fueling power, Zen's hands moved constantly and more quickly undulating unpredictably from pausing at random to a tightly wound blurring figure eight with both hands, a practice to strengthen and tone while increasing the ability to strike with amazing speed and power. The practice had become an unconscious part of Zen's art and a tell that his rage was close to surfacing. Zen edged closer and closer to Grink. Zen weaved back and forth, in and out of Grink's range. *BAM*!

Grink stepped backward, blinking from the straight punch he'd received to the mouth. Zen's uncanny ability to irritate while analyzing his opponent was never more apparent. On one hand, he darted on the other he circled. Without saying a word, Zen challenged and withdrew, stepped in close, dodged, and was out of range, grinning without fail. *BAM*! Zen's rear leg round kick landed firmly in Grink's solar plexus. Grink bent and grabbed air trying to capture Zen's foot. *BAM*! The second kick of the double round kick combination hit Grink in the forehead standing him back up.

Zen's circular motion, geared to mesmerize opponents, had lulled Grink into a predictable pattern of movement. Grink was aware of the technique. He'd been beaten severely each time his movement became predictable. Try as he may, he could not stop himself from making the mistake. Grink very gradually unconsciously fell into a predictable pattern. *BAM*! *BAM*! Right front kick to Grink's left knee, right straight punch to Grink's nose. *WHOOSH*! Left leg jump spin sidekick to Grink's chest. Grink's tentacles flailed, hands gripped emptiness, Zen was out of range grinning, circling, a predator. Zen frustrated Grink, always feigning movement and attitude. A constant charade laced with consistent punishment.

He outwardly challenged. One moment looking as if he was overconfident stepping a bit too close in another moment, looking a bit out of balance on the next, then delivering a series of blows or a single devastating blow from an odd position, ultimately returning to the charade of "just being lucky." The entire process was a weave of ruse and reality. Zen imagined he'd always been very patient in this aspect of his life. Though he would take advantage of an opportunity, exploit it for all it was worth, he would not overestimate his ability or the lethality of his opponent. He did not attack; instead, he waited for Grink's attack. Zen was confident Grink would provide an area of vulnerability, become more predictable, and lapse in concentration. *He refuses to move that right arm! He refuses, and I can't stop him quickly without a clear shot at the link.* Zen continued to circle frustrated with his opponent's caginess. Grink lowered his right arm slightly. Zen struck. Grink had allowed Zen just enough room to place the ball of his left foot firmly behind Grink's right eye. The force was noteworthy. The lead leg round kick would have rendered a normal man unconscious, but Grink, far from normal, simply turned his head without losing concentration or composure. Grink quickly reposed, raising the arm to its former position.

Zen smiled, whispering, "*Brace yourself, Grink. This is going to hurt!*" Zen growled, hissed, then barked simultaneously side kicking Grink just hard enough to cause Grink to lower the arm in a blocking motion. Zen resisted, widening his grin as Grink's arm passed where Zen's lead leg should have been. Zen blasted Grink's temple with a round kick. The kick had been performed, once again, in combination with the sidekick, without putting the lead leg on the floor. The kick's force turned Grink's head ninety degrees. Zen's foot carried through. Zen again, in nonstop motion, hook kicked back with the same leg catching Grink firmly in the left eye crushing the cheekbone. Automatically, Grink raised his hands to his face. Zen stepped in, next to Grink's right breast. He spear-handed Grink's throat with his right hand then reverse punched Grink, with rib-cracking force, just below the armpit with his left hand. The left hand's force sent ripples in all directions from Grink's rib. His fist was centered in the area of vulnerability—the mind link. Grink screamed in agony and anger from the defeat, shimmered, and was gone. Zen's left eye was slightly swelled from the earlier punch. His left shoulder already bluing from the back fist.

Zen saluted the shimmering remnants of Grink. "Much better, Grink. I may actually begin to enjoy this competition!" Zen's remarks were without humor. He had, in his peculiar way, begun to respect Grink's abilities. "But I am truly getting sick of being your entertainment!" Zen turned to Ablis cold with rage. Zen stopped short of exploding, crossing arms, and staring at Ablis. While she appeared perplexed, pain invaded her face.

"Damn you!" Ablis burst.

"Me?" Zen exploded in anger as well as genuine confusion. "Why are you angry with me!"

Ablis opened her eyes squinting with pain. "We're finished for today," she retorted.

"Answer me," Zen requested with a tempered hint of concern.

"No!" Ablis angrily responded as she stumbled from the perch on which she meditated. Ablis dropped to her knees, clutching her right side. Zen rushed to her side, very gently lifting Ablis to her feet. Shocked, he stepped away. Ablis's left eye was black and blue.

"What happened?" Zen asked panicked by Ablis's pain. Ablis faltered momentarily. Zen was quick to support. "Take your hands off me!" Ablis pulled away shakily.

"I-I didn't do that...did I?" Zen asked quietly while assuring Ablis he would not enter her space. Zen's eyes dropped. He hadn't meant to hurt Ablis, but he had meant to get rid of Grink once and for all.

"Of course not, you idiot!" Ablis snapped. "It was my fault, and quit being a child about my feelings," she added, regaining strength.

"Your fault?" Zen looked up confused.

Ablis explained, "I was so surprised by your method of attack I didn't adjust the link sufficiently. I was unable to absorb the blows!" Ablis voice and anger continued to slap Zen.

"I'm sorry... I really wouldn't have hurt you."

Zen's concern caused Ablis a moment of distraction as she looked deep within Zen's consciousness. What she saw came as much a shock as the pain of Grink had. Ablis's blinked the tears away nearly as quickly as they arrived, regaining control. "I'd have had Grink kill you if he could have."

Taken aback by the cool matter-of-factness of Ablis's response. Zen barked, "You are a witch, a ruthless, uncaring, cold, lifeless witch! I should have broken Grink's neck. Maybe that would have settled our arrangement!" Zen attempted but was unsuccessful in masking his hurt.

Ablis smiled. "You'll be better off keeping that attitude. I don't need a soft-hearted, lovesick, stable boy. I need a seasoned fighter that will survive regardless of feelings for anyone...least of all feeling sorry for me!"

Zen's jaw clenched. "I'll kill Grink tomorrow"—he stepped forward close to Ablis's face—"with force you'll never." Zen stopped himself. "If it's a line in the sand you want, witch, it's a line in the sand you'll get," Zen stated ominously. He turned to walk out of the room. "I wonder if you'll smile as nicely if his head is tilted at a permanent forty-five degrees!" Zen moved closer to the doorway.

"You'll not meet Grink tomorrow," Ablis added coolly yet less antagonistically. "I'm satisfied that your physical skills are sufficient for fighting normal adversaries. You're still an infant in most of the realms you'll need to be skilled in. We have much to do." Ablis walked to the doorway, paying little attention to Zen's mood. "Your supper will be ready in an hour. I expect the sanctum to be spotless by that time." Ablis pointed toward the door and waited for Zen to proceed through.

Zen cringed. "You push me beyond my limits, woman."

Ablis laughed. "You have your limits mixed up with your pride. We've not discovered your limits, but we're constantly rediscovering your pride." Ablis took two steps toward the kitchen then turned back to Zen. "You have great potential, Zen, so did a few before you. Pride and other self-limiting characteristics relieved them of their humanity. You'll not need pride when and if you accomplish the tasks at hand. You'll be content with your awareness. An awareness that will view pride as an enemy, a risk to inner peace, or your ability to focus, and finally a risk to your existence. I hope to see that day."

The door closed, confused by Ablis's suggestions of hope and, what he perceived to be, a vague hint of caring, Zen slammed a small pot into the door. Ablis's voice hummed through the door. "Again, you'll find yourself cleaning up your own mess before attending to others. Someday, I hope you'll outgrow that."

Zen's face reddened with outrage but said nothing. He simply picked up the broom and began cleaning. *Maybe she's right*, he thought.

Zen swept the sanctum floor while heating water over the hearth. Impatience plagued Zen. *How many days do I have to remain here? How many days until this puzzle is solved? Why shouldn't I just leave...? Because you don't know where you are, and she might have the answers you're looking for, that's why*! he thought, mumbling to himself as he set the broom in the corner.

"Scrub the floor, I'm a damn maid. Worse, I don't get paid!" he grumbled out loud all the while pouring hot water into a wooden bucket. Zen wrinkled his nose as he mixed in the lye, stirring carefully with his hand covered by a rag of sorts. Resigned to having to complete the chore, he bent down to the floor, arriving on hands and knees, and began scrubbing.

ZzzzzzzzzzzzzzzzzzzzzzzzBBzzzz. Zen instinctively ducked his head. "What the hell is this?" he exclaimed, rolling to the sanctum wall narrowly missing the bee's sting. Grabbing his quarterstaff, Zen yelled for Ablis. No answer. "Thought so," Zen whispered, watching seven lark-sized bees, noting the large slick twin stingers. The bees buzzed in a tight formation just out of the staff's range. "Will this ever end? Can't you allow me at least to do one thing at a time?" He listened intently for a response but failed to receive one. Zen returned his full attention to the bees. *Ablis, you come up with the damnedest sort of bugs*! He smiled, watching the formation watch back. *There must be a mind link somewhere*, he thought. *Where is it*?

Staring at the bees, Zen muttered, "Whoa!" realizing the stingers were nearly five inches long and undulating back and forth in and out of their abdomen. Each bee possessed a single eye and very large mandibles. Each of the six legs was hooked for gripping where a foot should have been. The wings were ten inches long, four inches wide at their base. Each bee could move horizontally or vertically with amazing speed. They seemed a bit sluggish when moving diagonally. "Great," Zen said aloud. "Quicker than Grink and just as mean. I wonder if they're as tough." Zen slowly stood up. Just as Zen started to move the staff, one of the seven bees struck with blinding speed. The force of the blow practically ripped the staff from Zen's hands. Shocked white, Zen could not miss the two ice pick-sized holes completely through the staff's end. *My god!* Zen thought. *How am I going to get out of this one with all of me intact?* The bee returned with blazing speed slightly miscalculating Zen's ability to evade.

Zen swiped toward the bee with his left hand, stopping short just as the right hand struck the bee's wing knocking it to the floor. Before moving to attempt to crush the bee, Zen eyeballed the regrouped formation. They moved in a group about a foot closer but did not attack. They looked uninterested in anything but observing. *What the heck is going on?* Zen stared in fascination, noting the formation still had not moved, but the injured bee was making its way back toward the formation. The fascination turned to agitation.

Zen exclaimed after several minutes, "Come on! Come try to kill me! If that's what you want!"

The bees hovered without apparent interest. Zen decided to creep to the hearth where his poncho was hanging. *It won't stop them, but maybe I can catch them before they try to kill me*, he thought to himself. Zen leaned on the staff, sliding his right foot toward the hearth. Zen shifted his left foot, causing the staff to scrape the floor. Instantly, the formation shifted and spread several feet apart staring at the floor and the staff. Zen froze. "What the hell are they doing?" he whispered aloud.

Ablis opened the door. "Zen, BEES!" She slammed the door shut just in time to avoid the oncoming formation. Each bee struck the door from a different angle then regrouped, hovering and staring at the door. The oak door shook violently from the bee's impact. Twelve holes remained. The door was cracked in several places. Small pieces of wood were scattered near the sanctum wall. Zen stood speechless, realizing the bees were not Ablis's creation. Even more terrifying was her obvious fear of them.

"ZEN, DON'T MOVE AND SAY NOTHING! Those are moribund hornets. They sting only after drawing blood by piercing their victims. They attack in unison, and the venom does not kill. It rots the flesh in pint portions!"

GREAT, Zen thought. *Any more cheerful things I need to know! What am I supposed to do? Sit on my thumbs until they get hungry. Ablis!* Zen screamed mentally.

Ablis laughed nervously. *Those damn bees scared me so much I forgot we could mind speak if we're this close. If you're finished giggling, tell me what the hell to do!* Ablis sobered quickly. *They can't see, but they hear and smell very well.*

Zen's mind chuckled. *I'm not getting close enough to know how they smell.*

Ablis's tone and response were unmistakably unamused. *Stop trying to be a comedian! I'm serious! Once angered, they attack the slightest sound or movement*, Ablis finished.

Zen could not believe what he'd just been told. *They can't see! You've got to be out of your mind. Those damn bugs are unbelievably accurate!*

So is a bat, Ablis responded.

True, Zen agreed, resisting the temptation to scratch his head. *What is the big eye in the front of their face for then, decoration?*

It's some sort of vibration sensing organ. When they buzz, it's like they are pouring water across the floor, looking for anything that changes the shape of the water, and they watch or sense that area for vibrations. That's the only way I can explain their behavior, Ablis offered.

You said they attack any sound or quick movement after they've been excited, right? Zen asked.

Yes, Ablis responded.

Zen thought a moment. *I have an idea then.* Zen slid almost imperceptibly toward the bucket of lye soap. Each movement, though extraordinary minute, caused the bees to flare their wings edge a bit closer hovering in obvious agitation. The entire formation eyeballed Zen. *BANG ON THE DOOR!* Zen mind spoke. Ablis kicked the oak door.

The formation, in a blaze, struck the door a second time, knocking out thumb-size chunks and cracking it to the point of near collapse. Simultaneously, Zen threw the staff toward the ceiling above the door and leaped to the bucket full of lye. Zen lifted the bucket to his chest. Five of the bees attacked the staff ricocheting it into the wall and striking it again before it tumbled to the floor. The sixth bee peeled off toward Zen, striking the bucket about six inches from the top causing lye to spew forward. At the sound of the spewing liquid, the bee spun and attacked a second time. This time striking the bucket above the previous mark and emitting a high-pitched squeal. Venom spurted into the bucket, causing the lye to hiss. The aroma almost gagged Zen, making it difficult to remain still. The bee then gulped a large portion of lye as the rest of the formation faced Zen and the bucket. Zen understood immediately when the bee squealed it was signaling a kill as well as calling the others to his side. "Why aren't they coming?" Zen mind spoke.

The bee that had gulped the lye hung motionless from the bucket spittle running from the mandibles. *It looks paralyzed,* Zen thought, again very gradually moving toward the hearth. *I hope there's enough of this left for the rest.*

"What are you doing?" Ablis asked without masking the sense of urgency.

Zen explained.

You're not going to try to get the rest to do that, are you? Ablis asked incredulously.

I'm not an idiot! Zen retorted, silently sensing Ablis's desire to argue the point but holding back. Standing next to the hearth, Zen held the bucket chest level amazed and grateful the dying bee continued to stem the flow of liquid. *When I say NOW, I'm dropping the bucket into the hearth. I'd appreciate any help I can get if any of the hornets decide to get intelligent or survive this.* Zen inhaled slowly and deeply tensing in the process of readying himself for the feat.

What do you think dropping the bucket will accomplish? Those bees are practically death-proof, Zen! Ablis believed Zen was going to die—if not from hornet's stings but from stupidity.

Their wings aren't death-proof! Think, Ablis. Think instead of command for a change, Ablis!

Before Ablis could retort, she heard Zen's mind exclaim, *Now!* Zen dropped the bucket into the hearth. As if able to travel the speed of lightning, the hornets hit the bucket plunging it deep within the hearth. All six bees screamed and squealed. Though their torsos remained intact, as Zen had guessed, wings and legs were quickly consumed. Zen breathed a sigh of relief reaching up to finally scratch his head.

"Yᴇᴇᴏᴏᴡᴡᴡ," Zen exclaimed while spinning full circle, unconsciously preparing for a second attack, but ill-prepared, Zen dropped to his knees clutching his right forearm. The hornet descended for the same forearm. The entire room bleached white from the bolt of energy emanating from Ablis's left hand exploding the hornet five inches from Zen's arm, knocking Zen to his back. Shocked by the concussion of Ablis's energy bolt, Zen barked, "What the heck are you doing?"

"Saving your rump!" Ablis retorted.

"Thanks! You damn near killed me!"

"Damn near just means I'm just a much better shot than you expected. How's your arm?" Ablis moved toward Zen.

"Just fine, I always wanted a hole or two in it!" Zed offered sarcastically, shaking his head.

Ablis turned to lift the large hammer she'd armed herself with just in case and crushed each of the bees one by one as they departed from the hearth. Zen got to his feet and cautiously examined his arm. After crushing the final bee, Ablis leaned the hammer against the side of the wall next to the hearth, then picked up a second bucket containing cool water. She returned to Zen, looking very concerned.

"I think that could use some water."

"My arm's fine!" Zen retorted, turning away.

Ablis inhaled deeply. "I know your arm's fine, Zen." She smiled. "It's your head that's swollen." The smile widened as she emptied the contents of the bucket over Zen's head. Ablis turned, walked through the door to her favorite walnut table, sat, and wept after making sure she was out of Zen's sight or earshot. Zen pulled the bucket off his head, grimacing from the grazed puncture wound.

He wiped the water from his face with the bottom of his shirt then examined his arm. "I suppose you'll turn black and red and fall off next." Zen cussed the injured arm and, as usual, was miffed at himself for not realizing the rogue bee was still about.

The irritation with Ablis for dumping the water on his head faded as he grabbed another jug of lye from the small bench he'd been keeping cleaning supplies and utensils in. He searched the shelf above the table for something he could use to clean the wound. "Aaahh"— he nodded in satisfaction—"there you are." He lifted a large sewing needle and strip of cloth from the shelf. After wrapping the needle, Zen dipped the needle and cloth into the lye then swabbed out the puncture wound, grinding his teeth with every insertion. Despite the pain, he was very grateful the puncture was only a minor flesh wound. Zen realized he was very lucky to have quick reflexes and the distraction caused by Ablis or the bee to puncture would have been deep into the flesh rather than just under the skin. He had managed, by successfully rotating the forearm away from the stinger, to avoid what would have been a serious injury. Recounting the events in his mind, he both realized he was very lucky and needed the practice to be more aware of his surroundings. He would have only received a scratch if he'd been a tad bit quicker, he thought to himself.

Ablis wiped her red eyes clean as quickly as she could, splashed cool water on her face, and took a deep breath. *No time to get weak-kneed,* she thought to herself. After successfully regaining composure, she heated the stew over the kitchen's open hearth, stirring ever so often between sampling and seasoning. The cooking served as a welcomed diversion from the training and the fiasco that had just occurred. Zen cleaned the sanctum for a second time then sat in his favorite corner, eyeballing the room.

How did they get in here? he thought to himself. *The windows are shuttered and closed. Ablis must have closed them.* Leaning the back of his head against the wall, Zen recalled the very strange event. He recounted each moment in an attempt to recreate the happening in his mind. *She couldn't have shut them in. Either she's one heck of an actor, or she didn't create them.* Zen got to his feet, checked his body and clothes for additional signs of damage, then walked into the kitchen, believing things had gone fairly well considering the circumstance.

Ablis paid little attention to him appearing occupied with cooking and her "own little world" as Zen would have described it if he'd had enough nerve. Ablis concluded the final taste test, filled the bowl a quarter full of stew, and sat in the lone chair next to the table. Zen grabbed a bowl, filled it, spooned one spoon full into his mouth, grabbed the chair that had been next to the wall, and sat down beside her.

Ablis scowled. "I don't remember requesting your presence."

Zen refused to look up. "You didn't."

Ablis put down her bowl, taking a deep breath. Without looking up, she said very quietly, "Zen, you've pushed and pushed me. I've advised you several times to treat me with respect. I've had patience. I've attempted reason. Will you force me to use stronger methods, or will you change your attitude?"

Zen looked up, his face a combination of confusion, hurt feelings, and consternation. "Do what you will."

Ablis closed her eyes. Zen felt himself being lifted from the chair. Before having an opportunity to verbalize his regret for earlier remarks, he was slammed into the wall and pinned with tremendous force. Ablis finished her stew. Zen could not move. *Okay*, his mind spoke, *I'm sorry.* Ablis released him. Zen landed firmly on his rump.

"Did you send them?" Zen inquired.

"Send who or what?' Ablis responded.

"The hornets," Zen returned.

"The HORNETS! Of course, I did not send the hornets! Why do you ask such a foolish thing?"

Zen's face reflected his confusion and his irritation with her mood. "Because they could not have come in by themselves."

"Why not?" Ablis asked.

"Because the windows were closed." Zen stared directly at Ablis. "You didn't open them, did you?"

"No…no, I didn't," Ablis answered now as curious as Zen, stopped her preparations, and seriously considered his deduction. "Are you sure they were closed?" Ablis looking back to Zen.

"Yes, I latched the shutters before sweeping. They just appeared from nowhere," Zen recalled without consciously considering Ablis's presence.

"At first, I thought you conjured them, but I could not find the link. I was amazed at their speed. I thought you'd been holding back."

He turned and faced Ablis. "Are there many more like you?" Zen turned sideways, rubbing his arm.

"Sorceress? Well, yes, there are a few, but none close enough to pose a threat. I would sense their power in any case."

Zen frowned. "You can always sense their power?" Zen raised a curious eyebrow.

"Unless they're much more powerful than I or it's demonic."

"Demonic." Zen's eyebrows raised further.

"Yes, demon's wizardry." Ablis frowned. "What did you mean when you said you couldn't find the link?"

Zen's face flushed as he frowned in self-abasement, thinking, *You idiot, this woman's bewitched you.*

Ablis's face was serious and threatening. "What did you mean?"

"Well, I could see the link on Grink."

"What do you mean? Describe it," Ablis offered anxiously.

"It was a small acorn size abnormality. It sort of resembled a pockmark. Whenever I disrupted it, Grink dissolved." Zen turned to face Ablis.

Ablis looked ominous power radiating. A pulsing aura silhouetted her body. She stared at Zen. Zen's stomach quivered. *Fear*, he thought. *Why am I afraid? She never really planned to transform me unless I failed. I have not failed.* Zen could feel Ablis's eyes upon him. Her aura enveloped him. He felt calm yet transfixed. All he could comprehend were her eyes.

"How long have you been aware of the link?" Ablis compelled.

Zen answered, "Since the third battle with Grink." *How odd,* Zen thought. *I'm talking on one hand and observing myself talk on the other.*

"Strip," Ablis commanded.

Zen automatically began taking his clothes off. He could not stop despite the tremendous embarrassment. "Do not do this to me." He steeled anger rising as he was dropping his shirt to the floor.

"All the way," Ablis commanded.

Zen protested, "Kill me rather than subject me to this! I'm no sideshow for your amusement!"

Zen continued to remove clothing as he was compelled. He could not stop. With of his mind, he focused on pressing back against the compulsion. Zen could feel resistance build wax and wane, but he could not free himself from the compulsion. Zen's mind ached. His flesh felt as if he were on fire. He pressed and pressed, resisting Ablis to the best of his ability. Sweat trickled as he clenched his teeth. Ablis increased power.

"Take off the trousers and undergarments."

Zen did as she commanded. While Zen stood suspended, Ablis brewed an elixir. Zen tried to calm himself yet remain focused on his predicament, thinking back to the times his rage took over and the times he was able to regain control. He remembered the first time he'd communed mind and spirit. He'd nearly been able to project himself out of the Octagon but could not hold the focus sufficiently. Zen attempted to duplicate the process. He cleared his mind, to the best of his ability, of all distractions. *Focus,* he thought. *Focus for all you're worth.* Zen began the reenactment, the melding of mind, body, and spirit. Though not conscious of the movement, still completely enwrapped in focusing, Zen raised his hands. Startled, Ablis increased the power. Zen's concentration broke. Again, he stood transfixed. Ablis was more determined.

"Drink this," she commanded.

Zen had no choice but to swallow the entire concoction. Ablis pulled the bowl from Zen's hand, commanded him to open his mouth, then placed the stem of the wood rose in his mouth. She stepped away after forcing Zen to bite down. Walking what she believed to be a safe distance, she turned and faced Zen. Standing heels together arms spread wide, Ablis chanted,

> *Brace of Hedge, Spirit of Shoal,*
> *I call thee forth through mortal soul,*

(Power raised and arced from Ablis's aura.)

> *Aid of goodness, Wisdom Miser*
> *Spirit of Truth, Messmorizer*

(Zen felt heat radiate from his chest.)

> *Let fire dance and Wood rose bleed*
> *If this Zen be the demon's seed*

The wood rose did not burn or bleed—it seemed fresher. Ablis was relieved yet curious at the occurrence. She released the compulsion. Zen collapsed. Ablis stared at Zen's fallen body. Clutching the wood rose, Ablis thought, *Could this be the one father?* She crossed her arms, leaning against her favorite oak table. "Messmor," she stated aloud. "Father told me never to call his name without true necessity." Ablis fidgeted and paced. "I must know. I've waited too long." Ablis continued to pace. Zen groaned. Reconsidering, "I must be more certain. Lemious made it this far." Ablis smiled to herself. *Who'd have believed that Lemious would befriend this human…then earn a title… G. G., a fitting nickname.* Returning to the matter at hand, Ablis continued mumbling aloud, "How can I truly test him?"

Ablis's face brightened, remembering a story of courage and ingenuity taken from another world and told to her by her father: "**Stem the Torrent.**" Exactly, he will have to stem the torrent. *A final test! I've waited longer than I thought was possible*, she thought, still fearing that her hopes would be dashed again and knowing that Zen's failure would hurt much more deeply than those before him. Ablis stopped pacing and began trimming her fingernails with her teeth. Nipping the side of a fingernail, she bit off a sliver at a time, placing each remnant of the fingernail on the palm of her opposing hand. She unconsciously continued the ritual as she contemplated her next move. "He isn't ready... He will be! He must be!" she mumbled. Ablis squatted down, slipping her arms beneath Zen's and lifted him waist level. After dragging him to her bed, she replaced his undergarments. "I'm sorry, Zen, but I had to know you weren't my nemesis' creation," she offered with genuine regret.

Zen woke in Ablis's bed, quickly realizing he was wearing his undergarments. Zen sat up back against the headboard, thoroughly embarrassed. Zen felt deeply shamed, abused and powerless, demoralized. He tried to muster anger or rage, anything to dispel this feeling of hopelessness.

"You're awake," Ablis interrupted his self-depreciation with a smile. Zen said nothing. "You slept a day and a half! You should be more than ready to get out of that bed." Ablis kept her hands on her hips, eyebrow cocked. Zen said nothing, staring forward. Ablis sneered, "What's this? Pouting?" Zen said nothing. Ablis's anger became more apparent as she pressed the conversation. Zen said nothing. Ablis concluded she could not cause him to speak voluntarily. "Suit yourself. I don't care whether you speak or not, but I do expect the kitchen cleaned and a new stack of woodcut for the week." Zen said nothing but moved mechanically toward the door and finished what Ablis had asked without speaking.

Several days had passed. Ablis could not engage Zen in any conversation. She was equally unsuccessful at mind speaking. Though she'd attempted on several occasions, much to her dismay, she was unable to penetrate the defensive barrier surrounding his thoughts. Her inability to penetrate his mental barrier was nearly as frustrating as his refusal to speak to her. "Damn you! I had to know, okay?" she screamed, pulling at her hair. "Zen, say something, anything. I'm sorry I hurt you." Ablis cringed at her apology. *This is too much*, she thought. *I don't apologize to anyone*. Ablis exhaled through her nose. "Can't you hear me? I said I was sorry. Are you going to pout forever?" Zen's eyes steeled. *Life at last*, Ablis thought finding it difficult to conceal her relief or the flash of mist that she blinked away before it could be considered.

"Had to know what?" Zen asked quietly while sharpening his knife.

"Whether you were real or a well-made apparition or a doppelganger."

Zen shook his head. "You are an idiot."

Ablis bit back a retort. She was grateful they were at least speaking. *It's time to begin*, she thought without changing her expression. Zen sat behind the sharpening stone, peddling and grinding the second blade. He felt that familiar anger building inside toward Ablis. *There's something different*, Ablis thought, watching Zen closely. Zen's emotions were much more controlled. His recovery was more complete than Ablis could imagine. The spell cast to determine his identity had also awakened another ability. Zen could feel his fingers tingle as he concentrated on the knife's edge. He could sense the knife shine a bit brighter and those he'd sharpened a bit deeper than one would expect them to. During the term of his silence, Zen had practiced controlling the energy pulsing within.

First, he managed to block Ablis mind speech and her repeated probes. Second, he managed to push the energy to the tips of his fingers. Zen could cause the phenomenon with a moderate degree of concentration—much less than it required in the beginning. Ablis stared at him curiously.

"What exactly are you doing?"

Zen continued, "What's it look like?"

Ablis responded quickly, "You know what I mean!"

Zen stopped. "No, I don't," he lied. "I'm sharpening a blade. Does it annoy you?" he added without looking up.

Ablis stepped closer. "Why are you concentrating so hard on something you do with ease?"

Zen shook his head, examining the steel. "Just want an excellent edge," Zen replied. He smiled while allowing the knife to slice through a cucumber, powered only by the weight of the blade.

Ablis, though not satisfied, did not suspect Zen's true intent. "I suppose you're still recovering." Ablis sat on the table's edge. "I cannot wait much longer, Zen," her voice even and very serious.

Zen glanced up. "I suppose you're right." He stood up, placing the blade in his boot.

Ablis tossed him the second knife. Zen caught and quickly placed the blade in the sheath at the small of his back. "What now, my lady?" Zen asked very courteously.

Ablis looked intently at Zen. "What's going on with you?"

"What do you mean?" Zen responded innocently.

"You know what I mean. You've gone from a skulking little baby to a cooperative little boy in less than ten minutes!"

Zen's face reddened. "You are an ungrateful ass!" he barked.

Ablis smiled. "That's better. Familiar territory." She laughed. "I have an errand for you to run."

Zen bowed, deeply in an exaggerated flourish. "Zen the Pledge at your service," he cracked sarcastically.

"Take the bushel of apples from the cellar, load them in the cart, and harness the mare. I'll join you shortly." Ablis turned to go to her study.

"Where are we going?" Zen inquired.

"We aren't going anywhere. I'm going to Battersea. You're staying here."

Zen perked up, "Battersea?"

Ablis turned to face him. "Yes, Battersea," she asserted.

"I must go with you." Zen stepped forward, not quite pleading, but he could not mask his anxiousness.

"No!" Ablis retorted, returning to the door to the study.

"I'm going," Zen stated flatly.

Ablis turned to look back to Zen, her face an illustration of curiosity. "What's in Battersea for you?" she asked.

"An innkeeper," Zen returned, staring into the distance.

"Back to your quest again"—she placed her fists on her hips—"forget it. You're not going," she finished.

"Bu—" Zen started.

"It's final, Zen!" Ablis interrupted, glaring with an absoluteness Zen had learned to respect.

"Agreed," Zen whispered, not breaking eye contact.

Ablis did not flinch. Zen's eyes steeled for a moment then the steel turned to an absence of feeling—a cold absence of respect, value, or caring. Zen smiled a lifeless smile, broke eye contact, and proceeded to the cellar. Ablis stood for a moment, trying to make sense of what had just occurred.

"Something's different." Nodding, she added, "I'll have to find out what it is."

Zen finished loading the last bushel of apples into the cart. Wiping sweat from his brow, he whistled for the mare. She bounded from the woods, shaking her head like a newborn colt. Zen smiled, patting her head.

"You're a good-looking nag you are. It's a good thing you're not human. You'd make life difficult around here."

"If you're done making passes at my horse, harness her." Ablis laughed. "I don't have all day."

Zen rubbed the mare's neck. "Well, sweets, time to earn your keep." Zen harnessed the horse as Ablis climbed into the cart.

"I'll be back just after dark. Make sure the shelves are cleaned and new hickory gathered before I return."

Zen nodded in silent subservience. Ablis smacked the reins.

See you, sweetie, Zen mind spoke.

Ablis did not move, though her face pinked. Just as she was about to scold Zen, she discovered the mare's eyes seemed to twinkle. Ablis startled, as the cart rocked forward. *What's this? He's charmed the mare*, she thought to herself. *So it begins. He's found an affinity. I wonder what else he's found.* Ablis nearly reigned in the mare, then relinquished, *I'll find out soon enough. This is not the time to let him know I know.* She smiled to herself. *Maybe, just maybe, Father.* Ablis took every precaution to assure the thought would not travel to Zen, knowing she must be much more careful than she'd been thus far.

Zen picked up and dusted off the riddled staff. "You're pretty much ruined," he offered as he examined the holes and missing pieces. "Those godforsaken bees…" Zen twirled the staff one last time. "Well, my friend, I'll not burn you, but I need to build another. No time for it now…chores."

Zen placed the staff back in the corner. After cleaning the sanctum, kitchen, and bedroom, Zen entered Ablis's study, discovering a library of sorts. He stood in silent adoration as he ran his fingertips down the edge of the redwood shelves. "Immaculate," he said aloud. "The workmanship is magnificent." Zen eyeballed the expanse of books lined neatly in alphabetical order. "Mania, Manifestations, Metallurgy…manifestations?" Without thinking, Zen did a double take. "What does that mean?" Looking both directions before moving forward, Zen removed the book from the shelf.

"*Manifestations,*" Zen could not contain his curiosity. Surprised, realizing the depth of his interest, Zen read the first few pages then stopped.

> *Manifestations are created by manipulating available sources and resources into an intricate weave of psychic, kinetic, physical, and magical energies. Manifestations are substantially different from illusions or glamours. They exist independent of the mind of the beholder and can be granted or actualized through a methodology that allows a modicum of independent action, which of course is dependent solely upon the skill of the caster. Individuals highly skilled in transmutation or metamorphosis will find striking similarities between the processes. Transmutation binds existing strands of physical reality to the most active strands of projected psychic imagery in order to cause the original substance to metamorphose into the desired form.*
>
> *Manifestation works very similarly though the order in which the strands are bound proceeds differently. Manifestation is possible when the strands of psychic imagery are excited to the point of visual perceptibility and projected from the caster's mind to a specific location. The image that coalesces, however, is incomplete unless the caster is skilled with a sufficiency that allows kinetic energies to also be*

projected from the caster or drawn from another source of musculature where kinetic energy naturally is generated and fused to as well as within the projected psychic imagery. The combination of the bonded projected imagery and the kinetic infusion allows the would-be manifestation to move and perform functions that require mobility. The manifestation, however, is still not complete until physical energy is applied in a way that the image can sustain its shape and offer resistance to the environment to which it was introduced; in other words, a being of air would diffuse into the air unless an exterior shielding or other "physical" barrier existed to allow the being to sustain a specific shape; shape-shifting is a relative to this art that we will not address at this time. The application of physical energy is a very delicate procedure—too much and the result is a rigid, slow-moving, though substantially durable manifestation, too little and the result is a very fragile, wisp of a being that could diffuse at any moment into the environment to which it is introduced, particularly if the primary physical makeup matches the physical reality of the environment to which it was introduced.

Zen closed his eyes, trying to embrace the complexities of the information. He opened his eyes, scratched the back of his head, took a deep breath, and embraced the book a second time.

Physical reality bound by magical energy allows the outer layer of containment, or skin if you will, to respond to the environment in a very natural way if the caster is sufficiently skilled. The Manifestation, dependent upon the amount of energy and the nature of the being created, can either be projected from the creator and controlled through a psychic link or tendril, or the Manifestation can be fused with a time-limited amount of energy through which it operates independently, apart from the creator, until the energy dissipates or the creation is destroyed. In either case, the success of the manifestation, including the distance a manifestation can be projected with the psychic tendril attached, and the amount of energy necessary to fuse an independent manifestation is solely dependent upon the skills, natural abilities, and store of energy possessed by the creator.

A caster possessing the discipline to focus and control the process necessary to harness the energies can create amazing Manifestations with very useful abilities. In fact, Apotheosis was known to create Manifestations so complex that the onlooker could not determine the difference between the Manifestation and the animal it was intended to duplicate.

The process for linked manifestations, though evolving from complicated origins, uses the most basic rituals associated with even the simplest magical manipulations. The initial step involves clearing one's mind of distraction, requiring only a small bit of discipline, while focusing upon the central point to which the image is to be projected. If the caster can form a psychic tentacle and extend the tentacle from the caster to the focal point, the caster is ready to begin fusing the strands of energy through the psychic links to the manifestation. This manifestation innately forms a receptacle, much like a fetus with an umbilical cord, through which energies (mana) can be fed. The focal receptacle is the port through which the mental image and associated energies flow to the point of realization. Additional strands of mana are woven to enable the caster a means of controlling the Manifestation or apparition.

The focal receptacle serves as a conduit for cerebral commands as well as a regulator for amounts of energy dispensed during any given manipulation of, or activity by, an apparition. The duration of an apparition's existence is dictated by the skill of the caster and the ability to sustain the psychic link. The caster should always exercise caution assuring one does not reach a point of psychic depletion resulting in a wavering or premature breaking of the link. Disrupting the link causes the immediate immolation or dissipation of the apparition. Manifestations can be useful in a variety of ways, but as stated previously, one must be cautious in their employ. The sustained output of psychic energy, if channeled incorrectly, can severely deplete the caster's life force. It should be noted the link itself can be seen by others gifted in the arts, including neophytes, peers, and superiors. Peers and superiors, if aware of the link, can block or disrupt the links by physical or mental means. Again, the ability to do so is directly proportionate to the peer or superiors' innate ability not necessarily the refined skill. A blockage will either disrupt the link thereby destroying the apparition or shift the focal receptacle to the next compatible psychic force…giving control of the manifestation to a peer or superior caster if one is present at the time the blockage occurs.

Zen slammed the book shut. "Grink!" Zen exclaimed. "I saw his link!" Zen's mind was abuzz. He managed to resist the compulsion to read on. The temptation to continue, however, pressed substantially on. He managed to return the book to the shelf, assuring it occupied precisely the same space at precisely the same angle. "What else do we have here?" He scanned the shelf. "*Chants, Demons, Incantations, Witchery, Wisdom… Wisdom?*" Zen pulled the book from the shelf. "*W.I.S.D.O.M…Witchery, Incantations, Sorcery, Demons, Omens,*

Magic…or Will, Intuition, Stealth, Druid Lore, Obfuscation, and Magic… The Choice Is Yours. Quite a title," Zen mumbled, turning the book over in his hands. "The choice is yours, huh." Zen opened the book. The page just inside the cover read:

Manuscript for those who are mage born

—Messmor

"A fitting name for an author of such as this." Zen laughed, glancing at the entry of the dwelling as if half expecting Ablis to be standing in the doorway. After reassuring himself she was nowhere close, he tucked the book inside his cloak. Anxiousness and curiosity about the book's contents did not detour Zen from completing the cleaning of the shelves. He worked as quickly as he could without compromising the standard he knew Ablis expected. He peeked one more time at the book before he stepped away from the shelves, smiling to himself.

"Shew," Zen muttered, wiping sweat from his forehead. "I'm glad to be done with that." Zen closed the large oak door to the study, stretched, then removed the book from his cloak. Glancing out of the window, *Plenty of daylight*, he thought. Zen grabbed for the riddled staff and an apple. "Security and food, what more can a man ask for?" He laughed again, walking through the doorway to large sugar maple.

The noon sun, in its prime, demanded that all within its influence slow down and nap. If it weren't for a slight but steady breeze, Zen would have fallen victim to the sun's command. As it were, Zen removed his cloak and sat leaning against the sugar maple, occasionally wiping sweat from his brow. "WISDOM, huh? This guy must have had a high opinion of himself." Zen was not sure he respected Messmor yet proceeded to spend the remainder of the daylight reading *W.I.S.D.O.M.* To Zen's amazement, the book turned out to be just that. Zen was fascinated by the book's simplicity yet an immense wealth of insight. After reading several pages, he realized, though each subject had been mentioned, only those in the second acronym were being addressed. There were no examples of spells, incantations, or rituals to follow in conjuring, only ways to discover the depth of your powers. The book alluded to building strength as well as endurance but had not expounded about any methods of mastering power. Each of the disciplines within wisdom was addressed independently. The information intricately described each discipline as a world on to itself to be traveled by each mage born in a different yet mutual way.

Any mage who had traversed one or more of the disciplines could recognize the signs of a fellow traveler past or present. Even with as much information as was provided, the book did not expose a given discipline. It tantalized the reader. Challenged the reader to explore one's inner strengths to determine whether they had the desire, skill, physical prowess, endurance, and intelligence sufficient to accept the challenge of any one or more of the disciplines. Even if one believed he possessed the skills, the book suggested there were no guarantees, yet the reward, if the reader could master even one discipline, would be beyond the reader's comprehension. Adrenaline pumping, Zen realized he'd spent much too much time dreaming of powers to be and not enough time doing the necessities of the day. Zen closed the book, still reeling from the excitement. Something about it looked different, but he could not quite decipher the abnormality. Shaking his head, painfully detaching himself from the book, Zen muttered, "I don't have time for this!" He slammed it shut. "Time to collect wood. Dusk is upon me."

In an hour, Zen accomplished collecting the wood and splitting enough of the limbs and cut sections into chunks of wood that could be stacked against the side of the dwelling. Zen looked at how much he'd already carried, calculating he'd chopped enough to keep the occupants of this meager but homey dwelling cozy for a week. Sweat rolled off his brow. In an instinctive motion, Zen ran his forefinger over the right eyelid, gathering the salty moisture and flicking the bulk of sweat off to the side of his axe hand as he continued to chop. He wished he'd made a bandana to catch the sweat before it made its way down his forehead and, now, dripping from his nose. Zen straightened, leaned the axe against his leg, and wiped the sweat from his face, with both hands, then patted his hands on the apron.

Zen's ritual concluded with dunking his head in a bucket of fresh water, exhaling, causing bubbles to rise in all directions, bumping gently against his face. Zen lifted his head with a shake, droplets flying in all directions yet maintaining the flow down his face, neck, and throat. He covered his head as quickly as he could with a drying cloth, swatting deer flies away from his bare skin, then proceeded to towel out his ears, face, and neck. Zen finished by hanging the cloth on the edge of the shelf and picking up the now-half-full bucket of water. Zen strolled leisurely through the doorway and emptied the bucket by pitching the water to the base of an oak tree close to the dwelling.

Zen felt the subtle shift of temperature as the setting sun lengthened shadows that highlighted and silhouetted in the door's frame. Zen stepped to the doorway, shirt in hand, and paused to take in the dusk's beauty. He closed his eyes, reveling in the caress of warm sunlight and the coolness of wind against wet skin. Goose bumps sprung to life despite the warmth of the sun. He smiled, thoroughly enjoying the fragrance of freshly split pine. "Going to be a warm night," he remarked, taking in as much as his senses would allow. Zen leaned silently against Ablis's domain, catching the final glimpse of the sun's departure through the trees. He straightened. *I'll give her another hour*, Zen thought for a moment, adding, "I guess she's big enough to take care of herself, big enough to take care of me as well." He chuckled then laughed aloud, his last remark bringing an unrelenting smile and finally a grin.

The sun had been down about two hours before Zen, who was no longer measuring time by ear positions, began to seriously wonder what had been taking Ablis so long. Boredom and worry combined to create an anxiety that made him uncomfortable all the while it pressed him to leave the dwelling and find Ablis. "No!" He pounded his fist on the table. "I will not leave or allow myself to be bothered by some self-righteous, self-centered, self-indulgent female! No matter how she looks in the moonlight," he added pacing back and forth. *Maybe I can sleep*, Zen thought. He grinned as he plopped himself on

Ablis's bed, knowing he was not normally permitted to do so. Before long, Zen was up wandering through the storage and supplies, running their inventory through his head.

Zen's wakefulness refused to relinquish, and his anxiousness continued to grow. Rummaging through supplies did not take his mind off Ablis, but he did manage to occupy and enjoy an hour of target practice. Zen and the mice of the dwelling had developed a relationship since his arrival—a relationship that the mice were not so sure they liked but ultimately benefited from. "Zen and Mouse," as Zen referred to it, would begin with Zen placing corn kernels between thumb and pointer then torquing the somewhat-feeble projectile at the persistent and determined mice who, with all their being, wanted to dive headlong into the sacks of nuts and varied grains that were situated next to the table. Zen had strategically located himself between a crack in the wall next to the fireplace, an apparent temporary hold for his foes, and the foe's cache of goodies.

His stubborn friends routinely peeked out, hoping to catch him by his unawares, and, as if lulled into overconfidence, would burst out, scurrying faster than their feet could take hold across the wood floor. Zen giggled as he watched the most recent would-be victim dash toward their goal, hoping Zen would notice neither the sound of scurrying feet nor their lack of traction. It was great fun, and all parties seemed completely committed to the game. *Zzzzziiinggg...* *Crack!* "Almost gotcha ya, you little turd!" Zen laughed aloud. "Pretty cozy for a mouse in a cat's domain." He aimed another kernel.

"What's taking that woman so long?" he mumbled as he torqued the latest in a barrage of corn kernels that ricocheted against the wall. This one clipped the mouse just behind the ear as he prepared to burst. With a squeal, the little vermin jumped a foot and a half in the air, landing after a 180-degree turn and leaping again, almost instantaneously, to the crack in the wall while his partner stepped smoothly to the side as if to say, "I told you, sooner or later, he'd hit you, but noooo...you just had to do it one more time!"

Zen straightened. "Well, little ones, you'll have the rule of the place in a moment." He picked up the several sacks and placed them high in the cupboard after tying the tops together. "But I can't have you eating everything. Besides, you have enough corn to last you for a month on the floor!" Zen paced back and forth a few more times, finally concluding he could not stand to worry any longer. Checking his knives, he grabbed the riddled staff, deciding to search for Ablis. *Enough is enough*, he thought.

Zen stepped under the archway, worry furrowing his brow. "No moon…great." Fingering the staff and staring into the blackness, Zen decided, pitch black or not, Ablis had not returned from Battersea. She was definitely capable of taking care of herself, Zen thought, but that was also her vulnerability. She tended to overestimate her ability to recognize and prepare for everything and anything. The wooden step creaked its resistance as Zen's weight pressed against its strength. "I've waited long enough to find the owner of that inn. Besides, why should I worry about a woman that can more than take care of herself?" he asked the stars. His resolve waned as quickly as it had formed. She was not back, and he would have to find her. "Because she may have found trouble," he muttered, thoughts spinning. Zen looked back into the dwelling. "One last check before I go searching. You don't mind, do you?" he asked his staff. "I didn't think so." He backstepped through the archway. After taking a few moments to walk back through the house, he was confident that all was in order.

His mind continued to battle both sides of the conundrum. Being torn between searching for Ablis and fulfilling his quest was more difficult than he would have once imagined. Zen realized that no matter which course of action he ultimately decided, he would still need to go to Battersea. The one pressing compulsion he could not shake was the need to proceed. He knew that Ablis could deal with trouble and likely was not in any danger. Ablis, though nearly as important as his own life, was still secondary—the little bit he knew of his destiny had steadily nudged, pressed, and pulled him toward an innkeeper and a town called Battersea.

Zen was determined to discover the reasons for the bounty placed upon his head as well as to meet this innkeeper face-to-face. The innkeeper's name escaped him, but he clearly remembered the arrogance abounding from the scroll Frank had carried. Zen pulled the door shut quietly. Without hesitation, he moved into the darkness, pulling the wolf skin cloak close to his throat, his decision finally made. "I am no one's slave, but it is time to find out what and who I am," he offered the darkness. The night was not cold nor bright, but Zen was taking no chances. Detection was to be avoided at almost all costs. He knew no one, but Ablis who, at this point, was the last person he wanted to meet. He would experience relief to know she was safe, but he would not stop to do her bidding. Zen replayed the events that seemed years previous. *A bounty on my head*, he thought, *and why? What was the name...John...John...John Rippion!* Zen smiled. "It's time we meet John," Zen offered so quietly he was not sure he'd spoken aloud.

Zen walked quietly, unconsciously sniffing the night air, attempting to ascertain anything unusual. His entire sensorium on edge, Zen's eyes adjusted to the lack of light while his ears and nose adjusted to the sound and smells of the evening. Checking the horizon, Zen noted a light from Battersea flickering dimly to the southwest. He could also make out the wagon path that appeared to run just outside Ablis's house toward Battersea. As a precaution, Zen delayed a moment and considered triangulating the location of the dwelling to make certain the dwelling's place in the woodland would not be lost to him. The process was very difficult in the darkness, but he managed beginning with Ablis's rock. "The 'rock' is visible," Zen muttered ever so quietly. "Let's see where is it... Hmmm...there it is." Zen nodded to himself as he located the Northern Beacon.

Zen finished by adding Battersea to the triangle. Confident he could find the dwelling no matter where he might find himself, Zen continued to make haste toward, what he expected to be, the village. Ablis's path was relatively easy to follow. Though the light was minimal, the cart's tracks were not difficult to locate. The weight of the cart disfigured the grassy meadow marking Ablis's progress steadily toward the flickering light in the southwest. Zen double-checked the cloak's single pocket. One of the moccasins had nearly fallen. "Can't lose these," Zen mumbled, taking out the jerky he'd made earlier in the week. Zen emerged from the woodland, moving deftly and silently barefoot through grasses of varying heights. Even in the darkness of no moon, the starlight was sufficient to allow Zen to make out portions of his surroundings as he made his way down the wagon trail.

Zen hesitated in response to a sound in the far distance. He believed the sound he was hearing was the faint creak of a wooden wagon's wheel scraping rock. Squatting low, he strained his eyes while listening closely to locate the sound. On one hand, he wanted to know that Ablis was okay; on the other, he did not want to be noticed. The compulsion was upon him. "Shhhhh," he chided himself. *It must be Ablis. I can't hide from her out here*, he thought anxiously to himself. Hearing the squeak of wagon wheels drawing closer, Zen knelt in a tall tuft of grass, trying to remain somewhat hidden while thinking through how he might solve his dilemma. Zen surveyed his surroundings by conducting a very slow 360-degree turn. "No cover," he whispered flatly. The grass was only about a foot tall. Zen felt the sweat bead on his forehead and temples. "Knock it off! You've been in worse than this," he whispered. Zen took a deep breath and concentrated on calming his heart, removing any emotion that could distract him from the task at hand. Still standing motionless, he contemplated, "The woods are too far."

The wagon creaked, bounced, and hopped over clumps of sod, ruts from carts whose memories were long gone, and rocks that tend to resurface from ground pressure. Ablis hummed a song from her youth. The lilt echoed her delight, and enjoyment of her unusually carefree, spirited mood, smiling at the thought of John Rippion. How naive he was to think of her as a common peasant girl. Ablis's smile widened, recalling how much more difficult it was to convince him she was different from most of the girls he'd been accustomed to. He was not altogether repulsive, and she had not been altogether unattracted, but that sort of pleasure only detoured her from the resolution she had been seeking for what seemed an eternity. John was an unusual man—none quite like him in these parts. Ablis thought for a moment, *None quite like John in any of her escapades*. If she had not been guiding the wagon carefully through the ruts that might entangle or damage the wooden wheels, she would have stopped to follow the train of that thought to the end.

Ablis's thought process was disrupted as she noticed the mare's ears perk. Without an outward sign, Ablis opened her senses ever so slightly, examining her immediate area then reaching forward. The mare continued an instinctive vigilance. Zen felt the touch of Ablis's probe. *Dang*! he thought as the probe passed. *But how can that be? Zen* hesitated, knowing that any weakness in the wall against Ablis probe would draw Ablis to his thoughts. *How could she have missed me?* The probe's power strengthened. Zen concentrated more vigorously, remembering the book he'd read earlier. WISDOM...*stealth and obfuscation...* Very slowly, Zen brought himself first to his knees then prostrate in the grass. *Spread your presence to your surroundings. Do not hide but rather make it be part of your surroundings. Cream blends in butter, salt blends in porridge, blend...blend with your surrounding. Think not of what observes but of all that is being observed. Concentrate, lose yourself but not so much that you no longer exist within your environment.* FOCUS, *blending...blending...blending.* Zen lost conscious connection with Ablis's, with self, blending into his environment without thought of consequence or fear of reprisal.

Ablis hesitated, "There!" Her ears perked unconsciously. She strengthened the probe and shifted it back toward the abnormality. Her body leaned in the direction of the probe. "That's odd." She frowned. "I felt something. I know something was there, but it's gone," she whispered to the mare. "So what was making you perky?" she asked the mare, patting her mane. "Probably nothing but your nerves after dark." She smiled about to snap the reigns. "Wait a minute." Ablis turned back toward the area she'd thought to be occupied earlier. "That's it! Nothing. Nothingness." Ablis tensed inwardly, assuring that anyone or thing that could have observed would not have observed her shift in assessment and return to the search. *You idiot girl! Nothingness is as obvious a something as anything could be*! she scolded herself inwardly.

Ablis nudged the mare forward in a manner that would provide any onlooker a sense that all was well simultaneously assuring her actual intent remained guarded. All the while, she searched the meadow as thoroughly as she could. *There it is again.* Ablis formed a pattern of essence from the nothingness then reigned the mare. *Zen?*

It was Zen, she realized, smiling to herself at his accomplishment. *An interesting twist…obfuscation. Well, he'll enjoy this lesson. He's not the dolt I thought he was that first day.* She smiled again outwardly. Snapping the reigns, Ablis urged the mare forward, anxious not to interrupt what Zen had initiated. Ablis remembered the first time she'd read the book. *A new freedom, wondrous, terrifying, irresistible. I wasn't naive enough to try this first though*! she thought. Ablis could hardly contain herself. *It took me two days to gather myself together after the blend.* She snickered. *He thinks he's so clever.* She laughed aloud. *Just the same, I'd better prepare for his coming home.* Still having difficulty not laughing loud and most certainly disturbing the night, Ablis headed the mare home. *He's never had a hangover the likes of what he's going to feel when this is done*!

Ablis thought back to her beginnings, the first time her father presented the book of *WISDOM* and his surprise that she could read both sides of the book. Her father, Ablis's eyes misted at the memory of their companionship, told her she was a rare exception, as was he, that most people did not even notice the book. A rare group could read it. Very few could glean anything from the pages, and only the truly gifted, the exceptional, could read both sides. Those rare beings were normally beings of legend, dark times, and unique trials. She didn't feel gifted or exceptional. She felt the loss of her father. His disappearance, a mystery, one she could not unravel, but one she was convinced she could solve if she could find the right partner to assist her through whatever would need to be faced. If someone or something had taken her father, it would be truly formidable. She wondered if Zen could read both sides of the book. The possibility of his full departure failed to register at any point of her ponderings.

Each hour, after the second day of Zen's experience, Ablis visited the prostrate mage born ensuring his safety. Ablis's humor had turned to vague concern. *He's been out longer than me, and he'll not make it back if he goes much longer. Stemming the torrent is no easy task,* she thought. Looking at Zen reminded her of another valiant but unsuccessful candidate—G. G. failed the first day. His body could not sustain the immense draw of resources nor could his mind withstand the compulsion to blend beyond even one's own psychic recognition. Ablis watched and waited, hoping Zen would succeed where the most promising had failed before him. Ablis was hopeful but not optimistic.

Zen reveled in the majesty of his surroundings. The night air was magnificent. He felt every ebb, every impulse of the meadow. He stretched senses further and further embracing the forest, feeling the sun's rays, the wildlife, knowing the sureness of the earth, the strength of nearby rock masses. Zen felt one with all. Zen's spirit soared at being part of such an immense reality. He felt the moon's rise, the owls launch, the pain of an impaled rabbit, the lust of an angry boar. Amidst his genuine revelry, Zen's mind began nagging with more and more intention to wake him from the blending. Zen realized he could be in danger. He sensed his exhaustion. The nagging sense of danger continued through the sun's second and third pass. Zen began to understand the power of obfuscation—it's surrealistic splendor, it's unending and deadly compulsion to meld further. He was becoming addicted to the splendor, wanting to believe he would die without its caress, its special union with his spirit. Addiction pure and simple, he realized. He was addicted to the blending. His mind began to press back against the stimulation, the pleasure of blending, to thoughts of danger and an inability to gather himself together. Zen's mind battled, one side wanted to immerse into the pleasure, the other side wanting freedom.

Though successful in achieving obfuscation, he had been unsuccessful in controlling its allure and, now, its compulsion. As in all addiction, the message, of perpetual peace and promise of being forever in harmony with the cosmos by bonding with the power of the drug, was false. Continued bonding would eventually deplete all his energy and, in the conclusion, take his life. Zen became more and more conscious of himself as a separate entity among the multitudes that existed. His mind vacillated ambivalently between recognizing his reality and simply surrendering to the pleasure of Obsfucation. His mind broke free. As his mind cleared and sharpness returned, he became aware of his spiritual formlessness. His spirit had spread over miles in circumference, barely held together by the strands of psychic energy that dimmed progressively as Zen weakened. He attempted to pull from within which seemed to deplete rather than restore energy. Panicked by the awareness he may not recover, he closed his eyes and searched his surroundings for a solution. He may have already gone too far, sacrificed too much of his strength, hopelessness seeped through the cracks in his subconscious.

Never one to give in to hopelessness, despite the exhaustion and pall of no resolution, Zen was determined to get through and recover from this dilemma. *No way back... I...must...concentrate.* Zen felt his strength ebb as his reserves dwindle. *It is just a mental intoxicant. There is no hopelessness. Hopelessness is an illusion.* He pressed to find the outer limits of his blending. *An illusion that causes one to believe one is not capable, but obfuscation is...I...will...not...yield.* The psychic echo of his last remarks silenced the meadow. He'd pressed himself to the limit extending this far, how could he contain the blending? How could he return to his original state?

Zen's panic escalated, his psychic distress humming the air. Ablis cringed. She'd not slept in the past thirty hours, expecting Zen was to soon join G. G., then she heard him. *Ablis...ABLIS.* Zen's mind resounded from all directions. Ablis remained silent, wishing he would not expend the energy. Zen called again and again as his panic grew. *I know you're there! Damn you... Help me! I would not abandon you in a time of need!* Ablis's eyes teared. She covered her face with her hands, shaking her head as she responded, "No, Zen. The battle is yours."

Zen's hurt, anguish, and rage echoed to the boarders of Three Ward. *You leave me to die! Am I so much less than you?* Zen's mind choked in agony.

Ablis wiped the tears from her eyes, staring skyward, "Father, I cannot bear this much longer." Ablis breathed deeply. "I will allow him one more hour. Should no sign of composure be seen, the transformation will begin." Ablis's hurt deepened. She'd waited so long to find the key to her dilemma. The search could begin a new in less than an hour, and Zen...yes, Zen had been the best of her prospects. The only one to come this far. The only one who touched— she blocked the remainder of the thought chastising herself for even allowing such a thought, let alone risk believing it.

Do you hate me so...? Am I truly nothing...nothing to you...? Zen's psychic despair ebbed while Ablis's silent retort flowed down her cheeks, dripping into her hands, and stained her soul.

G. G.'s eye and ears shifted. He recognized the despair. The suddenness of his shift caused his troops to form rank and file, awaiting his orders. They'd witnessed this behavior before. He tensed, grimaced, tensed again then, realizing the troop had been observing him, chirped at ease. The troop relaxed but did not break rank. All seemed to be wondering what was occurring, but only G. G. recognized the talent and the test that was occurring. He could only wonder and hope his friend faired better than he had. He knew that Zen was doomed either way in failure. He would either die a human death or join G. G.'s rank. If he joined G. G.'s rank, G.G. would kill him immediately rather than risk a rebellion and lose his place among the lizards. G. G. wished his friend only the best—a victory or a quick death.

Ablis set off to the cabin to prepare for the transformation, believing there would be no other recourse. Once in the sanctum, Ablis approached the redwood chest, blocking tears, breathing deeply, she knelt. *Well, Zen*—her hands shook—*it's almost the end of this life for you. If you are at all able to do it...do it now.* She opened the chest, very carefully removing her father's folded robe. Ablis selected the appropriate wards and runes. Trembling, she stood, tears streaming, she could not stem the tide. Wiping the tears with the back of both hands, she could hardly contain herself. She could barely see, yet she managed to remain standing. Her hair, normally well-preserved in a tight braid, hung loosely around her face, sticking to her cheeks and neck. She felt a tightness in her chest and light-headedness. Ablis's heart was breaking, and the exhaustion of searching without respite seemed too great to carry on. Knowing she had to begin the transformation was weight enough, but this other emotion, an emotion she was not accustomed to, slowly overwhelmed. She'd always prized those who proceeded Zen, treating them all similarly, seeing them all as a tool, a solution to her puzzle, but Zen was different.

WHY, ZEN? Ablis pounded her fist on the wall. *Why did you*— Ablis cut the thought short a second time. She drew the runes on the archways then set the wards to the north, east, south, and finally west. *It's time*, she thought, turning to the doorway for a final glance to the meadow.

There in the doorway, he stood. Zen's face distorted in a mixture of anger and pride. Ablis dropped to her knees, clutching her face and weeping uncontrollably. Zen's mouth open, then closed, then open again. "For me?" His eyebrow rose. His face softened. His mind spoke the second time while he reached for her. *For me, Ablis?* Ablis wept more forcefully but did not reply. Zen knelt down, drawing her close, nestling her cheek against his chest. He stroked her hair. The smell of her closeness was intoxicating. He could feel his body call out to her. His spirit reaching to her. He said nothing, yet his warmth radiated to her.

Ablis clung to Zen, despite not wanting to show her weakness, despite how much she needed to find a person who could help her. At this moment, this small respite, she let go. She needed Zen—his warmth, his touch, his compassion. She was not able to speak. She held him close until the trembling stopped all the while keeping her mind guarded. Finally, she pushed herself free.

"Thank you, Zen," she offered, wiping tears. "I do not deserve your kindness. I would not have stopped you from dying," she choked out.

"It's enough to know you do not wish me dead," Zen replied, feeling overwhelmed and vulnerable, mystified by this feeling of connectedness, desire, desperation to remove Ablis's hurt occurring all at once.

"No, IT ISN'T!" Ablis barked, raising her hands fiercely, disengaging from Zen, overwrought with emotion. "I do not have time for this! And I'll leave you to die over and over until you die or are ready!"

Zen stepped back. "I know," Zen offered quietly. "No love is lost unless love is gained, and you will not allow yourself its luxury. I don't understand nor do I have control over what I feel. It is foreign. It should not be there. It gets in my way and muddies the water, but…I will not die. In fact, because of you, I live." Zen smiled, turned, and walked away from a speechless and confused Ablis.

Zen hesitated at the archway. "I have my own quest that needs doing. For a reason beyond my ability to unravel, we've been thrown together. You needed to find me, and I needed you to hone me. I've given you your time. Now it's my time. You and I can begin again when I return from Battersea."

Ablis did not move or answer. She was numb from the experience. She watched Zen walk out into the darkness then sat on the chair near her father's wooden chest, contemplating what had just occurred. *Love? Is this love? Dear god, I don't have time for this.* She stood, pulled her hair back from her face, walked to the kitchen, and splashed the cool water from her favorite basin upon her face.

Dabbing the droplets from her face with a towel sown by her mother, Ablis shook her head, attempting to deny the emotion that was welling within. *Pain and pleasure...pain and pleasure... I have no time for either.* Ablis closed the door to her bedroom and stared at her bed. Exhaustion, as well as this strange immobilization, pushing and pressing her consciousness, she knew she needed sleep. She was physically and emotionally exhausted. Ablis lifted the sheet, opened the bedding and laid back both quilt and comforter, then crawled into her bed nestling under the two. She stared at the robe, her father's robe, hanging on the wall, and felt the tears come again. She rolled to the edge of the bed closest to the robe and pulled it to her. Clutching her father's robe close, she asked him for guidance as she drifted into a much-needed sleep.

Morning broke, finding Ablis sleeping soundly. Zen had finished gathering supplies and was about to leave as he quietly opened the door as to not disturb. Without a word, Zen stood and regarded Ablis. Her natural beauty astounded him. He drank in the curve of her lips, the shape of her cheeks and chin, the way her hair cascaded across her shoulder, and the absence of worry that only came with restful sleep. *Why we met and why it had to come to this, I do not know, but if I do not return, this time has been worth the memory of you,* he thought to himself. *Neither of us can afford the other, yet I feel incomplete without you. You're hard-headed, arrogant, and hell to live with.* Zen smiled. *But you are strong and independent, driven and committed, valiant and forthright. Underneath that brashness is a woman, a glorious woman who has not discovered she can love as deeply as she can be brash…and she says I'm the fool.* Zen so wanted to kiss her gently before he left but did not want to do so without her permission.

Zen smiled once more. He picked up a piece of parchment and proceeded to quill a note. Careful not to wake Ablis, he placed the note on the chest next to Ablis's bed. *I hope you understand,* he thought, again to himself. Zen turned but before leaving quietly paused to once again etch Ablis's form in his mind. "Thank you, my lady," he whispered and very slowly quietly closed the door.

Zen gathered a change of clothes, provisions for one day's journey to Battersea, and his armaments. Looking at the staff, he smiled. "You'll remain here, guardian of my past. I'll never replace you, but I must have another at my side. Twirling the staff a final time, he leaned it against the sanctum wall and proceeded through the cabin, slipping silently into the morning air. *A beautiful morning indeed,* he thought. Zen had gained a new awareness of his surroundings since the blending. It was difficult to readjust after beholding then bonding with the intricacies of his surroundings.

Ablis stood near the bedroom window, wordlessly watching Zen's departure. She made no move to stop him. Still in shock, one lone tear made its way down Ablis cheek to her chin. The note Zen had written rest softly in her hands. "Father, what am I to do?" she muttered. The tear continued its course, not knowing whether its roots were in joy or sorrow. Ablis etched Zen's form into her mind, fighting back the ache of his departure. Ablis reread the note.

Ablis…

If love is tendered by soul's breeze,
I am leaf caught betwixt its gale
With force full wrought to send what frees,
my hearts ship sings full winded
sail
joyful tears filled to outward seam
no measure accurate quite
to gauge

the exhilaration like unending dream
love's pure life abounds
this mage…

Zen, Mage born

* * *

Crack! Wigan's face turned abruptly. The blow rendered her practically unconscious, spinning her perpendicular to the bolder. She groaned, tasting her own blood.

"Do not move," a familiar voice stated. "I am going to touch your face. You must not resist." Wigan's body trembled. "Calm yourself, girl," Apotheosis whispered, gently placing his hands, left first then right on each side of Wigan's face. Very slowly, Apotheosis encouraged Wigan to her feet. "You will begin to feel the warmth of my palms." Simultaneously, Wigan felt Apotheosis hand warm. "As you see, my image open your eyes."

Wigan screamed, "They burn! They buurrrnn!" Her knees tried to buckle, but she managed to remain standing.

"I know they burn, girl! Have courage. Do not close your eyes no matter what you see. Do you understand?" Apotheosis held her face firmly.

"Yes, yes, I do," Wigan responded.

"Good," Apotheosis continued. "Do you see my image in your mind?"

Wigan nodded. "Yes, I do."

"Watch my hands closely. Do not close your eyes. Your sanity depends on it."

Wigan, concentrating not to blink, watched Apotheosis move his hands in patterned ritualistic figure eights. Apotheosis hands blurred to molten spheres formed within the figure eight. Suddenly, the uppermost sphere streaked toward Wigan's left eye, shortly followed by the second sphere aimed at the right eye. Wigan's head jerked back. Miraculously, she kept from blinking. Just before striking, the spheres stopped. Each hovered and undulated simultaneously in the air. It was nearly impossible to stop the muscles in her eyelids from twitching to a blink. Wigan concentrated on Apotheosis's face. She'd never seen an aged sorcerer in action nor witnessed such concern. "Look deeply into my face, Wigan. Concentrate on my forehead."

As Wigan's tear-filled eyes shifted the spheres pulsed then entered, Wigan screamed, dropped to one knee but was unable to close her eyes. Mist flowed from the portals of Wigan's mind to the foreground. Apotheosis quickly stepped between Wigan and the demon's seeds forming nearby. Wigan's eyes began to focus. Her vision cleared in time to witness bolts of energy fork from Apotheosis as well as Apotheosis's walking stick. The first bolt forked, striking both creatures center the chest. It separated limbs from the trunk. The second bolt removed the first being's head. The third blast from the walking stick cremated the two beings. Apotheosis breathed a sigh of relief then turned to Wigan who was still weeping. Looking stern only for a moment, Apotheosis reached out and embraced Wigan. He hesitated, hand over her head, then gently caressed her hair. "You'll be fine, girl. Get hold of yourself."

Wigan shook with fear yet took great relief in Apotheosis's kindness. Wigan slowly regained composure, wiping the tears from her face. "What happened to me? What was that you burned?"

Apotheosis smiled. "They'll be plenty of time for questions. Let me just say you have powerful enemies…and"—he cocked his left eyebrow, staring into the distance—"powerful friends. Breeze."

Yes Apotheosis, she responded.

"A portal," Apotheosis concluded. Breeze nodded as the wind swirled tightly around the two combatants. "Wigan comes to my abode. The Stoneguard shall be healed as the sun rises. Inform him of this night, and from henceforth, we are picket against the source that summoned this fright."

Breeze nodded and vanished in unison with the rest of this newly formed troop.

The sun rose slowly, patiently blazing new life to the dawn, streaming prisms of love light gently through the valleys and peaks of Vrazenthorn. Stoneguard rejoiced at the sun's warm embrace. He had not believed the agony would stop and was more than grateful when the healing began.

How strange this feels… It's as if I were my old self. Stoneguard smiled, remembering his youth, his stubbornness, his half-witted dream of immortality. *I received what I requested*, he thought without bitterness. Bitterness had been the better part of an early Stoneguard. Since the transformation, bitterness had ebbed into memory not so much unlike the memories of being human. *How special being human was*, he mused. *A gift so grand one could not fully appreciate its splendor.* That had always been his curse—to have so much and recognize so little. He had been impetuous, running after the dream of Apotheosis. None of the others had ever returned, but he was unique, gifted, courageous…and extremely thick-headed. He chuckled.

I haven't lost that. He continued to chuckle, smiling inwardly, momentarily thinking of Wigan. *Nor my way with women.* Stoneguard's mind wandered back to an earlier love. *I've lost so much.* He pictured his first love, remembering the feeling of being completely mesmerized by her glance, charmed by her touch. His love had been pure and total. She had not felt the same. Even so, the memory brought back a joy that Stoneguard had not felt in many years. *Such a pure and innocent thing…transformed into stone with the rest of me…from a lion's heart to Stoneguard.*

The healing continued as Stoneguard dozed. In the distance, Breeze watched curiously as the bluff pulsed ever so slightly. Boulders had been reforming more and more rapidly, paced with the sun's rising. Stoneguard was mending. Breeze contemplated the guard ambivalently—so cold yet constant, arrogant yet ever protective. *What an unusual man he must have been*, she thought. *I wonder what lies beneath the stone. What is it that died with his humanness…? Why had Apotheosis done this to him?* Her story was much simpler. She received what she deserved. Her reward, though bearable, had been just that. So self-centered, preoccupied with her beauty, she challenged Apotheosis to withstand her charm—her seductiveness, only to find she had been charmed by her pretense.

She smiled in respect and maturity at Apotheosis's retort. She had never forgotten those final words. *That which you are, you can-*

not free, your visions obscured by your vanity…without this mirage just what would you be—a spirit, hot wind, a breeze for no one to see… Then it had happened, smiling ruefully. *Yes, then it happened. You're a shrewd and cruel judge, Apotheosis.* Breeze hesitated briefly, *I wonder why, after all these years, you've shown mercy to the 'guard.'* Breeze lilted shapelessly. Wonder turned to contemplation, contemplation to uneasiness. *What is on the horizon if he should now need us?* Breeze shivered, causing small whirlwinds in all directions, whisking leaves with each tremble. *If he needs us, I don't think I want to be needed. I must speak with the guard,* she thought. Breeze despised the thought of actually conversing at any length with Stoneguard. His belligerence was unending, at least in her experience. The core of their relationship had been antagonizing one another, almost ritualistically not cooperating even to have a single civil conversation. That had changed when Wigan arrived, but Breeze still felt uneasy. These were not ordinary times. The fear of what may be in their future, and the need for consultation with a peer compelled Breeze to ensure the change continued—she knew she must alter her relationship with Stoneguard even if she did not know exactly why.

After spending precious minutes agonizing, Breeze decided she had no other choice but to confer with Stoneguard. Breeze cautiously approached the bluff. *Stoneguard?* she whispered, looking for some sign of awareness.

"The guard sleeps. Leave him be."

Breeze spun to face the curious eyes of Apotheosis. *Where's Wigan?* Breeze asserted, attempting to mask how much Apotheosis had unnerved her.

Apotheosis scratched his chin, tilting his head to the side. "Resting, and what are you up to this fine day, my lovely?"

Breeze grimaced, clenching her jaw, knowing only Apotheosis was aware of and could see her true form. *You certainly think you're something, don't you!* Breeze asserted.

"I know who I am. Answer my question." Breeze had learned early on to respond quickly when Apotheosis's patience dwindled. "Truth…the truth, Breeze."

Breeze exhaled with resignation. *I was going to wake Stoneguard.*

"Why?" Apotheosis asked.

To examine your change, Breeze offered.

Apotheosis's eyes twinkled. "My change? What of yours?" he asserted then vanished.

Mine? I haven't changed! she spouted half-heartedly. *Have I?* she said, tilting her head slightly to the side.

••

Zen strolled leisurely through the meadow. The blending had not only awakened a strong thirst for knowledge, but it had also loosened a second gift—an unusual understanding and awareness of the land of Three Wards. He had been personally introduced to, communed with, and touched the incredible diversity of life that existed within three square miles of the meadow. He sustained an awareness of life, though not as intimate as the life close by, that extended for several miles in a radius from where the blending had been initiated. Obfuscation had been much more than simply obscuring himself. *It could be a lifetime of experience... W.I.S.D.O.M.* Zen's smiled briefly then frowned at the fleeting thought. *It could be a quick death without reprieve as well.* Zen shivered, knowing he would never repeat obfuscation near the extent to which his ignorance had led him. He was more than grateful to have survived the experience.

The meadow reached up to gently embrace his feet, seeming to welcome his fellowship. Zen felt strange, not alone but among friends. All his senses were alive in a marvelously heightened sort of clarity but not all the sensations were pleasant. He understood the grass's determination to withstand its environment, particularly bearing Zen's weight, absorbing the pain of Zen's tread without complaint. The aggravation mites emitted, having to change their course to avoid this human intruder. Birds that gawked and hooted, not realizing he understood their commentary. Zen squinted from the cacophony, deciding he would need to discipline this newly found ability at least to an extent, allowing him to think clearly and find silence when either was truly needed.

Shortly after entering the wood from the meadow, Zen located a long and weighty branch of an oak. Lifting the branch, Zen tested its strength, observing it was freshly separated from the trunk from lightning. *Tempered by lightning*, Zen thought. *This will do fine*. He whittled as he walked. Several hours passed. The afternoon sun was warm and unyielding. Sweat trickled down both sides of Zen's ear as well as pooled on his brow. The basic rough of the staff was complete. He smiled at its shape. *A near-perfect octagon*, he thought. "Still needs some preserve, curing at the very least, but it is a fine piece of weaponry." The edges, though not razor-sharp, would inflict greater injury, allow sharper blow, and resist rolling. It was balanced close to perfection. The staff sizzled in the air. Zen's familiarity with this kind of weapon allowed it to be an immediate extension of self, as Zen practiced several forms. "It's good to have you in my hands, friend. I hope you're as good as your brother," Zen offered aloud, staring at the staff, admiring its internal strength. "And you'll double as a fine walking stick for the poor old man of a monk that I intend to be." Zen focused energies until his fingertips sparked, sending millions of minute arcs forward caressed the staff as he infused a part of himself to its exterior. The edges sharpened a bit, the texture of the wood smoothened, the staff lightened and seemed to balance well in his hands as it hardened to a remarkable extent. Zen spun the staff one last time. "Perfect," he muttered as he gathered himself for the journey.

Checking the sun's light, Zen guestimated about a half day's, formerly two ears worth, of daylight. He believed the time left should allow him to arrive in Battersea with time to spare. Zen calculated he would have about a quarter of the day left before sundown. He would see the town in full sunlight before entering John Rippion's after dusk. The thought gave him comfort. He had no idea why he would be uneasy arriving in darkness, but he never disregarded that sixth sense when it was working.

Zen reflected on the note taken from Frankey, still wondering why someone wanted his life when he knew no one…but Ablis. He ached at the thought of her, a vacuum existed in his heart that could only be filled by her presence. He gritted his teeth then proceeded forwarded, not indicating his newly found wounding.

Zen's mind shifted from retrospective consideration of the events to contemplating the mystery of Battersea as the ever-present press to continue on his quest asserted itself. In all that had been experienced, Zen's new appreciation for the world that surrounded him did not diminish. His awareness of danger and abnormalities in his surroundings was pronounced. He recognized and was warry of predators nearly immediately, always choosing to avoid them. He wondered if it would be the same with human predators. "I wonder what John Rippion has in store for me? Particularly if he suspects my killing Frank." Zen contemplated. *The entire affair seems predictable…too predictable and too predetermined…too well-arranged. A trap of some sort.* "Guess I'll find out when it's time to be enlightened." Zen laughed to himself and proceeded onward.

Battersea was unusually dusty for a forest town. The buildings were small and worn, though sturdily built. Zen spotted John Rippion's Inn. Several horses were tied outside. Biting off a mouthful of jerky, Zen decided to pull the cloak's hood up and over his head. He knew it would look a bit suspicious in the heat, but he would not be close enough to the inhabitants to warrant concern. Double-checking to ensure he had not been seen, Zen slipped behind and past the livery and leaned against a large apple tree. Leaning his back against the bark, bending slightly, Zen dropped the hood, pulled down an apple, and waited for the sun's descent. He was confident of his ability to handle John Rippion as well as orchestrating an easy exit from town. Obtaining information about his would-be assassin and financier would be a more difficult and intriguing problem. *No answers…only questions…but a solution to many things may be hidden in the nooks and crannies of this town*, he thought to himself. Zen bit off a large chunk of apple and contemplated his situation, careful not to fall asleep in the heat from a dwindling but powerful sun.

The sun dipped predictably behind the horizon, obscuring the wood and cloaking the town. Zen stretched then pulled the hood up into place. *Not a time for foolish chances*, he spoke to himself. Staff in hand, Zen soundlessly entered then crossed the road. Zen sensed the horses' uneasiness at his approach. He anticipated their discomfort but could not reduce the intensity slowly building inside, the very same intensity that pressed the horse's unease. It was the part of him that was automatic, calculating, emotionless, unconscious…and deadly. Zen neither liked nor disliked the characteristic, only understood its necessity and predictability. It was as resistant to restraint as his love for Ablis and as intense as Zen's life itself. He'd been able to tame it a bit but not completely.

The door resisted slightly then opened. The festivities hesitated momentarily as Zen entered John Rippion's Inn. Several patrons did a quick assessment of Zen as he shuffled in slightly stooped, slowly and harmlessly making his way to a dimly lit table. All returned to what they considered to be much more interesting occupations for the night.

What a collection, Zen thought. *Old, young, scruffy, manicured, wimpy, and bull-necked…all kinds.* The ale flowed continuously. The mood vacillated between near hostile explosions to hilarious camaraderie. In both cases, the intensity caused Zen to be more vigilant than normal. Despite the diversity, all patrons seemed to move with an air of confidence. Zen remembered a past instruction of Sensi. *Let not your eyes destroy what your inner self perceives. Every man is capable of killing, remaining silent, or walking away, every man is capable of dying, being unduly noticed, or charging foolishly into battle. Your life is dependent upon avoiding death…within life, and in every journey, the adventure unfolds as it is intended.* Zen grinned behind the protection of the hood. "I wonder what John Rippion's master said to him," Zen muttered without being heard. *I wonder how I can remember what my Sensi said, but I cannot remember my Sensi. Odd that I can remember the echo of the Sensi's voice in my mind but have no recollection of the relationship or actually, the training.*

Zen sluffed off the thought like he had so many others that pointed to the senselessness of his existence. He concluded it was a waste of energy. It was more important to follow the compulsion to learn what this existence was about, to conclude what his true purpose was or is, and how this might be a part of it. *What a deal*, he laughed to himself.

"Ale," he muttered to the maid as he brushed her hand from near his face protecting the hood. "I'm in no need of company or conversation, only something to quench my thirst." Zen peered cagily through the smoke-dimmed brothel, watching each patron closely gauging how each distributed their weight. Experience demanded he scrutinized the surroundings for danger, possible adversaries, and to avoid surprises. Danger and potential danger comes in all sizes and shapes—from the least threatening and often most deadly to the obviously threatening and often, though most noticed, the weakest of adversaries. Three of the twenty-plus patrons and the barmaid appeared worthy of closer observation.

Zen stood up slowly as if having some difficulty, being careful to keep his hood in place and project a caricature of feebleness. He swallowed the last bit of ale, wiping the dribble from his beard, simultaneously burping loudly, staggering, and selecting the most advantageous route to an unpopulated portion of the inn. The barmaid noticed his advance, but no one else paid him the slightest bit of attention. Most were preoccupied with lust or liquor—all but the three at the opposite end of the bar drinking slowly, standing semi-tensed. Zen glanced from the barmaid to the threesome. None had given an indication of being aware of or concerned with his presence. Finally, the barmaid eyed him momentarily then cordially ended the conversation she'd been having with the three promising a quick return.

"What'll you have?" the barmaid inquired a bit more cheerfully than necessary, never really taking her eyes off the three at the end of the bar.

"Just another mug of ale or untainted cider," Zen offered quietly in an aged voice.

The barmaid smiled. "Ale, huh? Why the hood?" she asked while picking up the mug and wiping the bar.

Zen smiled to himself, replying scruffily, "It doesn't pay to be ugly in a place such as this."

The barmaid laughed. "The girls aren't exactly interested in your face." She leaned forward elbows on the bar, cupping her chin in her hands. "There's your cider." She smiled. "I don't know if you can handle the ale." Zen dropped three coppers on the bar. The maid made no attempt to move. "Where do you come from?" her curiosity more than apparent as she glanced at the fellows at the opposite end of the bar.

"From the south," he responded a bit unfriendly.

The barmaid pressed further, "I've lived in the wood most of my life. Strange I haven't seen you before."

Zen's hood bobbed. "As I said, it doesn't pay to be ugly."

The maid laughed cheerfully, shaking her head. "So it doesn't... so it doesn't."

She straightened up as she swept the coppers quickly to the fold of her apron. "Town seems full tonight," he pressed his advantage.

"Yes," the barmaid answered, glancing at the three at the end of the bar. "Since John offered the reward for Witch Mason's death, several have reported her killing."

Zen shrugged and continued the conversation, "The three at the end of the bar?"

The maid stared curiously at Zen. "You're a sharp old codger, aren't you."

Zen sipped the cider then replied while wiping his beard. "I'm ugly, not dimwitted. Besides, you seem to spend more time with old men than you should," he said, tilting his hood slightly toward the three at the end of the bar.

The barmaid inhaled a bit more deeply than normal. Stepping back, she tilted her head as she turned toward the three at the end of the bar. "Just how old are you?"

Zen grunted then sipped more cider. "Old enough to know my limits." He allowed her to glimpse his eyes yet managed to cover the rest of his face.

The barmaid could not miss the twinkle. She laughed. "Ugly or maybe not." She smiled a wide and experienced smile. "Midnight-blue eyes...with a twinkle, you might be worth investigating!" she added as she ambled toward the three at the end of the bar.

Zen noticed the sway in her walk, suddenly feeling the stirring of his youth. "There will be plenty of time for that," he muttered, returning to the more comfortable tasks of hypervigilance, assessing, and measuring the physical prowess of the patrons. Amidst pressing away a not-so-subtle twinge of guilt for thinking such a thing after confessing his love for Ablis. "The arrow knows not where the archer aims. It simply stands ready to be launched." He laughed to himself.

CHAPTER 9

──────── ❧ ────────

Messene and Nanling

An eternity of contemplation, frustration, hope, and despair…Peace strained day after day, attempting to successfully achieve the birthings without success. She searched her mind for some clue—a statement by her mother, a vague memory of her father talking about his parents, old pictures and odd conversations to the point she could barely decipher what was actual, what was confabulated, and what was simply a transient delusion. In times of frustration, she examined her body for a clue or pathway similar to that which spawned Wigan. She contemplated her personal characteristics, strengths, and weaknesses. Peace resigned herself to exercising then relaxing in her favorite chair. *Abkhas has not been back in days. I doubt that he's forgotten me. I wonder if he's discovered Wigan,* she thought. Peace pondered the possibilities, deciding that Abkhas could do practically anything he wanted with or without her permission. She smiled picking up "Forever Full" and swallowed a large gulp of water. "At least this is fresh," she offered to the cup.

Peace's life had changed dramatically since her entrapment, yet the patterns of her former life permeated her captivity prevailing even against the unlikely odds in hopes that life would return to normal. Peace unconsciously measured and detailed her surroundings. She could not determine the exact length of time in minutes or hours, but she was able to accurately predict when food would appear for consumption, the space of time a droplet of water would take as it rushed to the floor from her cup, even how many moments were required for the self mending process that both blessed and burdened her captivity. She enjoyed her meals though the food was varied in attractiveness. The slugs were still part of the menu, but several other nourishments, if that is what you could call them, appeared from time to time instead of or in addition to the shell-bearing animals. Substances resembling mold were not uncommon. Neither was the more recognizable foods such as poultry, fish, pork, vegetables, fruit, and beef. She enjoyed the tastes even the bitter and nearly repulsive, both were a departure from the usual yet repetitious existence she'd grown accustomed to. She enjoyed brushing her teeth nearly as much as eating the food. Her cherished toothbrush had been abused to the point of losing the bulk of its fiber; nonetheless, Peace was determined to use the brush until it was useless or her teeth fell out. She eyed the toothbrush.

"Hmmm, about time for my next feeding." As predicted, the sustenance appeared. "Roast beef... Must be a holiday." She smiled, pulling off a chunk in a manner more indicative of the unsocialized than a cultured woman she believed herself to be. She smiled as the juices flowed across her tongue when she pressed the savory piece of roast against the roof of her mouth. Peace was so absorbed in consuming her nourishment she did not notice the being shimmering into existence behind her until an experienced hand reached past her shoulder and snatched a large piece of beef. Peace leaped sideways, startled and utterly silenced by the shock of the intrusion as well as the presence of another human being. Her mouth moved before her voice finally emerged.

"Who are you?" she barked out, keeping her back against the wall.

"Why you know who I am? Miry...has it been that long since we parted company?" The intruder continued to munch on the large piece of meat as if he were a taste tester in a cooking contest.

Peace stepped a small distance away from the wall. "Ab—no, you can't be Abkhas."

Peace frowned, the stranger retorted. "That's correct. I am not Abkhas, though we have a great deal in common."

The compulsion to say nothing about Abkhas shot pain through Messmor's spine. He grimaced though he'd had it happen so many times before that the pain was nearly of no consequence, a very, very minor distraction at best. Seemingly undisturbed by the environment, the stranger continued to tear small pieces of beef away then began reaching for a second large portion of beef while consuming the last piece of the previous portion taken.

"LEAVE THAT ALONE! Who are you was the question I asked." Peace snatched the beef from the unwanted guest then pushed the intruder's hand away from her food.

The stranger smiled, knowing he could have easily avoided her assault but released the beef without a struggle satisfied to lick his fingers and enjoy the moment.

He appeared to be an aged yet supple man with an intensity to his gaze. She felt his mental probing, his attempt to reach into her mind. Peace could feel the intensity of the gaze. It was uncanny, almost searing. She wondered why he observed so intently. He continued to stand in front of her measuring, pressing mentally, all the while smiling as if to disarm her. Peace felt the mental press a second time and had no intention of being disarmed by the smile. She took note of his eyes. Those strange deep blue eyes. *Those eyes...it can't be.* Peace's face shifted from recognition to astonishment to extreme agitation.

"Yes, Miry, I am the Messmor."

"You BASTARD!" She stepped forward with intent, staring down her pointer finger. "YOU BROUGHT ME TO THIS! HOW DARE YOU DO THIS TO ME! HOW DARE YOU KEEP ME IN THIS HELLHOLE!" Her anger was beyond tears.

"I can understand your discomfort, but I cannot begin to explain all that is involved. Your captivity is necessary. It is extremely important to Alluvia. More importantly, as far as you are concerned, it could also be important to the population of earth." Messmor snatched yet another piece of beef and ducked, stepping away, narrowly evading Peace's left hook. He raised his left hand to block her right and grabbed her wrist. "I'm sorry this is the way the game is unfolding, but I have little control over the majority of it."

Peace kicked Messmor firmly in the shin. "DAMN YOU!"

Messmor grimaced, dropping the meat back onto the tray. "I suppose I deserve that, but settle down, Miry...or am I going to have to restrain you?"

Peace laughed. "RESTRAIN ME." She laughed while tilting her body forward, demonstrating her anger. "RESTRAIN ME." Peace laughed nearly hysterically. "What the hell do you think you've been doing?" Her finger pointing like an ice pick. Peace stepped forward, slapping Messmor firmly across the right cheek.

"Okay, that's enough." Messmor's hand twitched, and Peace found herself unable to move, transfixed as if frozen at the moment. She realized she could make sounds, but that was the extent of her ability to move. "I regret having to do that, Miry." He reached for the piece of roast he dropped a moment before. "But as I said, your success is extremely important to Alluvia and possibly the last chance earth will have to be free from the abomination." The pain from the compulsion reasserted itself, but Messmor continued.

Peace laughed again. "Right, I'm supposed to believe that? I suppose you're Merlin's baby brother and I'm the last hope for an endangered species." She resisted his press and began to move slowly toward him, though the mental bonds were not quick to loosen. She could move only a slight bit, but she could move. "You've been reading too many B-rated magazines." She raised an eyebrow. "Eat all of the food. Trap me and keep me here for god knows how long. Leave me to attempt to make sense of the senseless, and NOW you want my cooperation? You truly are beyond rationality." Peace bit back the tears aggravated that they would even emerge at this particular point in time.

Messmor moved to comfort Peace. "Miry...I know it's difficult."

Peace jerked backward away from his reach. "Don't patronize or touch me. You have me here. There is absolutely nothing I can do about it. I can barely tell the real from the unreal, and most of the time, I'm unsure that I have deciphered which is which. Considering that I have made myself believe I've given birth to a thought, my god, a thought that speaks to me and brings me cups that I believe are real." Peace leaned against the wall as far from Messmor as she could situate herself.

Messmor stopped his forward progression. "We both know that you are not hallucinating, that this place is real, and so are your birthings…at least Wigan is."

Peace squeezed her temples. "It's impossible…but somehow… it's true…" Regaining the composure, she stared at Messmor. "You owe me an explanation…a complete explanation."

Before Messmor could respond, Peace changed the subject. "What exactly does earth have to do with this? And don't get so swept up with my cooperation to think I'm going to believe everything you're going to tell me, but go ahead and deliver your best line. I don't get much entertainment here." She smiled.

"As I offered previously, I do not have time to tell all this to you. Abkhas"—the pain seared this time causing him to suck in wind—"is well advanced in his plans. It thwarted Wigan's effort to contact you or Zen." The pain nearly dropped Messmor to his knees as he reached out to the wall for support.

Peace interrupted, "WIGAN! How is Wigan? Is she okay?"

Messmor pitched the last piece of beef to the plate on the table ahead of him. "Yes, for the time being, she is with an acquaintance of mine, but enough of that." He licked his fingers a second time. "Wigan's training is well in hand, but the point is she should have made contact with Zen by now and has not."

"Who is Zen?" Peace interrupted a second time.

"Never mind," Messmor directed.

"Never mind? NEVER MIND! How can you stand there and tell me never mind? If—"

Messmor interrupted, "SHUSH, WOMAN! I have much more to do than to explain everything that will eventually be yours to sort through! I need your second birthing."

"My second birthing." Peace laughed aloud. "I've been trying to figure that out for days."

Messmor's eyebrow raised. "I am aware of your predicament. I've come to help you free her and get on with the game. If we don't hurry, there will be no game to go on with. Abkhas has found a way to evade the rules and provoke injury to one or all the birthings!" This time, Messmor was driven to his knees with pain.

Peace stepped forward. "What's wrong? Are you hurt?"

Messmor raised his hand to fend off Peace's advance. He stood up. "A necessary consequence to breaking the rules and telling you more than I am granted leave to about the situation." Messmor braced himself on the wall.

"There are rules? Rules against you talking to me about Abkhas?" Peace asked.

Messmor smiled through the pain. "You have a knack for the obvious, Miry."

Peace grimaced. "You are really a smart-ass, aren't you?" She stepped back.

Messmor remained silent, seemingly occupied by thoughts beyond Peace and the captivity. He began wringing his hands, pacing back and forth. He stopped, faced Peace, arcing his hands as if choreographed to emphasize each of his statements, accenting the appropriate syllables. Messmor continued, "He has attempted to immobilize both Wigan and Zen. He has been able to prevent you from sending your second birthing. I must act quickly, and you have no choice but to trust me." Messmor concluded, standing close to Peace.

"TRUST YOU! ARE YOU DRUGGED?" Peace blurted.

"Enough is enough!" Messmor stepped forward staring deeply into Peace's eyes.

"OH NO, NOT—" was the last sound to drift from Peace's mouth.

Messmor slid past her mental barriers, penetrated her psyche, and began his search. He knew this visit was time-limited but necessary. He searched Peace's past, her parents, her brother, sisters, all currently living relatives to no avail. He could not secure the correct attributes. Several hours passed before Messmor decided to search through Miry's genetic pool, to travel back through the bloodline in search of a kin bearing suitable characteristics. Messmor was surprised by the vastness of Miry's genetic past as he crossed pathways, leaped through the genetic history line by line. The technique he employed was unusual and called for only in extreme conditions. According to the rules, it could only be enacted if Abkhas or a similar player evoked a condition that was not addressed by the normal rules or had violated the game. Messmor was sure one or the other had occurred. He was bound to inform the birthing of their immediate danger, orient them to the proper time, and set them forth in close proximity to another birthing. He was allowed to do no more and no less. Unfortunately, Messmor was able to use this technique only one time during any contest without direct intervention by the Grand Council, which had not ever occurred in the history of the game.

"Just one...why now? Why couldn't 'It' have waited a bit longer?" Messmor mumbled his frustration, continuing the genetic search. Almost passing a very dark part of Miry's ancestry, Messmor stopped, returned to the abnormality stepping into this small space in time. After a moment's observation, Messmor realized this was the birthing he was looking for. Sometime between the tenth to sixteenth century, she was born and lived only a short time. An earth woman named Messene, he could not determine the exact point of her birth. A frail-looking woman with an extraordinary sense of reality. An avid fighter much more capable than her appearance would insinuate and an expert with bows and throwing weapons. "EXCELLENT!" Messmor exclaimed as he removed himself from Peace's mind.

"Awaken," he commanded, and Peace opened her eyes just in time to observe a small acorn-size sphere floating next to Messmor. "How did this one emerge from such a dismal line?" Messmor murmured out loud.

Peace noted energy arcing back and forth between Messmor and the sphere, some sort of energy transfer she surmised, but she remained silent, satisfied to watch very closely. When the exchange was completed, Messmor stepped away, and Messene shimmered into form. She bowed to her mother of sorts.

"I come from your past, fine lady. I thank you for my second life and an opportunity to be of assistance in this matter of great urgency.

I hope this life brings us both much happiness." Messene smiled with complete sincerity, catching Peace unprepared.

"Remember her face well," Messmor stated to each of them. "She goes."

The two shimmered and were gone. Peace reached for Messene but reacted too slowly to detour the departure. Messene winked out just as Peace touched her arm.

Messene found herself outside a small town after dusk. For a moment, she saw Messmor wave. She felt the medium touch her arm. The warmth lingered, then she was alone. She was aware of her basic surroundings, that she was entering danger, and was seeking the birthing Zen who did not know he was a birthing or that he was being sought after. Messene grimaced. She was given no description but was told she would recognize him by her sense of the truth. She smiled. *The sense of the truth... It had been a curse that forced her into solitude, and now she was to be grateful for it. Well*—she adjusted the bow—*it brought me back, a second chance...maybe a real chance this time.* She had the uncanny ability to see what was real. Shape-shifters, spirits, vampires, and witches could not fool or befuddle her with illusions or glamors, charisma, or persuasiveness. She could always surmise the true intent.

She breathed in the afternoon air. The only weakness in her unnatural ability was deciphering natural disguises. If the disguise was created or maintained by non-magical means, she would not necessarily be able to determine its existence. Most magic used for mind control, to mesmerize or influence others were easily deciphered. A good disguise, one implemented without any kind of magic, was her bane, which worried her a bit, made her even more suspicious when something or someone seemed out of place. In any case, the gift forced her to continually be wary, never let anyone catch her unguarded or unaware, never trust, and never show weakness...but maintain cordiality, avoid manipulations including those she would be tempted to press forward.

She proceeded very slowly down the dusty road, looking for some kind of life. Messene reached the outer limits of the town very quickly. She noticed a small sign above the blacksmith's shop "Battersea Smithy."

Battersea, I presume. She nodded silently to the sign. Messene located the central part of town almost as quickly as she'd entered the small town. The voices carried clearly from the inn to the street. Just above the doorway, a fairly expensive sign was hung.

"John Rippion's Inn. Looks like an interesting place," she spoke to herself. "I hope it is permissible for a monk to use a bow in this time."

Dressed in a monk's attire complete with a hooded robe, necklace, and amulet to a deity, Messene proceeded to the inn.

Straightening the robe just before entering, Messene commented one last time to herself, "Not my first choice of a disguise, but it'll do for the time being." Messene opened the inn's door very slowly. She took a deep breath and assumed a stance as casual as she could muster, then entered the inn.

Messene's disguise, coupled with her relaxed demeanor, eliminated any suspicion the patrons may have had. The noisy crowd took little notice with one exception. Zen eyed the stranger with a quick glance, almost dismissing him as one of several non-threatening patrons. Zen noticed the stranger, however, carried his small frail frame with confidence. He exhibited agility similar to well-trained martial artists—a soldier at the very least, but something was wrong. Before he was able to accomplish more scrutiny, Zen was interrupted by the barmaid, "Another ale from your friends." She smiled.

"Friends? I have no friends in this town," Zen replied.

The maid looked curiously. "They said every stranger is a friend as long as their bounty remains theirs."

Zen glanced to the end of the bar where all three patrons saluted Zen with mugs of ale.

Messene made her way to the table earlier occupied by Zen. The barmaid approached. Without speaking, Messene dropped three coppers on the table and pointed without exposing her hand to an empty mug. The barmaid clairvoyantly swept the coppers into her apron and headed back to the bar, muttering her thoughts about the bizarre and unusual patrons of this past week. Messene meticulously examined all the patrons, making certain all was as true as it seemed to be.

"No illusions," she muttered. Messene began looking for Zen. After minutes of examination, Messene narrowed the obvious choices to one of the three standing at the end of the bar. All three looked capable of handling themselves without difficulty. The largest of the three was indeed large, just shy of seven feet and weighing a muscular three hundred and fifty pounds. His hair was cut short and greasy. His hands showed recent combat. Two short swords dangled on his hips and a large spiked combat axe over his back. His counterparts were smaller yet large men. Each carried daggers in their boots. Each wore spiked gloves and wrist bands. Messene cringed inwardly. *How are we going to accomplish our goal when you bring that much attention to yourself?* Messene took a drink of the ale and nearly spit out the swill. She managed to swallow. Spitting it out would have drawn too much attention.

The threesome was dressed in animal furs. The smaller two of the three carried broad swords. Messene decided she liked none of the three. All were barbaric, yet one of them must be Zen. Despite the urge to approach them, better sense prevailed. *I'll wait to see which one of the three is the one I seek,* she thought.

As the evening continued, Messene's dislike for the three increased. The triad had alternately pinched, pulled, and fondled women that passed them by, and they were currently harassing the old man at the end of the bar. Messene grinned in spite of herself at the old man's stupidity. He was actually antagonizing them. She took a deep breath, trying to decide whether she should get involved, particularly considering the task at hand. *Always a failing to help the weak and spare the victim, to offer fair fight, and honor to an enemy... Will I ever be beyond these constraints?* Finally, she decided she would determine which was Zen then dispatch the remaining two. Messene very quietly and cautiously moved to a dark corner table. Once arriving, she removed an arrow, assuring no one had observed her movements, and laid it across her lap as she placed the strung bow in front, across the tabletop.

Zen eyed the three. "They claim the killing of Witch Morgan?" he asked the barmaid.

"Yes, yes, they do." The barmaid nodded in affirmation. "John will be out shortly to pay them." She continued to wipe the bar clean, attempting to look busy as to justify not going back to the other end of the bar.

"How will he know they are the ones that killed her or even if they killed her?"

The barmaid laughed. "Only strangers come here after dark… and John Rippion is the reason. John's a man of…um…many talents. One is knowing the truth from fantasy," she concluded, standing up straight.

"An interesting man indeed," Zen relinquished, as he lifted the mug eye level, saluted the threesome, then poured the ale slowly, purposely to the floor, never taking his eyes off the threesome. The largest grinned maliciously. The smaller two stared angrily. The barmaid backed up, aghast at the old man's gesture.

She whispered, "You're going to get yourself killed, old man!"

Zen grinned. "Who'll miss one more ugly old man? Tell me more of this Witch Morgan."

The barmaid looked back to the three, noting they were growing more anxious. "Well, not that it will do you much good after those three finish with you, but Witch Morgan lived not far from here. The village folk says that she captures and enslaves men of all ages… turns them into beasts that run wild in the swamps. They believe she should be killed, but none have the stomach for it. John's offered a reward for the Witch and the balding man for some time with no takers till now. I doubt they've killed her from what I've heard of her, but no one will challenge them except John himself. The middle one, Beylog, is John's man…or at least seems to be."

The barmaid turned as a mug slammed against the bar top rang out. "Woooman, you gonna play with that old man or test the flesh of his better?" The largest signaled for the barmaid to attend to him immediately as his grin continued maliciously. "I'd better go…and you'd better watch yourself."

Within a few minutes, the barmaid returned to Zen, carrying a second mug of ale. Ale spilled from the rim as the barmaid's shaky hands placed the mug in front of Zen.

"Please don't cause yourself any more harm and accept this."

Zen unlocked his eyes with the largest of the threesome to look at the barmaid. "Go about your business. I'll take care of mine."

She stepped away then turned back. "But…"

Zen smiled kindly at her concern then motioned her away and returned to engaging the largest of the threesome. Beylog lifted his mug in salute. "You are a gutsy old one, but I grow tired of you." The bar began to quiet as word spread of possible trouble. The barmaid pushed the mug to Zen.

"The big one likes your courage but not your brains. He's promised to spare you…your life it is…if you drink with him."

Zen's eyes met the barmaid's. She stepped back, suddenly chilled by the steel that emerged. "I drink only with friends, and I have no friends, except maybe you, in this town."

The barmaid shook her head. "They'll kill you she offered matter-of-factly.

"We all die sometime." Zen took a deep mouthful of ale.

The large man smiled and relaxed. The inn began to become noisy then quieted abruptly as Zen spit the ale on the floor, saluted directly to the threesome, then poured the remainder over the bar. Zen had had enough of the threesome's theatrics, their rudeness, and their ruthless behavior. Besides, it was time to see if the practice would pay off. Calculating the movements of all three, Zen felt the draw to combat burn within. Pre-combat adrenaline pumped, pressing and heightening his awareness, he could feel the sweat trickle down his sides.

Messene could not contain her laugh at the old man's manner. *You're intent on being killed*, she thought, *but you'll go out with style, old man.* The large one lowered his mug slowly to the bar. The inn was silent, customers moving away from the three at the bar and Zen. Zen deduced from the patron's reactions that the three had established themselves as the local kings of cutthroats. Zen offered the barmaid a silver coin as he leaned his elbows on the bar. She made no effort to pick up the offering but put distance between her and the site of a probable altercation. Zen did not move from his perch until one of the three grinned and arrowed a dagger directly at his chest. Zen waited until the dagger was within a few feet then fell from his stool in a seemingly uncoordinated fear-generated act of stumbling. The dagger whistled passed, sticking two inches into the support beam directly behind where Zen had been sitting. Zen was even amazed he was able to pull off the charade without having his hood fall from his head.

He grinned inwardly. Having a firm grip on his staff, he returned to the stool. The entire inn was in an uproar. Zen had looked so ridiculous all but two people were at least amused. The dagger's owner stared viciously at Zen and John Rippion who just appeared at the upper-level stairway. The establishment's owner stood looking regal in riding breeches and short topcoat, highly polished boots, and a kerchief tucked in one sleeve, stared down at Zen from his perch. Rippon's clothing did not in any way distract from the strength possessed by their owner.

"So"—his low voice carried with such authority it literally extinguishing the conversations throughout the inn—"you have arrived." John leaned his hand on his saber and grinned, the light dimming eerily near his body. Zen was caught. He was amazed and a bit unsettled that the man not only recognized him but was speaking to him as well. The patrons began backing as far away from the bar as they could comfortably reach. Zen decided hiding was no longer necessary—it was pointless.

He stepped away from the bar and slid the hood back from his head, rubbing his balding crown. Zen smiled, withdrawing the note describing Zen and the bounty. He looked up to where John was standing.

"Frank wasn't good enough. Neither are your hirelings," Zen asserted, nodding toward the threesome without taking his eyes totally from John.

John shifted his gaze to the three. "Interesting." John walked to the intersection of the stairs angling down to where the patrons stood. "It seems our 'old man suggests you are inadequate for the job, Beylog. I think he's challenging you."

The largest swallowed the remainder of his ale. "Do you want this one, Rip, or should I rid ourselves of his presence?"

John scratched his chin, cocking his head. "I think I'd enjoy…," he hesitated then frowned. "Have your fun. I have something else to tend to." John stared in Messene's direction.

Messene's laugh was cut short by the tone and implication of the man's voice. She felt his eyes upon her. *Uh-oh*, she thought. *Times have not altered as much as I would have liked.* Messene knew better than to look up. She could only hope the "not-so-old man" could survive long enough to cause John Rippion to take notice. She knew she would have a difficult time with the likes of John. She'd seen them long ago—in terrible times. They were not above slaughtering anything that opposed them. In the very rare instance, you find one who was not arrogant or self-absorbed, you would have found one just as deadly, all the same this certainly was not one of those times. *A wicked adversary*, she thought shielding her mind to the best of her ability, knowing only too well that death would occur soon. She hoped it would not include her own. The bow had been setting neatly across her lap, arrow notched. *You'll only get one shot*, she thought, knowing the timing and distance adjustment must be perfect. Less could make this new life much shorter than she'd anticipated.

Zen caught John's stare following it to the man of small stature. Zen suddenly realized the man was, in fact, a woman, strands of her blond hair protruded slightly from the cloak's hood. Beylog had also noticed.

"Well, John, I see your distraction. I think I'll have a look at the wench before you do for a change."

Beylog and companions moved toward Messene's table.

John asserted himself, "No!" Hissing, "Beylog, the woman is MINE!"

Beylog stopped, a bit surprised at John's intensity, giving Zen time to make his way between Messene and the threesome. He did not feel any allegiance toward the female but could use the diversion to his advantage. Beylog looked up at Rippion. "You can have any woman, Rippion. Let us have this one." Beylog started to walk toward Messene a second time.

Rippion hissed, "That isn't just any woman. She's a menace, a menace I will enjoy taking care of very slowly. Would you prefer to join my minion Beylog, or would you graciously offer me the opportunity to meet the woman first?"

Beylog could feel John's eyes upon him. He stopped, waved his two companions back toward the bar. "We've been friends a long time, John. Help yourself to the spoils."

Rippion relaxed his stare. "Why, thank you, Beylog. Kind of you to reconsider."

Zen leaned as if winded, on his staff. "No one shall have the girl unless she so chooses."

Rippion's eye burned ember red staring powerfully at Zen. Zen felt the intensity of the stare for a moment then the room swirled. Zen steeled himself.

"You shall not have me so easily, Rippion. You'll not bend my mind or my back."

Zen prepared for combat.

Messene watched the not-so-old man' curiously. She sensed his inner strength, a vague yet authentic aura of magic, and something else—something like she'd not experienced before. Her choices were muddled. Zen could be any one of the four but definitely not John Rippion.

"So mage born, you steel yourself well, but how will you deal with the four of us?"

Zen's eyebrows twitched. "Mage born? What would you know of mage born?"

Rippion took two steps down the stairs. "Surely you are aware you are mage born, or are you simply more ignorant than other birthings?"

"Your attempts at distracting me will not work, Rippion. You are just moving your mouth to get closer to me."

Rippion laughed. "I can kill you outright. You don't have the means to dispatch me. I am surprised to find that they kept you ignorant of your fate. All the better I guess." He fidgeted with the saber at his side. "It does not change the outcome of our meeting any, and since you know nothing about what you are, then I need not waste time answering any questions."

He must be Zen, Messene thought, listening to his retort.

"I live for reasons I do not know, but I am not willing to die before finding out. I do not wish to kill any of you, but I will if need be."

Rippion took an additional step. Beylog and his companions edged to Zen's left. "All this for the honor of a wench you don't know? Or do you?"

Zen cringed. "The 'woman' not 'wench' is not known to me, but all the same, the woman shall go free, and the four of you can meet me."

Rippion's laugh shook the building. "As I stated before, I am far your better. You cannot possibly survive me, let alone the three to the left of you."

Zen lifted his finger slowly to his nose. "Three?" He shifted his stance. "You overestimate the odds!" Zen's hands were lightning quick. In a single motion with the left hand, he removed the knife nestled in the small of his back and fired it at one of the smaller men while removing the knife from his right boot and firing the second. Beylog's underlings were just beginning to move in Zen's direction when the daggers arrived. The first knife penetrated the assailant's left eye, sending him horizontally across the table. The second knife took the second assailant directly in the ear before his hand could lift the broad sword. He staggered, still grinning in amazement then fell face first directly on his nose, bouncing once and lying still. The first lifted his head as if to comment then convulsed. Beylog pulled the axe from his back in a single motion, still shaken but determined to not give way to Zen. Beylog stepped forward.

"I fall not so easily, little man."

Rippion's smile was gone. He'd underestimated Zen.

"Guess we're down to two. The odds are in my favor." Zen grinned, shifting from a rooted stance to a relaxed shortened fighting stance edging his way toward Beylog without fully losing Rippion from his view.

John responded, exhaling slowly, "Things are never as they seem, Beylog. Be careful with this one."

Beylog grinned, spittle, from too much ale dripping out of the edge of his mouth.

Zen circled Beylog, pressing, lulling, and calculating his movements. "You remind me of another of my adversaries, Beylog. Grink was his name. He was bigger than you, though."

Beylog's grin widened psychotically. "Remember this as you face death, little one."

Beylog bellowed and charged slashing vertically. Zen stepped sideways and kicked Beylog firmly in the groin with his right leg bending Beylog slightly.

It'll be a reach, Zen thought as he crescent kicked Beylog on the knowledge knot with the same leg stepping through at the conclusion. The second kick did little damage but sent Beylog passed Zen toward the bar. Beylog caught himself, then turned back toward Zen, not quite as anxious as in the beginning to engage with Zen.

"One more chance, Beylog. Walk away and we can end this without pain."

Beylog made no sound as the axe sang forward. Zen nearly did not evade the slice as it traveled horizontally in a full circle. The axe adjusted slightly as it sang a second time in a diagonal slash vertically toward his head. Zen managed to evade to the left, thinking, *This one's no amateur.* Zen concentrated, losing track of John Rippion's position. The axe shifted horizontally. Zen ducked, sweeping toward Beylog's ankles. To Zen's dismay, the leg sweep only angered Beylog who was able to evade the sweep by lifting his left leg. Beylog regained balance as the sweep bashed his right leg. Beylog pressed forward with a vengeance. Zen glanced upward. *His intensity is unbelievable, yet his eyes say he's not in this.*

Messene was startled by Zen's speed and the accuracy within which the daggers reached their targets. He moved like a wolf, patiently and deadly, circling. She felt Rippion's gaze upon her. She'd been able to manipulate the bow into a much more comfortable position since the old man had been involved. *He is Zen...* She decided finally. "We lose the game if he dies here. He is more important than me. I am grateful for my second life, but if one should die, it should be me," she whispered to herself as she prepared to assist. Before she could move forward, she felt Rippion's power press more diligently in her direction. So was her curse. She could sense their presence but had no other than natural means of defense. She could only wait for the unlikely moment of chance and not look into his eyes.

Zen stepped forward, taunting Beylog to swing the axe again vertically. Beylog responded as planned. As the axe proceeded forward, Zen waited until the arc of the axe swing reached the downward movement. Zen stepped left of the axe, side kicking Beylog with right foot to the side of Beylog's right knee, then sliding next to Beylog's body Zen's arm coiling for a strike to the ribs. Beylog cringed as the heel struck the right side of his knee, not quite buckling but shooting pain in all directions. Zen did not pause, taking advantage of the shock as well as his nearness to Beylog. The punch beneath Beylog's outstretched right arm smashed directly into the least fleshy ribs under the armpit so hard that Zen felt the pressure in his right elbow.

Without stopping, Zen left hooked Beylog's kidney then right leg round kick through the gap left under the right arm to Beylog's chin. Zen followed with a left straight punch to the knowledge knot and a right hook to the ear. Unbelievably, Beylog staggered backward out of Zen's range and faced Zen. Beylog dropped the axe but did not go down. Zen lunged forward with a hop front thrust kick. The kick was risky, putting him firmly within Beylog's reach. The kick struck Beylog in the solar plexus, causing him to bend forward and, and though winded, allowed Beylog to latch a right hand on Zen's throat and to cradle Zen's right foot in his left arm. Beylog lifted Zen into the air by his knee and throat. Zen responded immediately by grabbing the thumb, rotating outward with his left hand, bending his right knee to bring Beylog's face into range, and palm heeling Beylog to the chin.

Before Beylog's chin returned forward, Zen launched his body forward off his left leg, putting all his weight on his right leg, causing Beylog to grip the leg harder as to not allow Zen to spring free. Zen used Beylog's strength and support to stabilize Zen's torso now near chest to chest with Beylog as Zen spear handed Beylog in the throat. Beylog blinked, let go of Zen, and grabbed his throat with both hands. Zen landed and immediately jump spin side kicked Beylog in the sternum as he traveled out of Beylog's range. Beylog's lungs whooshed air forward as he lost his breath, dropped to his knees, then to his stomach attempting to get air, curled in a near fetal position.

Zen kicked Beylog firmly in the ear. "Stay down, Beylog!" Zen advised as he stepped back to make sure he did not lose sight of Rippion again. Beylog began to rise, first to an elbow then to hand and knee. Zen sighed in frustration and regret. "You're forcing me to hurt you beyond repair, Beylog. Stay down." Zen decided he would need to finish Beylog before he could attend to Rippion. Losing sight of Rippion, Zen stepped forward toward Beylog. Zen felt Rippion's eyes upon him. Zen knew Beylog was already hurt in ways he was not aware of—ways that, without attention, would likely end his fighting career if he survived. Zen resisted Rippion's compulsion and moved to end the altercation with Beylog. Rippion magnified his power. Zen felt himself slow as he watched Beylog rise. He attempted to take advantage but could not move quickly enough through the psychic energy that pressing and restraining him with greater and greater efficiency. Zen felt as if he were surrounded by water and forced to move through a river current.

His legs and arms were more and more difficult to lift and turn. Beylog did not retrieve the axe, he instead reached for one of the broad swords with his right hand and pulled a short sword for his left hand. Beylog advanced very deliberately toward Zen. Beylog sensed Zen's sluggishness. Zen noted blood dripping from the edges of Beylog's mouth, and the telltale wheeze of filling lungs. Beylog proceeded as if undisturbed by his vulnerability. Zen continued to evade the sword slashes by placing chairs and tables between Beylog and himself. Zen could not afford to shift his attention to Rippion even though it was Rippions psychic manipulation that caused his sluggishness. On the other hand, though he could not maneuver toward Rippion, he could still avoid death for the time being. The giant's swords had nearly taken him several times before he could adjust to the weight of Rippion's psychic chains. Zen's arms and chest were burning with sweat and several sword nicks, yet Zen could not press for an advantage.

Messene regained strength as Rippion's stare shifted to Zen. John had proceeded to the first floor and was standing behind Beylog yet chest exposed to targeting. Messene measured the distance as only a trained archer could. She was aware that several variables could alter the trajectory from the mark she intended to hit. Messene realized the window for action was about to close, and to miss would end the purpose of both birthings.

She lifted the bow, drawing the arrow simultaneously. John spun meeting Messene's eyes penetrating deep into Messene's mind obtaining control almost instantly. His challenge, though sufficient to mesmerize Messene, was not quick enough. The archer's bow dropped from her hands. She could no longer see. Rippion's response was incredibly quick. Messene awaited the end, but the end had one remarkable flaw—almost is never good enough; the arrow was on its way. Messene, frozen mid stance, could not move. She prayed the makeshift, slightly oversized, arrow flew true. Her consciousness was captured, boxed in, and trapped, shelved where she could observe and feel herself move but could not control her actions. She could not see, so she listened with every aspect of her being. The silver-tipped projectile hummed an odd sound as it split the air then. *Thud!* It penetrated the center of its mark, plunging Rippion backward until the arrow was gripped ever so tightly by Rippion sinew. The silver-tipped arrow twitched to the last beat of Rippion's heart. Rippion's vision wavered, his concentration broke. He looked down in disbelief. The fletching protruded from the chest surrounded by hissing tentacles of the dissipating membrane. Messene felt the power shift. Rippion's mouth opened, initially silent. Still staring in disbelief, he screamed in agony. Tearing desperately at his chest, he staggered further backward. His bony hand leathered, frozen in a death grip, the body atrophied quickly. The hideous caricature of a man's shape-shifted, dripping flesh and ooze from his bones, plopping on the hardwood floor. Rippion's scream was lost in the roar of screaming patrons panicked and horrified by the sight and repulsed by the smell. Like a poisonous invisible cloud, the haze of Rippion's death, stench nearly unbearable, pushed its way into the street taking the majority of onlookers with it.

Zen, though thoroughly exhausted from fighting Beylog, gazed peripherally in disbelief. He'd managed to evade Beylog's final thrust just as Rippion hit the floor.

While a portion of Zen's mind absorbed the shock of Rippion, the martial artist continued without pause with a crushing ridge hand to his opponent's throat. Beylog dropped to a knee. Rippion's scream seemed to take with it the tenseness that had marked the Inn from the beginning. Rippion's influence gone, an eerie silence prevailed. Zen's concentration lapsed as he leaned against a nearby table. He watched in awe as Rippion decomposed in front of his eyes. Zen turned back to Beylog who was now very near death smiling.

"You've done well, little one. Better than I." He coughed. "My freedom, alas, I cannot enjoy, but I've seen the Rippion die. 'Tis worth it."

Zen flinched forward at the vibration of the bowstring. The arrow penetrated Beylog's breast. His death was quiet and efficient. Zen spun in anger. "Why did you KILL HIM!" Zen barked, stepping intently toward the bowman, spittle flying.

Messene looked up. "I simply ended his pain. You killed him." Zen blinked, a bit winded, knowing her perception was as correct as her feelingless reprimand. He stopped the advance and turned back toward the assailants.

Zen collected his knives and the coin from the dead men. He offered half to Messene who frowned.

"I am no thief," she offered flatly.

"Nor am I," Zen responded. "Dead men give freely. I prefer not to steal, and I don't have time to work for coin." Zen stared at Messene sternly, giving full measure, then grabbed his staff and headed toward the door, tossing a silver piece to the barmaid who stood in awe. Zen tilted his head in her direction. "A silver coin for your trouble, friend," Zen concluded, walking through the door.

Messene watched Zen closely. *A challenge this surely is*, Messene thought to herself, *but a part of a greater good, it seems.* Messene paused, contemplating her next statement.

"Zen Murcada."

Messene's voice carried an air of assuredness without taunt or intent to command but a directness very difficult to ignore.

Zen slowed, feeling a sudden ache in the back of his head, turned to face Messene. "What did you call me?"

"I called you by your rightful name, Zen Murcada, first birthing of Omurcada. I am Messene, second birthing of the woman Peace, your counterpart in this quest. I am to join you. The rest will reveal itself to us. I know that our time grows shorter each day. I know no more than that."

Zen stood for a moment, mulling over her statements silently. For a reason, he could not make sense of... He believed this woman. Even more curious was an urge to trust this woman. Why would or should he trust this stranger? There were no reasons of course... well...beyond the fact that she'd saved his life for no apparent gain. He hadn't trusted anyone before, not even Ablis fully, and did not like trusting this one. Zen's left eyebrow raised. His stance shifted as his mind battled suspicion, curiosity, resistance, and a press to trust each with a logic that was not refutable.

"Omurcada?" His head ached at the sound of the name. One side of his mind searching for the reason he could not recall something that obviously was within his awareness that would not fight its way to the surface. The other side attempting to fully appraise the woman in front of him. "I know no one of that name. It seems odd you would know anything about me. I'll not wait up or fend for you. I have enough to take care of myself."

Messene nodded, silently preferring an arrangement with no ties and no obligations. She did not understand why they were partnered, but for the first time in two lives, she was not offended by it.

"Suit yourself. I will not object as long as you proceed in the direction you are intended to proceed."

Zen stopped. "And you intend to stop me from moving in any direction I choose?"

Messene, unflinching, simply stated, "No."

Zen returned to taking lead and heading northward. "That's good," he replied.

Messene, without losing any distance or hesitating in any way, said, "I will only stop you if you travel in the direction that was not intended."

Zen did not detour from shifting paths and heading back to Ablis's cabin. "You think you could stop me from going the way I choose if it's different from the path you think I should take?"

Messene's quiet but firm statement hung in the air like a damp fog. "I can, and I will."

The two proceeded silently through the wood.

* * *

Peace rubbed her eyes purposefully in an attempt to remove a small irritant. She was more than a bit unsettled and remained disturbed at the ease in which Messmor had subdued her. Despite the irritation and the forced truce oddly required between the woman and the wizard, Peace was pleased that Messene had been born. Peace experienced a twinge of loneliness thinking about Wigan, her firstborn and who had been such a blessing in this captivity. She pressed the thought to the side. "Only one birth remains..." Peace wondered where, in her past, Messene had existed. There were unanswered questions, and in some ways, answers that were more confusing than the questions. *How had Messmor known Messene was one of three mentioned by Abkhas?*

Though Peace much preferred Messmor's manner, she had not stopped trembling since his visit. She could not decide which one was the most frightening—Abkhas in his cruelty or Messmor in his omnipotence. Peace's eye continued to itch. *The game must be well on its way*, she thought to herself, sitting quietly, legs crossed, head leaning against the chair's back. "I wonder when or if I'll be a player? Or will I simply be the broodmare?"

Peace frowned in disgust and frustration. Her eye continued to irritate more persistently. "Damn thing!" she muttered again, attempting to remove the irritant. After several minutes, Peace removed an eyelash that had abraded and caused her left eye to redden. "Gotcha finally," she admonished the lash lifting it eye level then laughing at herself. *Messmor*, she thought, clenching her teeth, popping knuckles in her fingers. "I wish I at least knew why I was here, just something to make sense of it all." Peace uncrossed her legs and stood up. Her leg tingled and resisted control. "That's all I need... You go to sleep right when I need support!" Peace could not contain herself, thoroughly delighted with her humor she giggled to herself, laughed out loud, finally laughing so hard she had difficulty getting her breath. Peace, in time, regained control, knowing the stress was as much to blame as her humor. After patting her leg to make sure it had awakened totally, she walked to the area she'd named the aerobics section. Peace was relieved her company had departed, but she was feeling more and more physically uneasy. *Must have been the beef*, she thought as she stretched her back and neck.

Peace normally exercised for an hour after waking, but she was not feeling well—not feeling well at all. She poured water into her palm and plashed it upon her face. Her stomach lurched. "I suppose I'm pregnant." She laughed. Her stomach swirled in a way suggesting she'd better lie back down. Peace returned to her favorite chair. She glanced at the couplings on her wrist. They'd become second nature since her captivity. She'd appreciated the extended length of the chain but would have preferred freedom—at least to move throughout the room. *Oh well, a project for another day*, she thought, resigned to the fact she was powerless to do much. She had always detested being sick, and this was not an exception. She unconsciously fingered the couplings leaning back into the chair, her eyelids heavy.

Peace had just begun to drift into light sleep when a familiar voice interrupted her respite. "Miry? Miry, you must awaken."

Peace opened her eyes, caught between fear and anger, stared at Messmor. "Back so soon?" She started to move out of the chair then decided better of it and sat back, exhaling and attempting to steady her stomach as well as the lightness in her head. "Just visiting or have you decided to take up residence with me?" She tried to laugh sarcastically in an attempt to mask her fear. She would have preferred to keep her illness just as hidden as her fear but she doubted that would be possible.

Messmor's eyes twinkled. "An interesting offer, Miry." He smiled.

"You're an ass!" Peace asserted, chin out, impatiently.

As she sat forward, she covered her mouth with her left hand swallowing down the volcanic offerings of her stomach. "What exactly do you want from me?" Peace directed at Messmor.

"Your third birthing, Miry."

Peace inhaled deeply, resigned to the fact the Messmor could proceed as he pleased regardless of her opinion. "Well, help yourself, but unless you have a bucket, I wouldn't get too close to me."

Messmor frowned. "Are you physically ill? I'm sorry this has caused you so much discomfort, Miry. I do not control the game or its rules. I am only a player. I can influence but not literally change the game."

Peace looked up meeting Messmor's eyes evenly. "Is this an apology?" Peace laughed. "It certainly does not change my position or ease the situation, does it?"

Messmor grimaced. "No...no...it doesn't." He looked down at the floor. "Again, I'm sorry your conditions are as they are. I have seen worse however."

Messmor concluded, not looking away from Peace but not intruding on her mental barriers. "Is that supposed to be comforting?" Peace raised an eyebrow, cocked her head, and crossed her arms as much as to show resistance as to quell the rumbles in her stomach.

Messmor smiled. "I suppose this is pointless. One only sees their own pain doesn't one... You, by no personal fault, are unable to see the situation as I. You are in captivity, and your experience extends not past even this cubicle. When, god willing, you see the picture as it is, you'll forgive me and understand my plight has been long-standing...near hopeless until now. You'll never know the extent to which I depend on you." He concluded the oratory, looking distant, without his normal arrogance, never vulnerable but close to humble for the first time in Peace's memory.

Peace, however, did not relinquish her position. "Am I expected to consider this an honor and a privilege or one of each?" Her eyes narrowed. "You must be insane." Peace looked away.

Messmor smiled tightly. "To you, I suppose I am. My time dwindles, Miry. As you imply, my presence offends you, so shall we proceed?"

Peace was afraid to admit, though far from pleased with the situation, she yearned for company, any company but Abkhas.

Peace lifted her hand, stopping short of reaching the tear dribbling down her cheek. "These chains...," she muttered, regaining her composure.

Messmor watched Peace, closely contemplating his next move. Messmor stepped quickly forward and removed Peace's chains. Peace was stunned. Sparing Peace any embarrassment a thank-you would cause, Messmor stepped back and instructed Peace to sit in her chair and prepare for the birthing. Peace tried to gather herself then waved her hands.

"Wait," Messmor retorted. "No stalling, Miry. Nanling needs to be born."

Peace waved her hands a second time, obviously in distress. Her stomach wrenched as she vomited. "Gosh, I'm sick."

Messmor jumped backward to avoid being splattered. He hesitated, torn between concern for Peace and anxiousness to send the birthing forward, Messmor lifted Forever Full and handed Peace the cup of water.

"Okay, deep breaths, then drink this slowly."

Peace said nothing. She placed her hand over her mouth for a moment before following Messmor's instructions. Messmor watched the floor undulate and shift absorbing and cleansing the putrid offering Miry had expelled.

"Interesting abode, Miry...very interesting abode."

Peace rinsed her mouth, spitting the tainted water to the floor that, again, absorbed her offering. Peace lifted her head. "It has its perks. I'm sure I could make you a good deal, or would you like to trade this home for yours?" She chuckled, still trying to manage her stomach.

Messmor glanced around the room before continuing. Messmor knelt and made eye contact.

Peace shifted, suddenly raising her hand between the two. "Before you take this one, please know I care about Messene." Her head dropped. "I miss Wigan's company, and I don't want this one ripped from me." Peace looked up and nodded her head, signaling Messmor to continue.

He took a moment to stare curiously. "You are a strange one, Miry. Honor, strength, intelligence… You and your birthings teamed with another, and his birthings are all that stand between this world and another's domination. I am happy you represent earth. We may have a chance."

Her face brightened slightly. "Quit mumbling and get on with this…before I have to breathe on you again." She giggled and reengaged eye contact. Despite her anger and desperation, her eyes twinkled in the way that would indicate the makings of friendship if the circumstances were different. At that moment, for some strange reason, she thought of Greyson Mirphey, wondering whatever became of the little Irishman. She briefly contemplated his existence in this sort of circumstance. Grinning to herself, she all but dismissed the thought. *After all, he was less than this would require, an ordinary man…yet rare integrity…and a hidden strength…a meeting sooo long ago.* She shook her head. "Why am I thinking of a nobody at a time like this?" she mumbled to herself.

Messmor grinned, listening too the mumblings. "Somebody was a nobody and not just anybody. He was the nobody that somebody needed when anybody wouldn't do."

Peace blinked and laughed aloud. "What kind of circular logic is that?"

Messmor's grin continued. "Not all is as it seems, and the moment you believe you have reality captured, it slips away. The present is the present only because it is not yesterday and a certain somebody, not anybody, yet a nobody could just save tomorrow." He laughed. "Child games in a wizard's schoolyard." Peace blinked. Messmor smiled a last time. "Which is it, Miry? Am I an ass? A friend? A poet?"

Peace grinned back. "You're a politician…and that's not a compliment."

They both laughed.

Messmor rolled the sleeves of the robe up to his elbow as he returned to the ritual of midwiving a birthing most unusual. Messmor peered deeply within Peace's psyche, pressing, dodging, turning in an attempt to find the one he needed to find. Suddenly, without prompting, an acorn-size phosphorescent orb appeared. Messmor's eyebrows raised.

"She almost made it here on her own, Miry."

The orb pulsed then, just short of instantaneously, located itself between Peace and the Messmor. The orb radiated warmth. Peace was awake and observant. "Why doesn't she appear in full form?" Peace inquired.

Messmor's eyebrows raised in surprise. "I had nothing to do with this one's birthing, Miry. She's pretty much on her own."

Peace nor Messmor, both preoccupied, observed the dark shroud shimmer into existence a few feet behind Messmor.

"What's it's name?" Peace inquired.

"Nanling," Abkhas retorted in a rasping yet booming voice, simultaneously striking the Messmor firmly in the back of the skull with the ridge of his atrophied hand. Peace stumbled backward tripping over her favorite chair.

"A-AA-Abkhas," she hissed.

"Yes, my pretty…to borrow a phrase." Grinning broken teeth fully exposed, ember eyes twinkling yellow emanations. "It's so nice to feel your greeting. I see you are amazed." It laughed sardonically, bending slightly backward, spreading both arms. "You tremble pleasantly since our last meeting."

Peace said nothing, slowly edging herself past the unconscious Messmor inserting herself between Nanling and Abkhas.

Abkhas continued its phantasmal grin. "Stand not between us, earthling! You are incapable of protecting the birthing." It glanced at Messmor, still unconscious. "Foul miser, I thought you wiser than to be so easily dispatched!" Abkhas smiled. "Of course, this is the consequence when you are fully outmatched."

Abkhas raised an open palm, very slowly pushing Peace aside and reached for the orb. The sphere hissed, squealed, then whizzed in short zigzag patterns about the room. First in front, then side to side, then passed Abkhas, who taken off guard by the orb's intelligence, frantically swatted in an attempt to catch Nanling. The orb appeared to be a small very bright comet whose tail lengthened as the orbs increased its speed. The tail seemed to coil around Abkhas as Nanling speedily flew circles around its nemesis. It took a moment to regain composure. Abkhas began to concentrate energy. The sphere began to slow against It's will, stopping chest level directly in front of Abkhas. It was drawn left and finally centering precisely between his two outstretched hands. Abkhas grinned in victory.

"A time to live... A TIME TO DIE!" he bellowed, bringing his hands together in an echoing clap.

Abkhas's face twisted in bewilderment and agitation when he realized he'd missed the sphere. Peace attacked Abkhas with a fury. Nanling hovered for just a moment between Abkhas's chest and the heel of his clasped hands. The little orb emitted a very high-pitched rapid laugh then disappeared through a small hole in the chamber's wall. Jeb materialized in front of the hole Nanling had entered. Abkhas roared furiously, stepped beyond Peace, intent on crushing Jeb, who immediately winked out, and capturing the birthing who had escaped. Billowing, Abkhas turned toward Peace.

"You'll pay for that distraction with your pain, wench!" He forced through clenched teeth.

An aura rose and shielded and interceded between Abkhas and Peace. Abkhas spun. "You interfere with the game for the last time!"

Messmor, adding the mana being generated by the room to his own, easily fended off the energy bolt. "I'm not sure you're in any position to accuse much less dictate terms." Messmor continued. Peace pushed herself as far into the corner as possible. "The Grand Counsel convenes on the third moon's rise. You have violated the game." Messmor's smile widened. "I've waited years for this moment, this circumstance, this alteration of the rules..."

Abkhas began to shimmer into translucence, "You do not threaten me!" he bellowed, though noticeably less confident.

Messmor's comment hummed throughout the chamber echoing in Abkhas's mind.

"The game is the game, the rules do rule, unless so altered by the Omnipotent fool who chooses himself as the master guide and loses his choice, as the Council abides…"

"Your quotes are meaningless to me," Abkhas declared omnipotently. Messmor was not intimidated. "Your facade of Omnipotence is just that, a cover for a frightened being who lusts for control and power to shield the need to compensate for an inadequacy well-guarded. You've overplayed your position concerning the Grand Council. I will discover your secret before this game is over and share it with all of Alluvia, beginning with the Grand Council. We'll see how well you proceed when the facade fades and the black hole of a heart is exposed."

Abkhas started to respond then bit off the remark, discovering that Messmor had vanished. Abkhas hung in the air, realizing the stakes of the game had increased incredibly, but Abkhas could not quite understand why such uneasiness should occur from Messmor's comment. He'd violated or improvised under natural limitations as he'd explained to the Grand Council, in games past, but had never experienced such unease with the Messmor's remarks.

"He knows nothing of what has occurred…my secret? What is Messmor thinking?" He vanished.

Peace remained sitting back against the wall, trying to make sense of what had just occurred. Nanling seemed to escape safely, but she had no idea if she could be contacted. She rubbed her eyes. *Was that a lizard with wings or a bird?* she thought. Grateful for the assistance to Nanling, whatever it was. She still was not certain it was real rather than an illusion or hallucination caused by her sickness. Too many questions and too many answers causing more questions. She rubbed her wrist unconsciously, realizing suddenly the chains were actually removed. "Now I need to think escape!" She tilted her head. "But…escape to where?"

CHAPTER 10

─────── ✿ ───────

Progression

A dark figure loomed in the shadow of It's Alluvian keep. An atrophied finger gnawed not so gently against It's chin as he contemplated Messmor's remarks.

"A secret? A black heart! Bah!" It rumbled, standing then spinning and de-illuminating the room with energy. The walls pulsed from scarlet to violet. Energy arced in all directions from the darkness that invaded the center of the room—the absence of light, the abyss in the center sucking the light away from the room even as mana arced and shone the silhouette of Abkhas. Abkhas's mood undulated, orchestrating the pulsing and the deepening of the dark nexus. "It is time to gather those who serve," Abkhas offered in a tone that further edged the darkness. Abkhas thought of Messmor past and present. *He is but a flea...*, it swatted, *a bothersome one still...an irritant to me... I must wait to kill.* Finishing his thought, a peculiarly dark and poetic revelry, Abkhas shifted focus back to the process of aligning his campaign.

"First to order..." Abkhas climbed the stairs of the keep. "*Yes, King, your home is now mine...so is your underdeveloped mind.* It smirked, reaching the uppermost floor of the castle staircase. Abkhas proceeded to the parapet, then finally to the Guardian's Tower. It

253

examined the castle's surroundings. The night air captured It's swirling fetid breath. Like smoke rising from a funeral pyre, the breath spun above Abkhas and escaped unnoticed by the nemesis. Its vision penetrated the darkness as it assured itself that none would notice its presence before opening its mind to set the spell.

Abkhas started then stopped the spellbinding, still uneasy from Messmor's comments. Messmor seemed to be aware of much more than Abkhas had anticipated, which compounded Abkhas's irritation. It surveyed its surroundings once more to determine with certainty Messmor was not within a distance to observe or strike. Confident its foe could be sensed if present, Abkhas stretched its mind, allowing it to diffuse slowly, quietly, through the knoll, over hills, beside the river. Satisfied that Messmor was not within range nor with the means to interrupt the spellbindings, Abkhas removed the demon chain from around its waist and set it before him. It patiently and carefully manipulated the links to form a near-perfect circle on the stone floor of the Guardian's Tower.

The chain was around what would have been assumed to be its waist, weighing nearly thirty stones, was obscured by swirling gray-black tendrils of darkness. The links, highly polished yet absent of light, were twisted into symbols individually representing each of his three lieutenants and their minion.

The buckle, similarly obscured, was constructed from finely polished onyx that seemed to swallow light rather than shine. Four figures were etched in its half-moon shape—Abkhas, Niphyus, Breyfirr, and Lucanus. The top figure was Abkhas representing unyielding command. Abkhas rubbed the etching remembering, the second figure, the first lieutenant was Niphyus, second-in-command, commandant of the Legion of Brume. He had been with Abkhas since the beginning. A sorcerer of great magnitude, always lusting for power, died at the hand of Abkhas after issuing a challenge… It didn't like to be challenged. Niphyus survived beyond the final seconds by trading the inhabitants of three dimensions and swearing allegiance to Abkhas. Abkhas accepted the inhabitants as well as Niphyus's allegiance, but to seal the pact permanently, Abkhas transformed Niphyus into a hideous being many believed to be a demon and placed Niphyus' soul into a sealed and warded chamber of the chain.

Hence, Niphyus was transformed. Niphyus's lust for power was second only to his fear of Abkhas. He was bound to Abkhas less out of loyalty as out of the understanding he would never regain his soul without Abkhas's cooperation. Niphyus was the master of horror, shock, and awe, and his command, the Legion of Brume, trembled in his sight out of fright. Forty thousand troops who feared his reprimand to an extent compelling all to be utterly faithful. The Legion of Brume, unspeakable horrors, all honed into a formidable fighting force. Niphyus and the Legion existed as Abkhas's right arm.

The second lieutenant and third in command was Breyfirr—a master of mind control and illusion. Breyfirr preferred to work alone. Not entirely human, or anything else for that matter, a shape-shifter who sought out and joined Abkhas two dimensions ago after causing the Messmor to build mind blocks within his birthings to withstand Breyfirr's influence. Messmor was successful in building the mind blocks but lost the world. Abkhas rewarded Breyfirr with the third command and a legion of combat troops major and minor. Though Breyfirr's troop was small, less than two thousand, it was unusually efficient, continually supplemented by inhabitants of any given dimension—most could not withstand Breyfirr's compulsion to yield their very person to his cause. Those that could resist were singled out and eaten. Breyfirr's legion loved him. They had no choice.

Rippion had been one of Breyfirr's lieutenants. Abkhas had recently been advised Rippion had died at the hands of one of the birthings. The death of Breyfirr's lieutenant was an irritant but not nearly as unsettling as Messmor's remark. Abkhas shook the remark from its consciousness. It was angered the comments were still an issue.

The third lieutenant was Lucanus. Lucanus was a mystery to everything that ever encountered him. Lucanus joined Abkhas, once the hive, a loose description of the insect-like social structures of the Lucanidae civilization, was conquered as signified by the killing of the queen. In full adherence to the Lucanidae Code of Honor, Lucanus and his forces aligned with Abkhas's forces following the defeat. Their loyalty was as absolute as their lethality. Abkhas had not ever been completely comfortable with Lucanus but could not deny the lethal efficiency within which he dispatched adversary after adversary. There were times when Abkhas wondered how the feeble pittance that followed It could have conquered the Lucanidae, but It knew that It had masterminded the assassination of the queen, one of the more delightful memories of It's domination. The queen's death by the hand of Breyfirr was truly satisfying to both of them. Abkhas prepared the calling.

> Breyfirr's minion lead the way
> Niphyus to final the stay
> Lucanus to align the scourge
> Minion three conjoining the purge

Abkhas laughed, lips cracking, it placed both hands inside the chain circle carefully touching the third in command's emblem. Energy arced from Abkhas's atrophied nails to the emblem. The stone beneath the chain smoldered, shimmered, then faded into the portal it was destined to create. Abkhas lifted his spirit chain from the floor while watching the swirling mass of endlessness. "An abyss of such dark beauty save... A cauldron black and cold and grave." It fastened the belt's outer chain back around its waist and turned to the being standing in the darkness. A silent immobile near mindless caricature of the being it had once been. Abkhas motioned to the king who immediately shuffled forward, eyes glazed, muscles limp.

> First conquest, a lovely thing,
> Remnants of a would be king.
> Your spirit no longer yours to keep,
> A secret from those who seek.
> The source of darkness, sickly pall,
> No rescue comes, no clarion call.

Abkhas turned toward the portal then glanced back to the king...

> No utterance, no word, nor sound,
> of this arrangement to be found.
> Lest death enter through portal door,
> You live to serve, nothing more...

The king shook despite the compulsion. Abkhas sent the king's spirit back to the king's body then reached through the portal and was gone. Only the illusion of nothingness to protect the inner chain and a broken mindless king remained.

* * *

Omurcada continued to grope in the darkness, wondering if his eyes would ever experience the delight of color, clouds, the moon, or the sun. The chains though mysteriously loosened from the couplings on the wall, hung burdensome on each of Omurcada's chaffed wrists. Scratching and digging at the dead skin, Omurcada wondered when and if Camen's birth would ever come. He had spent thirty-seven mealtimes worth of thought and energy attempting to cause Camen's birth but was not successful. When he was not thinking about Camen, which had become an obsession, he exercised. Though he could not see in the darkness, he could feel the muscular bulk of his chest and arms. Both had gained in size and strength during the weeks of captivity. The thought of the birthings and the exercise were his only anchors to sanity—sanity that continuously edged closer to obliviousness. The lack of company and the eternal darkness made sanity a very difficult endeavor. Omurcada constantly pinched, pulled, and tested himself to assure he was not sleeping. The darkness was unrelenting even when dreaming. Dreams were a natural hazard in the darkness. It was nearly impossible to know whether he was dreaming of darkness or standing in it. In some instances, where he had been forced to consider the dreams simple hallucinations, he could not determine whether he was awake.

Omurcada spent several days mapping the walls with his fingertips and pacing the distance the chains allowed in an attempt to build a mental picture of his entrapment. His fingertips were calloused from touching the limits of his prison. He knew every crack and cranny. He expected to encounter cobwebs or bugs or bats—anything but the lack of life he noted in the room. The presence of chairs and table were still a mystery to him. In the early recollection, just after their discovery, Omurcada experienced euphoria. He hoped a visitor—any visitor—would come. His delusion stretched into the hope of rescue, freedom, light—anything but this infernal darkness. His optimism lasted longer than one would expect, given the circumstances, but eventually, the hope of reprieve dwindled and relinquished. His focus returned to the game and the birthings. He did not look forward to any additional encounters with Abkhas or Messmor for that matter. So…he concentrated on Camen.

He not only wanted the birthing to be successful, but he also wanted Camen to remain as his company—someone he could share his thoughts with long enough to achieve a mental balance, a voice beside his own to rest his weary mind from the constant assault of his unconscious. His desire, his obsession, fueled the ongoing battle between sanity and insanity. The more driven in his obsession, the more present his unconscious. The thought of company provided Omurcada the impetus to sustain the hard-fought and delicate balance as well as generate enough energy to deal with his heightened cerebral activity. He was much more disciplined in controlling his inner self, but that did not reduce the fear of being lost in the foreverness of insanity.

Omurcada shook his head, concentrating on an old and filthy rhyme he'd learned when he was fourteen. "Cocktail, ginger ale, five cents a glass, and if you don't believe me, you can kiss my royal, ask me no questions and I'll give you no lies, but if you get hit by a bucket of shit, be sure and close your eyes…" *That…that dream was too much.* Still shivering from seeing gargoyles and Abkhas riding a two-headed dragon chasing down and devouring humans. The rhyme, though he hated to admit it, had become a reality test. For some reason, he could not recite it in its entirety when he was sleeping. "Time for push-ups." He squatted, quickly adjusting to the appropriate prone position. "Knuckle busters first," he announced loudly, enjoying the resonance of his voice. "Yes, I've been talking to myself... Well, just answering my echoes." He grinned an unseen grin. "Four, five, six... Camen, is today your birthday, or am I chained to another sensation-filled day in this demon's playhouse?" He laughed loudly, again finding security in the echo of his voice.

After 150 push-ups, Omurcada was becoming board. He'd lost his original enthusiasm about being in shape and was finding it difficult to consider the number of push-ups he could do without stopping any feat at all. *If only she could see me now*—thinking of his childhood sweetheart—*I would not have to worry about a conversation or competing with the ninth-grade football team*, he thought. Again, aloud, "Five thousand one hundred and twenty-six multiplied by two hundred and forty-seven equals...one hundred and twenty-three thousand twenty-four... Three hundred and twenty-five multiplied by four hundred and fifty-one equals one hundred forty-six thousand five hundred and seventy-five... Got to keep this mind sharp," he muttered, trying to smile but unable to forestall the boredom. "DAMN THIS PLACE!" he screamed, pounding his fists on the floor. Tears ran in an even flow, burning his eyes and leaving salt residue on his cheeks. Omurcada knew the outburst was just that—an outburst. It would not change his captivity, bring light into the room, open doors, or gain his freedom.

Omurcada closed his eyes and lay his head upon his forearm. He'd grown accustomed to letting the stress ooze out of his system when he rested this way. Despite the constant battle between his conscious and subconscious, his thoughts slowed, and he slipped into a much-needed sleep.

The room shimmered a very deep purple, then violet, then red—carnal red—lips appeared stretched agonizingly over broken yellow teeth. Abkhas silently observed Omurcada.

"Yes, knave, the second birthing's life is spun. An interesting sort he'd be...this one... Aaaaa... Yes...his calculation, stealth, and cunning... My Celtic knave will weep this day's coming." Abkhas continued his quiet musings. Its expression reflected its twisted delight as it prepared for the destruction of Camen. It's chuckle sent shivers and ripples across the atrophied muscles in its face. Abkhas, in this state, could only be described as demonic. It had waited with uncharacteristic patience for the birthing to occur, but waiting was no longer possible. The game had been progressing too quickly.

Omurcada stirred as Abkhas placed an atrophied hand atop his head. Omurcada felt the touch. His heart soared only to be strangled by the sight of Abkhas—a sight that was as quickly lost as perceived. Abkhas's pulsing ember eyes enveloped and rendered Omurcada helpless. Smiling what could have been perceived as a kindness, if one had not known the nature of Abkhas, it pressed greedily forward, forcing Omurcada to sleep while he searched for the birthing. Abkhas burrowed deep, deeper, and finally was thoroughly in control of Omurcada's thought process despite considerably more resistance than it had expected. In anticipation, Abkhas hummed to itself. "A spirit of deviousness this birthing, such a waste of mortal means, but its death will bring me closer to killing Messmor's dream," Abkhas remarked as it narrowed the possible places the birthing could be hidden.

It reached a tendril, finely spun magic guided by Abkhas's thought, down into the hidden crevasses of Omurcada's mind in search of its quarry. "THERE!" it bellowed, removing the orb maliciously. In the same instant, Abkhas, so pleased with his conquest, forgot about Omurcada who, once released, lunged forward swinging his chain forward nearly destroying Abkhas's skull, shattering remnants of its neck. Abkhas's hiss of shock chilled the air but was instantly replaced by his bellow, that deep, guttural, echoing sardonic laughter. Had Omurcada not known he'd struck it with a lethal blow, he would have believed it all to be a dream. Still holding a squirming orb in its left hand, Abkhas's skull reformed and materialized on its original perch. "You impetuous little speck, you intended to hold ME in check? You're as pathetic as the grave, you worthless Celtic knave."

Abkhas began rolling the orb between his finger and thumb. Omurcada could hear the muffled tiny voice of what he presumed to be Camen. Abkhas grinned as only Abkhas could grin. "You believed you could hurt this shape you see? It is merely a shape that pleases me…" Abkhas threw back its head, emitting a deep rumble, a would-be laugh distorted by Abkhas voice and the harmonics of the room. Omurcada's heart sunk though, even to his amazement, he felt no fear of Abkhas. Abkhas continued, "Your birthing has arrived in time for you to enjoy its short existence, its wonder, its pain as I destroy. Yes, squash its tiny shape. I wonder, will it ooze like a grape or simply splatter…? It doesn't matter. Its pain I cannot enjoy. The game is engaged. I have no time to enjoy its sweet cries or tears of the father into the night." Abkhas roared, believing himself wicked beyond comprehension and comedic without equal. All four walls resonated, vibrating the shackles on Omurcada's wrists. Abkhas thrust his face close to Omurcada's. "Your hatred feeds my fire. Your desperation quenches my thirst. You are indeed the knave, the crier I surmised at first."

Abkhas stepped back one step and raised its hand. Omurcada looped a length of chain in each hand then began twirling chains. The chains began to glow. Omurcada ignored the heat whirling the chains faster and faster. The room began to lighten dimly as the chains heated, and Omurcada accelerated the rate of each rotation. The chains had become a blur of soft orange and yellow light. The walls vibrated. The cave rumbled with Abkhas's voice. It continued to roll the birthing back and forth through his fingers.

"You cannot kill me…" Omurcada concentrated as to not show weakness or the pain in his wrists from the heat of the chains. "It is not the time for my death. If it were, you'd have killed me outright and taken the birthing." Omurcada accelerated the chains, causing the air to whistle and his hands to blur.

Abkhas's face began to shift to seriousness, evil, ominous. "The pain I render is much worse than death, earthling."

At that instant, Omurcada struck the hand holding the birthing. Camen's scream, though very high pitched, was deafening. The minuscule orb whizzed over cranny and crook, seeking some method of escape. Abkhas hand reformed mid-reach, and he darted his arm through the air. Omurcada could hardly believe Abkhas could be that agile. His eyes hurt from the light generated by the chains, but he knew he must continue if Camen were to live through this encounter.

Several times, Abkhas nearly gripped the orb only to have the orb slip out of harm's way by the narrowest of margins, or its hands destroyed mid grip, enabling the orb to find freedom once again. Omurcada continued his assault with the chain. Though no permanent damage could be inflicted, the time and energy It required to reconstruct body parts gave the orb a bit more of a chance to find an escape, to fulfill its destiny. For several moments, the three battled. Omurcada steadily attacking Abkhas, Abkhas paying little attention to Omurcada while focusing on reforming hands and reaching for the tiny orb, and Camen searching with all the freshness of his new life for a means of salvation. The little orb zinged to the wall behind Omurcada and paused momentarily. Abkhas struck. As his hand clutched, it felt the heat of the orb. A grin of victory and satisfaction rippled across the remnants of It's face. Just before realizing the heat was simply a very close call, Abkhas witnessed the mighty little orb dash through the hole that had days before contained the chain. Abkhas, stunned by disappearance, stared into the hole, simultaneously backhanding Omurcada with enough force to leave a man-sized imprint of Omurcada in the dirt wall to Omurcada's left. Abkhas could sense the orb had successfully found the second chamber. It growled and shimmered into a haze then reformed into a translucent tendril appearing like slightly visible fog then proceeded through the hole seeming to be sucked into the orb's escape route.

Abkhas arrived in Peace's chamber only to see the orb escape through a small crack in the wall. Abkhas raged with anger, wanting and needing vengeance, knowing the orb had truly escaped. Peace raised her head toward Abkhas, grinning at It's discomfort. Abkhas set her to fire, turned, and shimmered into apparent nonexistence. Peace screamed and smoldered for a few minutes before the healing returned her to normal. "What in god's name was that?" she wondered out loud. "Where did it come from?"

Omurcada lay unconscious on the dungeon floor. Several of his bones were broken. His healing was much slower. Abkhas's voice lingered in the cell. "You shall suffer a thousand deaths for your trouble this day, and when the deaths are done, your birthings shall pay!" The voice was gone—only Omurcada remained. Beneath an unbearable pain, a glimmer of hope burned slightly but brightly. A smile of satisfaction pinned to his lips and a small victory warmed the soul of a knave—a brave knave at that...

* * *

Messmor's concentration broke. He sensed a shift in the game. He had been aware of Abkhas making contact with his minion, but this was different. Abkhas was unusually absent—either no longer on Alluvia or in a place secluded even from Messmor's ability to sense. *Wardings?* Messmor thought.

CHAPTER 11

※

Camen

Camen blinked, not knowing exactly what might have happened to cause him to be sitting on a high stone ledge in the middle of a country that was unknown to him. He sat contemplating the entirety of his existence seated firmly upon the stone ledge. Strong and sturdy, the ledge had survived centuries of abuse from the elements and was not without evidence of its struggles. The ridge face was pocked with oddly shaped smooth depressions, some large enough to be converted to small sleeping quarters, others barely noticeable. Camen had immediately reached the closest depression, which was large enough to press his body into and huddle safely. The shadow from the ridge side obscured the depression and, to a remarkable degree, shielded Camen from detection by anything close to his position. The natural rock walls redirected the wind away from his face. He sat, back tight against the stone yet with enough space to be able to scan the landscape without obstruction. The wind whistled its way, chaffing and withering whatever lay in its path. It seemed to take particular notice of Camen. The steady press of its gait nudged and pressed the indentation swirling eddies all about Camen's face to no avail. Even with unanticipated gusts, it could not pry Camen from his refuge. Camen cautiously pulled the collar close to his throat. He could have sworn the coat bit him as he wiped the last bit of blood from the back of his neck. Camen chuckled to himself despite the odd situation he found himself in. "Bit by a coat, that makes about as much sense as my arrival in this place." He unconsciously adjusted his position while pressing the topcoat more firmly against the momentary respite. Still struggling with the abruptness of the events that had transpired and his complete disorientation with time and place, he stared silently at the shards of the orb that had shattered on the ridge face, leaving him undamaged but utterly alone.

Camen stared at the base of the ridge that he had climbed to escape notice and to find safe cover, finally believing he was safe enough within the escarpment to contemplate what had just occurred. The remnants of the orb dissipated quickly, sending ringlets of dust covering aspects of the ledge scurrying in all directions. What once was his entrapment was no longer—in its place stood a simple stand of grass quietly reshaping itself after having the weight of the orb removed. He pulled the black hood up over his head and fastened the black leather topcoat securely. Even his clothing represented a portion of the mystery. He blended into his surroundings nearly perfectly camouflaged. His rib cage itched and burned from the touching of Abkhas.

"Yes, Abkhas. I know you... I know nearly nothing else, but I know you," Camen muttered aloud.

Camen felt unease at the mention of It's name and the memory of an encounter with it—whatever it was it was named Abkhas.

Camen recounted his inventory, mentally reviewing all that he'd taken from the orb—a single set of clothes (his only set), a small bit of rope and what appeared to be a piano wire coiled but not so tightly as to lose its spring, rations for three days, and flint and stone. He felt the compulsion to go south. Camen trusted nothing. Even his instincts were suspect, but he had no choice but to leave these surroundings and journey forward. He climbed back down the ridge face to the ruined orb to take a final accounting.

The descent was difficult, but not so much so that his mind was prevented from its routine of calculation and recalculation. Bits and pieces of the puzzle were becoming apparent as his memory cleared.

The man in chains had saved his life…but for what purpose? He felt a kinship to the man without explanation. Camen was not particularly fond of kinship with anything but surmised there was a purpose behind whatever the basis for the feeling. *Abkhas…? Well, Abkhas is the enemy, but to what end and for what reason is also part of this riddle*, he thought to himself. Camen stopped momentarily. Sensing eyes upon him, he immediately pressed himself firmly against the ridge face. The cougar blinked…then blinked again, deciding that whatever had been there was no longer. He would need to look elsewhere for his meal. The large cat picked its way down the rock face, sniffing for some sign of nourishment. Lifting its nose to the wind, the cat turned, once again looking downwind in Camen's direction then proceeded westward at a progressively more rapid pace. Camen unstiffened. He had not seen the cat but sensed its presence was no longer near. He proceeded down the rock face dropping gently to the ground below when to do so would not cause harm or create notice.

Camen landed in a crouched position surveying his surroundings. After a moment, satisfied he was unobserved, Camen stretched his lithe elven-like frame to a full standing position. The wind continued to assault but much less vigorously than it had been at the top of the ridge. The escarpment, a lifeless blackened monument to the sheer tenacity of its existence, provided a steady path and a break in the snow line against the ever-pressing forest. Though narrow, the distance between the ridge and the forest provided enough of a gap to allow clear vision for a great distance in either direction. Camen proceeded south along the base, listening intently for any sound, watching closely for any sign of life, and occasionally stopping to dispel the eery feeling that he was never quite alone.

Camen periodically placed his hand upon the cold rocky surface to become more acquainted with the texture of the landscape and to note any vibration that might suggest the presence of others or life beneath the ridge. Camen had noted during the initial examination that the area had been volcanic at one time—volcanic or dragon burned to a substantial extent. Much of the rock face was smooth and mirrored like finely polished black onyx, surrounded by baked, scarred, and rough-cut cinder, the combination of which was at once extraordinarily beautiful yet stark in its presence. As he walked, he continued to observe the landscape for another high point from which he could attempt to gain bearings sufficient to mark this place as the beginning and triangulate locations in the future. He remained curious about life beyond the wildcat that had earlier sensed his presence. There had not been any other signs of human life, but he was sure that human or humanlike life existed, and he would eventually find it. Camen was not particularly bothered by being alone, essentially weaponless, but he knew for some reason he preferred to be among people—well, among them but emotionally close to no one—to observe but to not engage unless a purpose existed to support the entanglement.

Camen finished his ascent to a perch just above the tree line. He could see in several directions. Camen's eyesight, keen and distanced, picked through the baron treetops and the ridge face hesitating to mentally mark undulations in forest density and height, changes in land textures, movements of any kind, but found no certain signs of city life only wisps of smoke that probably meant small dwellings and simpleminded beings. He continued to feel the urge to roam south, but no paths were apparent at the junction between the ridge and the tree line. If trails existed, they were now snow-covered. Camen guessed it would be another quarter of the day before sunset. He surmised he would have time to journey a considerable stretch forward before either stopping for the night or locating life somewhere in the distance. He decided when all else failed, he would ask someone who lived in one of the small dwellings for directions to the nearest town. He was not particularly pleased with the thought of relying on another's perspective or directive, but the choices were limited.

Facing a night in the snow with nothing but a makeshift shelter was equally distasteful. Camen decided to continue toward the wisp of smoke emerging from a place hidden in the woods but where the smoke was the most notable in a southerly direction. He climbed a tall birch tree, thinking it was strange a birch would be in this terrain. Camen triangulated the wisp of smoke using the ridge points as the base and two baren treetops as part of the triangle, then shinnied down the tree.

Camen made his way through the wood at a steady careful pace. His footsteps were remarkably silent, and his path never perfectly straight. He was uncomfortable leaving tracks in the snow, but it was unavoidable. He observed the sparse wildlife, noting the sparseness was likely because of the time of year, had not taken notice of his passing, which pleased him for some reason. He found himself uneasy whenever a bird stopped chirping or a squirrel raised a chin responding to something different in its environment. Camen realized that he was not only very cautious about his movements in an automatic unconscious kind of way, but he was also picking out certain withered remnants of plants and determining sediment types of the landscape by the flora it presented. The forest floor would not be as dense with undergrowth as he expected given the types of withered plants he'd observed. He assumed the dense canopy, that would be present in late spring through late fall, combined with the acidity of the oak trees, kept the competition for sustenance to a minimum through a few elms and a few maples managed to gain a firm hold next to what appeared to be a dry run or a creek bank not that far in front of him. Camen assumed the soil was rich from years of deciduous droppings with an occasional bit of sand where the water that could not be absorbed would run more easily. All the while, he assessed and observed his mind continually wandered back to his existence and his persona.

Why on one hand he needed to be with people yet, on the other, preferred to be alone among them? Why did he seem to want to be in the city yet also seem to know the plant life in the forest in more detail than would be commonly expected? "Mysteries," he said aloud, hushing the birds closest to him. He nodded to the sparrow eyeballing him closely. "Better to keep my thoughts to myself, I see," he whispered.

Camen negotiated the creek bank, stood silently for a moment. He stepped to the edge of the very narrow frozen creek, noting weak points in the ice along the bank. Placing his left foot on the ice edge, he very slowly applied pressure until the ice nearly gave way. Realizing the cracking ice would echo a small distance, he looked for something to muffle the sound from the ice he intended to break.

Nothing but tree bark, he thought to himself. He looked at his coat and for a moment thought of placing it on the ice but could not bring himself to risk damage to the coat—a curious decision in and of itself. He resolved to risk the noise. *No choice*. He reasserted pressure with his left foot, using his heel to press the ice downward and the ball of his foot to brace the opposite side of where he believed the ice would break. *Pop!* The ice broke with relative ease and near silence. He quickly surveyed the area then relaxed after being satisfied that he was not being intruded upon. Camen knelt, removed the chunk of ice, and tasted the frigid water never relaxing his vigilance continually reviewing his surroundings. *Seems safe enough. No odd tastes…very clear.*

He swallowed a small amount, enough to sustain fluid but not enough to become very ill if the water were tainted, he hoped. Camen unfastened the topcoat, not wanting to experience the intrusion of the cold but understanding it was necessary, and removed a small water bag from one of many hideaways in the long coat. He dipped the water bag at an angle that reduced the gurgling sound of its filling. Once filled, he carefully placed the small water bag back inside its particular pocket. He stood slowly then noiselessly refastened his topcoat. *Useful coat*, he thought as he checked the pockets and *definitely mine*, it seemed tailored to fit. Camen pulled the collar tight, jumped the narrow stream, traversed the opposite bank, and continued his way toward where he believed the wisp of smoke originated.

The evening was near upon him when he spotted the small but well-constructed dwelling. He could hear the humming of what he thought to be a woman. He continued to inspect the surrounding. *No livestock. Hmm…farmers maybe…but no major clearings*, he thought. With additional observation, he detected a series of plots where trees could have been formerly but no longer existed. The areas encircled the dwelling, and though snow-covered, the absence of trees and the common shape made the plots very distinguishable once one noted their presence. Camen noticed three well-traveled trails in the snow. Two of the trails headed southerly and one to the northwest not too far from his current position. He scanned the paths, attempting to determine the distance from his position as well as the distance they traveled into the wood. While scanning, he heard the door creak open. A small squat creature, with a large ax, stepped forward then turned facing the dwelling. It motioned another squat creature, that appeared to be female, forward. *Dwarves? What sort of land is this?* he wondered to himself. Though it was not totally illogical… *The ridge was very unusual… but what would they be doing in a wooden dwelling instead of the mountains… Mystery upon mystery…*, he thought as he scratched his nose then unconsciously rubbed his hands together to bring his fingers warmth.

Camen quickly scanned the trees closest to him and moved quietly to a very large oak. Satisfied the dwelling and the inhabitants would remain in view, he leaned his back against the tree, feeling more comfortable with the black-gray background as opposed to the white snow. As he waited and watched the couple converse, he surmised it was time to get wood to keep the dwelling warm, but it was late enough in the afternoon that the male did not want to go far from home. Camen continued to press himself into the tree. Feeling more and more at peace with his chosen cover, he decided he could remain there a bit longer. The northwest path was only a few feet from where he had positioned. He could make himself known once he was more comfortable with the creature's intent.

"Aye me, darlin', its gettin' aboot time ta get thot rick o wood from the west. A chill's upon us again tho spring'll be comin' soon." Shim grinned at his wife, Brianae.

"Off with ya then, and DON'T be carryin' all thot wood down the hill. Take the sled with ya." Brianae waved Shim on, half pushing him, out the door.

"Boot carryin' them is easier woman!" Shim protested.

Brianae laughed. "And you'll be complainin' more about the slivers ya get in your fingers than you do those that you get in your arse."

Shim winked at Brianae then kissed her gently. "Yer never gonna hear me complain aboot slivers in my arse when 'tis yer soft and gentle fingers thot pull 'em out."

They both laughed, then Brianae shushed Shim and sent him on his way, closing the door behind him. Shim hoisted the ax upon his shoulder, walked around to the back of the dwelling, fastened the sled's pull rope to his waist, and proceeded up the path.

Camen watched the exchange, determining the two must be mated. He was surprised he could make out their language though the male's low guttural rasps were more difficult to understand. His observation was nearly interrupted by his growing feeling of comfort, a oneness, next to the large oak tree. He looked to the tree and noticed his sleeve was nearly the same texture as the tree bark… With a quick and startling review, Camen realized that his entire topcoat was nearly a complete match for the tree. He also noted upon disconnecting from the tree his coat was changing rapidly, and the feeling of comfort was absent. He pressed his back to the tree a second time and waited. The feeling slowly returned, and Camen observed the very, very gradual change in the texture of the coat. *Amazing*, he thought.

"Ye lake thot tree, laddie," Shim's voice boomed.

Camen jumped away from the direction of the voice. Cat rolled then reached deep into his coat for something that evidently was not included. Realizing how absurd he must look, Camen straightened up.

"You startled me, sir."

Shim laughed aloud. "Sɪʀ, is it! Haʀ, I dinnae grow these whiskers, carry an axe, and marry a hofling ta be saddled with that soort o title. Am no sɪʀ, laddie. M'name is Shim. Me and m'wife, Brianae, live in tha hoose." He pointed. "And yer name moost be Joompin Jamie O'Floops an Rools, haʀhaʀ." Shim leaned on his axe, glanced at the house, grinned mischievously, the pulled a flask from his belt satchel. He lifted the flask and tipped it slightly, taking a small drink then sucking in air and blinking the tears away offered the same to Camen. "Ye woont a nip o tha good stuff, laddie? It'll warm yer boones and take off tha chill."

Camen took the flask and smelled the contents—sweet and sharp at the same time. "Fine brew…elderberry and…corn whiskey." Camen handed the flask back to Shim. "That's quite a combination, Shim… Very skillfully prepared."

"Then DRINK it, laddie. Doon't be turnin' a friend away," Shim instructed with a wide grin.

Camen resisted the urge to tell Shim they were not friends. "I stay away from the dwarven brews. They tend to make a fool of me." Camen smiled convincingly.

Shim hesitated then gulped some more. "But thot's the reasoon ta drink it, laddie, ta act lake a fool even when yer nut."

Camen laughed. "I'll try to remember that. Thank you for offering, but I'll have to pass."

Shim eyeballed Camen. "Yer knew ta these parts, laddie. I knoow nearly oll tha payple froom tha region, and ye look a bit elven, half-elf I'd guess."

Camen smiled, knowing he needed to continue the conversation to secure haven but was very intent upon giving little information and gaining as much as he could. Giving little would be easy.

I don't know much, he thought, but even letting that be known would give up more than he'd like. "No I'm not from these parts, and I've never seen one like you. Are you a dwarf?"

Shim nearly spit out his fine homebrew. "O' COURSE AM A DWARF." He laughed. "And PROOUD OF IT" he bellowed to the wood, turning a pirouette and bowing to Camen.

Camen could not help but chuckle. "Why do you live in a wooden house then instead of the mountains?" Camen asked.

"Mountains?" Shim scowled. "Myyyy laddie, they be telling ya stories lake that where ye come from? Next thing ye knew, they'd be tellin' ya thot we're affeered of spirits and faeries." Shim suddenly quieted and looked both directions. "Ye dinnae see any on the way, did ye?" he whispered to Camen.

"No…no, I didn't," Camen replied.

"O' COURSE YE DINNAE SEE ANY 'CAUSE THEY DUN LIVE HERE!" Shim bellowed, turning another half circle as if to announce his proclamation to the entire world.

Camen grimaced. "A little loud, don't you think?"

Shim pulled the flask from his lips, not looking at Camen but whispered in a voice that Camen could understand easily, "Not everything is as it seems, laddie. FAERIES AND SPIRITS, HAR, ye never knew who's listenin' or watchin'. Why bri an' me eat faeries fer breakfoost ond fart spirits afta sooper, and am shure I appear ta be soomethin' quite different from what I am"—*burp*—"much like ye…a thief or assassin ye be I know not which, aye, faeries and spirits all be splittin' lake tha rick o wood 'ave piled in tha snoow… Yer not froom Tent Town, but ye may as well be. Yer welcome ta spend the night, knew questions osked if ye help me with tha wood, but let it be known that all cut yer throat befoore ye can squeal if ye decide ta do anything I or me missus disapproove oof… Am droonk as a dorf can be… A moog o' ale an' a good place ta peeeeeee"—*burp*. Shim unfastened the rope from his waist. Camen resisted comment—"Thot is an interesting coat, laddie. One not seen ooften in these parts…or anywhere near here. 'Ave oonly seen one…the wearer of thot coat woould nut find himself in these woods without a reason. What's yer reason, laddie?"

Camen did not move as Shim positioned the tip of the dagger, with an admirable amount of stealth, near Camen's kidney all the while whispering and watching. "I don't remember who I am except that my name is Camen."

Shim's feet were well above his head before he realized that Camen had gained leverage, swept Shim's legs while wrist locking Shim's right hand with Camen's left and dislodging the dagger that had been aimed at Camen's kidney. Shim's shoulders were hitting the snow as Camen snatched the dagger from the air. Camen knelt next to Shim with the point of the dagger touching the crease between Shim's throat and the bottom of his chin. Camen smiled a very cold steeled smile.

"Where's the wood?" he asked as he stepped away.

Shim stood up and brushed off the snow. "A wood mule is what I am, a wood mule. Nicely doone, laddie. Can I have tha dagger back?"

Camen flipped the dagger and tossed it to Shim handle first. Shim caught the knife and pointed to the woodpile.

Before long, the two had the sled and two sacks full of wood, but neither said a word till just before they reached the front door. Shim stopped and looked squarely into Camen's eyes.

"Am a changed mon b'cause of me wife. There's still a bit o' thief in me. I doon't want her hurt."

Camen nodded without feeling. "I have no intention of hurting either of you. I have no reason to," he stated flatly.

Shim nodded. "Aye... Yer kind oonly needs the reason. Be it mooney, principool, or yer foon."

Camen's eyes remained devoid of emotion. "If I wanted to hurt you, we wouldn't be discussing this."

Shim rubbed his chin. "True. But even ye have to sleep, remember that." They both grinned. "Am hooome, woman, ond the woods are safe from faeries and spirits," he bellowed.

The door opened. Brianae smiled at Camen. "Company, dear?"

Shim kissed her. "Aye, a guest for tha night. Camen...is...an acquaintance of mine froom tha oold days. He's harmless enoof tho."

Camen bowed. "M'lady Brianae, I've heard nothing but good things about you from your husband. A lucky man he is indeed."

Brianae blushed and kissed Shim. "He's a liar but a fine one at that. Supper is near cooked. Fire is stoked, and there's a cradle for guests near the fireplace end. We're not used to folks as tall as you. The chairs are a bit small, but the fire's warm, so ya might want to set yer boots near the fire."

"Very much obliged, m'lady."

"Bah, m'lady, sir, next thing ye knew, he'll be callin' us lord and...and...hmm—" Shim's voice was lost to Brianae's interruption.

"Hush!" Brianae admonished Shim. "He's been more respectful than most the sots you run with, so shush and help me finish supper."

Shim grinned, then winked at Camen. "Ain't she tha livin' end, har!"

Camen pulled his boots off, expecting the stench from feet without air, mixed with wet leather, but to his amazement, the boots were not wet inside or out. They repelled the water yet allowed his feet to breathe. His socks were dry. Brianae glanced in his direction.

"Go ahead and take your socks off. Warm yourself by the fire."

Camen nodded. "Thank you, m'lady."

Shim shook his head while raising an eyebrow then walked to the fireplace, bent, took a long stick from the fire, and lit his large pipe.

Puffing just a moment then inhaling deeply, he coughed smoke out of his nose and mouth. "Dam, woman, this year's botch is a bit dry, doon't ya think?"

Brianae smiled then motioned to her husband to come hither. Brianae handed Shim a large spoon. "Keep the stew from burnin' if ya can manage and give me that pipe."

Shim laughed. "Shure…am ta stir the steew and yer goona have a smoke. A fine lady ye are, HAR." Brianae giggled and took a long draw from the pipe. After a moment, she exhaled through her nose. "Ya put that dam corn whiskey in the tabacca again, didn't y? O Lord of the Booze Barrel!" She turned eyes narrowed but twinkling.

Shim's face reddened. "Just a we pinch, m'dear, a dinnae think ye would notice sooch a small amoont." Shim laughed self-consciously.

"Well, it's all you're gonna get to smoke till it's gone, and I'm smoking the ring barrel tabacca all the while you're sufferin' and a coughin'."

"THE RING BARREL! Why…why… THOT'S PURE GOLD yer smokin'! I was goona sell thot barrel ta Loyd McNamara fer one hundred gold pieces!"

Brianae pulled the pipe from her mouth. "One hundred gold pieces! You said seventy-five gold pieces the last time we talked about it? What's this about?" She turned to face Shim, pointing the pipe at him. "And just what were you gonna spend the twenty-five gold pieces on? Ale? Corn whiskey? That putrid elven swill they sell at stubs?" She pushed him backward, jamming the pipe into his chest. "No candies for the missus. Nooooooo. No linens or cloth or food stores. Just that putrid swill that you think makes you act and smell manly!" She placed her hands on her hips, cocked her head. "Deny what I'm sayin', Shim Patrick MacDonaugh."

Shim, without taking his eyes off his wife, dipped the soup ladle into the stew behind him, swiveled it to his lips, placing his left hand beneath to prevent any stew from hitting the floor and gulped a large gulp of stew.

"Why, me love, this stew hos ta be sooom of tha finest stew ye ever made. Come taste this, Camen." He stepped away from his wife. "Here, laddie, haave a taste o the woorld's finest stew." He winked at Camen.

Brianae, wise to her husband's tricks, nodded. "Go ahead, Camen. Taste the stew. I'll season it to your taste. You just tell me what it needs." She swatted Shim. "And you…"

Camen raised an eyebrow. "Zeason to my taste? You have a store of different seasonings out here?"

Brianae smiled. "Yes, yes, I do. We have a small cellar for roots and dried plants. I'm a bit of a healer for these parts, so as I collect herbs and roots, I also pick up seasonings or trade for such whenever possible."

Camen nodded. "Very resourceful," he said as he took the ladle and tasted. Camen's mouth watered immediately. The stew was divine.

Brianae waited, tapping her toe. "Well, what is it missing?"

"Nothing. It's quite good," Camen replied.

"NOTHING, IT'S QUITE GOOD!" Shim bellowed. "There's NONE better, and it is still missing something!"

Brianae's mouth dropped. She turned to square off with her husband for a second round when Shim's booming dwarvin' laugh thundered, "IT'S MISSING A BOWL, WOMAN, A BOWL! HARHAR."

Brianae's eye's twinkled. "Ya old fool!" She swatted him with her apron.

Brianae filled a bowl full of stew and handed the bowl and some sweet bread to Camen.

"Thank you, m'lady," Camen offered.

"You're most welcome, Camen," Brianae replied. She started to walk back toward the stove then turned. "Our custom is to bed for the night after supper, but there is plenty of light by the fire, so make yourself ta home."

"Thanks again, m'lady, but I need the sleep as well. With my belly full of stew and sweet bread and my feet next to the fire, I think sleep will take me quickly." Camen spooned a large chunk of beef into his mouth.

"Blanket's under the cradle, and there's a hook for your coat on the wall above you," she hesitated, "or you can just cover yourself with it whatever makes you comfortable."

Camen nodded and slowly chewed the stew analyzing the tastes.

"Be shore and keep an eye oopen, laddie. Ya never knew when a sprite or faerie might try ta take yer boots, HARHAR!"

Camen's face only hinted the steel his eyes aimed toward Shim while his smile masked all emotion from Brianae. "I'm not too afraid of sprites or faeries with you in house." He finished the stew, but before he could set the bowl down, Brianae swept it away to the washbasin. He couldn't help but notice despite the humor and homi* ness the couple provided, they both were very agile and intelligent in their own way, both attributes masked to a remarkable degree by the nonchalance of their manner.

Shim scratched his beard and fired the pipe he'd managed to slip away from the table while Brianae was occupied with putting dishes away. Brianae expressed her good nights and retired to the couple's small bedroom adjacent to the kitchen.

"Don't be long, Shim," she added as she pulled the makeshift curtain across the entryway. Shim pulled the stool closer to the cradle Camen was sitting on. Though remaining faced to the fire and rubbing his hands as if to warm them, Shim renewed his conversation with Camen.

"Soo...ye never been ta Tent Town, have ye?"

Camen finished pulling off his socks and setting them across the cradle's headpiece. "No, I've not ever had the pleasure."

"Pleshure, hehe, well, I wooodn't call it pleshure. Ye really dinnae come froom around these parts, do ye?"

Camen watched Shim closely. "No, I'm not. So tell me how far is the nearest town from here?"

Shim exhaled a large cloud of smoke slowly. "Journeyman's Sleep is aboot a half day's walk from here...straight sooth. Ye knew tha difference butween noort and sowt, laddie?"

Camen nodded yes as he leaned his back to the wall and set his bare feet closer to the fire.

"Journeyman's Sleep is an odd toon split butween thoose thot have near noothin' and those thot have soomethin'. There is a coonstant war butween tha two factions. Tent Town is coonsidered tha sloom of tha region. Fool of brigands, thieves, pickpockets, and tha lake." Shim hesitated.

Camen noted the subtle shift and the twinkle of memory spark Shim's eyes. "You from Tent Town, Shim?" Camen asked.

"Aye, many years ago… A different life…a different time, laddie. Aye, a different man was I." Shim shook his head. "A thief and a brigand I woos. Cut yer throat and pocket yer purse withoot a care in the woorld aboot whoo ye looved or whoo loved ye. I hod no Da or Ma ta teach me tha ways of tha woorld, soo I joined tha MacAndrews"—Shim smiled, puffing his pipe—"and friends."

Shim cleared his throat and resituated his position on the stool. "Was a loong tayme agoo, laddie, boot there are days thot tha oold life pulls at the whiskers of an oold dwarf."

Camen nodded. "Hard to let go of who you are no matter what the reasons to change may be."

Shim laughed quietly for a change. "And how woould ye knew about thot, Camen?"

Camen frowned. "A boy believes he's someone by the voice of his friends. A man knows he's someone by the voice of his heart… A killer knows he's someone because anyone who disagrees is already dead."

Shim grinned nervously. "A philosoopher ye are, laddie, knew thot I woouldn't a guessed…especially froom one such as ye." Shim shook his head.

"One such as me? You don't know me from anyone, Shim. You make assumptions and act on your calculations. You've experienced some success doing such, and now you believe you can, in a glance, determine who I am and who I am not. It's a dangerous game." Camen sat forward. "One that will get you killed in the right and the wrong places."

Shim watched Camen closely. "Aye, I make assoomptions true enough…so do ye, boot back ta my questioon, O Lord of Philosophers, how woould ye knew about the heart?"

Camen smiled an emotionless smile. "There are many ways to obtain the information you desire. You could release a captured moth to see which way it travels and follow it for months to see how strong it is…or…you could stick a needle through its back and watch closely for exactly how long it would take for it to expire. The same conclusion from differing points of view."

Shim nodded. "Yer a coold-hearted bastard ye are, Camen."

Camen smiled. "Worse, I'm a heartless bastard, Shim. I don't care whether I'm a man by the measure of my peers or my heart. Both are tools to an end, and the end…the end is what I decide, and the conclusion is what I determine. I'm satisfied with that."

Shim nodded, feeling more uneasy. "Soo…what doo ya plan ta doo next, laddie…O Joodge and Joory?"

Camen sat back. "Sleep, Shim…with one eye open, not because I'm afraid of you or your missus." Camen smiled. "'Cause I need the practice."

Shim cleared his throat. "Ye knew what I mean, laddie."

Camen opened both eyes. "No, I don't intend to harm you or your wife, but I would not assume that I can be trusted. My motives may have changed the next time we meet. I do appreciate the hospitality, but do not mistake it for affection or a feeling of indebtedness. I carried the wood. I earned my keep. Tomorrow, I'll be gone."

Shim scratched his beard. "One thing poozzles me, laddie."

"What's that?" Camen responded.

"Why woould ye be soo free in sharin' yer philosophy with me?" Shim asked.

Camen closed one eye. "Why do you think I would be so willing to share with you, Shim?"

Shim scratched his ear. "I dinnae know, laddie, oonless yer thinkin' ye can shoot me up permanently whenever ye want."

Camen chuckled. "When's the last time you practiced?"

"Practiced what?" Shim responded.

"Sleeping with one eye open."

Shim coughed. "I think a'll be dooin' thot this night, laddie." Shim stood, pointed the pipe at Camen. "Aye, I think all be dooin' thot this night."

Camen leaned his body to rest at a forty-five-degree angle with his coat pulled to his neck and the blanket he'd been given by Brianae over top. "No worries this night, Shim...no worries...and tell your missus the dagger she slipped under her dress will not be needed unless of course it was meant for you."

Shim grinned then shook his head. "I might groow ta lake ye, laddie, if thar woos one redeemin' quality ta pick from."

Camen laughed despite himself. "Rest easy, Shim."

Shim shook his head and entered the small bedroom. "Oouch, gods, WOMAN, woot in Bridget's name ya dooin' with a dagger in BED!"

The three slept the night without incident.

CHAPTER 12

---　✿　---

The Artist

A small crowd gathered around what appeared to be an injured woman, unconscious, just inside the castle's courtyard. The Captain of the Guard had been summoned to the scene.

"Back! Back away! Let me through!" the sergeant of the guard cleared the way for his captain. "Out of the way!" he bellowed, not quite shoving the royal visitors but making it apparent that he would not stand for any more interference. The onlookers—dukes and duchesses, earls, knights from distant lands, and their squires alike—moved back to let the sergeant and captain through.

The sergeant finally pressed his way beyond the last ring of gawkers discovering that what had been reported to him by Sir Edmund's squire was true—a woman dressed in the finest of silks lay unconscious in the king's courtyard. A woman who no one could identify but obviously was of royal origins. The sergeant stood silently looking at the woman, wondering what, if anything, he was supposed to do when his captain shoved him aside.

In an instant, the captain barked, "Water and a priest, Sergeant. Send Corporal Danahee for the water, and you fetch the priest."

Sergeant Timmer didn't hesitate. Raised in the woodlands by Colonel Lanzo, he felt out of place serving as sergeant of the guard, but he'd been recommended by Lanzo himself, so rather than serving in the woodlands of his home, here he was, doing his duty in a different way. *At least they allowed me to keep my bow*, he thought.

"Danahee! Get your lame butt over here on the double. Grab a canteen of fresh water and take it to Captain Montgomery now!"

Danahee saluted. "Yes, sir! On the double, sir!" as Danahee turned Sergeant Timmer caught sight of the grin and kicked Danahee squarely in the rump.

"And don't call me sir again, you little weasel!"

They both laughed while neither slowed in accomplishing their duties. Corporal Danahee had gotten along well with "Timmers" from the start. The sergeant was not like many of the others. He was not afraid to work as hard as any underlying nor was he afraid to tangle with any member of the ranks if the need be...officer or not. All respected his skill with a long sword and dagger, but some had laughed at the bow until he put three arrows in a would-be assassin before anyone could move to interrupt the attempt on the king's life. If it hadn't been for Timmers, King Edmund II would no longer be on the throne. His promotion to full colonel was planned to take place next week. No one expected a nonroyal to be elevated to royal status and be given lands, but then again, no one expected a nonroyal to be the one to save the king's life. Timmer's good fortune had not changed his disposition a bit. He still was Timmer and likely would remain that way regardless of his station. Danahee worried that Timmer may have difficulty dealing with the ogre assigned to protect the royal family since Timmer would be the first colonel assigned to the same function in the history of the kingdom.

Sergeant Timmer arrived at the castle's infirmary to find the White Wizard was gone and the Holy Cleric of Constradista absent as well.

"Great," he muttered to himself. *My choices are now Herb or that idiot Sylince John S... Poor woman... Well...a poor healer is better than no healer at all*, he thought as he headed out the castle gates into the city of Constradista.

"Where's that water, Danahee?" Captain Montgomery turned, looking for the corporal.

"Here, sir." Danahee saluted and handed the captain the canteen.

"Where's the healer?"

Corporal Danahee shrugged. "Sergeant Timmer was heading through the castle gate the last I saw him."

"Good god, man, the Holy Cleric isn't in the castle again? What's come over the old geezer these days? He's never where he should be when we need him, which seems more frequent every day."

Corporal Danahee shrugged a second time. "Anything else, sir?"

Captain Montgomery knelt, poured some water in the palm of his hand, and splashed it on the lady's face. *No reaction*, he thought. The captain laid his hand on the woman's abdomen and felt the very slight rise and fall. "She's still alive. WHERE'S THAT PRIEST!"

Sergeant Timmer burst into Herb's Herbs, the local apothecary. "HERB! YOU HERE?" The halfling peeked over a set of potted shrubs he was about to set on the second shelf of his greenhouse.

"Yes, yes, I'm here Sergeant Timmer! Must you yell and disturb my plants? Have some respect for the beings that offer their life to sustain you, man!"

Sergeant Timmer grimaced. "This is no time for lectures, Herb. Come with me immediately. We have a lady in distress in the Castle Courtyard and no priest to attend to her."

"No priest? Where's His Hooooliness? Out baptizing virgins into womanhood again?"

Timmer couldn't help but smile at Herb's insinuation. He wasn't the first nor would he be the last to make the not so veiled accusation. "If His Holiness were available, I would not be here to obtain your services now, would I?"

Herb acknowledged Sergeant Timmer's assessment, wiped his hands on his apron, and asked Timmer, "What is wrong with the lady that you would require my services?"

Timmer laughed out loud. "If I could answer that question, why would I need you to come with me? Now get your rump movin', man! The cap'n's waiting!"

Herb scurried ahead of Timmer without complaint. The two made their way back to the Castle Courtyard in no time.

"Out of the way!" Timmer barked to the onlookers as they moved a little too slowly for his liking.

The captain spotted Herb. "Here, Priest, over here."

Herb stopped. "I'm a cleric. I am not anything like His Holiness."

The captain frowned. "I need a healer. I don't care whether you're of the same order as His Holiness or a backwoods cleric. Can you heal?"

"Well," Herb offered, "it depends on the condition. Let me see the lady."

The captain stepped aside.

Herb knelt close to the woman, placing his ear to her chest to listen for the strength of the heart—weak but steady, he noted. He looked over the woman's arms for bruises or marks. Seeing none, he began to reach for her dress and decided against it with so many onlookers. He placed his hand under her head slowly. Intending to feel the bones in her neck, he noted a lump on the back of her head above and to the left of her knowledge knot. He lifted her eyelid then the other, noting the pupils were different sizes.

"Hmm, she either fell and hit her head or was attacked judging by the lump on her head," Herb offered the captain.

"Well, what are we to do?"

Herb stood. "She appears to be from a well-to-do family or royalty even. Does anyone know who she is?"

The captain shook his head. "No. No one has ever seen her before. I guess it would not harm to take her to the queen. Maybe she'll know what to do."

Herb nodded his head. "Good idea, Captain. I'll send a poultice to the castle with instructions as to how it should be applied to the back of her head and some herbs that are to be added to boiling water and given to her to drink once the concoction cools."

The captain nodded his head. "Timmer!"

"Yes, Captain, behind you, sir."

"Go with Herb and gather what he needs. Bring the poultice and the herbs to the castle post haste."

Timmer saluted. "Yes, sir," and followed Herb as ordered to his shop.

The queen chastised the captain for assuming she would take in any mongrel that happened to faint on the castle grounds as she passed the captain on her way to the maid's bedchamber where the captain's men deposited the unconscious now-moaning woman. The queen stepped into the chamber, still disgusted intending on getting a good look at this vagabond then sending her on her way like she would any uninvited trespasser. Herb and Timmer were already there. Herb had applied the poultice and was attempting to force the woman to drink his concoction but was not having much success getting the liquid to seep into the woman's mouth. Timmer was busy trying to prevent the odd-colored liquid from reaching the silk gown the lady was wearing. Seeing the texture of the silk, the multitude of complexities in the fabric, and the intricate weaves applied to the outer and undergarments, the queen stepped forward quickly.

"CAREFUL, you idiots, that gown is worth a fortune."

The queen noticed the silver amulet—amethyst set with emerald. "When was she discovered, and who was near her?"

Timmer relinquished the towel to the queen who pushed Herb to the side and proceeded to makes sure the woman, the gown, and the amulet were protected.

"I asked a question, Colonel, I mean, Sergeant Timmer."

Timmer snapped to attention. "Sir Edmond's squire found her and reported she was unconscious with no one near."

The queen frowned. "Sir Edmond's squire? Sir Edmond's squire has not returned from Largo's Trader. Are you sure?"

"It was reported to be Sir Edmond's squire by one of Captain Montgomery's men, Your Highness. That is all I know. We rushed to see whether the report was true and found the lady in this condition."

The queen nodded. "It's no wonder she received a bump on the head strolling around with a king's ransom worth of gown and jewelry." The queen stood up. "Take her to Princess Elyanna's bed-chamber. Oooblem Silvershadow will be close by. I will instruct him to guard the woman personally. Timmer, you stand with Oooblem until I can determine a course of action."

Timmer nodded. "Yes, Your Highness." He bowed then hesitated. "Shouldn't the king be advised?"

The queen's expression failed to change. "Timmer, haven't you noticed the king has not been himself? I have instructed Commander Ebon to find His Holiness to examine the king, but His Holiness is nowhere to be found. Until the king is feeling better, I am acting on his behalf. Do you have a problem with that?"

"Of course not, Your Highness."

Timmer bowed again, masking any opinion he might have in deference to the queen's authority. The queen touched Timmer's shoulder. He halted and turned to face her immediately. "Your Highness?"

Queen Myranda smiled. "We've known each other since I was a girl, a would-be princess, and you were the peasant boy sneaking into the castle to catch a glimpse of the castle guard."

Timmer smiled, thinking back to those times then regained his composure as a soldier in the service of His Majesty. "I remember well, Your Highness. Is there something else you desire?"

The queen looked directly into Timmer's eyes, causing him to flinch a bit. He'd always been loyal to Myranda. They'd been childhood friends and would always have a deep affection for each other, but both knew and only desired the friendship, that be as it may, it was a closeness that was a bit more than a brother and a sister and a bit less than lovers.

"What's your opinion of the king? Tell me honestly."

Timmer gulped and looked in both directions. "Well."

Just then, a shadow blocked the sunlight that had been beaming into the room. Timmer reached for his sword only to find a very, very large hand swallowing up his hand, arm, and elbow, and a second hand firmly grasping his opposite shoulder and arm.

"Yooze dun wunt ta do dat, Timmer. Dis is meez place o' duty, not yoooz place. Meez dun wunt ta hurt yooz, but meez will if yooze dun take dat hand of o dat sword."

The ogre stood nearly eight feet tall, easily six hundred pounds of knotted muscle, hair, and flesh.

"Gods, Oooblem, you could announce yourself before you scare the life out of me!" Timmer's face turned red, then the shock registered, and he knelt quickly in front of the queen. "Begging your pardon for the outburst, Your Highness. My deepest apology."

She giggled. "Stand up, Timmer. Release him, Oooblem."

"As yooz wish, ma lady." Oooblem set Timmer free and bowed as only an ogre could.

Timmer frowned. "I should have your head, Oooblem. The queen should be addressed 'Your Highness,' not like a common maid in waiting!"

Queen Myranda began to protest but could not get Oooblem to stop before he'd followed Timmer's command. "Okay...if yooz say dat's what meez supposed ta do, den dat's what meez will do..." Oooblem took a deep breath. "As yooz wish, Yoooz Hine-ass." He bowed again as only an ogre could do.

Timmer's face flustered, not knowing whether to simply be angry or draw his sword. Queen Myranda burst out laughing.

"I tried to stop him and to tell you, Timmer. Never ask Oooblem to address me as Your Highness. It always comes out that way." She giggled again. "And he is trying to be as respectful as possible. Our language is still difficult for him even though he's quite bright for an ogre."

Oooblem smiled wide, his large yellow eyes the size of saucers danced with pride and affection for his queen. "Yooz is too kind ta meez, Ma Lady Myranda."

The queen stopped him from bowing again. "What do you think, Oooblem?"

Oooblem hesitated. "About da king?"

Oooblem clarified. "Da king is da king, but da king isn't where he's supposed ta be."

The queen nodded.

"What is that supposed to mean?" Timmer asked.

Oooblem looked down at Timmer. "Meez always hab liked yooze, Timmer, but yooz is actin' like yooz is meez commander. Meez dun tink yooz ebber be meez commander, so yooz needs ta settle yooz self down sum. Yooz know what meez means, or does Oooblem have ta wack yooz one so yooz knows what Oooblem means?"

Timmer's face turned red. The queen covered her mouth. Timmer looked up at Oooblem. "ARE YOU threatening me?"

Oooblem looked startled. "Nope. Meez just tellin' yooz du truth and makin' sure yooz understands du truth for what it is. So yooz understand, or does Oooblem have ta wack yooz one so you knows what Oooblem means?"

Timmer shook his head. "I understand perfectly."

"Dat's gud. Weez shud get along gud den."

Timmer cleared his throat. "What did you mean before?"

"Meez thought yooz just said yooz understood!" Oooblem responded.

"Not that. I mean, about the king," Timmer clarified.

"Oh, du king. Wull, du king is du king, but du king is not du king like du king supposed ta be."

Timmer shook his head and looked helplessly to the queen. Myranda stepped past Timmer. "What do you mean the king is not 'du king like du king is supposed ta be'?"

Oooblem grinned. "Yooz kin talk just like du ogres, ma lady." He took another deep breath. "Meez is meanin' dat du king is still du king. Yooz understand?" he asked the queen.

"Yes, I believe I understand dat part."

Oooblem nodded as if he were addressing two infants, he spoke very slowly. "But du king is not du king like the king is supposed ta be. Yooz understand dat?"

The queen said, "No, how can the king be the king and not be the king he is supposed to be? That makes no sense to me. I saw him earlier sitting on the throne."

Oooblem interrupted, "Nooooo. Yooz saw du king dat wus not du king sittin' on du throne."

The queen's eyebrows narrowed. "You mean there's an imposter on the throne? Impossible. I know my husband well."

Oooblem took a deep breath, looking a Timmer and the queen as if they hadn't a brain in their heads. "Dat King is yooz husband, but yooz look close du king is not dere," Oooblem stated flatly.

Timmer started to realize what Oooblem was saying. "Not an impostor. It's the king, but someone or something is controlling him…sort of keeping the king prisoner inside his own body."

Oooblem's large yellow eyes danced as he patted Timmer on the head, nearly knocking him senseless. "Dere's hope for dis one, ma lady." Oooblem grinned. "Dis one ain't as stupid as sum of dem guards yooz hab."

The queen, still puzzled looked at Timmer, said, "Is he saying the king's possessed?"

Timmer shook his head. "I think he's saying the king's controlled, not really possessed or you would see it more clearly."

Oooblem smiled again. "See! Dat one's petty smart. Meez took du little ones to da safe place yooz and meez knows about. Dey will be safe dere, ma lady. If yooz wunt meez ta watch du new petty lady, meez will make sure she's watched gud."

The queen, still in deep thought, motioned Oooblem and Timmer to guard the woman. "I'm going to my children. Timmer, you assist Oooblem, and, Oooblem…"

"Yes, ma lady?" he responded.

"Send your emissary to keep guard of my children as soon as it's possible to do so safely." The queen stepped then turned. "And I want you personally to keep an eye on the king." She hesitated. "Put your battle armor on. I want whatever decides to come into this castle without permission to understand the meaning of fear."

Oooblem bowed. "Yes, ma lady. Meez will dress in meez light battle armor, ma lady, mezz queen." Oooblem straightened then turned to look down at Timmer. "Kin yooz watch du petty lady for a little while? Meez needs ta grab meez armor, sword, and hammer."

The queen interrupted, "Not your heavy battle armor?"

Oooblem nodded, "Duh hebby armor will hab eberyone in duh castle running away."

The queen thought for a moment and chuckled, "You're right, of course." She turned to Timmer and said, "Stand guard while Oooblem gets his light battle armor."

Timmer agreed, wondering if Oooblem could look any more frightening than he already did to someone who'd not seen an ogre. Oooblem set off to get his armor and shield.

Timmer looked in at the woman and could not help wondering if her arrival had something to do with the king's recent odd behavior. He half wondered if she was the cause of it. Timmer contemplated the conversation between Oooblem and the queen. He'd underestimated the intelligence of the ogre. He smiled to himself. *Not the oaf I thought he was,* he thought. Timmer turned, hearing the rattling of armor and looked back down the long hall to the armory. Timmer spotted the lumbering mass of armor, muscle, and weaponry. Even to ogres, Oooblem would have been a giant, and the giant was heading in his direction. Oooblem pulled the oiled cloth from the breastplate, and the armor glistened. *In the king's name,* Timmer thought to himself, *I hope to never meet him in battle as an enemy.* Oooblem's enormous shield set comfortably in the back harness, protecting Oooblem's back from knowledge knot below the tailbone. The breastplate was an alloy of platinum and steel brightly shined. His short swords were swords that humans would consider two-handed, were strapped to his legs like a short sword on a human, and that monstrosity of a battle hammer, oversize just for Oooblem dangling from his hip to near the floor.

"Okay, meez ready to help yooz guard, Timmer. I know dere is nuffin' in dis Castle dat scares yooz so meez in gud hands guardin' wiff yooz." Oooblem grinned.

Timmer grinned back at Oooblem but couldn't figure whether that was humor or the ogre's way of saying they were friends in any case Timmer was glad the Ogre was happy. "Hammer instead of great sword?" Oooblem smiled. "Meez, great sword goes wiff meez hebby armor and its to big ta carry in duh halls."

Timmer blanched. "Anything scares you, Oooblem?" Timmer asked.

"Yup," Oooblem responded.

Timmer looked puzzled. "Like what?"

Oooblem adjusted his armor one more time, then swung his battle hammer around to set it on his shoulder. "Queens."

Timmer laughed out loud. Having known Myranda the majority of his life, he said, "Wise answer, my friend...wise answer."

The woman groaned, pushing the damp towel from her face. "Stop," she muttered. She opened her eyes. "Where am I?"

CHAPTER 13

---　🌸　---

Gerald the Good

Omurcada's breath was shallow, and his lungs burned from the exertion required to move. He closed his eyes, digging in with his fingertips and pulling with his hands while pushing with his feet, he crawled to the wall. Omurcada rested a moment before bracing on one elbow, shifting his back toward the wall, and bracing his back against it. He managed to push himself to a sitting position. After taking a deep breath, he adjusted his body one more time to finally lean fully against the wall, wincing at his weakness. For once, he found himself enjoying the wall's coolness though his muscles ached. The healing had been much slower this last breaking. The anomaly had been angered to such a pitch Omurcada doubted he would ever be allowed to mend, but Abkhas had finally retreated and Omurcada had healed. The ordeal left him physically and mentally spent.

The "ordinary man" needed sleep and food, yet he found a moment to contemplate his existence once again. He noted, in retrospect, several things about his captivity had changed over time. He had discovered the chair and the table that could not have been there at the beginning of his captivity. There were subtle and not-so-subtle differences in how he was treated as well as the reaction of the room that he was beginning to believe was alive. The healings occurred differently depending on the severity of the wound and the presence of Abkhas. His diet had changed from purely slugs to a variety of vegetables, nuts, and fruits. Meat on occasion but primarily other food sources and a water skin had appeared on the chair about the same time the food appeared on the floor. His chains remained, but he was nearly free to roam the circumference of the room. The darkness was not always so dense that sight was altogether im'possible. There were times when he could make out silhouettes of the chair and table. He was very comfortable with the layout of the room and could navigate without stumbling or bumping into things. Though he'd prefer to be elsewhere, his entrapment seemed more manageable even though the memory of the last birthing was such that imagining another was exhausting in and of itself.

After gaining his breath back and a bit of strength, he crawled to the chair he'd discovered not so long ago, found the water skin, and drank deeply. Omurcada coughed a bit of the water out, wiped his mouth, took another sip then capped the skin. "Another birthing to go… I doubt I'll survive another," he offered the darkness. He returned to the wall. After being sure his back was adequately braced, he curled up as if to conserve heat though he was thinking too much to rest. "Comfortable coma," he mumbled to himself. "That's what I need." The pain ebbed, the healing continued, Omurcada finally drifted into a much-needed sleep.

Messmor set the candle down on the table and observed the sleeping "ordinary man." Messmor adjusted the water skin, setting it on the table near the candle, then made himself comfortable on the oak chair after moving it closer to the table. Messmor took in the surroundings, wondering to himself if he would have the constitution necessary to survive this entrapment and all it entailed if he were Omurcada. *We each have our roles…Greyson…*, he thought to himself. "Greeeyson…awaken, Greyson," Messmor requested telepathically, softly yet with authority. Omurcada heard Messmor's voice.

"God, I hate these dreams. Messmor or Abkhas, one about the same as the other," he mumbled and began snoring a second time. Messmor pushed aside the comparison Omurcada made, understanding that to anyone entrapped, the two would look similar in the beginning.

"Awaken, Greyson," Messmor instructed with greater volume and equal command.

Omurcada stopped snoring. "No, I'm tired, and I hate this dream, so get lost." Omurcada returned to a deep sleep, his snoring reverberating the entrapment.

"Greyson! WAKE UP!" Messmor commanded, kicking Omurcada's foot.

Omurcada sprang to his feet, not fully realizing what or who had touched him and began swirling chains while his eyes attempted to adjust to the brightness of the light. Messmor quickly stepped out of range.

"Stop this nonsense, Greyson. It is time we get the last birthing on his way."

The chains finished their final rotation and hung silently from Omurcada's hand. "Messmor...? You look like a skinny Santa Claus...all that white hair." Omurcada grinned, still squinting trying to adjust to the light and finding it difficult to concentrate with light in the room flickering shadows in all directions. "I don't know that I'm happy to see you...am I?"

Messmor pulled out a pipe, packed it with tobacco, and lit the packing. "First"—a magician's smirk followed by a retreating sorcerer's smile, Messmor inhaled, then exhaled the wizard blend through his nose pointing the pipe at Omurcada—"a question only you can answer, Greyson, but the result will be the same in either case. I need to free the birthing, Gerald."

Omurcada laughed. "How do you manage to be both gracious and obnoxious at the same time, Messmor? What are you anyway? Are you human?"

Messmor's turn to laugh. "Well, yes, I am human, but in a different sense than you are. I am a wizard. My tissue was fused with magic before my birth much in the same way your birthing Zen's is."

Omurcada perked up. "Zen? Describe him. All I remember is being raged full when he escaped this godforsaken abyss."

Messmor shook his head. "This is a terrible place in your estimation, but trust me, this is not a godforsaken abyss." Messmor's expression turned to seriousness. "Lest you and I hope you never have to experience such a thing." His face softened. "Zen…hmmm, Zen is an unusual man…mage born, and the last I was aware, he was not aware of it. He is physically agile and remarkably efficient in martial arts, particularly for one his size. Stubborn, determined, feelingless, and yes, rage full at times. I have not observed him in several days. He was, let me say, 'lethal' in our last encounter."

Omurcada responded, "He killed someone or something? Gods, I knew he had the worst part of me."

"Not so," Messmor responded. "Yes, he killed, but only that which required killing"—Messmor scratched his head—"but he has the potential to kill out of rage as well as reason…very unpredictable in that fashion. Different from Camen."

Omurcada leaned forward. "Camen, you've seen Camen?"

"I can understand that you would like to know of Camen." Messmor coughed, blowing wizard's blend smoke through his nostrils. "But I am not aware of Camen's whereabouts at this time. He was set in the northern climates. I have not had the time or inclination to discover more."

Omurcada stepped closer to Messmor then sat on the table corner, feeling the heat rising from the candle flame with his left hand and clearing his mind. "Miracles both…light and fire. So, Messmor…what's next. I've tried to find Gerald and have not been successful. I can sense him from time to time, but I can't seem to find him. He's not all here, if that makes any sense." Omurcada laughed again. "Why should I expect it to make sense?" he mumbled aloud, reaching for the water skin.

Messmor pulled at his beard. "Well…let's trade places. You in the chair. I'll sit on the edge of the table."

Omurcada nodded. "After you."

Messmor stood and took his place at the edge of the table. "Why are you being so cooperative? I didn't expect you to simply allow this to occur." Omurcada picked dirt from his fingernails then rubbed his wrists.

"It makes no sense to resist you when resistance is simply a waste of energy. There may be another time when I won't be so easily persuaded, but this is not one of those times. One more birthing and I may have a chance to get out of here or at least have one of the birthings return this direction."

Messmor nodded. "I see." He tossed Omurcada a fresh apple. "Chew on this while I step through your lineage, that is if you're prepared for the intrusion."

Omurcada bit a piece of the apple. "Prepared? I'll never be fully prepared for that, but do what you must. I don't think Gerald's here."

Messmor frowned. "You may not have realized but this place has transformed you as well. You are not the Greyson you were when you arrived. You've been changed physically, spiritually, emotionally, behaviorally, and cognitively. Your transformation will continue as long as the birthings live." Messmor grimaced as the pain of the compulsion to never share this information pressed ever more intensely. "I don't know what the conclusion will be only that you will be part of battle beyond what you have experienced if the birthings manage to have initial success."

Omurcada nodded. "A conversation for a different time."

Messmor slid the psychic probe past Omurcada's barriers. Meeting no resistance, he proceeded deep into Omurcada's history, gliding down pathways of genetic and intuitive memory, Messmor searched. The traces of lineage undulated from being brightly illuminated to barely perceivable. Messmor noted most of the birthings had been from near the same time period, which was not necessarily unusual, but they aligned to the game and each other in ways he'd not seen before. He'd been surprised by the birth of Messene. Not that she was so aligned to the game but the fact that she nearly freed herself from Peace and arrived nearly in full persona rather than sustained inside the orb. He wondered how Gerald might be different from the others. If Messmor's theory was correct, Gerald would not only be aligned to the game and different in how the birthing would occur, but he would also, in some way, represent the final piece necessary for Abkhas's destruction.

After several hours, Messmor withdrew. He blinked and rubbed his temples, feeling exhausted mentally from the search. Omurcada noticed the candle had burned down a long way and the apple had turned brown where he'd bitten last.

"Long trip, Messmor?"

Messmor smiled, squeezing his eyes with his fingers attempting to lessen the strain. "Yes…and no sign of Gerald."

"That normal for you?" Omurcada asked.

"What do you mean? Eye strain or not finding the birthing?"

"Not finding the birthing," Omurcada clarified.

"Yes…yes, it is. This round has been strange in several ways, but I only do my part. You said you didn't think he was here, what did you mean by that?" Messmor asked.

Omurcada stood up and stretched. "I sense he's here at times, but then he's gone. He's here just before the first feeding then gone. I can't explain it. I just sense it, but I cannot communicate with him"—Omurcada paced—"and I can't make him aware of my presence. It is…it's…it's like he doesn't want to be discovered."

Messmor nodded. "Okay… Strange things have happened before."

Omurcada stepped back unconsciously, as Jeb winked in landed on Messmor's shoulder and, as usual, took the initial moment to groom Messmor by yanking a long white ear hair from Messmor's ear.

"Ouch! Stop that, you buzzard!" Messmor waved Jeb away.

Jeb landed lightly on the table, eyes bulging his aggravation with Messmor's greeting. Omurcada stared at Jeb, wondering what kind of a beast it might be.

"A wyvern?" Omurcada asked.

Jeb squawked. Messmor chuckled. "This is Jeb, my familiar." Jeb bulged his eyes more ferociously at Messmor. "Okay, okay." He nodded toward Jeb. "Jeb thinks I'm his familiar. We've been having this argument since we claimed one another."

"It communicates with you?" Omurcada questioned.

"Well, yes, in a manner of speaking, Jeb transmits images that are accentuated by sounds he makes in order to convey his thoughts to me."

Omurcada nodded, shaking his head in disbelief. "Can this game get any stranger than it is already?"

Messmor laughed. "I'm thinking it will get much stranger before it changes course, and I don't know when or if that will occur."

Omurcada exhaled. "Thanks for the optimism."

They both laughed.

"Let's get back to Gerald. I'll wait till you sense him again." He tossed Omurcada another apple.

Omurcada caught the apple and tossed it back. "I'll take the pipe this time."

Messmor grinned. "Aaahh, yes, the affliction of addiction never quite allows one to live in peace."

Omurcada snapped his fingers. "The pipe, Messmor."

Messmor handed Omurcada the pipe. Omurcada lifted the lit candle to the bowl and fired the packing while drawing air through the pipe. He continued puffing the packing to flame then inhaled the smoke very very slowly. "A very good blend...smooth beyond smooth."

Messmor took the pipe back from Omurcada fairly abruptly. "Yes...my own blend."

Omurcada smiled. "A little possessive, are we?"

They both chuckled.

Omurcada's expression changed to seeming search somewhere beyond his vision. He blinked. "He's here...early."

Messmor looked startled. "Gerald?"

Omurcada nodded. "Gerald or something else. I cannot explain, but you'd better hurry."

Messmor put down the pipe and quickly slid past Omurcada's dropped barriers. There, before him at the edge of Messmor's sight, a being turned and looked directly at Messmor. The being seemed to sense Messmor was attempting to entrap him magically. Messmor recognized the shape to be a man. The man slowly shook his head in dismay then, as if an everyday occurrence, simply reached into the fabric of existence with both hands, separated the would-be reality, and slipped out through the hole he'd created a dimensional rift before Messmor could move or do anything to object. Stunned, Messmor did not know quite what to say or do.

Messmor, remaining safe in the byways of Omurcada's mind, contemplated what had occurred. *That must have been Gerald, which means, there must be a hint to where he exists in Omurcada's lineage. There must be a trail to this being's origin. I must have missed it,* he thought to himself. Messmor spent the next several hours searching Omurcada's lineage and memory for abnormalities, strange occurrences, cataclysmal, or simply unusual but noted happenings. He was about to withdraw and rest when he noted a very minute silver line burning bright, dimming, then turning translucent...not to be seen with the naked eye.

No wonder I couldn't find it. The line disappears here...but it must go on. I simply cannot see where it goes, he thought. He pressed deeper—visions of a castle and a paladin standing on the mote bridge, Holy Avenger burning brightly against the forces of evil. The paladin was facing a young woman surrounded by an aura of darkness. The young woman's arms were raised high—lightning sped from the dark aura to the parapets, the guard towers, and the mass of soldiers behind the paladin. The vision flickered rapidly, making the vision progressively more difficult to understand. Messmor watched the paladin step forward and cleave the young woman nearly in half at the waist, immediately followed by a curious exchange that was not completed as the aura winked out and the young lady died.

"I wonder...," Messmor startled.

"What she said?" the being asked, finishing Messmor's sentence.

Messmor turned his psychic self completely around to find the being standing a distance away, cautiously observing the vision through Messmor's eyes. Messmor slammed his barriers close and stared ominously at the being, a man in priestly robes. The being's defensive shield sparkled as it absorbed Messmor's minor probe. "You'd be better served to ask your questions, sir. I am but a wretch of a being, but I have sustained certain advantages that prevent the intrusions you would have upon me." The being sat down cross-legged. "If you have questions ask, this form will dissipate soon and you'll be forced to wait for another darkness to continue the conversation if I choose to continue."

Messmor pulled on his beard. "Who are you?"

The being frowned. "A wretched soul punished by the god he once served for a deed unspeakable, a deserved punishment that I can neither resist nor renounce because my guilt is true and steadfast."

Messmor scratched his ear. "Why are you in Greyson's lineage."

The being smiled. "Isn't that obvious? I am of Greyson's lineage because I am part of his line though not often remembered."

Messmor was perplexed. "You appear to be alive still…how can that be?"

The being frowned. "I am not undead, but I cannot die until my god releases me to do so. I am a man but not a man. I am from this reality, but I rarely remain. I return when the darkness comes and leave when the light takes my humanity."

Messmor decided to ask the being directly, "Are you Gerald the Good?"

The being stood up quickly, looking a bit anxious and pained at the same time. "I have not been called or heard that name for god knows how many years. I once was Gerald the Good, but…I killed her, an innocent, with my sword…with my hand. Her blood is upon me, the wretched being that I am and my god has punished me for my transgression."

"What transgression?" Messmor asked.

"You saw the transgression, wizard. I nearly cleaved the young woman in half. The innocent that she was, reached out to me and in that instance, I realized the evil was a glamour, a very fine and complex spell, but a glamour nonetheless. The woman was an innocent used by an evil being, and I cleaved her nearly in half." The tears trickled down Gerald's short-cropped beard. "I deserve this wretched existence for my sin against all that is good."

Messmor shuttered at the raw powerfully authentic despair that emanated from Gerald.

"Gerald," Messmor soothed, "your pain is nearly visible like a dim pallor in your aura. I would not disturb you, but I…um"—

Messmor scratched his chin—"we need your help, Gerald. I am a bit confused about why you would be considered a birthing in the game, but you are of Omurcada's lineage. That is why I have been seeking you."

Gerald frowned. "How can that be? You knew not who I was or what I was."

Messmor explained the game, the history, the domination, and finally, the rules. Messmor's psychic pain from resisting the compulsion to not share any aspect of the game with the birthings was apparent, measured in stops and starts in his speech and the trickles of sweat beading up on his forehead. Gerald stood patiently. He could see Messmor was in pain from a source not of his own making, yet Gerald's observation was purely objective.

"I don't know that I am willing to visit my shame upon any others, though I sense your need of me. I am not compelled to follow."

Messmor noticed that Gerald's lower half was slowly fading away as if dissipating into nothingness. "DON'T LEAVE!" Messmor asserted.

"I am not leaving. It is part of my consequence. I will fade into nothingness during the day and become flesh and bone during the night. I wander the planes of darkness to feel myself real and the planes of light to observe but to not be seen or touched."

Messmor grimaced. "A wretched existence," he whispered.

"A fitting end for the stain upon my soul," Gerald offered feelingless.

Messmor watched Gerald's form fade into nothingness a moment before he observed a rift in reality open as if the cloth were being torn seemingly by itself. On impulse, Messmor followed.

Gerald stood whole on the rocky bluff of this darkened scarlet land. "No sun...no moon...no daylight in the abyss. I come here to contemplate my reality and to do penance for my sins. You should not have followed. You know not how to return. You could be doomed to walk the scarlet path for the rest of your existence." Messmor smiled yet feared Gerald to be correct unless he could convince this odd birthing to return with him. "You were once a paladin. Are you still bound by the laws of good?" Messmor asked.

"No," Gerald responded. "My life has become much too chaotic to sustain the Holy Avenger. Am I good?" Gerald's laugh echoed in the semi-darkness. "I suppose I am, though not as abiding by the letter of the law and the compulsion to destroy evil wherever it may be against any logic or at any cost. A lesson learned."

Messmor stepped forward and placed his hand on Gerald's shoulder. Gerald flinched at the touch. Messmor returned his hand to his side. "We may be more alike than different, Gerald, though I do not carry the same burden I know that following the path of righteousness is laden with sacrifices that I understand and some that I do not."

Gerald turned to look directly into Messmor's eyes. "Did your god forsake you for sinning against the very purpose for which you were created?"

Messmor did not break eye contact. "No…and yours may not have either. You may simply be on a path of tempering, as wretched as it seems, for a larger purpose. Your demise might not even be a consequence of your god's wrath but a result of something else that is now being used to shape you for a larger purpose."

Gerald's eyes twinkled for the first time. "It has been a long while since I've spoken with a wizard. You weave spells with your tongue nearly as well as those I grew up with. I doubt what you say is true, but I cannot deny thinking the same from time to time. The logic is flawed by the stain of the innocent. I cannot forgive myself or bring myself to harm another. Your journey…the game as you describe it…would require that I harm others in defense of myself, and I am unwilling to do so no matter their evil intent."

Messmor continued to maintain eye contact without flinching. "The game requires nothing of the sort though avoiding such may take remarkable ingenuity. You may be the first person I've met since the game's beginning that could avoid it."

"So…I would not have to kill or harm any creature?" Gerald asked.

Messmor, not wanting to give any assurances, said, "I do not know what the game will bring you. I can only say that you will not be compelled by me to kill or harm any creatures."

Gerald smiled. "I don't think you could compel me, but I know very little about from where you come. I am inclined to walk the plane of your game, but I cannot begin in the daytime. I would not be seen nor my voice heard. I would need to begin during the nighttime. I assume I would be required to begin in Omurcada's chamber...like a...birthing...correct?"

Messmor nodded affirmation. "You would not have to arrive as the others, but you would need to step from the path created by Omurcada's lineage."

Gerald returned the nod then reached both hands into the reality of the plane and separated existence. "Step through twice and you will be standing in front of Omurcada as you left him."

"Tomorrow night?" Messmor asked.

Gerald nodded. "Tomorrow night. Now go while I am still able to brace the partition and stem the torrent."

Messmor stepped through twice as instructed. As Gerald promised, Messmor was standing in front of Omurcada. Omurcada was sleeping soundly. Messmor tugged at his beard. "Strange...very strange... This one is more than I anticipated, and I'm not at all sure...not at all sure"—he glanced around the room sensing for any other being's existence—"I'm comfortable with what is occurring."

Messmor placed a second candle, four stick matches and a striker, and a packed pipe on the table. After rolling the last apple around in his pocket, he placed it on the table as well. "Enjoy, Omurcada of Celtic origin. You deserve a much greater reward, but this will have to do." Messmor shimmered out to a destination of his unique desire.

CHAPTER 14

❧

A Paladin's Contemplation

Gerald thought back to Messmor entering the rift and disappearing through the ethereal door. "Odd beings wizards, allegedly human yet nearly bloodless in their obsession to whatever cause they are bound. Is it Messmor or Abkhas or the Council that manipulates so many to which this evil emanates or is sustained?" he asked himself in a whisper as he began to reach to open the void.

Gerald's hands returned to his side, hesitating a few moments more not at all comfortable with what he was about to engage. "The game is not of my making or my concern, 'tis true, yet"—running his hand over the top of his head—"I cannot deny the presence of evil or the opportunity to atone or prevent my lineage from bearing the weight of my transgression." Taking a deep breath, Gerald proceeded to open and step through the rift. "Kindred are kindred… My blood is their blood."

Gerald took in Omurcada's drab abode. He slowly examined the room, from left to right, analyzed in detail what he believed to be a magically enhanced cell, though the spell shifts were subtle and of neither good nor evil origin, it became obvious to Gerald that arcane had been involved. He surmised, by the limited space, the peculiarities in the room's construct, and the chains on through the wall, the room had been designed exclusively for Omurcada. The dirt floor should have been cool, but it was neutral to the touch. The rock walls should have been much cooler than the floor, but the two were nearly the same, fluctuating a bit warmer or a bit cooler in different areas. The room's temperature was neither cool nor warm—it was precisely the difference between the two. Even though the wall temperature undulated slightly, the air temperature did not. The room seemed livable, manageable, not comfortable yet not uncomfortable, with the exceptions of the chains that stood out as a testimonial to the insanity of the game.

Gerald wondered, not for the first time, why he could feel the things he touched when he was translucent, not visible yet, at the same time, could not be touched by other beings. As odd as the conundrum was, there was no resolution and the inability to be touched by others had, at times, been near unbearable. He could feel the presence of others though they could not feel his presence. He could touch their arms, but they could not feel his touch. He had long surmised that touch required a physical resistance of some sort to trigger the sensation of physically feeling. He further surmised that his sense of touch, while in the state of translucence, was as much an echo in memory of what should occur when his fingers or feet came in contact with something rather than truly the sense of touch. He postulated that the magical barriers he'd managed to generate around the substance of his existence created, a sort of physical barrier that served as a thin, yet flexible, magically induced skin. When pressed against something, the magical barrier undulated much the same way actual skin would. Gerald could sense the changes in the flow of magical energy, creating an artificial sense of touch. His inability to be touched by others remained a mystery in his punishment.

"Stop that," Gerald muttered aloud. The years of existing alone had resulted in an undisciplined luxury of allowing his mind to wander in whatever direction it decided to take him. On occasion, he would catch himself have a full conversation with himself, including disagreements at various decibels. He was not pleased that it had taken this particular moment to contemplate whether his feeling of touch was actual, imagined, or magically induced. He had more important issues to attend to. Gerald shifted his concentration back to examining the room. He wondered if the neutrality of the temperature worked only for the guest or if the same were consistent with the captive. The surroundings would have depressed most men, but Gerald had seen and experienced much worse, at least from his perspective.

Gerald's face remained devoid of emotion as he simultaneously stepped cautiously through the room and contemplated the Game Messmor had spoken of. Messmor's description of Abkhas echoed an evil surpassing even the darkest evil he'd engaged in combat in his previous life, more than he'd experienced or observed since his punishment. He was surprised that even after all the years of living within the bounds of his punishment, he could still feel his pulse quicken with the compulsion to run headlong into battle with this entity. He had managed to resist the compulsion for several years, staying true to his vow to self, but this evil—an evil that walks all paths without fear of reprisal, an evil that would suck the light of goodness from the mouths of the gods without hesitation or trepidation, an evil that appeared to be nearly completely unchecked and openly arrogant— was particularly difficult for the once paladin to resist.

Gerald was not as naive as he had been in the beginning though. Too many times there were unanswered questions, untold implications, treacherousness that would or could never be identified without luck or a twist of fate that resulted in a chance meeting, or a much deeper look at what presented itself as obvious. Gerald smiled to himself, a rare occurrence, remembering the words of Ema, the seamstress of the Emerald Sun, as she'd been remarking about intrigue among the ladies of the court.

"Gerald, come sit." She motioned to a padded stool next to the loom. "The intrigue of good and evil is not always what it seems and is rarely uncomplicated, particularly between the sluts and harlots that frequent this court, but honor, true honor, shines forth like a beacon in the night if you simply take time to notice and focus away from the glamour of evil." She frowned. Gerald had always been amazed at this woman's insight into, what seemed to be, all things. Ema continued, "Evil, on the other hand, except that which is so arrogant that there is no caging the lion, presents itself in extravagance and deception." She raised an eyebrow. "Remember, always remember"—her eyes flashed to Gerald's, her iris, piercing, radiated with more intensity than usual—"extravagance is always deception…a cover or a mask for something that lies deeper. Look at this gown"—she pointed to the emerald green gown that glimmered with a sheen-like silver mist flowing through to the hems and seams—"look closely, Gerald. Threads upon threads, a weave of luxury and cloth that masks the bitch beneath the garment." He remembered her pause and the flash of those aged eyes as she looked up. "Gerald," Ema started.

"Yes, seamstress," Gerald responded, still surprised at the seamstress's language.

Ema hesitated a moment as if she were battling two thoughts at once. "Never underestimate the allure of a well-made gown or the possibility of death by hairpins." She seemed to let go of the thought as her mood shifted abruptly. "Now shoo yourself away from here. I have more gowns to prepare."

Gerald scratched his chin. "As you wish, seamstress."

After taking a few steps, Gerald turned and remarked to Ema, "Surely the one that wears that gown"—pointing to a particular gown hanging next to Ema—"could not be of evil intent."

She followed the direction Gerald pointed and discovered his finger arrowing to an incredibly beautiful white silk gown that had been hanging in the seamstress' workspace as long as Gerald could remember. Ema shook her head. "Boy, what did I just tell you?"

Gerald resisted, "How could evil wear such a pure bit of cloth?"

Ema glanced at the door, her facial expression twisting a bit toward gruffness, causing Gerald to quiet and follow to where the seamstress had shifted her line of sight.

"Your gown is hanging where it always hangs, Luceen," Ema remarked as Gerald stepped out of the duchess's path.

Gerald spoke before thinking, "That dress is yours, Duchess Luceen?"

Ema shook her head at Gerald, stifling a knowing smile, but the telltale twinkle in those eyes was difficult to deny. Luceen laughed aloud. "Yes, it is you silly boy. I'm to be married again next week to the earl of Leandra's Pass. White trappings of the virgin"—she laughed again—"the suggestion of purity to tantalize the court." She smiled at Gerald as her eyes drifted from his eyes to his crotch and back. "I'm surprised you haven't learned the ways of a woman of the court by now, Gerald." She began to reach toward him.

"The gown is finished, Duchess," Ema interrupted the would-be interlude as she cleared her throat.

"Now away from here before I lose my patience and this buffoon of a boy loses something even rarer."

Luceen tilted her head to the seamstress dropping her hand to her side. "As you wish, Ema though, dear lady, you should watch your tone with me. You never know when you might need the assistance of another."

Ema frowned her disdain and pointed the darning needle toward the entryway, motioning Luceen to be gone or suffer the consequences. Luceen proceeded through the entry, pausing close to Gerald and turning just long enough to slowly brush her breasts against Gerald's elbow and allow her perfume to strike deep into his loins. The moment the duchess was out of earshot, Ema turned to Gerald.

"GLAMOUR." She leaned forward in her chair, aiming the darning needle at her favorite pupil. "Gerald, what did I tell you, boy? Threads upon threads, a weave of luxury and cloth that masks the bitch beneath the garment. Careful of that one. She'll ride you hard then bury your heart in such despair that your god himself would have to lift you out." Ema's eyes flashed with a fire of conviction. "You understand me, Gerald?" Ema watched Gerald closely.

"Yes, m'lady seamstress," Gerald responded. "I-I understand." He nodded. Gerald glanced once more around Omurcada's room. *If only I had understood,* he thought. *Ohhh, the lessons I would have avoided.*

Gerald's smile in remembrance of Ema retreated as quickly as thoughts of the Duchess Luceen, both replaced by his intermittent preoccupation with the game.

Messmor seemed as much a part of the unfolding chaos as the dark one. Messmor's motives seemed more in keeping with what would be considered by most for the good of the people but Gerald was not convinced that Messmor was still aware of what would be the "good of the people." Gerald had seen the battles between good and evil over and over during his bereavement. He more than understood that believing you were doing good was not necessarily the best measure of what was truly good. Wizards, in particular, seemed to become so entangled in the battle and the intrigue that they would bend the reality of others simply to accomplish a goal that the wizard believed necessary. That sort of thinking was the aspect of Messmor's discussion, rather than the request to be part of the game, that compelled Gerald the most.

He could see the centuries of battle that raged upon the wizard's face. He could hear the conviction to defeat Abkhas and free the worlds entrapped. He could also see the single-mindedness from which Messmor proceeded to attempt to entrap Gerald without so much as an offering of an explanation or verbal enticement. Messmor had initiated the magical probes, believing he could penetrate Gerald's psyche but discovered, as many had in the past, Gerald was not without defense. An intellect existed in Gerald that Messmor would have enjoyed dissecting. Gerald had sensed Messmor's dismay when discovering Gerald's shields could not be penetrated. Messmor experienced further frustration having to relinquish the assault, understanding that increasing the energy and applying additional force would defeat the subtlety that Messmor believed would be required to pass the barriers, unusual barriers such as these. Gerald observed this very intelligent, driven, and skilled wizard make an understandable mistake all because of the single-mindedness that had been driving him, obviously, for centuries. Those were the sorts of mistakes that facilitated defeat and encouraged evil to flourish whenever allowed to dim the hopes of the poor souls caught betwixt. If Abkhas was what Abkhas seemed to be, those mistakes would cause the demise of another world…or two.

Gerald felt the "game" beckon him even before Messmor had arrived to press the request he "fulfill his destiny," as Messmor would describe it. Gerald sensed the shift in the planes, the imbalance that had occurred with Abkhas's ascension to power. The shift had not been sufficient to draw Gerald forward nor enough, in Gerald's opinion, to make his god abdicate the curse, but it had been enough to make Gerald take note. Something else existed. Something that he was destined to discover or perform or be a part of pressed him to this juncture. His punishment withstanding, a purpose larger than Gerald existed. The sort of purpose that was impossible for people like Gerald to walk away from. The puzzling aspect, as he continued to consider his surroundings, was his inability to determine whether the pull toward the game was derived from his experiences after the curse or from his paladinish former life. The possibilities were endless, but the nearly absurd chance that, after all these years of wandering and watching, a purpose behind the punishment that could result in redemption was too much to ignore.

Shaking himself free from the deeper thoughts about his existence, Gerald revisited his conversation with Messmor. He wondered why Messmor had been prohibited from disclosing details about Abkhas beyond advising Gerald of "its" existence, the depth of It's evil, and a brief history of the game. He was puzzled about why Messmor could explain the roles of Omurcada and Peace without penalty. Gerald mulled over other aspects of the game—the nature of the birthings in particular. Messmor had advised Gerald of the birthings by name but said very little about their persona or their talents. Messmor hedged anytime Gerald pressed for additional information. Glancing down at Omurcada he wondered what peculiar characteristics were present that would cause Omurcada to be chosen. Was it because he was part of Gerald's lineage? He had no idea how many generations were between him and Omurcada though they must be intrinsically connected for Messmor to follow the lineage path to Gerald. Gerald could not help but wonder if his punishment had affected the ensuing generations. He shuddered at the thought of others having to carry the burden for his mistake.

Gerald felt the tug go eastward but ignored it while he assessed, from a distance, one of two principal figures sleeping on the dirt floor. The darkness of the room parted exclusively for Gerald, as his punishment dictated, his sight was enhanced while he was in the translucent state, but he could not be seen by or communicate with anyone else. Gerald could view and comfortably observe Omurcada. Gerald knelt to touch the dirt floor and realized it must have been daytime on this plane. His substanceless fingers could not scoop a handful of the dirt. He could feel its neutral temperature but could not hold a mere granule of silt. Dismayed, momentarily, Gerald stood and reexamined the room with a thoroughness that only years of observation could accomplish. He identified the trace of magic that veiled the opening to the dirt room at the cave's end. Gerald realized the darkness must be perpetual for Omurcada. He considered removing the veil when evening arrived but decided that was something to be considered by the one, whoever that might be, destined to do the honors as the game dictated.

Gerald stepped within a few feet of Omurcada. Closely following the lengths of chains he discovered the holes in the wall from which the lengths of chain protruded. *One of the advantages of this wretched form*, he thought to himself as he shifted into a shapeless invisible anomaly and entered into the hole, much the same way water would a drain, all parts flowing and following through without hesitation or interference.

Oozing out the other side, Gerald immediately gathered his translucent self into the form that would closely resemble his actual form if he were not invisible to those who might be observing. Gerald startled a bit discovering he was standing next to a woman with whom he had no reference, stepped carefully sideways instinctively all the while realizing that Peace could not see, hear, or touch him. Some aspects of human behavior or near impossible to untrain. His hypervigilance, unconscious and automatic, was one of them.

Peace, sitting thoughtfully at the table in the center of the room, seemed completely occupied. She swirled in the small puddle of water, spiraling circles, and stirring figure eights, sending ripples in all directions with each of her fingers. The small puddle of water, one of her "miracles from Wigan," sustained its volume fed by the nearly not noticeable trickle of water over the chalices border, down the side, wrapping the stem, to finally join the pool at the base of the cup. An opposing stream trickled over the edge of the table to the floor below within which it was immediately absorbed. Peace's finger halted as she looked up and stared about the room feeling that something was there. She tensed but did not see anything abnormal. Peace tilted the ornate cup to return it to a level position that served to stop the flow of water and the trickle that was noisily distracting her from attending to the odd feeling she'd just become aware of. She understood, through experience, that not seeing anything abnormal was not a true indication that the abnormal was not occurring or present. She closed her eyes, freeing her mind, and reached within to embrace the feeling of uneasiness. Once located, Peace attempted to follow the feeling of uneasiness to its outward source. She turned sensing, sensing, reaching to the direction from where the disturbance was emanating.

She opened her eyes, staring intently at Gerald. Gerald, stepping backward, startled by the nearness of her face. More than a little uncomfortable with Peace staring intently into his face, he managed to step back against the wall. *She sees me? No...that can't be, yet there she is staring right at me.* Gerald, somewhat immobilized by the thought, realized though she'd looked in the right direction and stared intently into his face, she could not see him yet somehow was aware of his presence, but she was not certain what she was looking for. Peace could sense his presence but could not see his person. She continued to stare through Gerald. Peace stood up from the chair, sucked the water off the tip of her finger, and walked through Gerald then stopped and turned around. Gerald felt Peace pass through, simultaneously feeling his body disperse and reshape behind her. Peace reached her hand out and stopped next to Gerald's face. Gerald flinched but did not move. Peace continued to stare intently.

"Who is here? Abkhas?" Peace shook her head ever so slightly. *It can't be Abkhas*, she thought. Peace ruled out Messmor as well but could not determine what if anything was in the room, yet she did not feel quite right—something was amiss, but she had no idea what that might be. Gerald backed away.

"My name is Gerald, and your name is Peace, and though I can see you and you can feel my presence, you cannot see or even hear me as I speak. As frustrated as you may feel, I am afraid it pales in the wake of the frustration I've experienced from having this occur a thousand times in nameless lands with an endless amount of faces," he spoke aloud.

Peace looked more intently at the space that seemed to be causing her trepidation but could find no rational reason for the feeling. *I finally must be over the edge*, she thought as she walked back and sat in the chair. She sipped the rest of the water out of her cup. "Over the edge," she muttered.

Gerald took note of Peace's sensitivity to her environment. He was surprised she could sense him. Though the phenomenon had occurred in very unusual circumstances on other planes as well, the accuracy from which she determined his whereabouts resulted from very rare intuitiveness in his experience. Continuing the examination, he took in the construct of Peace's abode, wondering why this part of the cave had light and the furnishings were in better repair and noticeably of more durable quality than those provided to Omurcada.

Gerald had disciplined his impatience long ago, but it, on occasion, would press him to hurry along toward other important objectives. Gerald's experience taught him to not discount even the smallest detail when attempting to unravel a puzzle. Over time, he tended to catalog trivial facts in the far reaches of his mind until the total created a nexus of similarities. *A preponderance of evidence.* He'd been taught by the scholars of the Emerald Sun. Gerald had an uncanny ability to bring those seeming nonsensical unrelated twisting of fate forward when needed. He could and would shape them into a trend or possibility that made sense.

Satisfied that the quick perusal was sufficient for what he needed to learn at this juncture, Gerald decided it was time to return to his kin. *Back through to Omurcada*, he thought. *Then...I suppose the journey eastward.* Gerald moved toward the opening from which the chains protruded. He made an additional note that Peace was no longer chained. The loose ends dangled from the wall.

Though Messmor explained the game, the wizard failed to prepare Gerald for anything he might see or give a hint about what he was supposed to do including the direction he should proceed. Gerald had always been unconsciously and, at times consciously, sensitive to what he perceived as *the callings of fate, the mutterings of destiny*—the only failing, much to his chagrin, was an inability to determine whys or predict the outcomes. Even with thoughtful consideration and considerable preparation he could never rule out some twist, some oddity, some event, that was unaccounted for, influencing the outcome of any endeavor. *Such is existence... Wretched or otherwise, no matter the guise of stability there would always be a random...the substance of chaos...willing and read to alter anything that could naturally be expected*, he thought to himself.

The pull to travel eastward continued to assert itself with no consequence beyond, causing Gerald to conclude convincingly that he would need to eventually travel in that direction. Gerald understood, however, to keep the "game" consistent with the evolutions of the past. He was required to make contact with Omurcada before escaping Omurcada's entrapment. Gerald continued to wonder about the odd resurgence of his paladin leanings. He scratched his chin looking back in time, the unreal events, the progression to becoming a watcher rather than a member of the world. He'd paid the piper by sacrificing the want of emotional attachment for cold analytical detached observation. Gerald, over time, dimmed emotion with more efficiency than he originally intended, sealing the most influential aspects of his heart as far away from being realized as humanly possible. He noted, however, that in the past few days, the stirrings of his earlier life were pressing through, taking root in and influencing his decisions once again. He was not altogether repulsed nor completely settled with their intrusions. Gerald was aware that the evil of Abkhas was such that the longer he dwelled on the matter, the more he would be compelled to address the nemesis in some fashion. Gerald was also blessed or burdened, he was not certain, with the understanding that Omurcada was his kin. Therefore, the birthings were also kin. His only kin in his past life had been taken from him by the vows to the Emerald Sun. This new weight of obligation to family was compelling and disturbing at the same time.

His translucent form slid through the opening without hindrance, forming and reforming, bending, and twisting until ultimately arriving in Omurcada's chambers. His transparent body shifted shape and reformed near Omurcada's feet. He attempted to scoop a handful of dirt but still was unable to move even a speck. Gerald felt no loss as it was his method of determining whether the plane had progressed to night. He concluded that sitting on the dirt floor, back against the wall, and waiting would the best course of action. *Time rarely yields or deviates from its path. My musings will neither advance nor detour its course*, he thought.

Gerald slowly descended to a sitting position, back against the wall. He remembered the early years of his punishment spending hours, attempting to prevent himself from sliding through whatever substance existed below him, how impossible it was to simply lean against something without slipping through, the unfortunate, completely antagonizing reality of having to reform whenever the slipping stopped, then repeat the process. He most certainly would have perished had his body not been imbued with magical essence, the mark of a paladin of the Emerald Sun. More than once, he'd slipped through the upper crust of a plane into a pocket of water or oil, near misses in lava pits. His entire world had been quicksand except for nonporous surfaces. He remembered spending full days sitting on glass and full nights trying to determine a method to successfully stop the slipping and manage one of the more difficult aspects of his punishment.

In determining a solution, being a paladin, with a bit more magic in his lineage, than the priests of his birthplace had anticipated, worked in Gerald's favor despite his punishment. Gerald was able to discover how to focus and manipulate the energy that emanated from within as well as that which surrounded his person. He eventually discovered ways to manipulate the energy close to his person either generated by another mage born or from those natural paths of power that existed in all the planes. Manipulating mental barriers into defensive shields, as well as learning to command kinetic energy, had been a substantial part of surviving his punishment. In the present time, he managed to form physical barriers that were undetectable by the naked eye yet supplied the firmness necessary to create a stable somewhat-fluid containment field for his otherwise uncontainable gaseous form.

After girding portions of his body to resist the slipping, over time, he learned how to expand the containment field with skill sufficient to form a thin layer of shielding that sustained his original form. Sustaining a form while moving required the majority of his psychic and magical energy in the beginning. The years of punishment afforded Gerald the opportunity to practice the manipulations to the point the entire process was now largely unconscious, every manipulation, maneuver, and realignment orchestrated by an enhanced part of his brain with a minimal amount of energy or conscious regard. Gerald named that part of his brain the "tacit" region because that operated with remarkable efficiency and very little intrusion from aspects outside the central task of keeping Gerald's form consistent and safe. He no longer attempted to stop his shape from becoming translucent. Even with the substantial barrier, he still could not be seen by others or create a physical reality sufficient to pick up objects or touch another person. The punishment would not allow it. He was thankful that the punishment did not require him to sustain the translucence during the daytime or generate the energy to convert his substance to flesh and bone in the evening—the punishment simply occurred in unison with the plane's natural occurrence of darkness and light. He imagined that the energy required to perform such feats would be well beyond his innate ability. Gerald understood that he would not survive with the energy completely depleted.

On Alluvia, natural periods of dark and light varied according to the distance and the degree of pitch Alluvia rotated between its sun and the two moons. Gerald had often wondered why moonlight did not seem to shift his form nor did dark places during the daylight hours. Gerald understood that on this plane when the angle to the sun teamed with Alluvia's rotation along its axis caused nighttime to occur, the metamorphosis would happen as it had on every plane where the principles were similar.

Shaking himself away from thoughts of the past a second time, Gerald sat cross-legged on the abode's dirt floor to await the nightfall at which time he would meet with Omurcada. Gerald wondered how it would be to communicate freely with his relative several generations removed. A relative whose success or failure would shape the destiny of this world and possibly others. Gerald stood, believing the time was near, reached into existence, separated the fabric, and stepped into the scarlet path then back again to stand between the edge of existence and the trail of the lineage that he must step from to remain in keeping with the construct of the game. He would become a birthing. Gerald reminded himself of the man lying on the floor of the cave waiting for Gerald to arrive. For the first time in a long while, decided that he may not be the only wretched soul to have weight placed upon his shoulders by their god.

End Book 1

ABOUT THE AUTHOR

Mr. Murphy is known as Curt, a shortened version of his middle name. Curt is a Christian man, married to the love of his life, Janelle, the father of five children and is the oldest of ten children, eight still living. Curt's life experience is diverse. He is a Vietnam Era veteran, USMC, a licensed alcohol and drug counselor, also listed as a LADC supervisor in the state of Minnesota. Curt developed Addiction Recovery Inc. in 1991 and retained the position of CEO until January 1, 2020. Mr. Murphy is an accomplished tournament fisherman with several noteworthy top 5 finishes in regional bass fishing contests. In his twenties, Curt earned a first-degree black belt in Chung Do Kwan-Taekwondo, from Grand Master In Mook Kim as well as a first-degree brown belt in My Ja Quan from Grand Master Karl Scharff. Mr. Murphy is an avid photographer. A portion of his photos can be found at https:// Curt Murphy (curts968) Profile/500px.

His interest in medieval fantasy started in his early thirties and grew into role-playing games with his sons, and his son's friends, developing story lines, wild exciting adventures, conquering dragons over popcorn and chips with dip. He was encouraged to write and publish those adventures. Chronicles of Alluvia was born from the early beginning, developing a few pages at a time. Early drafts of the book were reviewed by friends who would be substantially critical (truthful) and who enjoy reading medieval fantasy as well as participated in role-playing, RPG, and MMORPG. Curt's oldest son pressed him to complete the work as soon as possible with the demand that no matter what occurred, the character G.G. would not be killed.